NATHANIAL
Dodging the Owlhoot

Nathanial: Western Promises Series, Book 4
ISBN-Paperback: 978-1-7366925-0-9
ISBN-Ebook: 978-1-7366925-1-6

Published by:
Fig Publishing
www.jbrichard.com

Editorial services by: Anne Victory, Editing and Gathering Leaves Editing

Cover and interior design by TLC Book Design, *TLCBookDesign.com*
Cover: Tamara Dever; Interior: Monica Thomas

Images: Wolf © cundrawan703/123rf.com; Mountain landscape © Wirestock/123rf.com; Leather swirls © Mario7/Dreamstime.com; Cowboy walking forward © Kanyakits/iStockphoto.com

Publisher's Cataloging-In-Publication Data
(Prepared by The Donohue Group, Inc.)
Names: Richard, J. B. (Julie Beth), author.
Title: Nathanial. Dodging the owlhoot / J.B. Richard.
Description: [Beaver Springs, Pennsylvania] : FIG Publishing, [2021] | Series: Western promises ; book 4
Identifiers: ISBN 9781736692509 (print) | ISBN 9781736692516 (ebook)
Subjects: LCSH: Adopted children—Family relationships—Fiction. | Runaway children—West (U.S.)—19th century—Fiction. | Orphan trains—West (U.S.)—19th century—Fiction. | Outlaws—West (U.S.)—19th century—Fiction. | Wolves—Fiction. | LCGFT: Western fiction. | Historical fiction.
Classification: LCC PS3618.I343 N382 2021 (print) | LCC PS3618.I343 (ebook) | DDC 813/.6—dc23

Printed in the United States of America

WESTERN PROMISES
~BOOK 4~

NATHANIAL

Dodging the Owlhoot

J.B. RICHARD

FIG PUBLISHING

CHAPTER 1

THE TRAIN RUMBLED along the tracks. Nate chuckled to himself, remembering the "pull the table runner" trick. What a mess he'd made. But his plan had worked. His stupid aunt and uncle were left in the thick, dealing with a pissed-off restaurant owner and upset customers, while Nate slipped out the door and hopped on the first train leaving Fort Sherman.

Steam hissed every now and then out of the smokestack on the engine. Nate stared through the fly-speckled window, his eyes fixed blindly on nothing in particular. His heart had stopped racing. Miles of tree-dotted countryside were behind him, as were the Fletchers. Sons of bitches.

Puffy clouds in the sky formed odd shapes. One looked similar to a turtle shell with a head poking out but no feet. Too bad there wasn't such a large beast able to stretch its head down and eat up Mr. and Mrs. Fletcher.

A bird soared near the cloud. Nate wished he had wings and pressed his palms against the glass. Its wings caught on the current. Nate traced the path with his fingertips as he watched it soar over a ridge. If anyone noticed the crimson on his cheeks—well, he wasn't the only one upset. Except anger burned inside him. Lots of the other kids were crying. This was, after all, an orphan train, and too many children needed a good home. Some of the boys and girls around him were missing families they didn't even have yet, a dream, their hopes of finding a loving mother and father, maybe siblings too.

Nate had all that, and then he was torn away. He'd lost everything because some stupid judge thought he knew what was best for Nate and ruled in favor of him going east with the damn Fletchers. How was that best for him? An aunt and uncle that he knew nothing about other than they were rich, which meant exactly squat to him.

Nate's arm got bumped. On the seat next to him sat a small dark-haired girl with a nametag that read: Minerva. Poor thing. Who named their kid Minerva? Sounded like an old lady name. Judging by the girl's small size, she was probably six or seven, only a hair littler than him.

"Sorry." She wiped at her red eyes.

"Don't talk to him." A tall boy, a head and a half taller than Nate and sitting in one of the seats facing them, kicked her shin.

"Ouch," she cried, rubbing her leg.

"She can talk to me if she wants." Nate ground his fists together, in no mood to put up with anyone's bull. There was no reason to be mean. She'd apologized; that was all. "Mind your own business." Nate glared.

The other boy wouldn't have known it, but he was getting Nate's version of the hard look Pa gave when he was mad. Eyes narrowed, jaw tight, and lips pressed in one thin line. Since forced to leave Gray Rock, Nate had been stewing, his anger bubbling right below the surface. It wouldn't take much for him to explode and feed the snotty kid a knuckle sandwich.

Nate's muscles were tensed, ready for a fight for more than one reason. His future—God only knew what lay ahead. At the moment, he was headed nowhere in particular, just riding the rails away from the Fletchers. Soon, though, after dark, he would jump.

He had a developed sense of direction for his age, nurtured by riding with a gang for some years, and his pa, Nolan Crosson, had taught him how to map by using the stars. Turning course, heading toward a life in Missouri where his so-called father, Jim Younger, had roots, Nate's innards were all in knots. If one of that family didn't take him in, however and whenever he got there, he honestly didn't know what he would do. It was a lot to roll over when his mind was stuck on those he missed. His real family, the ones left behind in Gray Rock. A place he could never go back to.

This bigmouth sitting across from him was a headache Nate didn't want to deal with, or he'd settle things right quick with a punch in the face.

"She's my sister." The boy arched back, eyes a bit wide. Maybe he was scared Nate was going to pound the teeth out of his head. "You don't have a tag." He twisted the hunk of paper pinned to his tailored coat. Leslie was the name on it. "I saw you jump on the train. You're not supposed to be here. We don't know you, and—" He eyeballed Nate from head to toe.

Nate had been wearing the same wrinkled clothing for more than a week, dirty from those hours he'd spent helping Dutch and Harvey, the stagecoach drivers, with the horses during the time it took to travel from Gray Rock to Fort Sherman. So what if he looked—Nate sniffed under his arm—and smelled as if he'd just crawled out of a ditch? That didn't make him any less a person. Just poor. Apparently, not good enough for Leslie.

"You better keep your mouth shut." What if this other boy told the conductor? Nate raised a fist an inch from the end of Leslie's nose.

Minerva burst into tears, hands covering her eyes. A few times when Pa hadn't bothered to drag Nate to the barn to give him a licking and wailed his ass right where they stood, Elizabeth had cried too. He reckoned Minerva didn't want to see her big brother get his nose smashed.

"What's going on here?" A man, who stood erect as if he were being measured with a ruler, wearing a railroad hat looked down the end of his pointy nose at the three of them.

None of them answered. He had appeared suddenly, and Nate couldn't remember for what dumb reason they'd been arguing. All he knew was that he didn't want to be there. He wanted to go home but couldn't because he'd just be taken by the Fletchers again.

Without warning, the man grabbed Leslie's shoulder and began to shake the marbles out of his head, whiplashing back and forth.

"Stop it!" Nate thundered. With both hands, he shoved the railroad man.

He didn't budge an inch, but he did let go. Tears rolled down Leslie's face, and his sister was bawling. Both of them were quivering. Nate's fists balled at his sides, he was just pissed off. All the other kids turned in their seats and stared with eyes the size of saucers.

"Why you little—I'll show you." The man drew his belt out of his pant loops, folding it in one hand.

No way in hell. That fella wasn't going to beat on him.

Nate jumped to his feet. "My father's a sheriff. He'll lock you up if you touch me," he blurted without thinking first. No one was supposed to know who he was. He needed to hide his identity in order to flee from the Fletchers.

"You mean you're not an orphan?" The man cocked his head, eyeballing Nate, probably wondering if he was lying.

An orphan train wasn't a joyride. No one would hop aboard unless they had no other choice. Nate didn't nod or shake his head to confirm or deny anything.

The Fletchers weren't dumb, at least not Mr. Fletcher. He would have wired the next town where the train would stop, and he'd have someone watching for Nate to step out of any one of the three cars. But while they were moving, there was no way to get a message aboard. This fella couldn't know about his escape back at Fort Sherman.

"Where's your nametag?" The fella snarled while rubbing at his chin. The belt was still folded tight in his other hand.

"I ain't got one." Nate wished Jesse was there. Pa was dead for all Nate knew. But his big partner was tall and strong and would have taken ahold of this fella for even thinking about hitting Nate with a belt.

Think, think, think!

He didn't have the help he wanted, and he had to get out of this. His plan had been to wait until dark, then jump off the train when it slowed to round a bend or stopped at a water station sometime before they reached the next town. Extra miles between him and the Fletchers were a good thing. He reckoned he had no choice but to get off before he wanted to.

"His nametag flew out the window." Leslie pointed to where the top window nearest their seats was open just a crack. "You can check your clipboard. Patrick Harrison. His name will be next to mine and our sister's."

Nate didn't know who Patrick Harrison was, but he assumed Leslie and Minerva had a brother who was not on the orphan train for some reason.

Why was Leslie sticking up for Nate? A few minutes ago, he wasn't good enough company to be spoken to. Something had changed.

"Our father was an attorney before he and Mother were killed. Father was good friends with a constable, the head of the department." Leslie had the man thinking. Yeah, those two were orphaned, but Nate looked a little closer and suspected the railroad man was doing the same.

Leslie's and Minerva's clothing was store-bought, not raggedy like one might expect children without parents to be wearing. On Minerva's feet were white button-up boots, not the standard black variety that all the kids he knew wore. The conductor had to wonder if there might be consequences for being rough with the Harrisons. They obviously had come from a family with influence. They wouldn't have been on that train had they had any living relatives, but they might still have some connections. Someone somewhere could be looking out for the welfare of the Harrison children, certainly their assets. They surely had retained their wealth, and the fella with the belt didn't want any trouble. He began to thread the leather strap through his loops.

Whew, that had been close. Nate's heart was still pounding. He plopped down into his seat. Minerva smiled at him. Her round, rosy cheeks reminded him of Elizabeth, making him miss his little sister something fierce.

"I'll make another tag. This time, don't lose it," the man snapped before he disappeared into the next car.

"Thanks, but you didn't have to lie for me. I would have done somethin' to get away from him." Nate wouldn't have wanted to in front of Minerva, but he would have knocked the man to his knees with a punch directly to the part of his body that made them boys and not girls. Then Nate would have jumped off the train. The situation had worked out better. This way, on the fast track, more miles were being put between him and the Fletchers.

"Is your father really a lawman?" Leslie leaned forward in his seat, his eyes boring into Nate.

He wasn't sure he should answer. He supposed it would be okay. Who would question a couple of kids if Nate was tracked to this train? The conductor believed him to be Patrick Harrison.

Nate nodded and pulled his deputy's star out of his pocket. Mrs. Fletcher had made him take it off. She wanted him to hand it over, but Nate had a screaming, cursing fit, throwing dirt at her. Mr. Fletcher intervened, saying he could keep the badge if he'd calm down, then softly scolded his wife for trying to thrust another change into Nate's life. They all needed to take things slow.

Nate pinned it on his shirt.

"Is he alive?" Leslie's eyes glistened, not for what he believed Nate might have lost—they didn't know one another—but because his own father was dead.

Minerva sniffled. The deaths must have been recent.

Nate hoped he didn't regret this. Inwardly, he felt a surge. He wanted to brag about his family. He hadn't really spoken about them in what seemed like a very long time. His lips tingled, ready to gush out his thoughts. "He was shot, so I'm not sure. He was the sheriff of Gray Rock."

There was an energy lighting him up as he began to tell these two about Jesse, Pa's deputy and the best big brother, always doing something with him, reading or riding horses. He explained about Ma and her great cooking, how she took care of all of them, and that she was going to have a baby. And he couldn't forget Elizabeth, his roly-poly little sister. By the time he was done, his stomach was growling at him. It must have been past suppertime.

The conductor walked into the car. Nate had a nametag thrust at him, and, along with the other kids, he was given a piece of hardtack out of a burlap sack that had feed and grain written on the side in black. It wasn't Ma's delicious cooking, but it would hush his stomach from rumbling for a little while. He nibbled, as did Minerva, taking care to brush off any crumbs.

"We need to get off this train. Do you think Deputy Adams will help us find our brother, Patrick?" Leslie whispered.

"Where's he at? What happened to 'im?" Nate's brow wrinkled.

Leslie looked over the seat tops. No one was watching them or listening. Then he ducked his head. In a soft voice, he said, "We don't know. He must be in the city, San Francisco. That's where we lived. We were told that Mother and Father were killed. Patrick was taken out of the house by a couple of men. They had guns. We'd never seen them before. And we were put on this train. But Pat never made it here."

"How do ya know he was supposed to be on this train?" Nate wasn't trying to be negative by doubting, nor was he calling the city kid stupid. But canny—inwardly, he shook his head. Judging by Leslie's silky white shirt, unwrinkled bowtie, pleated knickers, and polished brown leather shoes, which all screamed spoiled rich, he might never have had to make his own bed. Who in this part of the world didn't wear boots? Riding a horse almost demanded it.

"On the steps of the train, right before we were taken inside. A man. Papers blew out of his hands. I snatched one out of the wind. It was Patrick's nametag." Leslie sank in his seat.

That was solid proof. Nate wished he could be of help, but he had his own elephant-size problems. He couldn't speak for Jesse, but knowing the kind of man he was, Nate believed he would help these two. "Tonight after midnight, when the others are all asleep so no one knows where exactly, the three of us will get off the train."

"While it's still moving?" Leslie's face paled. "We could get hurt."

Nate rolled his eyes. "No kiddin'. I hadn't thought of that."

Pussyfooting around things that might scuff those shiny shoes on Leslie's feet wasn't going to help him find his brother any faster. Geez, he needed to man up. They were kids, but still ...

"San Francisco's that way." Nate jerked a thumb over his shoulder. "If Patrick's there, then staying on this train is only takin' you farther away from 'im." They were facing some tough travel, and Nate wasn't going to carry anyone else's load. By now, there were people out hunting him, but he would spare some time and help get these two turned around and headed in the right direction. Toward the last place they saw Patrick, where hopefully there would be a happy reunion. He, on the other hand, would be traveling south.

"There's something I'd like to know." Leslie handed his last bite of hardtack to Minerva, but his eyes were on Nate. "If you have a family, why are you on this train?"

He decided to be honest, his version of the truth. They already knew too much. He'd get them to the stagecoach line in Green River, which would carry them to Gray Rock and Jesse, who could coordinate their safe return home. Otherwise, these two might get lost. Both would have to swear an oath that they'd not tell Jesse of Nate's whereabouts.

"Some bad people kidnapped me. And now I have to run away. They'll go to Gray Rock huntin' for me. I can't risk going back."

"If your father's the sheriff, why doesn't he arrest them?" Leslie lifted his nose in the air.

The Harrisons might not like what he had to say, but he believed his thought to be the truth. "Because the people I'm dealin' with are stinkin' rich and think they can buy anythin' they want. Maybe they bought the judge who handed me over to 'em. I don't know." Nate shook his head. He hated to think about it, but he regurgitated how his so-called aunt and uncle stalked him before the trial. "Well, my love ain't for sale. I hate 'em."

He didn't know if Pa was alive. He hadn't been part of the trial because he'd been shot and was in bed fighting for his life when Judge Parker gave Nate away. There wasn't anything his father could have done.

They were quiet then. The sun dipped lower until it touched the horizon where the ground looked flat, one straight line ablaze in shades of orange. The deepest of the palate looked almost black as the fiery ball appeared to sink into the earth. Closer to the train, long blades of grass shimmered with red shadows, darkening as the day turned into night.

Nate yawned. Minerva was asleep, leaning against her brother's shoulder. Leslie, same as Nate, stared out the window. In a few hours, they would need their strength. It was a long road to Green River, and they would have to stick to the least-traveled path or make their own.

Three runaways, no supplies, and no weapons. What was he thinking taking these two city kids with him? Nate wrung his hands, the thundering wheels on the track matching his heartbeat. In the distance, a wolf howled.

CHAPTER 2

JESSE STUMBLED THROUGH the batwing doors of the saloon and onto the dusty boardwalk. His boots made a clomping noise on the planks, and he squinted thanks to the brightness overhead. "Damn you, Pete," he hollered over his shoulder while shaking his fist in the air.

"Go home, ya drunk!" Pete yelled.

The barkeep had cut Jesse off and shoved him toward the door. His money was good, gosh darn it. So what if it was barely noon and he was slobbering, barely able to sit upright? No one's business but his own. Though, judging by the number of eyes on him, folks were making it their business.

Gray Rock was filled up with the lunchtime crowd. Mr. Henderson was sweeping the porch in front of the store, and Big John and another fella, who were jawing near the town square, stared at him. Big John shook his head, his lips pressed into a straight line. The other fella's face wrinkled up just as ugly, and he rubbed his hand over the back of his neck.

"Go to hell!" Jesse waved them off.

All the other gawking towns-folk could kiss his ass.

One of his boot heels slipped off the edge of the boardwalk, his

knees dipped, and before he knew it, his rump hit the dirt. He groaned.

He rolled with a grunting effort to his feet, wavering for a minute until he gained balance by leaning against the hitch rail. His gut churned. He burped, wet and chunky, caught for a few seconds in the middle of his throat before he swallowed hard. Downing an entire bottle of whiskey could make a man awfully sick. He held around his stomach for a minute until the sweaty, sick feeling that had his upper lip beaded with perspiration passed.

Which direction was home?

He pushed off the rail, stumbling forward. It was too damn hot, unseasonably so. He wiped his head. The stock horses in the corral would need water. That was if Jesse could see straight enough to climb on Freckles and find his way home. His chores around the Crosson ranch never took more than a few hours to finish, and that included the extra work of now doing Nate's share. He typically worked during the cool of early morning, but today, he'd felt lazy and had only fed the animals before riding into town.

Jesse wasn't Gray Rock's deputy anymore, thanks to the damn Fletchers, those blasted city folk that took Nate away. Because of them, what else did he have to do? Nothing.

"Kiss my ass," he shouted at no one in particular as he staggered along the middle of the road.

Where was his horse?

More people, the same people he had protected as deputy, turned their backs on him as he lumbered along, kicking up dust because his legs were too heavy to lift, dragging his boot toes.

"Anyone seen Freckles?" He chuckled, but why, he didn't know.

Shorty and his bitch were there on the opposite boardwalk, packages in hand, eyes wide and staring at his every move.

Shorty shook his head. They hadn't spoken to him since Kristy left on the stage, the same transport that carried Nate away. They could shove their pity or whatever it was right up between their cheeks where the sun don't shine. He didn't care what they thought, any of them, the whole damn town. Judgmental arseholes.

None of them had a child ripped out of their arms or had to stare at an empty chair each morning at breakfast, then again at lunchtime, and at the supper hour. Ma would burst out sobbing any minute of the day. He hated it. And sweet little Elizabeth kept asking for NaNa, which was what she called her brother because she couldn't say his name.

He swung and punched a hitching post. "Dammit!" He rubbed the hot pain in his knuckles, which did nothing to console his heartache.

Sure as the sky was blue, he believed that Sheriff Crosson would've been healing a whole lot faster if the man wasn't grieving for a lost son. God, Jesse missed that kid. Nate would have arrived at Fort Sherman hours ago if the stagecoach was running on time. Soon, his little partner would get on a train headed east. Jesse wiped at his eyes.

"Jesse!" Ned, wearing his official striped telegraph visor, waved a small slip of paper in his hand. Big John marched up behind Ned, toward Jesse.

"Git away from me." He shoved Ned. Jesse's words were so slurred he barely recognized his own voice. "Just tell me where Freckles is." He did a spin, looking himself, and nearly fell over in the dirt, tripping over his own two feet.

"This is urgent." Ned held out the telegram, his hand shaking. "The sheriff'll want to see this right away."

"Well, thar he is. Give it to 'im." Jesse cast an arm in a flippant wave toward Big John, who was elected by the town council the day after Nate had been shipped off to take over as sheriff while it remained to be seen if Nolan Crosson could return to his duties. Jesse understood, but it pissed him off. It felt like the town was giving up on the man who had diligently protected Gray Rock and its citizens day and night until his bullet injury. Now it seemed they just wanted to fill his shoes, which, in Jesse's eyes, couldn't be done.

"Shut up, boy," Big John snapped. "I'm not takin' over permanently, just until Nolan's back on his feet. If he were here, he'd be mighty disappointed in the way you're actin'."

God only knew when Nolan would be able to return to his duties. The man was barely able to sit up straight and feed himself. Doc was still camped out in the spare room, helping Kate tend to his healing wound. No more fever, but he was weak, too debilitated to anytime soon think about pinning on a badge, and Jesse wasn't faring too well without Crosson's guidance.

"Unless that's the recipe for a magic potion that'll make 'im all better, I don't care what it is." Jesse belched.

He'd been the one to tell Nolan Crosson that his little boy, his son, had been taken away, awarded to another couple, a distant aunt and uncle that were strangers to the kid. Before that day, he'd never seen Nolan weep, a grief-stricken father. They'd held to one another, a needed crutch for both of them, and let out emotions that Jesse, for one, didn't even know he had. Ma had been there, crying her eyes out. Jesse loved the two of them as much as he did the half-pint and Elizabeth, and eating at him one day at a time was the pain of loss. Grief was turning him black, devouring him from the inside out. He turned back toward the saloon.

"Where ya goin'?" Big John's huge hand slapped down on Jesse's shoulder, spinning him. "Son, you need to pull yourself together." He held the telegram in his other hand.

Ned stood awkwardly at his side as though he'd rather be anywhere else. Ned was a pacifist. Jesse knew him long enough to know the fella definitely was not confrontational. On the other hand, John and Jesse, drunk enough to feel gamey, were ready to quarrel. All he had inside was anger. Time to let out some of it.

"Don't call me that." Jesse jerked his arm away. "There's only one man who calls me son, and it ain't you." Some time ago, he watched Sheriff Nolan Crosson hang his biological father and brothers for cattle thieving. It wasn't until the sheriff had taken Jesse underwing that their bond grew, and Jesse, more and more, realized how special a true father-son closeness was.

"Then start behavin' like you're Nolan's son." John grabbed Jesse by the scruff and shook him until his teeth rattled. "If I didn't know better, I'd think you were Hank Adams' son."

Jesse swung, missing by a mile, for John had easily ducked the sluggish punch. Ned jumped backward out of the way, his arms covering his face, though no one was aiming at him. Five thick knuckles smacked Jesse in the mouth. He stumbled back, twisted an ankle in a divot, and fell flat on his back. John grabbed him by an ankle and dragged him toward a water barrel at the corner of the leather goods shop. A few men nearby chuckled. Others stared with wide eyes at the two of them.

"Let go of me," Jesse hollered but was too damn drunk to do much about it other than gripe as he thudded across the hard ground, dirtying the backside of his clothing.

"Look at yourself. You're a damn disgraceful sight." Big John yanked him off the street and sank Jesse's head deep into the water.

Jerked back by the scalp, he gasped for air. His hat lay in the dirt at his feet.

Jesse didn't have to see himself to know his clothes were wrinkled, and he hadn't taken a bath since before the trial, which was over a week ago. Shaggy whiskers covered his face, but why bother with shaving? Kristy was gone. Why should he care about his looks? No one to impress. Did it matter if he reeked of whiskey? Nate was gone too.

Ma had grumbled at him, but she wasn't keeping herself so well as of late either. More often than not, locks of red hair dangled from the usually neat bun on the top of her head. Each day, fewer and fewer strands were tucked in. She was dismissive about his appearance but not the boozing. That made her plenty mad, and she'd given him an earful each and every time he stumbled through the door. A few times, he'd slept in the barn just so he wouldn't have to see her brow crinkle and her eyes fill with tears. How awful disappointed she was.

Jesse smacked his palms against the barrel lip, and dust fell off. His entire world gone when Kristy and Nate were carried off on the stage. In times like those, Sheriff Crosson had always guided Jesse, kept him thinking straight, was a father to him. Jesse needed that now in the worst way, but Nolan was too ill, and Jesse couldn't seem to come to terms with this mess on his own. His heart pained for many reasons. No appetite, the shakes—rock bottom was where he was.

After the third soaking, Jesse coughed, then sputtered out, "I'm sorry."

"Jesse, I know you're hurtin'. We all miss Nathanial. But you need to remember that ya haven't lost your entire family. Nolan ain't dead, so stop actin' like he is. And Kate needs your support, especially now with the sheriff down in bed." Big John picked up Jesse's hat, handing it to him.

Jesse brushed the dirt off the brim, his wet hair dripping onto his soaked shirt. He slumped onto a nearby bench. Not only was his head throbbing, which made him feel like hell, but John was right. Jesse was behaving like an ass. Grief had blinded him to his responsibilities. He wore the Adams name, but like Nathanial, Jesse was a Crosson through and through. It was time he started acting like one.

"Please help me find my horse." Jesse grinned at the two men standing before him. He still wasn't seeing straight enough to find his legs to walk and remained slumped over on the bench.

A few minutes later, John steered his buckboard, pulling up reins in front of Jesse. Ned came forward with Freckles and tied Jesse's horse to the back of the wagon. Jesse was tossed in the bed, where he rolled on his back, letting the sun beat down on his face, and closed his eyes, hoping to sleep off some of the liquor before he got home and Ma took one look at him. Maybe his clothes would dry too. He for sure was going to get an ear-chewing.

Jesse woke up in his bed. His wet shirt had been stripped off, his chest bare. He didn't remember any of the ride home or even how he'd gotten into the house. Lordy, his skull was thumping. He rubbed his head.

Ma walked in carrying a steaming cup of coffee. Her face was pale, eyes red. No doubt, she'd been crying. Whether it was over him or all the other hurtful stuff, Jesse wouldn't ask. He felt bad enough as it was, and not just because his gut was twisting from all the alcohol. He was smarter than this, knew better, was taught to be wiser. Only once had the sheriff ever crawled into a bottle to solve his problems, and that was after his first wife and son had been murdered. He'd told Jesse all about it, aiming to save him from ever coping in the same way. He had forgotten the story of Nolan's drunkenness until now, and Jesse had learned the hard way. He wouldn't forget again.

What he should have done was talk to Ma, since the sheriff was ill, but he hadn't wanted to burden her with his frustrations. She was in a delicate condition, and he'd overheard Doc saying that she needed to take better care of herself, that he was there to help with Nolan, so it was okay for Kate to take a break once in a while. She was losing weight instead of gaining.

"Your father would like to speak to you. He said as soon as you're awake." Ma handed him coffee. Her face was sober. "I watered the stock for you."

"Thanks." Jesse never doubted he'd get a tongue-lashing. John probably told Ma about the scene in town, and she likely had told the sheriff. Jesse wasn't a kid, but he did live under their roof, and there were rules. Children, no matter how old, were supposed to obey their parents. He was a man and often had a drink with the sheriff, though responsibly. Slobbering drunkenness was not tolerated—ever. Any way he looked at it, they considered him a son, and with that, there were certain expectations.

Ma tossed him a shirt out of the top dresser drawer. "You're too old for me to forbid you to go into Pete's, but you know my feelings on that matter." She wiped at the corners of her eyes with her apron. "I don't want ya to become a drunkard over all this. It's been hard enough to deal with everything."

He was supposed to be the man of the house while the sheriff was mending. Those responsibilities should have kept him in check. For the past week, Jesse had done a piss-poor job of dealing with anything. He just couldn't believe Nathanial was taken away from them.

He took a sip of coffee, then set the cup aside on the nightstand. "I'll do better. I promise." He kissed her cheek.

"I know ya will." A small smile turned up the corners of her mouth. "You can start by taking a bath. I'll heat up the water. Now go talk to Nolan." She shooed him toward the door.

Jesse stretched his shirt over his head on the way into the hall. He knocked once before entering the sheriff's room. Doc rose from his chair near the edge of the bed, soiled bandages in one hand and a bowl of red-tinged water in the other. A fresh wrap covered the sheriff's wound. Thank God the smell of pus was gone. That had turned Jesse's stomach a few times. His gut wasn't overly sensitive to odors, but whew.

Doc walked past and out the door. It clicked shut behind him.

The sheriff groaned as he scooted up, propping himself on a stack of pillows. He held to his side and winced until he made himself comfortable. "Have a seat." He nodded toward the chair Doc had occupied only a minute ago. Jesse sat, not saying a word. He knew why he was summoned, and the sheriff's voice sounded much stronger, madder than he'd expected.

Suddenly, Jesse felt as though he were the half-pint's age. He couldn't even look at the sheriff. He stared down at the floor as though his boots were the most interesting thing in the room. Guilt was about as bad as grief. Both took a toll on a body. For the past four or five days, he'd been avoiding coming into this room. Each time Ma would say something to him about visiting his father, Jesse couldn't do it. He'd made an excuse. Hard to say why. Maybe because it wasn't easy to see the man in such critical condition. Though, Jesse had noticed there was more color in the sheriff's face today than the last time he saw him.

Right after the lawman had been shot, Jesse was so focused on taking care of Ma, Nate, and Elizabeth during the trial for Nate's custody plus his duties as a deputy. All those things kept him on task, but now he had too much time to think, and losing his little partner was on his mind every goldarn minute of the day. That was no excuse. Doc had said the sheriff was on the mend, slowly, but things were looking good, and Nolan would have been at Jesse's side had it been him lying in that bed. He'd failed his family miserably.

"I'm sorry."

"Look at me." The sheriff reached and tapped Jesse under the chin. The bump was strong. The sheriff had gained strength. "You have embarrassed me, actin' like a fool drunk and me stuck in this damn bed. Kate told me you've been drinkin' but not to the extent of what John described after he dragged ya home. From what he told me, this has happened more than once—you drunk before noon. I wish someone had told me sooner."

He let out a deep sigh. "Kate probably didn't wanna worry me, so I don't blame her. But dammit, boy, you know better. I wish I could get out of this bed. I'd kick your ass across the room." The sheriff laid his head back into the pillows and closed his eyes for a minute. Then he sat up a bit straighter. Jesse believed for a second or two that he might leap out and lay a thumping on him.

Jesse's shoulders slumped. He'd expected this tongue-lashing, but actually hearing how disappointed the sheriff was, he didn't believe he could feel any lower.

"I miss Nathanial too, but ya can't let that ruin your life." The sheriff's tone lost its sharp edge. "I know I expect a lot from you and it ain't always easy, but if I don't know what's goin' on inside that head of yours, I can't help ya. Talk to me."

"Sir." Jesse didn't know where to start. Bothering the sheriff with talk of anger didn't seem right when what he needed was rest, to mend, so Jesse had kept his hate of everything surrounding Nate's custody battle all bottled up. That led him down the path of guzzling down whiskey every day to mask the pain. He wasn't sure how to spit it all out. His tongue didn't move.

"Did you think I was too ill to listen or care?" The sheriff shook his head. "Neither of those things is true. You are my son." Sheriff Crosson patted his hand. "I lost one son to an outlaw's gun, a second to the law, a judgment that turned over my little boy to another man, and I'm not about to let you stray down a sinful road and destroy yourself. Do you understand me?"

"Yes, sir." Jesse stared straight into the sheriff's eyes. "I've missed you." It was the absolute truth, so why was it hard to say?

The sheriff was more awake and with it than Jesse had seen in a long time. He sounded like his old self. No one that Jesse ever met owned the amount of self-assuredness that Nolan Crosson did. It was but one of the reasons he admired the man so much.

"Well, you're in luck 'cause I ain't goin' anywhere." The sheriff paused for a minute. "But you are. I have a job for ya. First, you'll need to pin a badge on."

Jesse's brows shot up. What was the sheriff asking of him? He did miss being a deputy, but he wouldn't feel right working for anyone but Sheriff Crosson. Big John was a good friend, and it was neighborly of him to pin on a star when the need arose, but honestly, he was no lawman. John owned a freight business, and he wasn't all that handy with a gun. They'd taken Nate and John's son Johnny hunting a few times, and the man couldn't hit shit, wasting more lead than anyone Jesse had ever met, not even close to bringing home supper. Not exactly a mentor when it came to catching criminals.

Sheriff Crosson handed Jesse a slip of paper, the telegram Ned had tried to give him earlier. It was from Lem Fletcher. Nate had run off. The commander at the fort had the grounds searched. Nate was no longer in Fort Sherman. The Fletchers were putting up a ten-thousand-dollar reward for his return. If Nathanial returned home, the Fletchers expected to be promptly notified.

"Good Lord. With this kind of money at stake, they'll have every outlaw and bounty hunter trackin' the kid down, and he's too savvy to consider runnin' home." Nothing about that sounded good to Jesse.

Sheriff Crosson nodded. Apparently, he saw it the same way, or he wouldn't have asked Jesse to go after the half-pint.

"What about you and Ma? In her condition, she can't take care of the barn chores and watch Elizabeth." Someone had to feed the stock animals, chop wood, mend fences if need be, and Doc's time would be spent tending to the sheriff when Ma wasn't able. "There's too much work for a pregnant woman with a toddler." He just didn't see how he could leave. Not that he'd been much help lately.

"I've already talked to Big John. He's willin' to help, and Johnny will come after school each day and see to the horses." The sheriff pulled open the drawer of the bedside table. He picked up a tin star, his star, the one that read sheriff, the one John had been wearing. He handed it to Jesse.

"But this is yours." Jesse didn't reach to accept it.

"Right now, it belongs to you. Make me proud. Find Nathanial and bring 'im home." Sheriff Crosson stretched forward, and out came a moan.

Jesse leaned in. The sheriff pinned the badge on his shirt, over his heart. He couldn't help but smile. He'd been too long without it. It felt like a part of him that had shriveled up was alive again, as though the dark clouds had parted and nothing but blue sky was shining down on him. He tingled all over until he recalled something sobering

"You sure about this? The Fletchers'll take Nate away." Jesse knew he would have trouble handling that a second time. It'd been bad enough the first time. They'd been crying and clinging to one another. But there was an excitement in him to see his little partner.

"I wasn't given a chance to say good-bye. No matter what, Nathanial's my son. This is his home. I want 'im to hear from me, his father, that he has a place here even though the Fletchers plan to take 'im east." The sheriff shook his head. "We both know they won't ever get 'im there short of hogtyin' 'im. Even then, it's doubtful they'd succeed. He'll keep escaping until he tires of runnin'. Then he'll turn right around and fight for freedom, which is a powerful motivator, especially when threatened. What I'm worried about is that Nathanial'll fall into his past." He took a sip of water, then a deep breath.

"The boy only knows two ways of livin', and the other was taught to 'im by a gang of outlaws. I don't want 'im gettin' into trouble he can't get out of, and this bounty on his head won't help matters. I'm afraid he'll run smack into some of the mean men from his past. As soon as I'm strong enough, I want to talk to Prescott about filin' an appeal. I'll never stop fightin' for my son."

Jesse's smile stretched from ear to ear. Behind him, the door squeaked, and they twisted their heads in that direction.

"May I come in?" Ma held a tray with a plate of eggs, and the smell of fresh grainy bread reminded Jesse of how hungry he was. She had likely expected to hear some yelling.

"I'm starvin'." The sheriff eyed the food as he began to scoot toward the edge of the bed. Jesse took him by the arm, aiding him to fully sit upright, his feet flat on the floor for maybe the first time. It was damn good to see. With such a strong will, he'd be on his feet in no time, or so Jesse hoped.

Ma's eyes then focused on the star on Jesse's shirt. "You be careful."

"Yes, ma'am, I will. Don't you worry." He dropped the telegram on the nightstand, then slid the table over in front of the bed.

Ma set the plate of food on the night table and fiddled with the napkin as she unrolled the fork and spoon. "Knowing our little rascal, he probably hopped a train to who knows where."

She was right. Hours had passed since receiving word that the half-pint had run away.

"Farther away from Gray Rock is a safe bet," Jesse said.

The sheriff stirred his food. "Nate knows the Fletchers would look here first. Don't count on 'im comin' this way." He met Ma's watery gaze.

They were all aware that other messages had been sent out, informing town after town about the ten-thousand-dollar reward. Most folks in these parts didn't make that much money in a lifetime.

"Anyone who considers themselves even somewhat of a tracker might go after that reward." Jesse grabbed his hat off his head and smacked it against his leg. Criminal or an honest man, most men west of the Mighty Miss wore a gun. Accidents happened.

The sheriff swallowed the bite in his mouth. "Nate'll fight. He always does. The kid's a survivor. He made it pretty clear by runnin' away that he has no intention of goin' east with the Fetchers."

Ma sat down on the bed and half hunched over next to the sheriff, holding her head. "I just want him to be safe."

The sheriff gently rubbed across her shoulders. "Kate, I need ya to understand. Nathanial could cross paths with outlaws, bounty hunters, or any other man lookin' to get rich quick, and that's nearly everyone. What the Fletchers have done by posting a large reward for his capture and return is put our son's life in danger. Every grubby lowlife in the territory will be huntin' him for a big payout. Men like that don't let anything or anyone stand in their way, so Jesse won't be any safer goin' after 'im."

"I'm more worried about what'll happen once I catch up with my li'l partner." Jesse had no doubt that the boy wouldn't just give up and come with him, knowing he'd be given over to the Fletchers again.

The sheriff set down his coffee cup. "Trasportin' 'im back ain't gonna be easy for sure. He's gonna fight ya every step of the way, but you already know that, so be ready for anything. If need be, treat 'im like any other prisoner. If you think you see a possible way of escape, you can bet he sees it too. Then you counter that before he makes a move."

Ma jumped to her feet. "Nolan." Her face reddened. "How dare you suggest our little boy be treated like a common criminal."

"Ma," Jesse said in a soft tone.

She turned her glare on him. "I suppose you agree."

"Fletcher's telegram doesn't say Nathanial has to be found alive. The reward will be given out upon his return. Nothing was stated about his well-bein'. I just hope I get my hands on the kid before anyone else does."

"Kate." The sheriff took his wife's hands. "You and I both know that Jesse would never hurt Nathanial. Anything he does'll be a hundred times better than what some greedy bounty hunter might do. And God forbid he run into someone from his past."

Ma sighed. "I know. This whole affair just makes me sick."

The sheriff nodded. "I hate the thought of anyone roughin' up our son, especially given his past abuses. That fiery tongue of his, I'm afraid, will get 'im into worse trouble. You know what he's like when he's mad or upset, and his whole world's been taken from 'im." He shoved his food away, nearly knocking over the table. "Dammit. I hate bein' stuck in this bed."

"If anyone puts a hand on partner … God help 'em." Jesse was dead serious.

The sheriff grinned. Ma swept her arms around Jesse's neck, hugging him tight for a minute.

"I'll do my very best not to let either of ya down." The half-pint meant too much to him to consider failure. He slid the nightstand holding the half-eaten plate of food back into place in front of the sheriff. "Don't you let me down. You need your strength. I'll be givin' this badge back to ya as soon as I can."

The sheriff gave Jesse's arm a squeeze.

"When will you leave?" Ma straightened, her hands on her lower back supporting her round belly.

Jesse laid a palm flat against her girth, anticipating a kick for good luck. Someday he wanted a passel of brats of his own, and he looked forward to meeting this little fella in a few months. Marriage and kids would have to wait. Kristy was on her way east, and he had no desire to court anyone else, not yet anyway. The letter she'd handed him before leaving on the stage was stashed in his vest pocket.

"As soon as the sheriff gives me the go-ahead." Jesse would need to pack extra ammunition, maybe an extra pistol in his saddlebags.

"I'll get some food together and bandages and such." Ma turned toward the door just as Elizabeth squealed from her crib in the next room. Ma headed for the yelling.

"Mum, mum, mum."

Another sweet baby girl would be okay with Jesse.

He grinned. "Bah," like a sheep sound, came out anytime Jesse tried to get Elizabeth to say his name.

"I think this one's gonna be a boy." He just had a feeling, or maybe he just missed his little partner too darn much. Another ornery little cuss much like Nate wasn't hard for him to imagine. Not a replacement. That's not what he was picturing but rather a strong-minded child. He couldn't fathom a son of Nolan Crosson's being any other way. Even Elizabeth, with her cute blond rings and her mother's soft blue eyes, had a hot temper. That peanut had a set of lungs, and everyone in the house knew when she wasn't happy.

"I believe so too," the sheriff added, a proud grin on his face, his fork in hand.

Ma looked over her shoulder from the doorway. "This one certainly kicks like a boy." She held her belly. "Lord help us." She chuckled. Her beautiful smile lit up the room, though her eyes shimmered with tears. "I hope Nathanial gets to meet this little one. It's hard to believe that just a few weeks ago, the heaviest thing on my mind was Nate's jealous streak."

A clinking noise filled the air, for the sheriff had dropped his fork. Ma disappeared into Elizabeth's room. A few minutes later, she stopped squawking.

Too many memories, good and bad. Nathanial was part of their lives, and Jesse so often opened a door or turned a corner and expected the half-pint to be there. Not a one of them was used to life without Nate, nor should they be. It had only been a week, seven days sent straight to them from the devil's doorstep.

None of them would ever forget Nate's jealous streak. Good Lord, when he and Jesse had first met, the kid had made life a living hell for everyone in the house. He had filled Jesse's boots with horseshit, one of his many attempts to run him off. The half-pint had thought he was getting a brother, and he had over time. It all worked out. This trouble of the bounty on his head and with the Fletchers would straighten out too. It had to.

If the boy were there, at home where he should have been, Jesse believed Nate would have reacted differently, realizing that getting a baby brother or sister brought more joy than headaches. Nate loved Elizabeth. Teased her with that damn Ticklebug all the goldarn time. Plus, he would have Jesse, and they shared a unique bond. The two of them were part of this family, although they would never carry the same blood as Elizabeth and the new baby. That meant there would always be a special tie between him and his little partner.

Jesse gently laid a hand on the sheriff's shoulder. "I promise I'll find 'im and bring 'im home."

"Son, I'm countin' on it."

When Sheriff Crosson pinned the badge on Jesse, he had initiated a plan, and every ounce of Jesse's being could be banked on getting that job done.

"What's the next step?" Jesse tapped his foot, raring with eagerness.

CHAPTER 3

NATE YAWNED, but he didn't want to risk napping and maybe not waking up before daylight. "Why don't ya get some sleep? I'll wake ya when it's time to go."

"I haven't been able to sleep since we left the city." Leslie rubbed his eyes, then stared once again out the window into the blackness. There were dark circles under his eyes, which were bloodshot.

"How old are you?" Nate was curious, and they might as well talk since they were both awake. It would help pass the time.

"Eleven. I just had a birthday." Leslie grinned, but the corners of his mouth were turned down. "My brother Pat gave me a toy boat, a big one, a ship with sails that worked. We were going to float it in the pond but never got the chance." He was silent for a minute. "Pat wanted to be a lawyer like  our father, who turned into a businessman. He went to work with him three or four days a week. Father allowed him, said he was nearly a man at sixteen, time to learn the business, to sit in on banking meetings. He even claimed to know the combination to Father's safe at his office. Said he figured it out on his own."

Nate didn't know what to say and wasn't so sure he had to say anything. Leslie was missing his older brother and just needed to let out the hurt. Nate had good ears. He would listen, and he hoped Patrick was okay, but it didn't sound good. Why would he be kept behind and his siblings shipped off? It might even be too late to help Patrick, but Nate wouldn't mention that. Pa had taught him that money was too often the motive for a lot of bad doings.

"Pat was good with numbers. He assisted Father with the business accounting." Leslie rambled on, but Nate's mind drifted elsewhere.

Maybe Pa was feeling better, on his feet, and he could assist these two when they reached Gray Rock on the stage. He was good at solving crimes, and Nate missed learning lawman stuff. And the repeated mention of a brother produced an ache in his chest for Jesse.

"You two quiet down." The conductor passed by, looking over all the other kids either slumped over or leaning against one another, asleep in their seats. He blew out the lantern hanging near the door. Then he left the car. A rush of cool air flew in while the door was open, the rattle of rails louder. Other than the moonlight, it was pitch black inside the car. The even breathing of those around them sounded like a soft lullaby.

"Tell me about these people who kidnapped you," Leslie whispered.

Over the next hour, the stars shifted across the sky.

"Right from the beginnin', they acted like I belonged to them, like I was a bought horse and they had the papers to prove it." Nate quietly shared his experiences surrounding the custody trial without mentioning the Fletchers' name. Theirs was a name that left a sour taste in his mouth, and he never wanted to hear them mentioned out loud again. "Can you believe they didn't even let me say good-bye to my pa?" Nate blinked back the wetness in his eyes.

Leslie shook his head. "I'm sorry."

Nate leaned back in the seat. "I hope I never see 'em again."

It had to be midnight or after. The conductor hadn't been back since blowing out the lamp. It was time.

"Let's go." Nate kept his voice low, giving Leslie a nudge. He then woke Minerva, who whimpered into the black space surrounding them.

"I'm scared." Panic raised her already squeaky voice. If she let out wailing, they'd be found out, and Nate couldn't have that. If he was caught, he'd be returned to the Fletchers.

"Come on." Her brother tugged on her arm, bringing her to her feet before Nate had a chance to tell her to shut up.

None of them had a choice. Patrick, who'd been taken first, had no idea Leslie and Minnie were put on a train. He wouldn't know where to search for them. They, however, had been witness to their brother being dragged, kicking and hollering, out of their home.

With Nate in the lead, they crept single file, though he'd bet Minerva was clinging to her brother's sleeve. Nate pulled open the door. A wave of cool night air spilled into the compartment. He didn't look back to see if anyone stirred. Ahead, the engine chugged. Puffs of smoke rolled up over the car roofs. Iron on iron, wheels grinding the rails, rattling as they sped forward at a faster rate than Nate had thought when sitting inside, staring out the window. Leslie pushed the door shut behind them.

At the steps, holding to the guardrail as the train vibrated, the three of them looked out into the night. Nate couldn't guess what the two with him were seeing ahead, but what he saw was freedom, a fork in the road that would lead him to a life without the Fletchers. Only, that freedom came at a cost, one he would've had to pay regardless if he had gone with his aunt and uncle. Never again would he see Pa, Ma, Jesse, and Elizabeth. It was time to forget those good seasons. That wasn't him anymore. He was on his own.

"Hey, what are you kids doin'?" The conductor rushed from the car ahead, arms outstretched, reaching for whichever one he could get his hands on.

"Jump!" Nate yelled, giving Leslie a shove. Minerva was holding on to her brother as Nate had suspected earlier, so the two of them fell as one off the bottom step. Nate dove, just missing the swipe from the conductor.

"Ahh!" he screamed as he hit the hard ground and rolled. Air burst out of him in a gasp. He coughed on dirt, and his left knee burned right on the cap where he must've smacked a rock. Flat on his back, his head spinning from doing somersaults, he blinked a few times and stared up through the treetops at the stars. The train whistle blew in the distance.

"Are you okay?" Leslie held his head and squatted next to Nate. A small cut at his hairline bled. Tears dripped off Minerva's chin. Her dress was torn at the hem, and both knees were skinned up, as were her palms.

Nate pushed to sit up. "Yeah, I'm okay. A little dizzy."

"Which way do we go from here?" Leslie looked in all four directions. Somehow, he was able to block out his sister's sniffling. She wiped at her eyes, but a steady stream poured out.

Nate glanced at the stars. Pegasus, the winged horse, always grazed in the northern sky, or that's how Pa had explained it. Nate pointed southeast. "Green River's that way."

How many times had he studied the map of the territories tacked up in the jailhouse in Gray Rock and imagined himself chasing down the bad guys? Every sketched-out mountain and river between towns that Nate recognized by name only were memorized. He grinned, recalling the time he had ridden shotgun with Jesse on the stage because the regular rider, Harv, was sick. Though, they hadn't gone nearly as far as Green River. The single passenger, a farmer's daughter traveling home after visiting a relative, had gotten off three stops before. What a late night that had been. A wheel had busted earlier in the day, which took hours to fix. The fish … Pisces had been bright overhead when Dutch, the stagecoach driver, pulled up reins in front of the hotel, and Jesse aided the young lady inside.

Nate now stared off in the direction of Pisces. He got to his feet, brushing off his clothes with confidence. Minerva's bawling needed to stop. He rubbed the goose egg on his skull. He understood she was scared. The knots hadn't loosened in his stomach either. Being in the woods at night was creepy, too many unseen noises, and she probably still hurt from the fall. His head was thumping, and the racket wasn't helping.

"You gotta stay quiet." He wasn't being mean when he said it.

"What's it matter?" Her brother stood next to her, straightening his coat. "It's not like there's anyone out here."

"We ain't alone if that's what you're thinkin'." Nate gave them a minute to let that statement sink in. "Not only are there Injuns but wolves too. Both are curious creatures. They hear an out-of-place noise, and one or the other might come snoopin' around."

Minerva and Leslie both swallowed hard. The little girl took a step closer to her brother. "What will they do to us?" She had lived a life of luxury, well-kept, out of the way of harm.

Nate didn't blame her for being ignorant of life outside the city, but they'd both better listen to him. Brutal honesty was the best tactic. It would leave little doubt in their minds about the seriousness of the situation they were in. They could die.

"Wolves'll make a meal out of us. Any warrior'll cut off our scalps and leave us for dead, if not kill us."

"I wanna get back on the train." The little girl wailed.

Leslie stared at Nate as though such horrors only lived inside the pages of a book, that nothing that bad actually existed. They were standing in the woods, tall timbers overhead, the moonlight filtering through the leaves giving a dim hue to the rocky earth at their feet. An owl hooted. Then a coyote howled somewhere on a ridge not far away. None of those noises were make-believe.

Nate slapped a hand over Minerva's mouth.

Her brother snapped awake. "Do as he says, Minnie."

The little girl quieted, though she was still shaking. Her brother was wringing his hands.

"How will we know if there are Indians around?" Leslie whispered.

"You won't 'til your hair's missin'." Nate led off, the other two following behind in his exact steps.

They'd wasted too much time. The conductor had seen where they'd jumped off. He'd report them missing to some-one and might give an account of an approximate mile marker. Nate didn't know if anyone would come looking for three orphans, but he didn't plan on waiting around to find out.

They made their way over fallen trees, waded through creeks, and now had wet feet. Cold, squishy socks were uncomfortable. They crawled under brush hedges and twisted one way then the other over several ridges and across a long, open meadow. Grass, somewhat browned by the changing of seasons, stood as high as Nate's shoulders, and a few times, a sharp blade scratched his face. No clouds dotted the sky as the morning turned a brighter pink.

Nate found a pool of water at the base of some rocks. On their knees, they drank, scooping water in their hands. Nate's belly growled, and he drooled on himself thinking of Ma's flaky biscuits with butter melted overtop. Even if he pushed them to make miles, it could take all of a week to hoof it to Green River. Back yonder, on top of the last butte, stretched far out of ahead of them were lines of hills, one after another, splotched with red and orange leaves. Keeping the sun in front of him, to his left, he was sure of their direction, but the distance ... How far was that town? Without food, they'd never make it. He barely had any energy after one night of walking, though going without sleep hadn't helped.

Nate splashed water on his face as the Harrison children gulped more down. He needed to find them something to eat. These two especially wouldn't last long without nourishment. He'd been a dunce for bringing them. Maybe he just didn't want to be alone.

They'd gone another two, three miles when Nate found a good place to rest behind a cluster of rocks and a few thornbushes.

"Don't build a fire." He doubted either one knew how, and their raised brows confirmed it. "I'll make one when I get back." He didn't want one or the other of them adding too many sticks. A signal fire was the last thing they needed. Meat was what he wanted to sink his teeth into.

"Where are you going? Shouldn't we go too?" Leslie hadn't relaxed enough to sit down. His sister lay under a tree on the dry needles, her eyes already closed.

"I'm gonna hunt. And no, I don't need help. Just don't wander off." Nate left then, and a sinking feeling came over him. Hunting might end up being a waste of his time. If he were to see any game, it'd be a surprise. Neither city kid knew enough not to tramp on sticks, so plenty had snapped, but it was hard to see in the dark. Even after the sun started to climb, Minerva had tripped twice and cried out both times. So all the game in that area had probably been frightened away. Maybe he'd be lucky and find a berry bush or wild mushrooms.

As the sun climbed higher into the sky, his mind was not on tracking rabbits, though at his feet were small, round bunny droppings such as Jesse had pointed out during their hunts. What was his family doing right then? Did they miss him? He drew in a deep breath and swore he could smell Ma's sourdough biscuits. Elizabeth loved them, always banged her dolly on the table until she got one. Nate wiped at his eyes.

CHAPTER 4

JESSE DRUMMED HIS FINGERS on the counter, waiting for the clickety-clack of the telegraph to stop. What did the message say? Ned was scribbling feverishly on a piece of paper. Finally, the tapping stopped. Ned pushed up out of his chair, the wire from Fort Sherman in his hand.

Jesse reached across the counter and snatched the note out of Ned's fingers. Sheriff Crosson was at home waiting to get this news, and Jesse was pacing, ready to get on the trail. It wouldn't be just one cruel hand after the boy like when Jesse had faced off with Tipsy, a gunslinger from Nate's past who had aimed to kill the half-pint. This time, there'd be too damn many snares in any direction the boy set foot. Only one party could collect the reward. A battleground was what his little partner could end up in the middle of, and being a runaway would keep the kid from seeking the law for help. The half-pint was truly on his own.

Jesse read the message. According to Captain Farnsworth, a friend of Sheriff Crosson's and the commander at Fort Sherman, the train they suspected Nate to have escaped on was an orphan train. The first stop would be Black Dog Valley at approximately noon, and the captain had men stationed there. Jesse looked at the clock. It was ten thirty. The next two hours would be the longest of his life, but he and the sheriff had planning to do in case Nate wasn't caught. And the half-pint was too damn savvy to make this easy on anyone.

Jesse shoved the message into his shirt pocket as he headed out the door. He mounted his horse and turned toward home.

To his surprise, when he entered the sheriff's room, the man was sitting at the edge of the bed for the second time in two days.

"Well, what did Farnsworth say?" The sheriff leaned forward.

"The train he thinks Nathanial's on will stop in Black Dog Valley, but I don't believe he's on that train. He might've left the fort on it, but he ain't dumb enough to roll into that town and not consider that someone'll be watchin' for 'im."

"I agree." Sheriff Crosson tapped a map laid out on a table in front of him. "I've been thinkin'." He traced a finger along a line that represented the railway. Jesse pulled up a chair. Crosson stopped halfway between the dot that was Fort Sherman and that of Black Dog Valley. "Here." The sheriff glanced over at him. "Nate would have stayed on the train as long as possible to space himself out from the Fletchers, but he wouldn't have wanted to come too close to that next town either. This is probably about where he hopped off. From there, which way do you think he went?"

Even at a time like this, the sheriff was schooling Jesse. He was positive the man had a good guess and wanted to see if Jesse could reason his way to the same conclusion. He studied the map. Nate wouldn't have stayed close to the rail line. So directly east or west were out. North, that was lonely country, wild and full of Indians. There was really no place to go up there but across the border. Jesse scratched his head. He doubted Nate would do that. Angling south, there were lots of possibilities as to where the kid could go.

"Green River," Jesse said, pointing to the name on the map. "It's far enough from the railroad that Nate might chance goin' in, bein' that it's the first town along the southern route." Jesse tapped his foot. Partner was too gutsy for his own good. "That's a lot of miles to cover. He might be itchin' to see people by then or at least hear news of any kind."

The sheriff straightened his back, then shifted his position, but he still held stiff. "Don't underestimate how many miles Nate can walk, fast. Remember I trailed him for a week before I adopted him, when he'd been hell-bent on revenge against Deegan Jones. Nate was afoot, and I was on a horse. Nathanial's as capable as most grown men."

"True." Jesse chewed on his lip. "I could cut across here." He ran a straight finger over a line of razorback ridges. "Bet I could cut my travel time in half. Instead of two, three weeks, it might only take me a week to two to get to Green River if I push Freckles."

"That's mighty rough country." Sheriff Crosson scratched the back of his neck. "But you're right."

There was simply no other way if Jesse wanted to get to Green River before Nate.

"There ain't no trail where you'll be travelin'. Any horse, even a good, sturdy, sound one such as Freckles, could falter. That would set ya back further than had ya just gone the long way." The sheriff wasn't a pessimistic person. He just pointed out the facts as he saw them, preparing Jesse for what lay ahead.

"Don't you worry, sir. I'll be just fine." Jesse confidently grinned.

The sheriff patted his shoulder. "You should leave soon, within the hour."

They both fully believed that Nate had gotten off the train. The captain's men waiting in Black Dog Valley was a waste of effort.

Half an hour later, Ma had Jesse's stake ready, enough for a few weeks. He tied the sacks on the back of his saddle. He'd taken all the extra ammunition in the house, plus the map. If he didn't get to Green River before the half-pint, then Jesse would have to figure out the kid's next step. This was a race against time, and he expected trouble. Too many dishonest people would be after that bounty on the kid.

Jesse sank spurs. The sky was blue, and there was plenty of daylight for putting miles behind him. He couldn't help but feel knotted up inside. There were too many variables that could lead to disaster, and Jesse didn't want to see the half-pint fall into the wrong hands.

CHAPTER 5

NATE COULDN'T BELIEVE HIS EYES. A calf stuck in the brush on its belly, kicking dirt and bawling for its mama. Its leg was broken, twisted in a funny way at the knee. Nate felt sad for the poor thing. There was nothing that could be done to save that leg. If the rancher who owned the animal didn't come along and shoot it, putting it out of its misery, then wolves would eat the critter. So why shouldn't Nate eat him instead?

He pulled his switchblade out of his pocket, his hand shaking. He had cut the heads off chickens before, but how was he going to go about butchering a calf with a two-inch blade? This was a task that Pa or Jesse normally would have taught him, walked him through a step at a time, and made sure he had the right tools.

The more the baby cried, the less hungry Nate felt. His stomach churned as he thought about slitting the animal's throat. It was going to die anyway. Why shouldn't he, Minnie, and Leslie benefit from it? He hadn't found anything else to eat, no game, no nuts or berries.

Those two back at camp had to be getting worried. He'd been gone a few hours, longer than he'd expected.

He shoved his knife in his pocket. He didn't have the heart to do it, not that way anyhow. He looked around on the ground and picked up a big rock. A bash on the head would kill it, and hopefully there'd be less blood.

A cow bellowed. Nate froze. Dust, a good-size cloud, hung in the air behind a hill not far away. He'd bet it was the rancher who owned this calf or some of his hands rounding up strays.

Nate dropped the rock. He wasn't about to lose this meal. His fingers worked quickly to untangle the calf from the brush. Damn sticker bushes kept pricking his hands. The baby cow bawled.

"Be quiet." He tried hushing the noisy thing.

The dust cloud drew closer. Voices. Three, four men at least. Shit! Even if he got the calf out of the weeds, he needed time to drag it off. An open twenty yards of grass stood between him and the tree line.

His hands were scratched and bleeding, but he wasn't giving up. A number of brown faces appeared over the rise, moving steadily at a trot toward him. All the hooves, the thousands of pounds, some fifty cattle, shook the ground under him. Sunlight shimmered on their backs along with all the dust. One by one, four men appeared on horseback. Their eyes fixed on him, and his widened. Sweat made their faces glisten. They glanced at one another with raised brows. They hadn't expected to run into anyone. Neither had Nate. His insides tightened.

They halted the herd not fifteen feet from where Nate stood directly in their path. A cry flew up from where the calf lay, mostly untangled but unable to stand or walk.

"What do ya think yer gonna do with that calf?" The fella with the mustache eased into a slouched posture. His saddle creaked as both hands relaxed on his pommel.

With Nate's blond hair and blue eyes and the fact that he was a half-pint, he didn't look like a threat. But he could play hell if he had to. Now that these edgy fellas had a good look at all forty some-odd inches of Nate, their hands lifted off their guns. Tension had been thick at first glance. Everyone was breathing somewhat easy again, but Nate's brain was turning fast. He had a keen eye for details. Pa had taught him how to look for clues, and he spotted a big one. None of these men were wearing chaps. Any cowboy he ever saw wore chaps and gloves a lot of the time to save their hands from rope burns. He needed to be smart. They were carrying weapons on their hips, and Nate was empty-handed.

"I'm gonna eat 'im," he stated, matter-of-fact.

"Is that right?" The fella smoothed the end of his mustache between his fingers. The others all snickered.

"What do ya have to pay for that meat?" A different dust-covered man sneered, his lip bulging with a fat plug of tobacco.

Nate rolled his eyes. Did they take him for a nitwit? Ranch hands didn't have fancy rigs and wear their guns tied down. Nor did it take four of them to move fifty head of cattle. That herd didn't belong to them. "Mister, you can go to hell."

They stiffened in their saddles as though Nate had just slapped one or all of them. Their faces were now as sober as a Sunday morning before church.

And he let them have it. "I'll pay for this meat when you show me a bill of sale for that herd." He had basically just called them rustlers without actually saying the word.

Laughter roared from the four.

"Kid, you're all right." But the fella with the mustache pulled his pistol. Nate cringed, waiting for a bullet to split him in two. The fella grinned and aimed, then turned his gun and squeezed the trigger. The calf stopped crying. "Enjoy your supper."

Nate stepped off to the side, closer to the dead calf. The four men, one of them giving a whoop to get the cattle walking, went on about their risky business.

When Nate got back to camp where he'd left the Harrisons, he dropped the calf and shook his arms. He wasn't so sure they wouldn't fall off. It had taken three goldurn hours to gut and drag that damn calf, and it left a blood smear over the entire mile. Any big scavenger would definitely catch the scent.

Leslie and Minnie jumped to their feet, their eyes stuck on the calf with a hole in its head. Nate's hands were smeared with red, as was his shirt. He mopped his brow with his sleeve.

"Here." He tossed his flip knife to Leslie. "I gutted the thing. You can skin it." Nate flopped down in the dirt, lay back, and closed his eyes. A week's worth of sleep was what he needed, and they weren't close to Green River.

"I c-can't," stammered Leslie.

Nate forced his lids open. "Then we don't eat." It was as simple as that. He couldn't do everything. These two needed to contribute, make an effort for God's sake. Nate had brought them food. They could do the remainder of the work and let him rest. That was fair whether they liked it or not. He lifted his chin toward Minerva. "Go gather wood, then stack it in a tepee shape right over there."

She hurried off.

"Don't get lost," Nate called after her.

"I don't know how." Leslie regarded the knife in his hand, then glanced at the dead calf.

"You'll figure it out. It ain't that hard. Just cut 'til all the skin's off."

Nate's muscles were jelly, too blasted tired. He just couldn't explain exactly how it should be done, how Pa and Jesse had taught him to skin an animal. He'd helped skin deer, they butchered hogs in the fall, and he'd seen it done on cattle at

Shorty's ranch. He rolled onto his side away from Leslie's teary eyes as he began to saw with the small blade, and he sniffled.

Sleep was what he needed, not to play teacher. He could hardly keep his eyes open. If he did, he might cry. But his brain wouldn't turn off. Judging by the sun drifting west, it was nearing the supper hour. They would have to eat, then git in case wolves or bears came sniffing for the carcass.

Just as Nate nodded off, Minnie shook him awake. The firewood was ready, and Leslie hadn't skinned the calf but had somehow managed to chop a tuft of fur and skin off its tail. In one blood-covered hand dangled the blob of brown fuzz, the knife held upright in his other as he stared at both pieces, his coat sleeves stained with red.

Nate grabbed the knife out of Leslie's hand. "Pay attention." He dropped onto his knees next to the calf. "Ya start at the back legs and cut only the skin down the inside of the hind legs until you meet together at the center of the thighs." Nate sank the blade.

"Eww!" Leslie slapped a hand over his mouth. A funny, wet gagging noise burped out between his fingers.

"Then you go throw up." Nate smirked and went about his business of sawing. "Now, go straight down the chest. The warmer the animal is, the easier it is to pull off the skin." He gave a hard yank. As flesh tore, Leslie's cheeks turned a queer shade of green, but Nate's stomach growled. "The longer ya wait and the colder the animal, the harder this is." With both hands, he jerked a flap of skin, tearing away from the meat beneath.

Nate shook out the cramp in his cutting arm while Leslie took a few deep inhales.

"I'd rather starve." Leslie mopped his brow with a section of his sleeve not blotted with red.

Nate ignored the comment. It had been a long day so far, and this, no doubt, was a first for the clean-cut city kid. Even so, he should grasp the basics of how to fend for himself.

"When ya get to the front shoulders is when it gets harder to cut and pull around the shoulders and neck."

Leslie stumbled back a few steps, then plunked down on his ass in the dirt, his arms wrapped tight around his middle.

What a baby. Nate rolled his eyes. Going without a meal, now that could bring on belly cramps. The sight of a little blood and guts, that was nothing. After he dropped the calf's skin aside, Nate chopped the meat into small chunks.

Nate got the fire jumping while Minnie searched for a flat rock that they could cook the pieces on. An hour later, all three were chowing down.

With each bite, Nate's belly stretched fuller and his lids became heavier. He hadn't gotten to sleep long, a few minutes. Unfortunately, he couldn't give in to that urge. Wolf tracks. He'd seen fresh ones while returning earlier, pulling the dead calf that left a wide blood trail. Big prints, likely a large male, away from the pack for some reason. Strange, wolves usually hunted in a group. No other tracks, but Nate hadn't taken time to search. He was too darn hungry.

"Give me your shawl."

They couldn't leave behind what was left of the meat, not if it was going to take him three, four hours out of each day to catch something because these two had scared all the game away. Leslie liked to whistle, and his sister kept beat by clapping her hands, making too much noise. Why couldn't they have some useful skills? They probably couldn't spot a bear track if they were on the ground with their nose right in it. Nate flicked open his knife. It wasn't too sharp. Pa had told him a couple of times weeks ago to sharpen the blade. Nate forgot, so filleting what meat was left on the calf would have him sweating.

"She'll need that. It's chilly at night." Leslie snatched the shawl out of Minnie's hand as she pulled it off her shoulders. He wasn't about to hand over the garment or let his sister.

"I doubt she'll freeze to death," Nate snipped. What a sissy Leslie was. "It hasn't been that cold. Now give me the damn thing."

"This was a gift from our mother when we were in Paris." Leslie shook the silky red material and said a few words in a language Nate didn't understand. Minnie giggled, and Nate had a feeling he'd just been called a name right to his face. He couldn't be mad since he honestly wasn't sure what had been said, and he wasn't going to ask.

Nate touched the badge on his shirt. Once upon a time, he wore it because he was Pa's deputy or would officially be one day. Now the star was there for the same reason Leslie wanted his sister to keep that shawl. "Fine," Nate spat. "Hand over your ugly coat."

Leslie huffed. His face pinched tight, eyes wrinkled at the corners. If looks could kill, Nate might have been lying next to that calf's skin. Though, Leslie did rip off his jacket and shove it at Nate.

"If I had anythin' of my own to use, I would," he snapped. He suspected these two were used to being catered to without ever giving of themselves. Though, Minnie had been willing to hand over the shawl. Now she clung to the damn thing as if that swatch of thin material were going to save her. If they all didn't die, it would be a blessed miracle. Lots of dangerous predators roamed about, and the country wasn't forgiving either. It was a rough leg they were traveling, picked on purpose to deter any who might be following by order of Mr. and Mrs. Fletcher.

Nate plucked a small branch off the ground. Leslie's coat wasn't the heavy wool worn in the wintertime. The blue fabric was lightweight. Nate tied the garment onto the stick, forming a sling sack on the end. He dropped the cuts of meat inside.

"How do you know how to do all this stuff?" Leslie hunkered near Nate.

"Pa taught me. Jesse too." Nate wiped his bloody blade on some grass, then closed it and shoved it in his pocket.

Minnie rocked herself near the fire. Tears glistened on her cheeks. She was likely missing her mother while she hugged tight to the shawl. Nate's chest ached too. At this time of day, Ma would be doing the supper dishes. Elizabeth liked to splash in the soapy water. Usually, Nate loved to talk about his family. At the moment, his heart hurt something awful. Talking about the mother and father he'd lost wouldn't get him any closer to Missouri, but it would make the trip harder to bear when all he really wanted to do was go home.

"It's time to go." He kicked dirt over the fire, outing the flames.

"Minnie's tired. So am I. Can't we rest here for the night?" Leslie sat down next to his sister.

Nate looked up. There was still light in the sky. Four or five hours before the sun would be down. They could cover some miles in that time. He might get an argument if he explained, and then Leslie might decide that Nate was pushing too hard, especially Minnie.

There was another way to get what he wanted, and it would be the truth. "If we stay, we'll have an unwanted visitor sometime tonight."

"What are you talking about?" Leslie's eyes squinted.

Minnie inched closer to her brother while staring at Nate. Both of them were waiting for an answer.

"I wasn't gonna say anythin' 'cause I didn't wanna scare ya, but have it your way. There's a wolf followin' us. He'll come for the carcass and maybe bring friends."

Leslie and Minerva exchanged a queer look, silently talking to one another, the same as Jesse and Nate could do. Leslie had his head cocked, and Minnie slightly shrugged. What Nate was reading between the two was that they weren't sure if they believed him. The dummies. He hadn't lied to them so far. Why would he start now? He wanted to live as much as they did, and he'd agreed to bring them. They should have been considering both of those things. This holdup certainly was making him regret his decision to let them trail along. But he couldn't leave them. These two would never survive without him.

A mean growl behind the three chilled the air. Nate twisted around. Minerva shrieked, and a puddle of piss formed at her feet. Leslie froze, not screaming like his sister but shaking worse than a leaf in a storm.

"Git!" Nate yelled, waving his arms.

A throaty growl roared from deep inside the belly of the gray beast, teeth bared. Be eaten or feed the wolf, it was the only thing Nate could think to do. He grabbed a slab of meat out of the sack he was holding and tossed the cut within three feet of the snarling animal. Its nose turned up, sniffing the air.

"Back away, slowly," Nate said in a low voice.

His traveling companions, one then the other, stiffly nodded. As they distanced themselves, the wolf came a step or two forward, then scooped up the meat with a crunch of its mighty jaws. Nate threw another hunk, this one aimed toward the carcass of the calf. There were enough bones and tidbits of tenderloin to hopefully keep the wolf distracted.

It tore into the calf.

"Run!" Nate led off down a slope and into a thick tree line. Leslie was on his heels, and Minnie wasn't too far behind.

The wolf was no longer in sight, but that didn't mean he wasn't still a threat. Biggest goldarn wolf Nate had ever seen, and calf remains wouldn't hold him over for more than an hour at best.

Behind a clump of evergreens, Nate stopped, hands on his knees and sucking air deep into his lungs. Leslie and Minnie bunched in around him, gasping for air themselves. Leslie's face glistened all over with sweat. Tears streaked Minnie's cheeks. No one said a word. They just breathed hard. Nate couldn't be the only one feeling damn lucky to have gotten out of that situation without being bitten or torn to pieces.

Nate pushed aside a thick, bristly branch behind him, glancing over his shoulder. At the top of the hill they had just fled down stood the wolf, its cold blue eyes focused. Blood stained the white fur around the animal's jaws. Nate quivered, and a soft squeak slipped out between his lips.

No way were they going to be dessert. There was only one thing he could do. Nate shot off through the forest, dodging tree limbs, jumping twigs on the ground, and pushing aside brush. Nothing was getting in his way of escaping. There couldn't be a worse death than being eaten alive.

Two sets of pounding feet crunched anything underfoot close behind him. Sticks snapped, rocks skidded, and Leslie's hot breath steamed the back of Nate's neck. God, he wished Pa or Jesse were there. That would be the end of the wolf. What was he going to do? The city kids weren't experienced in the field, not that he expected them to be. React with fear, that's all he figured they'd do, so it was up to him to think of a way to keep all their hides intact. Pa had taught him and Jesse never to panic. That would only make things worse, and sometimes the answer would present itself.

Nate slowed his pace, trying to calm his breathing by taking a deep inhale. Through the skylight of leaf-covered branches, bright rays of orange filtered through. The sun hung low over the mountaintop. Darkness would settle over the land in a few hours. That wasn't long, not when they needed a good place to hide, a safe shelter. Even if they were to find a cave, which was unlikely, that wolf had their scent. It would find them.

The fiery tones that rippled the length of the sky gave him an idea. They could build a good-size fire. Big jumping flames might keep that beast from sinking his sharp teeth into one of them during the night. But if anyone was searching for Nate, as he suspected the Fletchers to have hired someone, the bright light of a fire might bring that person snooping around. If that were to happen, he'd have no choice but to leave Leslie and Minerva behind and run for it.

Nate's boot toe caught on a rock. Down he timbered, palms and knees smacking the dirt. Only a step behind, Leslie fell over him and rolled into a ditch. Minnie hurtled Nate, then skidded through rocks to a halt. She grabbed her brother's sleeve and madly tugged.

"Get up!" she shrieked, yanking on his arm until he was on his feet. Both their chests lifted and sank at a fast pace. Nate's breathing wasn't any calmer, though he was trying his damnedest not to be afraid. There wasn't much that scared Pa or Jesse.

Minerva pointed. Nate turned his head. A flash of gray-white fur darted between several overgrown clumps of brush and disappeared into the tall weeds.

"Shit!" Nate smacked his fists against his thighs and grimaced. Both hands were scraped and burning from his fall.

That thing was still following them. No noise rose out of the bushes. It must have been watching them, stalking them, because Nate had that sense and the hair on his arms and legs stood erect.

Minerva had the right idea.

"Let's go!" Nate took off.

They were all running as fast as their little legs would carry them. Too afraid to dare look over his shoulder and see more than Leslie and Minnie, Nate steered them deeper into the hills. They splashed through a creek, an inch deeper than ankle high, soaking their feet inside their boots and up the hems of their pant legs.

On hands and knees, they scrambled up a steep bank, sand and pebbles breaking away under them. Nate slid backward a few times, diggings his fingers into the loose soil, hanging tight, hoping for a toehold to climb. Minnie tumbled, plowing right over him. Together, as a ball of arms and legs, they rolled into the water, splashing droplets into their eyes. Nate squinted. Every stitch on them was now drenched, including Nate's hair. Minnie screamed. She didn't look hurt, no blood, and she wasn't the only one who was wet, uncomfortable, and scared.

"Give me your hand." Leslie stretched his arm toward her from up top on the bank.

Nate snapped his fingers. A bath! That was it.

Leslie tilted his head and eyed Nate for a few seconds. Leslie no longer wore the bloodstained coat. Nate carried it, though he'd dropped it plenty, which would leave the scent on the ground. Plus, after gutting the calf, his pants and shirt had to be carrying the stink of death. That wolf knew the smell of a good meal—beef, not people. Mistaken identity. The odor of a man should have kept the wolf stalled unless one of them was hurt, and none of them were more than scratched up from falling.

Nate stood up, dripping wet, his feet still in the water. He grabbed the sack of meat he'd dropped. Most wild animals wouldn't approach a human. Rather, they'd flee or at least scurry out of sight. Maybe he could lead the thing away, then dunk himself a few times and wash out the odor as best he could.

Minerva scrambled to the top with her brother pulling on her arm. Nate had hoped to feed them for the next several days. Going without a few meals wouldn't kill them, but that hungry wolf certainly could. Nate tore open the coat holding the cuts of flesh.

"Come and git it!" he hollered as he tossed a piece within a couple of feet of the brush where the wolf's pale eyes watched amid leafy cover. Nate twisted around and faced the Harrisons. "Follow the stream." He lifted his chin. If his hunch was right, this was Blackbird Creek.

Before Jesse had become Pa's deputy, he worked on a cattle ranch for a man named Wallace. Jesse had told Nate about chasing cattle rustlers into this territory. Then they'd lost them in the woods. Not good for the cattleman, but maybe Nate could use the vast acres of forest as a maze and lose the wolf, or he could hide.

"Where are you going?" Leslie paled.

"Are you leaving us out here?" Minerva began to wail.

Nate was wishing he could turn off his ears. She was getting on his blasted nerves. He needed to think, and her bawling wasn't going to help him do that.

"I'll catch up." He nodded more for his own reassurance than theirs. "This stream flows south, in the direction of Green River. Just don't lose sight of the water. I'll find ya."

"You sure about this?" Leslie's hunched shoulders were a clear sign of him not feeling too confident. Minerva clung to his arm. She hadn't stopped crying.

"I ain't sure about nothin'." Nate didn't know what would happen once he ran out of meat. "The stage stops in Green River. Ask for Dutch. Tell 'im Nathanial Crosson sent ya. He'll see ya get to Gray Rock." After that, Leslie would know to ask for Deputy Adams.

"What about you?" Leslie was smart. There wouldn't be time to get help if Nate needed it.

"Tell my family I miss 'em." Tears flooded his eyes. "Now git goin'."

Leslie and Minnie disappeared into the shadows between the trees. Nate had his fingers crossed that those two didn't get lost.

He turned, and the wolf stood across the creek from him. Nate's breath caught, and he stiffened. Six, seven feet separated them. No bared teeth, that was good.

"Here ya go, boy." Nate tossed another piece of food. "Don't kill me." He took a step back.

The wolf snatched up the meat and swallowed in one great gulp. Nate was exhausted from everything, but instinct told him to run. Fast.

CHAPTER 6

NATE HAD RUN ABOUT A MILE. His quivering legs weren't going to hold up much longer. It felt like all he did today was hightail it away from that pesky wolf. On the mountaintop ahead sat the sun, which would soon be down.

Under the shadows of tall evergreens, Nate's chest heaved as he caught his breath. Where was the wolf? It wouldn't have taken the thing that long to eat one scrap of meat. Maybe it had given up and wasn't perusing him—its next meal. Or worse, what if the wolf caught Leslie and Minerva's scent and was going after them instead? There was nothing he could do about that tonight. Hopefully, the Harrison children found a safe place to rest before dark, up off the ground where the wolf couldn't get them.

Nate jumped, grabbing a branch, then swung his legs up. Once he had a good, strong hand- and foothold, he stretched for the next sturdy limb and started to climb. There wasn't time for him to gather enough wood for all night. A fire would have to be big in order to keep that animal away. It wasn't afraid of people, at least not anyone smaller than an adult. Maybe it'd been shot at before and recognized that they'd had no weapon. Sleeping in a tree

57

was the safest bet. Yet he wouldn't rest well even if he picked a thick branch. What if he fell out? That mean critter might be waiting in the bushes to pounce on him.

If only he had Buck. No stupid wolf could run as fast as the mustang. Buck was a fleet-footed horse, maybe the swiftest in all of Wyoming. Nate settled on a branch, sitting as though he were in the saddle. He could almost feel Buck running under his seat as the wind kicked up and the branch swayed. His body moved with the rhythm of the memory of his horse, and before him, he could image Buck's neck stretching forward with each long stride, his black mane flapping in the wind and Nate's hair blowing too.

A rifle boomed not far away. Two more shots followed. Nate twisted in the direction from which the sound had come, all thoughts of Buck pushed aside. Nate cursed the Fletchers in his head, fighting the urge to punch the tree trunk and likely break his knuckles.

"Probably a tracker out to get me." Because of them, he could no longer trust any adult. It was hard to tell who might be scouting for him, but this time, he had to risk it.

Nate scurried down the tree. If he could find that hunter, he might be able to get help for Leslie and Minerva before they got themselves lost. Plus, it would be some protection from the wolf, wherever it was. Nate's fingers were crossed that the shots had scared the thing off.

He dangled for a few seconds before he dropped from the lowest branch, unable to shake the sense that whoever fired those blasts was hunting him. Surely, not enough time had passed that someone could've picked up his trail that fast. The Fletchers couldn't have hired a capable tracker that quick— could they?

A wet, furry something touched his hand from behind. A scream flew out of him as he spun away. He'd been standing there facing the direction of the shots, staring off, thinking about what human danger could be coming, and in doing so, he failed to see the four-legged threat not an arm's length from him. Nate stumbled backward, dropping the sack of meat, and caught the heel of his boot on a stump. A second caterwaul burst out before he hit the dirt on his ass, and the wolf jumped back. They stared at one another for what seemed to be a long minute. It was cool on the mountain, but the animal was panting. Nate couldn't take a breath, couldn't move.

Boom! A bullet smacked a tree a hair above the wolf's head. Bark exploded, throwing fragments everywhere. Nate threw up his arms, covering his face. His eyes squinted tight shut.

"Damn! Missed that sumbitch!" came a voice out of the darkness between the trees.

A fading line of orange crowned the mountaintop. The sun was all but down, not much light, hard to see who it was. Nate's chest banged worse than a few minutes ago when he'd thought he was going to be a snack.

"Who are ya? What are ya doin' here?" A scruffy-bearded man lowered his rifle to his side.

Nate figured what the fella was really asking: Why was he way out in the middle of nowhere by himself? There were no wagon trails around there that he could have fallen off one and gotten lost, and there were no nearby towns that he might have wandered from. So how did a kid find himself deep in backwoods country?

Whatever he was about to say, he couldn't break eye contact. That was a telling sign of a liar, according to Pa. "I fell off a train." The truth would never be told.

The fella eyed him. Lying wasn't second nature to Nate anymore, not since becoming a Crosson, but he wasn't all that out of practice either. He liked to get his own way. What kid didn't? A little fib now and then never hurt anyone. Except for the times Pa and Ma had found him out. Nate rubbed at his backside just thinking about it.

None of that mattered anymore. Ma and Pa weren't there. He could say and do what he damn well wanted. Yet smart he needed to be. This fella could be a tracker hired by the Fletchers.

"Horse shit!" The fella turned his head and spit a long string of tobacco juice. "Why not foller the rails?"

His plaid shirt fit tight and was stained with God knew what. Tobacco drippings maybe or bloodstains, hard to tell in the dimming light. Nate swallowed hard. The fella snapped one side of his suspenders while waiting for an answer, his rifle in his other hand.

Nate doubted the man would believe him to be some bastard child left to run. His boots were too new. His shirt and pants were wrinkled and dirty now that he'd fallen umpteen times, but the threads were good material. Anyone could recognize store-bought wears, especially a tracker, a man who relied on his attention to detail to hunt his prey. Was this man hunting more than that wolf?

"I was hungry. Saw a rabbit, took chase, and before I knew it…" Nate looked about into the night as though asking where on earth he was. A few stars twinkled overhead. He wished he could fly right out of there and land in Missouri.

The man rubbed his bearded jaw. What Nate said had sounded reasonable, and any person who ever felt the pangs of hunger would understand the temptation of chasing anything that looked like a meal.

The fella's eyes narrowed. He sure was studying Nate, and Nate looked away, shifting weight onto the balls of his feet, ready to run.

Stay calm, he told himself, taking a deep inhale.

"Where's your horse?" Nate tried to take the focus off him, and it was odd that the fella wasn't riding one, no pack animal either, which led him to believe the man's camp was nearby. Perhaps Nate's scream had brought him hustling.

A crooked line of yellow teeth parted the man's lips until his face wore a stupid grin as cockeyed as those teeth. "Why? You ain't plannin' on eatin' 'im, are ya?" He chuckled.

"No." But Nate would steal the animal if this fella turned out to be working for the Fletchers. Doubtful, though. A predator didn't usually joke with its prey. Or was this casual attitude a trick?

"Name's Amos." The man pulled a small buckskin pouch out of his shirt pocket. Between two fingers, he pinched a plug of weed and shoved the brown wad inside his mouth. His lower lip stuck out like a sore.

Other than the carbine in his right hand, nothing about Amos's manner alerted Nate to danger. The fella hunkered, rubbed the end of his nose with the back of his hand, and then spit. There was only one thing he could be looking at.

He turned his head toward Nate. "What the hell were ya doin' playin' with that damn dog? He's a devil. You'll git bit." Amos lifted his gun hand. A wide, ugly scar wrapped around his palm to the dorsal side of his hand, clear up to his pointer finger.

Nate squinted, for it was growing darker by the minute. No pinky finger on Amos's right hand. Nate's stomach churned. "That wasn't no dog."

Without lantern light, could be that Amos hadn't seen right. There was such a thing as wild dogs. A few months ago, Shorty and his men and Jesse had killed a pack of them that had been attacking Shorty's herd.

Before Nate could say that it was a timber wolf, the fella shook his fist in the direction where the wolf had disappeared into the darkness between the trees into the forest.

"I know exactly what that sumbitch is. My partner found that wolf as a pup and raised 'im after I killed the mother. I swear that damn animal knows … everythin'. That I wanted to make pup steaks out of 'im that night Bill found 'im." Amos licked his lips. "Damn wolf has been a constant nuisance, never liked me. Won't come close to camp no more 'cause he knows I'll feed 'im a bullet."

"Where's your partner, Bill? Can't he tie 'im up or somethin'? Or at least make 'im stop chasin' me." Pet or not, the wolf had trailed Nate. The beast trusted only its master, not even his partner, and for good reason. He rubbed his palm where the wolf had nosed him. As long as that keen sniffer didn't catch the scent of the two Nate sent in the other direction and then go after them.

"Bill's dead. Got hisself shot a week or so back." Amos's gaze turned to the south. Moonlight snow-capped the tree-covered hills for miles.

"Damned ol' Crow woman, meaner than cat shit. Has a little shack three days walk from here. Runs a trade business." Amos shook his head. "I told 'im never turn his back on that ol' witch."

"I don't understand. If that wolf hates you and Bill is gone, why don't the stupid thing just run off?" Why stay where there was danger? Not that the Fletchers would physically harm Nate, but he recognized them as a threat and had taken full advantage of the first opportunity to get away from them. Why hadn't the wolf done the same? Nate would bet that this hadn't been the first time in recent days that Amos had taken a shot at his deceased friend's pet.

"Montana was never far from Bill's side, too used to being around a human. Ain't nobody 'round here but me, though he keeps somewhat of a distance. Tried a few times to bait 'im in with cuts of meat. Wouldn't fall for it. Bill spoiled that animal."

"How so?"

Who kept a wolf for a pet? Nate had nursed a sick squirrel for a week and begged to keep it for a pet with its puffy tail and the cute chattering it did as though it had been talking to him. Buddy would even sit on Nate's shoulder while he did his chores. As soon as Buddy was well enough for Pa, he made Nate set the squirrel free. Wild animals were supposed to be in their natural environment, not family pets. He had understood Pa's explanation, but that hadn't kept him from asking a few more times to keep Buddy. In the end, Pa walked out into the woods with him, and they returned Buddy to nature together.

"Bill's squaw was kilt by Injuns up in Montana. She had a month to go before the baby was to be born. We went out trappin'. When we returned, we found her. Her neck was slit and her belly sliced wide open. Those sick bastards pulled the baby out, left it there on the ground, the cord wrapped around her neck too many times for coincidence."

Nate's tongue wouldn't work. Sorry was what he was thinking, but the air in his lungs stuck there, his mouth agape. What a horrible thing.

Ma popped into his head. He prayed the baby was growing and healthy. Word must have reached his folks by now that he'd run away. No doubt they were worried. The strain wasn't something Ma needed in her condition, and who was to say that Pa was up and around to comfort her? For all Nate knew, he was dead. Jesse was there. He'd do what he could, which eased Nate's mind, or he might go mad thinking about it all.

"Bill went on a killin' spree for a while, revenge, and I stuck by his side. Then one day, he was just tired, so we left them high-up hills and wandered here. Bill had changed. He was quiet and sullen, put all his energy into his work." Side by side, they walked out of the clearing and into the dark tree line.

"The day we found that pup, something inside him fixed itself. His face brightened. His mood was instantly more lighthearted. He treated that pup like a damn kid, feedin' it small cuts of meat even as it grew. Bill always did that, but not enough that Montana wouldn't hunt on his own and learn independence." Amos stepped around a dead tree.

Nate was close behind. "My God, are ya heartless? After all that, tryin' to shoot your best friend's dog? I've met some bad people, but you beat all."

"Shit. I ain't as bad as some. And that mean critter ain't my animal to care for. I got my memories of Bill. What I don't need is that damn wolf scarin' off the game I'm tryin' to trap." Amos shook his gun.

A dovetailed log shelter sat in a hollow not a hundred yards from where Nate had climbed the tree to get away from Montana. Trees surrounded the small shack. A second building about the same size was nestled into the side of a bank, which served as the rear wall. The other three walls were built with the same river rock used for the base of the cabin. Skins were stretched in strategic spots on the ground where the leaves wouldn't cover them with shade during the day and the sun could dry the furs for tanning. A fire burned inside a stone ring outside the house, small puffs of smoke flowing up out of the chimney top.

Nights in the mountains were cold this time of year. Some of the leaves were changing color. But tonight, Nate was sweaty. All the stress and running. For once, he wouldn't have given Ma any crap about swimming in the tub. A warm soak would feel great on his sticky skin.

"You said you knew some bad people … Like who?" Amos knelt next to the fire, feeding in a handful of twigs, his rifle leaned against the door of the cabin about six, seven feet away.

The question was odd. Without thinking, Nate took a backward step. The flames were between them, but some sense was telling him to be cautious. His exact words were that he had *met* some bad people, not *known* them. Was this fella suspicious? Surely, any price the Fletchers had put on Nate's head hadn't so soon reached the ears of this mountain man.

"What d'ya mean?" Nate played stupid, shrugging.

Amos stood causally while scratching at his groin. The lines on his face were smooth. Not one jaw muscle twitched or tensed. Most of his weight was leaned into one leg, and his hands floated at his sides. By all accounts, his entire body was at ease. Only, his dark eyes bored into Nate.

"Can you read?" Amos reached behind his back and pulled a folded newspaper out of his waistband.

"Yeah, I can read." Nate found his voice, though it sounded frail to him. The night had become pitch black all around them, for the moon was hidden behind a cloud, except for the wavering light thrown off by the fire about four feet in circumference. Shadows from the swaying flames cast what had to be the perfect imitation of a sinister mask across Amos's face as he took a step closer to Nate and held out the printed paper.

Nate didn't move to accept it. After a few seconds, Amos tossed the paper at him, then turned and picked up a coffeepot, placing it over the flames, rattling the tin lid. Steam hissed. Water must have splashed out into the fire. For the moment, Amos's attention was on coffee, so Nate dared to unfold the paper. What would he find printed on the pages?

There had been a reporter from Birch Creek at Nate's custody trial, actually several reporters from different places all over. Lots of people knew that he'd been ripped away from home, reading about the fight between Nate's folks and the Fletchers for entertainment. Had this fella gotten ahold of one such paper? Even so, no picture of him had been taken, but the Fletchers likely had posted a description, and Nate's white hair was a dead giveaway.

"Ten thousand dollars!" Nate blurted.

His eyes stuck on the bold black prink front and center on the first page. Unbelievable. That was more money than most folks earned in a lifetime. What were those two ninnies thinking? They'd have half the country chasing him. No doubt, the rougher fifty percent. That would be a lot of ducking and dodging and hiding out. It might take him forever to get to Missouri.

A hard hand slapped around his wrist, squeezing tight, pinching his skin. Nate jerked, dropping the paper in the dirt.

"That ten thousand's mine!" Amos wickedly grinned, displaying his yellow teeth, all five of them. His tongue jutted out like a snake about to strike. And the man had taken pot-shots at his dead friend's pet, an animal he'd have played a part in raising. God only knew what he was capable of doing to make Nate cooperate. No town for miles, days away, if not more. That added up to a lot of unwanted time together.

With the rough edge of his boot heel, Nate thumped Amos on the shin. A yowl jumped out of his throat, sounding worse than an injured coyote. Amos grabbed for his leg while hopping up and down on the other. Nate shot off as fast as he could go with his drumming heart leading the way. Amos swung his arm, snatched a fistful of the back of Nate's shirt, and yanked him off his feet, dropping him flat on the rocky ground. A large knee began to drop toward Nate's chest. It was as though he were watching his life play out slowly before his eyes. Once Amos had the bulk of his weight holding him down, there'd be no escape.

CHAPTER 7

WITHIN NATE WAS A CROSSON, and Crossons never gave up. An ear-piercing scream thrust out from the deepest, most primitive part of him. And he kept screeching, playing hell on Amos's ears, his face wrinkled in a nasty grimace. Nate thrashed, bucked, threw handfuls of quickly grasped dirt at Amos's eyes, and he kicked and scratched at any part of the man within striking distance. Amos's arms flailed in retaliation, but his knee slammed down, pinning Nate against the earth, knocking his wind out. Gasping and choking on the stirred-up dust, unable to move, Nate was caught the same as the wild animals this trapper had captured and killed for a price.

Tears sprang into his eyes, yet he wasn't done fighting. With a twist of his waist, he drove a knee up into Amos's groin, buckling him over with a throaty groan, his weight now all on Nate. Unable to breathe a sip of air, Nate couldn't even scream.

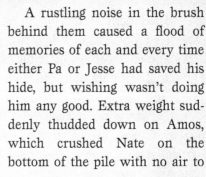A rustling noise in the brush behind them caused a flood of memories of each and every time either Pa or Jesse had saved his hide, but wishing wasn't doing him any good. Extra weight suddenly thudded down on Amos, which crushed Nate on the bottom of the pile with no air to

scream. Amos ripped left then right, and a vicious growl stifled the air. What in the hell? Nate tried to wiggle free but couldn't.

Amos's shrieks were deafening. His grip torn off Nate, he rolled across the dirt with the jaws of the wolf around the scruff of his neck, dragging him. White teeth sank in, some stained red. That was no pet. He was a killer by instinct. Cold-blooded in his own way, eyes black and hateful.

Nate pushed up off the ground. Amos's desperate cries filled his ears, and Nate wailed for the safety of home. He ran toward the shack. No way in hell would Amos live through that or even the next five minutes. Bones crunched. Amos's yells were cut off, and the roar of the wolf echoed triumphantly through the dark forest. Nate slammed the door behind him, and with one quick swipe, he had the bar locked in place.

Scratches at the door told him the wolf was out there in the dark and waiting for him. Nate backed away from the sound, bumping into a chair at the table. Then he turned and tripped over a bucket on the floor. He scurried on all fours to a stack of wood and tossed a few chunks into the fireplace. It took him a minute of blowing to get the flames standing tall.

The bright light and the crackling of the fire calmed his jitters a little, or at least he was breathing a bit easier. The scratching on the wood had stopped too.

He glanced around. The place was built sturdy. Had to be because of the harsh winters. Each log was notched, linked, and sealed tight to the adjoining one, no open seams. He stomped a foot. The dirt floor was packed hard as stone. That crazy animal wasn't going to dig his way in. There was also a haunch of salt pork dangling from a hook on the ceiling near the door.

If necessary, the bucket could be used for Nate to take a piss in. It was possible to hole up there until the wolf lost interest and went away. But this was home to that critter, and Nate knew how hard it was to leave that one place you felt a special tie to. It was more than just a roof over his head like the Fetchers wanted to provide him. That wolf might hang around for a while, and Nate didn't have the one thing he couldn't live without—water—especially if he ate any of the salt pork.

A howl just outside broke the silence. Nate jumped so that his head nearly whacked the roof beams. At the window, he pulled back the shutter and pressed his face to the smudged glass.

The fire outside was dying. Amos's corpse lay within the faint ring of light. Nate swallowed hard, his fingers digging into the windowsill. He'd seen dead bodies before, but it still gave him the willies. Worse than that was the spine-tingling feeling of being watched and knowing the killer was out there. He shrank until only his eyes peeked over the sill. It was too dark to see much of anything. What moonlight there was wasn't enough to unmask the devil hiding out there. But the hair standing on the back of Nate's neck was a telling sign that the beast was close.

Level with the windowsill stood a stockpile of firewood. Out of the dark, a gray-white blur leaped, its feet on the wood, standing legs spread wide apart but aligned with Nate's nose. Nate shuddered, his eyes raised. The wide jaw and flat gray head lowered. Yellow eyes stared into his mesmerized gaze.

Scream, dummy! But his mouth wouldn't open. Nate's arms and legs came awake with a wild flail, sending him tumbling backward into the table where he fell, knocking over a chair. Claws attached to a massive paw scraped the window once then twice. The spine-prickling sound jolted him to his feet.

Paper thin, the wavy glass groaned under the pressure. *Holy shit!* Nate twisted in every direction. No weapons. Amos's gun was outside, and he hadn't thought to grab the damn thing. At the hearth lay a long stick with the end charred black. No iron poker. There had to be a knife somewhere to cut meat, but most men carried their knives on their belts. Pa and Jesse did.

Amos probably hadn't been any different. This wasn't like home where Ma kept butchering knives in the kitchen.

Nate hurried, tossing stuff everywhere, hunting anything to protect himself. The glass creaked. He glanced over his shoulder. In the lower corner, the pane was webbed, ready to splinter any second.

Maybe he could whack the wolf on the nose with a frying pan. One sat near the stick fire poker. No, Nate wasn't strong enough to fight the wolf. But a few times, he had saved himself from being a meal by providing another source of food.

Nate grabbed a chair, then jumped up, standing on the seat under the salt pork. His fingers fumbled from shaking, not loosening the knot in the string fast enough. On the table, he sawed off chunks with his pocket knife, which was big enough for this task but nowhere near the size of weapon he'd need to fend off or kill a full-grown male wolf.

Nate took a deep breath before stepping toward the window, the wolf still in the attack position and keenly watching his every move. His hand trembled worse as he reached, holding globs of meat tight in the other. Was he out of his cotton-picking mind? At best, he'd likely lose a few fingers. He shook off the thought of the worst thing that could happen.

With a grunt, he broke the seal, lifting the window an inch. The wolf sniffed as his black nose pressed into the tiny space. Nate poked the pieces of meat through the slit as quick as he could. The wolf gobbled them. His focus was on the food, so Nate could actually think. He snapped shut the window, hoping to God it didn't shatter before he had time to close the shutters and lock them.

Nate turned his back and slid down the wall as the gut-sickening chewing sounds filled his ears and his heart with dread. What was he going to do? Outthinking a man was one thing, but to outsmart a creature so different from himself, an animal he didn't fully understand. How? With all his life experiences—and he'd had many that most boys could never fathom—dealing with a wily wolf wasn't on his list of been there, done that, not even a similar encounter to go off of. Instinct alone was telling him to run and hide, but he couldn't do that in the dark.

At least Leslie and Minnie weren't stuck there with a mad wolf lurking about. Hopefully, they'd been found by someone who could help them get where they were headed, but Nate doubted it. Out there in the hills were men like Amos and the ones who had shot the calf and left a kid in the wilderness to fend for himself.

The chewing stopped. Nate didn't dare peek, not wanting to see those yellow eyes. Instead, he stared into the flickering flames. How was he going to get out of there? Dying of thirst wouldn't be any good, but getting chewed up, he imagined, would be a whole lot worse.

Pa could think quick on his feet, though he was a planner. Jesse was rash at times but not often wrong. He had a good gut sense, and Pa taught him the rest, the same as Nate. There had to be a way out of this. It was just a matter of finding it, and if he didn't, then he'd come up with his own plan just like Pa would. But he couldn't erase the ugly picture of Amos's torn-up body, and it'd likely be the first thing the morning light brought into focus when he left the cabin. He just needed to remind himself to grab the gun. He wasn't going to end up ground chuck.

CHAPTER 8

NATE WOKE WITH A START, slumped against the wall under the window. He pushed up. In his dream, the big bad wolf had broken down the door and, just as Nate had backed into a corner, none other than the Fletchers waltzed in, arm in arm, smirking, and called off their hound from hell. Thank God the door was intact. No wolf. No Fletchers.

Nate yawned then stretched, easing stiffness out of his bones. Sunshine streamed in through the cracks around the shutters. Other than birds singing, it was quiet outside. No scratching or growling at the window or door. Nate's stomach rumbled.

After a few minutes of searching inside a dusty cupboard, he found a small jar of honey and a hunk of stale bread wrapped in cloth and crawling with ants. The tiny pests could have the hard bread. The golden-brown honey was all his. Licking his lips, he flicked the bugs off the jar, then took his plunder and sat at the table. The place was a mess, not exactly organized like Ma's kitchen, and Nate was too hungry to hunt for a fork or spoon. His pointer and middle fingers together would work just fine.

Nate lifted his hand and dug his first two fingers into the stickiness

while trying to forget the piece of salt pork on the table. He shoved another dollop into his mouth, then spit out a chunk of comb. The sweetness of the honey was good, but bacon was his favorite and would fill him better. But he couldn't eat the meat. It was ammunition against the wolf. It would keep that thing from munching on him once he left the shack, the same as the calf had. Nate had his fingers crossed.

With the elbow of his sleeve, he rubbed a clean spot on the window. Near the tree line, under the shade of limbs, sat a wagon. Last night in the dark, he hadn't noticed it. No corral or horse or mule. Where was the animal that pulled the weather-beaten buckboard? Perhaps Montana, the so-called pet, had eaten Nate's ride.

He found a satchel with several species of plant leaves stored inside. Some of the dried pieces were locoweed. When ingested by cows or horses, the animals acted crazy, staggering and such as though drunk. Would it work on a wolf? Nate grinned.

With the satchel strap slung over his shoulder around his neck, packed with the honey and most of the salt pork and the herbs left there, Nate slowly opened the door, allowing for the sunlight to spill inside the musty room. He blinked against the bright light. Held in his right hand, his pitching arm, was a cut of meat large enough to hold all three sprigs of the locoweed that he had poked down in between the muscle fibers. With any luck, the wolf wouldn't smell the weed, only the meat, and take the bait.

He took a deep breath and stepped outside, waiting to be pommeled and torn to pieces by the wolf. Nate turned his head right then left, trying his darndest not to stare at what was left of Amos. No sign of the beast. Thank God.

The buzzing of the swarming flies around the corpse was enough to set his heart to thumping. He hurried toward the wagon. It only made sense that the animal used to pull the buckboard would be kept close by. Back home, Pa typically kept the wagon housed in the barn or near about the corral.

He pushed pine limbs out of his way as he searched behind where the wagon sat. A hooved animal stomped behind a hedge of brush. Nate smiled.

It took him a few minutes to find a rope and loop it around the mare's neck. A quick turn about the yard, searching the one shed and the back of the wagon, revealed that neither Amos nor his late partner owned a saddle or bridle, but bareback was better than no horse.

An hour later, Nate yanked on the mare's mane, halting her. In the dirt near the horse's feet was a boot track, a partial print of a child-size shoe. It had to be Minnie or Leslie. This was backwoods country, too remote for most nesters. The soil wasn't tillable, awful rocky in the hills. It was doubtful that track belonged to some settler's kid.

"Whew." Nate let out a long exhale. He figured they'd have themselves lost by now, wandering in a circle, upping their odds of running into that mad wolf.

By noon, Nate found where the Harrisons had camped for the night and managed a small fire. His stomach rumbled, and his bottom hurt from the spanking trot, the only speed the nag of a mare would tolerate without bucking or rearing. He slid off the bony spine of his horse and rubbed at his behind.

After picketing the mare on the lead rope, Nate stretched out in the sun, letting the heat shine on him, and ate some honey. A chapping wind kicked up, hinting of the harsh autumn to come. Leaves turned over on the trees. There were more red and yellow ones among all the green than a few days ago. Why hadn't he thought to run away wearing a coat? Cold weather would settle in soon.

The mare lifted her head, grass hanging out the sides of her mouth. For a few seconds, her ears perked up. Then she went back to pulling what little grass there was.

Nate shielded his eyes from the bright sun. What had caught her attention? *Please don't let it be that wolf.* Nothing but trees. Some horses spooked easily, especially when it was windy.

Twenty yards above them on the ridge side, something moved.

The killer appeared, standing on a jetting of rock. Nate leaped to his feet, quickly scrounging through the satchel while keeping his eyes on his enemy. He felt the ball of meat concealing the locoweed.

"Here, boy. I got somethin' for ya." He coaxed in a soft, sweet voice, waving the blob of salt pork, hoping that mean critter caught the scent.

Behind Nate, something crashed through the brush. It sounded like a herd of buffalo. He twisted around. Not fifteen feet away, a big old granddaddy grizzly stood on its hind legs. Its muzzle was gray, but the thing must have stood ten, eleven feet high and weighed at least a few hundred pounds more than the mare. The bear's great jaws opened wide. A ferocious roar shook the forest.

"Ahh!" Warm piss tricked down Nate's legs, forming a puddle around his feet.

The mare screeched, bucking and rearing, pulling the picket looser with each jerk. Nate fired his meatball, bopping the grizzly dead center on its wide, flat head. The meat dropped to the ground. Lifting its nose, the bear sniffed, locating the tiny morsel of food. Nate stared dumbfounded at his hands. He was covered in the scent of honey and pig meat. From his feet up, his body began to almost convulse with the realization that he was about to be mauled by a giant grizzly with paws the size of frying pans and six-inch claws.

The mare panicked to the point of frothing at the mouth. Nate shook out the satchel. When the jar of honey hit the ground, it smashed open on a rock. What was left of the salt pork lay next to the shards of glass. Finally, he was thinking clearly enough to run to the mare, but he couldn't get near the worked-up animal. Damn thing kept biting at him.

On all fours, the grizzly charged. Montana leaped out of the brush, head down, teeth bared, and jaws snapping. That crazy wolf took a stand between Nate and the roaring bear. Growls and roars that sounded like war cries filled the air. No other noise could be heard. The forest suddenly appeared desolate. All other lifeforms had scattered or hidden. The two giant beasts lunged. Fur mangled with the clash of teeth and claws. A blur of brown and gray rolled across the ground.

Nate grabbed the mare's line just as she ripped free from the picket. She bolted, and he hung on with both hands. Smacked off a tree, he was seeing stars but managed to hold on to the rope while being dragged behind. Rocks, sticks, anything on the ground took a poke at him as the mare wildly ran. Crags of brush scratched at him, tearing his clothing, and twice more, he thumped against tree bark. With each frantic stride of the mare, Nate's hands slipped until he lost hold of his fast getaway.

He rolled five or six times, then landed facedown in the dirt. There wasn't a spot on his scraped-up arms and legs that didn't burn like hellfire. With a moan, he pushed over, remaining flat on his back, and stared up through the treetops into the blue sky. Puffy white clouds drifted past. It all looked so peaceful.

What a crock of crap. Life for him was anything but.

Nate forced himself to stand. Wooziness overtook him, and he leaned against a tree. Tears filled his eyes. The ache in his chest for home was worse than the cuts and bruises that covered his body. Blood oozed along his hairline. He touched gingerly at the knot on his skull where he'd bounced off a tree.

The mare was long gone, so Nate had no choice but to hoof it. But from there, which way should he go? He touched at his temple, his brain swimming. He closed his eyes for a few deep breaths. His aching body screamed for rest with the least little movement, but he couldn't stop now. His friends—they'd already been too many hours on their own. Two city kids, how long could they survive in the wilds without help?

Throughout the day, his pace faded. Not that he'd been walking with any gusto. More so, he stumbled along and had picked himself up off the ground a few times after a dizzy spell hit him.

He had decided to keep to the trail of kicked-up leaves left behind by the mare as she had fled, and he certainly wasn't about to backtrack toward the man-killing wolf and grizzly. He came to a shallow stream, which he then followed, winding downhill for no better reason than it was the easiest way out of the deep, dark woods. Every step, though, he huffed and puffed.

Near nightfall, Nate happened upon a set of wagon tracks. To his utter shock, a pair of larger and smaller child-size boot prints were there. He circled, studying the signs just as Pa had taught him. Leslie's and Minnie's tracks disappeared, but the line of the wheel pressed into the roadway remained. The wagon had stopped. The horse that pulled the wagon had stamped the dirt. He knew this because the hoofprint was deeper set in that one spot. A horse on the move couldn't have made that mark.

Nate pulled his shirt tighter, for this evening, the night air carried a bite. When it got too dark to follow the wagon's path, he curled up under the nearest tree. He was doggone tired. His head was thumping, his body ached, and if he didn't soon get something to eat, he might just chow down on the grass of the fields like King Nebuchadnezzar did in biblical times when he went bat-shit crazy.

Too much had happened in such a short time that Nate doubted his ability to handle much more. He wiped at his eyes. Had it not been for Montana, he would have been dead. Now that he really thought about it, the wolf had saved him twice. At first, he thought Montana had attacked both him and Amos. Now he wasn't so sure.

In the distance, a wolf howled. Chances were Montana hadn't survived the fight with the grizzly. Maybe not even a pack of wolves could have taken down that monster. But that wolf was a big one too.

Nate cupped his hands around his mouth. "Montana! Come 'ere, boy!" he hollered several times, then waited, listening into the night.

A coon chattered somewhere in a tree not too far off. Mostly, it was the wind that talked, long and hard at times. Nate shivered, never fully falling asleep. He drifted in and out of consciousness as the stars shifted overhead.

At the break of dawn, he followed the wagon tracks, his stomach loudly begging for a bite of anything. Around mid-morning, he stopped at a creek the wagon had passed through. Using his pocketknife, he whittled the end of a long stick into a spear.

It took over a dang hour before he speared a fish. One wouldn't be enough to satisfy his rumbling belly. Most of the afternoon was spent knee-deep in the ripple of current, stabbing at the water, splashing himself until he was wet from head to toe. But his work wasn't done yet. He gathered leaves and sticks.

The sun was well to the west when Nate licked the flaky remains of his second trout off his fingers, then outed the fire. What made him think of the wolf, he didn't know. Perhaps it was the comforting thought of not being all alone in the big bad world. On the ground near where Nate had taken his meal, he left the fish heads and tails for Montana, if he was still alive. If not, some other critter would enjoy the tidbits.

For two days, he lumbered after the wagon through the foothills. On the morning of the third day, fog hung heavy over a pond in the basin far below the outcropping of rocks on which he stood and stretched the cold night out of his bones.

A thick gray spiral of smoke caught his eye. Nate's insides fluttered. A cabin or camp. Someone was down there, and that stark line climbing higher into the sky meant they were home. The wagon tracks were headed in that direction. Nate smiled. It would be good to see Leslie and Minnie again. Then he thought of Amos, and his happy grin faded. He hoped to God the Harrison kids hadn't tied in with an underhanded weasel like him. Nate had been too easily fooled, almost captured for a price. And he owned an understanding of the ways of the men around him. Those two city dwellers were accustomed to the genteel, not grubby mountain folk.

Dingy gray, the weather-beaten cabin with a covered porch and curtainless widows sat silent under a spatter of tall trees. Long, leafy branches stretched over the roof, scratching the stone chimney each time a gust kicked up. Glass panes rattled a protest against the biting air. Fall had arrived overnight.

On the porch, a black and brown coonhound slapped his tail against the planks. Lifting his head from where he rested all sprawled out, he bellowed once. His job was done, and he dropped his head onto the porch. Those inside were now aware of the presence of a newcomer.

The door flew open. "Nathanial!" Leslie grabbed him by the arms, swinging them both around. Minnie squealed from the doorway behind them.

An old Indian woman, with more gray in her hair than black, pushed past Minnie. With each hobbled stride, she leaned heavily forward on a tall walking stick. Creased with deep-set wrinkles, her leathery face and sunken dark eyes appeared naturally unfriendly. Her digits and wrists deviated inward, each joint oversized, and the hump on her back was pronounced.

The old woman thumped the end of her stick on the porch. Her lips thinned, and she eyeballed Nate. The lazy hound rose and trotted off around the corner of the cabin, his tail tucked between his legs.

"Old woman."

Nate's gut rumbled. His throat was dry, and he hadn't slept well since being forced away from home. He'd nearly been mauled by a huge grizzly after slipping out of the clutches of a greedy mountain man, and the cuts on his arms and legs from being dragged behind the horse cracked open and bled if he bumped anything. He was in no mood to put up with anyone's guff.

"Get me somethin' to eat." He stomped a foot.

She snorted, then thumped her cane once again. "I am called Grannie." She then hobbled into the house, and the door slammed shut.

"You should watch how you talk to her. I can't believe she didn't hit you with that stick." Leslie rubbed the crown of his head. "She's basically made slaves out of me and Minnie. We've been going along with it, hoping you'd show up. We need to get out of here."

"She scares me." Minnie chimed in. "She's always mumbling, but there's no one there. It's spooky."

Leslie sighed. "I told you she's not a witch. Don't let that spirit world nonsense she goes on about get to you."

"Witch," Nate repeated, recalling that Amos had said his partner was killed by an old Crow woman, a witch. "You're right. We gotta leave."

"No." Leslie grabbed his arm. "You don't understand."

He peeked in the window. The old woman was at the cookpot hanging over the fire. Her back was to them.

"She has a newspaper. I saw it. It has a description of you," Leslie whispered.

"I know. I saw one myself." How many others were keeping their eyes open for him? Because of his trouble, his friends were in danger. He'd have to split from them as soon as he could once they were away from there.

"There's something else." Leslie wrung his hands.

Minnie clutched at her brother's sleeve, her eyes full of tears.

"Well, what is it?" Nate had to remind himself to keep his voice down.

"There was a man here looking for you. He and Grannie talked for a long time." Leslie glanced across the acreage toward the pond. "He camped there for a day or two. This morning, he was gone."

"You catch a name?"

"Luther Blackhorse."

Nate dropped to his knees and gasped for air. "Was he wearin' a buckskin jacket with fringe and duel bandoliers slung cross-style over both shoulders?"

"Yeah." Leslie nodded. "He had long hair as dark as midnight. A red hawk feather dangled from a braid behind his left ear."

The door creaked open. Leslie jerked Nate up onto his feet, though his legs quivered. He shouldered most of Nate's weight.

"What's wrong with you?" the old witch growled, eyeing him from head to toe.

"I think I'm gonna be sick." Nate rubbed his hand down the side of his face.

"Then git off my porch. Go on." She waved him toward the trees.

"I better help him," Leslie offered, keeping a tight hold on Nate. It was a good thing. Otherwise, he might have fainted. "Minnie, hold under his other arm." Leslie's little sister obediently grabbed Nate.

"Not you." Grannie yanked Minnie away by a fistful of hair. A shrill scream belted out of the little girl.

"Let go of my sister!" Leslie dropped Nate, grabbed his sister's arm, and jerked her in the opposite direction.

"She has dishes to do." Grannie ripped on Minnie's sleeve.

Leslie jerked back. A tugging war took place with Minnie yelling her head off between the two, but the old woman's yellow eyes were stuck on Nate. And that's when it hit him. Work wasn't the only thing on her mind. She was seeing him in the form of a fat payday.

Grannie let go of Minnie as though the girl were on fire, and the old woman froze, didn't even blink. Her gaze stuck on something behind Nate. Leslie turned. His eyes widened. Then his entire body stiffened. Minnie shrieked, though no one was seesawing her. Nate dared to turn his head, looking over his shoulder, praying to God it wasn't Blackhorse, the fierce dog soldier who had escaped being killed or captured during the Battle of Summit Springs.

"Montana!" Nate practically cheered but kept his distance. He still didn't one hundred percent trust the wolf. He hadn't expected him to survive the fight with the grizzly, but there the animal was, baring his fangs at Grannie.

Most of the fur covering Montana's one shoulder was stained red, and he carried a cut the length of his muzzle. Yet, with head down, ears pinned back, and his forelegs spread in a way that broadened his massive chest, he looked every inch the unstoppable killer.

Grannie stepped backward toward the door, bumping into the frame, drawing up her walking stick, ready to swing. "You!" she spat at Nate. "There is a powerful spirit inside you to be able to beckon the wolf."

In the Crow culture, the wolf was a symbol of strength. Old man Pike, owner of the livery in Gray Rock and longtime Indian fighter, had taught Nate lots about the many tribes he'd come up against over the years. That was how he knew about Blackhorse being a dog soldier.

Nate crossed his fingers behind his back. "If you lay a hand on either of my friends again, I'll sic my wolf on ya."

The old woman's lips curled. "The wolf is savage, but he is not evil. His intention is in his actions. He does not wish to harm me. Though, he will do what he must to protect you."

She had just described Pa. Why did he have to get shot all those weeks ago? He should have been at the trial with Ma. He should have stopped the Fletchers from taking Nate away. Now his life had reverted to a time when he rode with the Younger gang, when all he knew was struggle and heartache.

Nate kicked the dirt.

Grannie disappeared inside, the door left hanging open. Leslie put an arm around Minnie's shoulders, pulling her in close against his side.

"Will he attack us?" Leslie and his sister both were pale.

"I don't think so." Nate shrugged. He couldn't say for sure. After all, Montana was a wild animal.

"Can you make him go away?"

It was evident by the Harrisons' wide eyes that they weren't going to relax until Montana was gone.

"Here." Grannie appeared in the doorway before Nate could shoo Montana off, a plate of something in each hand. "This one you feed to your friend." Her eyes were but mean slits as she eyed Montana.

The wolf's nose lifted, and he sniffed. Nate couldn't help himself. Inwardly, his senses were all screaming to be cautious, but he was damn near starved. All he could focus on was that food. Venison stew, had to be. The smell was different than that of beef or pork, and Grannie had no stock animals that Nate saw.

He greedily snatched both tins. First, he set Montana's portion on the ground a few feet from where the wolf stood, his tongue out and panting. Nate took a seat on the porch and shoveled a big bite into his mouth. Leslie and Minnie kept their eyes on the wolf and hesitantly sat next to Nate. Grannie plopped down on a rickety chair that squeaked under her weight.

"Eat," Grannie said under her breath in a wicked, coaxing tone. Only, Nate had good ears. He looked up. She was leaned forward, gaze on the wolf and a small, satisfied smile on her face.

Montana nosed the food.

Amos popped into Nate's mind. Grannie had killed Amos's partner.

He dropped his plate and sprang to his feet while spitting out his mouthful. "No!" he screamed and ran toward Montana.

The wolf bolted into the tree line. With one mighty swing of Nate's leg, he punted the tin across the yard, chunks of venison stew splattering the ground everywhere.

When he turned toward the cabin, Leslie and Minnie were on their feet, holding tight to one another. Grannie had a shotgun aimed at all three of them.

"Get in the house." She jerked the end of the rifle toward the door. "And don't dawdle."

They hustled toward the door. When Nate got within arm's reach, Grannie poked him in the guts with the killing end of her carbine.

"I should have fed you the poison instead. You would be much less of a headache dead." She pulled a copy of the same newsprint Amos had shown him out of the waistband of her skirt. "This doesn't say you have to be alive to collect." She shoved him with the cold iron gun barrel through the door.

"Git over there against the wall, all three of you." She waved the gun, pointing the way.

Leslie fidgeted with the tail of his shirt. "What are you going to do to us?"

His little sister's eyes were magnified by the tears ready to burst out. Both of them shook from crown to the little pig that cried, "Wee, wee, wee," all the way home. And back in Gray Rock was where Nate wished to be.

Horses thundered into the yard. Grannie whipped in the direction of the porch. Her face smacked against the window. Her finger was still on the trigger, but the gun was held at her side. A horse snorted, and the clap of hooves on the ground as they pranced carried inside. Nate peeked out the window nearest him.

Five men, all wearing badges, sat their mounts in a line not ten feet from the porch. They all wore pistols and rifles in their scabbards. Not that Nate wanted to get captured, but this was the miracle he and his friends needed.

One of the lawmen stepped down off his horse. "Come on out, old woman. We know you're running guns to the Cheyenne north of here. Lame Dog talked once we got him in custody."

"You will never cage me!" Grannie packed her rifle into her shoulder, and the next second—*kaboom!* Glass sprayed out, tinkling all over the porch. Two of the horses reared, their riders grabbing for their horns as they slid near out of their saddles. Another horse jumped sideways when its rider pitched backward over its rump. The lawman hit the dirt with a hole in his chest, soaking the ground red.

Leslie and Minnie both screamed and ducked behind a table. Gunfire lit the air. Bullets pelleted the front of the cabin, both windows shattered by volleying blasts.

"Out the back!" Nate hollered over the booms of battle.

Leslie then Minnie crawled with speed toward the rear door, ignoring the slivers of glass all over the floor. Nate wasn't far behind, cursing the splinters pricking into his hands and knees.

"You're not goin' anywhere!" Grannie swung her gun around, aiming directly at Nate.

He dove off his knees and rolled behind a large crate just as the front door was kicked in, smacking the old Crow witch on the spine and sending the old bat flying across the room, her gun spinning across the floor away from her.

The Harrisons left the door open for him. The lawman glanced at Nate who was sitting dumbstruck on his ass.

"You're Nolan's boy," he said, but he should have kept his eyes on Grannie. She squeezed the trigger of a pistol, knocking the deputy backward, slamming into the door. His rifle boomed as he slid down the door, flopping on his behind. Red spilled out of his shoulder.

A second deputy rushed in, his pistol barking. Grannie jerked one way then another. A terrible screech bellowed out of her.

Nate jumped up, running out the door.

"Nathanial! Come back!" It was the pain-filled voice of the injured lawman.

Nate kept running. Leslie jerked on the rope he'd looped around one of Grannie's wagon mules. The stubborn animal reared, buddy sour, not wanting to leave his pulling mate in the corral.

"There's no time for that!" Nate yelled. "Run!"

The three of them hightailed it into the tree line. Nate glanced over his shoulder. One of the lawmen shouldered the weight of the deputy who had recognized him. Both stood in the rear doorway. The injured one met Nate's eyes. Something about him was familiar. Nate turned away, running faster, his heart pounding.

"Get 'im!" hollered one of the two lawmen behind him.

The only thing worse than thinking about that posse trailing him and sending him back to the Fletchers was the fact that he could run smack-dab into Luther Blackhorse. Dog soldiers were as mean as they come.

CHAPTER 9

NATE CRASHED THROUGH THE BRUSH. Twigs snapped ahead of him as Leslie and Minnie shoved through low-hanging branches.

"Over there! I see 'em!" A deep voice echoed amid the trees behind them. The posse's horses clambered out of a trench along the rocky hillside. On the flat, their mounts puffing, they spread out.

"Dammit," Nate mumbled to himself. It wouldn't take long for the posse to surround and corral them in a tight bunch. They were practically breathing down their necks as it was.

The wind kicked up. He shielded his eyes from the sting.

Nate gave a sharp whistle. "This way!" He changed course.

They were still climbing the ridge side, weaving this way and that behind any rock, stick, or clump of shrub that could hide the three of them. Nate grabbed Leslie by the back of his coat, pulling him down onto the ground behind a fallen pine that uprooted during a storm at one time or another. Minnie dropped down next to them, following, crawling in among the thick green branches smashed against the rocky shoulder of the mountain.

"I lost 'em! Anyone see 'em?" one of the posse members called out. Others shouted back and forth. None of them knew where the trio had disappeared to. Some cursing echoed through the chilly air.

Minnie sniffled. Her brother pulled her close, their clothing snagging on the sharp pine needles. It wouldn't be long until they were found, especially since Minnie was barely holding back from bawling. Her ankle was scraped and bleeding, her stockings torn, and she'd lost her shawl. Nate didn't blame her for being upset. But he couldn't risk getting caught.

He leaned over, whispering into Leslie's ear. "Those lawmen ain't huntin' the two of you, not like they are me. They can help ya."

Leslie shook his head. "We're not leaving you alone out here."

Truthfully, Nate was better off on his own, but he didn't want to hurt his friend's feelings. "Listen to me. They'll take ya to the nearest town. I'd bet on it. They'll see that ya get on the stage. Just don't forget. When ya get to Gray Rock, ask for Sheriff Nolan Crosson or Deputy Jesse Adams. They'll help ya find your brother Pat. They won't let ya down."

"I think you should go with us. What if that Indian, Blackhorse, finds you?" Leslie bit his lip. Minnie whimpered.

Through the branches, one of the posse turned his horse. "I think I heard somethin'." He gave a wave to his fellow lawmen. "Over here."

Nate's stomach tightened. "Leslie, you have to go. Those lawmen will have no choice but to send me with the Fletchers."

"The Fletchers," Leslie repeated, his head cocked. "I know that name. Our father did business with a man named Fletcher before we moved west." His lips curled into a hint of a grin. "Their son had a trunk full of puppets we played with. He did a different silly voice for each one, so funny."

Nate doubted that Leslie was talking about Lem and Deloris Fletcher. Lots of people probably carried that name. But Mr. Fletcher was a businessman. How big or small that world was, he couldn't guess, but Pa knew lawmen all over the country. Also, the Fletchers had once had a son.

"My aunt's and uncle's names are Lem and Deloris." He studied Leslie's face for signs of recognition.

Slowly, Leslie's head began to nod. "They were friends of our parents." His face suddenly wrinkled up. "I can't believe they're the mean couple you told me about." He grabbed Minnie by the hand. "They're good people...or were when we knew them. I don't understand. Ashton, their son, was my friend. They wouldn't hurt anyone." Leslie rubbed his head, messing his hair every which way. "We're leaving." He yanked Minnie.

They were outside the hiding spot before Nate could utter a word. Nice people, his ass. Apparently, he and Leslie defined good altogether differently.

"We're here!" Leslie waved his hands in the air, Minnie at his side twisting a strand of hair between her fingers, tears dripping off her chin. Two of the posse, one of them being the injured deputy that had recognized Nate earlier at the cabin, turned their horses, trotting toward the Harrisons.

"We got 'em!" the injured fella called. He had the straightest, whitest teeth Nate ever saw, and strangely, that was familiar. A few seconds later, the two other members of the posse rode through the trees. All four lawmen pulled up reins within a ten-foot circumference of him.

Nate couldn't breathe out. All it would take was one glance in his direction from either Leslie or Minnie, and he would be found, captured.

"Where's Nathanial?" The injured deputy searched near the downed pine.

His voice resonated in Nate's mind. He didn't know this man, did he?

He shrank back into the dark space between some full branches and silently prayed. Every muscle in him tensed to run. If Leslie wanted to get him in trouble—and he had rushed off at the mention of the Fletchers, family friends—this was the perfect chance. After all, Nate had described the couple as just horrible, no less than Satan's helpers.

Leslie stood silent next to a man wearing a sheriff's badge who lifted Minnie onto the saddle of his horse. He stared at the ground as though the answer as to what to do were written out in the dirt for him.

"Rhett, you sure it was Nolan's boy you saw?" The sheriff led the horse carrying Minnie closer to the injured deputy. Leslie followed, rubbing his head, still staring off.

"Burt." Rhett met the sheriff's eyes. "'Bout six months back or so, before you took over as sheriff of Pine Glen, I was sent on assignment to Gray Rock to assist Sheriff Crosson and his deputy. We transported some prisoners, and Nathanial was with us. Three weeks I rode with that kid. I'd recognize 'im anywhere."

Nate took a hard look, squinting his eyes. Rhett McCrae. Yeah, he remembered the fella now. Good man. Three or four years older than Jesse. Pa and Jesse both liked Rhett a lot, trusted him, and he'd bought Nate candy after they'd turned over the prisoners. Earlier at the cabin, with all the shooting and commotion, he hadn't recognized Deputy McCrae. His dirty-blond hair was longer now, hanging out from under his hat and almost resting on his shoulders.

The sheriff laid a hand on Leslie's shoulder. All four lawmen were eyeing him, waiting for him to tattle. Nate crouched on the balls of his feet, muscles tensed, ready in case he needed to bolt. He liked Rhett but not enough to turn himself in to be handed over to the Fletchers. Even though Leslie believed them to be not so bad.

"So you're friends with Nathanial's father, Sheriff Crosson?" Leslie cocked his head, studying Rhett.

Nate wouldn't call it a beard, but Rhett had the same dusty-colored scruff with a hint of red here and there. Not a tall man, average height. There was something in his doe-brown eyes that reflected honesty, a trustworthiness that could not be seen in every man.

"Yes, I am and proud of it." Rhett rolled his injured shoulder. "I'd ride the trail with Nolan any day of the week and twice on Sunday. He's a good man. True to family, a loyal friend, but tough when he needs to be, and I respect him for all those things."

"Nathanial said his aunt and uncle want to take him east, away from his father and mother." Leslie rubbed his hand over the back of his neck.

Nate knew what was best for himself—Ma and Pa. It wasn't Leslie's decision or the law. He would run until his legs fell off. Then he'd crawl. The Fletchers would never turn him into the son they'd lost. Leslie had to realize that Nate was nothing more than a replacement child. But he was cut from a different cloth. He'd never fit into their mold.

Rhett swatted a fly off his gelding's neck. "Heard 'bout the trial." He shook his head. "Those city slicks don't know what they're in for. Nathanial can be a handful. I've seen his ornery side. They'd have better luck tryin' to stick a wild horse in their pocket."

Leslie raised an arm, his pointer finger extended. Nate's heart thumped in his throat. He turned past Nate in the direction of Grannie's cabin. "Nathanial went that way. Said we were holding him up. He went back to steal one of Grannie's mules."

Rhett grinned. "That sounds like the half-pint." He gave Leslie a hand, pulling the boy up behind him in the saddle.

The four lawmen and Nate's friends headed in the direction of Grannie's cabin. When they were out of sight, he crawled out of hiding and took off in the other direction.

At some point, the sheriff and his deputies would realize Leslie had lied.

The sheriff, being in charge, also had the gun-running business of Grannie's to deal with. He surely hadn't expected to find three runaways, especially one that was involved in a high-profile custody case. He couldn't ignore that. And Rhett was Pa's friend. He would come hunting. Dodging the law was something Nate had experience with. Rhett was savvy, so it wouldn't be easy.

Luther Blackhorse would be tougher yet to shake off. Nate needed to get some miles behind him.

And where was that crazy wolf?

CHAPTER 10

SWEAT BURNED NATE'S EYES, though the leaves on the trees were blowing from the brisk afternoon breeze. He dropped to his knees next to a shallow, trickling creek and plunged his face in, lapping up the wetness. Six, seven miles. He wasn't sure how many he'd run, but it was a lot. God, his feet ached. By now, Rhett would be trailing. He respected Pa. No way would he just forget about Nate.

He shucked his boots. If he left any tracks behind—and he'd kept to hard ground when possible so as not to leave an easy trail—now wearing only socks, his tracks would be different. Maybe not enough to throw Rhett off, but the sudden change might confuse him for a bit, which would give Nathanial extra time to further open the gap between them. He couldn't guess that distance. Rhett was riding a horse, and Nate had only his two tired legs.

Just as his heart started to slow, it was time to go. His mouth was moist again. No time to truly rest. Seconds could mean the difference between getting dragged east into hell or... He looked over his shoulder at the stretch of sun-bronzed canyons speckled with sycamore. Blue sky touched the treetops everywhere along the vast hills and valleys as far as the eyes could see. Being on his own wasn't

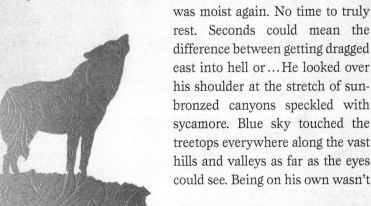

exactly the freedom he longed for. Going home to Gray Rock wasn't an option. He had to stay running. He was Missouri bound, Lee's Summit, the birthplace of Jim Younger, for whatever that was worth. At least it was away from New York, the city the Fletchers called home. Who knew if any of the Youngers would even accept him since he had changed his name? What if he ended up walking all that way for nothing?

As Nate pushed up off the stony creek bank, a rope fell over his shoulders. With a hard yank, his feet flew up. Before he realized it, his spine hit the dirt. A mean laugh cut through the air. The lasso drew tight, pinching his skin, holding his arms down at his sides. He kicked and tried to flail, rolling across the ground.

"Hold still." A corner of Luther Blackhorse's mouth curled into a wicked smirk. He stepped down off his horse.

Luther kneeled next to Nate, grabbed him by a handful of hair, and jerked him up onto his ass. Hell couldn't have made Nate bead with sweat any quicker, but this wasn't the time to panic. His nostrils flared. If only he could loosen the snare, he'd grab a rock as big as his hand and bash that bastard upside his damn skull. Instead, he arched his neck and spit with force, hitting his target right between his hate-filled black eyes.

Backhanded across the mouth, Nate flopped ass over tin cup, his face stinging, and he tasted blood. Before he could catch a breath, Blackhorse grabbed his face with one hand, pressing his cheeks together, breaking the seal of his lips, his mouth involuntarily hanging open.

Blackhorse raised a bone shaped much like a needle. "This is how Cheyenne teach children manners."

With a flick of his wrist, Blackhorse jabbed the razor-sharp marrow into Nate's tongue.

Between his screams, he fought, squirming and bucking, and tried biting down but couldn't force his jaw closed. Blackhorse was too strong.

Without warning, Blackhorse held Nate by the hair, shaking the mustard out of him. When he stopped, Nate's head still did circles. His mind cleared the instant Luther raised the bone tool level with his eyes. He blinked back tears.

"Dogs fastened tight cannot run away." Blackhorse poked what Nate thought was weird string through the eye cut out on the small bone. "This is sinew," Luther said. "Leg tendon from an antelope. Very strong. Does not break easy." He finished threading.

Nate knew this wasn't an educational session the same as when Pa taught him things. But it was clear, right in front of his nose, that the bounty hunter wanted him to understand. Escape would not be easy.

"What are ya gonna do with that?" Nate didn't really wish to know. Whatever that devil's intention, it was going to hurt. Inside his veins, the blood turned cold, and he began to shake all over. But he couldn't help but ask.

"I'll show you." Blackhorse pushed Nate flat against the dirt, rolling him onto his stomach. A knee pressed into his spine, pinning him down. "If you squirm, it'll hurt worse," Luther said without remorse for whatever pain he was about to inflict upon Nate.

Blackhorse brushed the white strands off the back of Nate's neck. He pinched more than an inch of his scruff between his big fingers. "Once I thread the sinew through the skin, I'll have you on a short leash." He grinned.

Nate let out hollering. There was no escape. No one knew where he was.

Blackhorse thumped the back of his head, using his fist like a hammer. Nate's forehead smacked the gravel. Luther pressed his face into the pebbles, pricking into his skin as the bounty hunter leaned down.

His lips touched Nate's cheek. His hot breath steamed the side of his face. "No one can hear your screams."

"You're wrong 'bout that, Blackhorse." A familiar voice came out of nowhere.

Nate shifted his eyes.

Rhett sat his sorrel, his pistol aimed at Luther. He squeezed the trigger. Blackhorse flew backward, bleeding just above his elbow.

Nate hurried, wiggling the rope off over his head, then jumped to his feet, snatching his boots off the ground.

Blackhorse pitched a ten-inch blade from his hip. The knife sank into a tree next to Rhett's shoulder. Sun glinted off the sharp edge. Rhett's mount reared, and he jerked on the reins.

Nate spun on a heel, one foot stretched to run when a thick hand slammed down on his shoulder. By a fistful of shirt, he was jerked off his feet and thrown facedown over the saddle across Luther Blackhorse's lap.

"Rhett!" Nate screamed so loud that his throat hurt.

Rhett's pistol barked behind them. Blackhorse pitched forward with a deep groan, nearly dropping Nate off the side of his prancing horse. Blood spilled out of Blackhorse's shoulder. The same arm Rhett had drilled him in the first time dangled queerly.

With his good hand, Blackhorse skinned his six-shooter, taking aim at Rhett. Nate thrust both fists balled together into the Indian's gut. Blackhorse choked out what air had been in his lungs. His bullet flew wide, missing Rhett by fifteen feet.

Blackhorse swung the butt of his revolver, and Nate caught a harsh whack on the side of his head above his ear. Suddenly, church bells rang inside his skull, and there were two of everything swimming around him.

As his head spun, he felt himself sliding, but his arms and legs wouldn't work the way he wanted them to. Gunfire cracked. Back and forth, the sharp zinging of lead flying through the air kept him somewhat aware of the danger and that he couldn't allow himself to slip into the blackness that so wanted to drape itself over his eyes. His lids were almighty heavy. He blinked and blinked, his head bobbing.

The ground rushed toward his face. Nate thudded in the dirt. Blackhorse's mare jumped sideways and just missed trampling him. The mare's reins dangled as it trotted off into the woods. Luther lay in the stones not far from him.

"Ya okay?" Rhett pulled Nate off the ground, standing him on his feet. His knees did a dip, but Rhett caught him by the arm. "Maybe you should sit down." He lowered Nate.

He wasn't about to argue. His head was pounding something God-awful. At least he wasn't seeing double anymore. But he wasn't so sure he wouldn't lose his stomach any minute. He held to his guts, rocking himself.

"Just breathe." Rhett awkwardly patted his shoulder. Nate recalled that he had been expecting his first child when they'd met those months ago. Bet he wished he was there, at home, with his family instead of here, bleeding and mixed up in this trouble.

Nate wasn't in any shape to run away, and at the moment, he was glad to have Rhett at his side.

He turned his head. His eyes widened. "He's gone!"

Rhett twisted. They both stared at the bloodstained dirt where Luther Blackhorse had lain.

"Thought I kilt 'im." Rhett reloaded his pistol while Nate rubbed his aching skull. "Let's git ya somewhere you can rest for a spell." He shoved his loaded gun into his holster.

Nate wanted nothing more than to lie down and sleep. "Can't I close my eyes just for a few minutes?" he begged.

Rhett eyed him. "That's a pretty good-size gash on your head. Ya might need a few stitches. Maybe a doc."

"Fat chance." Nate smarted off, regarding the blood on his fingers where he had touched the sore spot. Getting stitches hurt like hell, and going to a doc meant explaining who he was. The fewer people that could pinpoint where Nate had been, the better. Luther Blackhorse probably wasn't the only bounty hunter scouring the land for him.

"I ain't gonna fight with ya 'bout it. If that cut don't stop bleedin' in the next few minutes, I'll hold ya down and take care of it. Simple as that." Rhett handed Nate his bandana "Why don't ya wash up at the creek? Soak that and hold it against the cut."

Nate's tongue burned where he'd been stabbed with the needle, and the cold water felt good.

"Let me have a look." Rhett squatted. Nate opened his mouth. "Damn, that had to hurt."

"Not as bad as my head." Nate didn't think he'd see straight for at least a week.

"I gotta say you held up under Blackhorse's torture better than a lot of men would have. That punch to his guts likely saved my life." Rhett filled his canteen. "Ya think ya can ride?"

Nate stiffly nodded. "Where we headed?"

He accepted Rhett's hand, lifting him onto the back of the saddle. If they were headed to Green River, and that was the closest town, then Nate had a day or two to plan some type of escape. But in the meantime, he could rest easy knowing Rhett was watching over him.

"Green River. I'm purdy sure they have a doc there." He pointed to the knot on Nate's head.

"Is that where Leslie and Minnie are goin'?" Nate wanted to be sure they'd be put on a stage to Gray Rock. And Green River was the only town within a hundred miles.

"Yeah, I'm to meet Sheriff Coleman there. When I left them, they were going that way."

Nate kept an eye on their backtrail while they rode. Blackhorse was hurt, but that didn't make him any less of a threat.

The sun was beginning to retreat over the mountain. Nate caught sight of movement. "Rhett!" A shadow to the right of them, among the trees. "Over there." He pointed.

Rhett swung his rifle up out of its scabbard. "I don't see anythin'."

"I swear there was somethin' there." Nate yawned. Maybe his mind was playing tricks on him. He had taken a hard knock to the head.

A wolf howled nearby.

"Montana!" Nate called.

"Who?" Rhett's top lip curled up.

"Never mind." Nate stretched, arching his achy back. "I just need sleep."

Rhett kept his rifle across his lap as they rode.

Nate didn't remember closing his eyes. When he woke, moonlight filtered through the branches overhead and shone on the rocky dirt. The fire crackled, and he pushed back the layer of ground blanket wrapped around him. Rhett was resting against a tree, his hat down over his face, his legs stretched out in front of him. And the well-kept Winchester was within short reach.

Nate stirred out of his blanket. A pot of coffee sat near the flames. Anything hot to put something in his stomach would be great. Next to the brew lay a frying pan, cooling. Nate scurried over. Beans. He damn near cried for joy. Saliva thickened in his mouth.

He didn't even bother using his fingers to scoop the food. Headfirst, he dove in, licking every smear. When he came up for air, he gulped a few swallows of coffee, burning this throat, but oh well. He was too darn hungry to care.

"Them's some table manners, ya hog. Save a little coffee for me."

Nate peered out over the frying pan at Rhett, who was grinning.

"Go on. It's all yours. I had my fill of beans earlier." Rhett picked up the cup Nate had been using and filled it with coffee, taking a sip.

Nate buried his face in what was left of supper.

"I don't believe I've seen anyone so eager to eat my cookin'." Rhett pulled a piece of jerky out of his coat pocket. "Here, this'll stick to them ribs better than mushy beans."

Nate dropped the empty frying pan and snatched the dried beef, ripping off a hunk between his teeth. It didn't take him long to gobble down the treat.

His eyes drooped. He yawned, ready for more sleep now that his belly was full. "Rhett, will ya tell me a story?"

"Reckon I can try. Don't know if I'm any good at that sort of thing." Rhett scratched his head.

"Jesse's the best. Bet ya ain't as good as him ... Don't worry. I'll still like it." He smoothed out his ground blanket.

Rhett chuckled.

"How old's your baby now? Don't ya tell your son or daughter stories before bed?" Nate loved when Ma would snuggle under the quilts with both him and Elizabeth and read them a bedtime book. Sometimes Pa would join them.

"My boy would be 'bout six months old, but he and my wife died durin' the birth." Rhett rubbed his hands through his hair.

"Sorry." He hadn't known and didn't know what else to say.

"Unfortunately, things like that happen. I ain't the only man who ever lost his wife and child that way." Rhett's eyes glistened in the firelight.

Nate laid his head to the blanket. Why was life full of sadness? Why were families torn apart for one reason or another? He wasn't ready to accept that he'd never see his loved ones again. Not if he were honest with himself anyway.

He glanced away from the flames and stared at Rhett. "You rode posse with my pa three or four different times before the trip when I got to help transport the prisoners. Pa tells me all about his work. Jesse does too. If ya don't mind, I'd like to hear one of those stories."

Rhett rested his head against a patch of soft, mossy earth, staring up into the starlit night. "I got a better story for ya. One I'll bet you ain't heard before."

Nate was all ears. He scooched a mite closer, not wanting to miss a single detail. This wasn't exactly like home, but Rhett was a lawman. A flicker of belonging popped into his head. Ma and Elizabeth all snuggled up. Pa walking in the door, giving them a smile even after a hard day's work. Nate should have been in that picture. Bouncing into Pa's arms, asking too many questions about Pa's day and lawman stuff, like always, until Pa sat down and Nate soaked in every word.

"We might as well ride. We ain't sleepin'." Rhett stood and stretched.

Pink streaks began to climb over the horizon. A bluster of wind carried a few leaves across the ground. Nate rolled the blanket while Rhett saddled his horse. One by one, the stars disappeared as dawn covered the landscape with a soft red glow.

"I like ya, Rhett, so I'm gonna give ya fair warnin'." He wouldn't do this for just anyone, and he might end up regretting it, but he didn't want any hard feelings between them.

"I won't be given over to the Fletchers."

Rhett laughed. "Did ya honestly believe I thought ya would? You jumped off a train. That's a purdy damn bold statement. Obviously, you don't wanna go to New York City, and I don't blame ya none."

They eyed one another from across the smoldering ashes.

"Ya acknowledge my position as a deputy, the oath I've given to uphold the law?"

"Yes, sir." Being the son of a lawman, Nate understood better than most. "And I'm a fugitive thanks to the Fletchers."

"Noted." Rhett pulled his cinch strap tight, then straight-ened. "We're square, then. We both have to do what we must."

"We're square." Nate extended a hand. Rhett accepted, and they shook.

"All right, let's go." Rhett stepped into the saddle. "Blackhorse has probably been up for hours and on our trail."

Nate didn't want to think about that. "How 'bout that story?"

"Before I met my wife, I come west from Kiowa, Kansas, with a wagon train. One of four hired by the wagon master, a man named Frank Kennedy. Our duties included keeping the peace between families, protecting 'em, and doin' whatever chores needed done to ensure those folks got where they were going."

"So in a way, you were like a deputy to the wagon train boss?" The wagon train Nate had been part of with the Harpers never had a man in charge, not the way Rhett described.

"Yeah, you could say that." Rhett nodded.

Nate liked the story so far. "Sounds excitin'"

Rhett steered Banjo down over a bank, following a narrow game trail. "Not at first. 'Bout seven days into our journey, a wagon joined us out of nowhere." Rhett turned his gaze away from the ridge ahead and glanced over his shoulder at Nate.

"I wouldn't have thought a thing of it except four men were travelin' in that wagon, armed men. Sodbusters don't usually wear six-shooters on their hips. No women or kids either." Rhett suddenly pulled his rifle out of his scabbard alongside the saddle.

"What it is?" Nate twisted in all four directions, expecting Blackhorse.

Rhett lifted his chin toward a large wolf track in the dirt. "That's fresh."

At least it wasn't the dog soldier. Nate's heart started again. Did that print belong to Montana? He crossed his fingers.

"Banjo would be actin' up if a wolf was close by, don't ya think?" He waited a few seconds, letting Rhett come to that conclusion himself, or he might not put away the gun. "Why worry about some wolf that'll run if he has a chance?"

Unless rabid or cornered, most wild animals, even predators, would shy away from the unfamiliar smell of humans.

"Blackhorse won't give us the warnin' of a print." Death would just strike.

Nate shrank into a cringe.

They skirted a ridge. A rabbit bounded across a short open area of grass the second they appeared. No more wolf tracks.

Rhett slid his weapon back into the leather boot. "I ain't seen any sign of that damn bounty hunter."

"Amen," Nate muttered to himself. He hadn't spotted any horse tracks or boot prints. Luther had been bleeding when he got away. No blood drops on the ground, or at least not along that path.

"Go on with your story." Nate prodded. He couldn't let fear stew in his mind too long. Fear made a body weak. Then a bad decision might follow. What if he missed the opportunity to slip away from Rhett, back on his own and hell and gone from the Fletchers? He couldn't forget that.

Rhett pulled up on the reins, took a swig out of his canteen, then handed it to Nate. "Kennedy, my boss, said he'd helped those fellas fix a busted wagon wheel." A corner of his mouth curled up. "It don't take five men to replace a broken spoke. Even if the axle had been snapped, two, three men tops to set a new one."

Rhett secured his canteen over his saddle horn, touching spurs to Banjo's sides.

"How well did ya know Kennedy before ya hired on?"

A hint of movement on top of a cliff off to their right caught Nate's eye. If he pointed it out, Rhett might take a shot. What if it was Montana? What if it wasn't? He bit at his lip. It was four, five hundred yards away and above them. Sun glared off the stone wall. He squinted. Maybe he hadn't seen anything at all.

"Not well enough. So I kept a close eye on that wagon. Studied the habits of the men guardin' it. At night, when the wagons circled, they always kept their distance. Not far but not among the families. When the men entered camp to get grub or talk with Kennedy, it was in pairs. Two stayed behind with the wagon."

"There was somethin' in the wagon they didn't want anyone to know about." Nate took an educated guess. His skin tingled when he pictured himself lifting the canvas flap and discovering whatever it was the outlaws were hiding.

"Damn right." Rhett patted Banjo's neck. "Over the next few days, I recognized their folly. Another matter had emerged. By noon, their horses were tired, far worse than the other teams in the train. Usually, they'd fall behind. A good twenty-five, thirty yards."

"Whatever they were carryin' in that wagon must've been heavy." Nate scratched behind his ear. "Gold? Maybe crates of guns?"

They crested a tree-covered rise and started down the far side, veering between evergreens and juniper. Leaves that had fallen crunched under Banjo's hooves.

Rhett tapped his noggin with a finger. "My brain went the same direction yours is now. But I had me an idea hatchin'."

Nate smirked. He hadn't a clue as to where this story was going.

Rhett winked at him. "It was my duty to ride over and inform those fellas that they were runnin' them wagon horses into the ground. Those ponies were too thin."

"You didn't?" Nate chuckled. "What did they say?"

"I was to mind my own damn business." He chuckled. "Instead, I offered to help unload some of what was killin' their animals. I took exactly one step toward the bed of that canvas-covered wagon, hopin' to sneak a peek, but before I knew it, all four men were aimin' guns at me."

"Were ya scared?" Nate would have been, and he'd seen his fair share of gunfights over the years.

"I'd be lyin' if I said I wasn't. But I kept my wits 'bout me. My instinct was to draw. I fought down that urge, knowin' that standin' out in the open in front of four armed men and startin' a gun battle would only get me kilt."

"Holy shit." Nate sighed.

Rhett's brow furrowed. "Your pa don't let ya talk that way. Don't do it around me."

"You curse. Every other sentence," Nate snapped.

Rhett flicked Nate's nose. "I'm a grown man. I can talk any way I damn well please. You just do as I say. No cussin'."

Nate rubbed the tip of his nose. "Yes, sir."

"Now where was I?" Rhett pondered a minute.

Banjo scrambled up a rocky incline. At the top, the land leveled off, and Nate loosened his grip around Rhett's waist.

"You were facin' four armed men." Nate threw out a clue.

"Oh yeah. Kennedy rode up, asked me what I was doin'. I explained. He told me to git back to the other wagons. I wasn't to bother those fellas again, or I'd lose my employ."

"Did ya fold up?" Nate didn't believe Rhett would, but five against one was bad odds.

"Hell no." Rhett chuckled. "I stood my ground. Told Kennedy that four grown men who couldn't fix a wagon spoke might not recognize that they were pushin' their animals too hard. Thought I was doin' 'em a service by mentionin' it."

Nate snickered. "You sure got backbone. No wonder Pa asked for you."

Rhett cocked his head. "What do ya mean?"

"When we took those prisoners into Laramie a few months back." Nate shaded his eyes against the harsh reflection of sunshine where he'd thought he'd seen movement a few minutes ago and again just now. "Pa let me send the wire. Jesse usually does that."

"Your pa requested me? Sheriff Coleman never told me that." Rhett scratched his scruffy chin.

Nate shrugged, his focus keenly on the here and now. "Rhett, you see anythin' up there?" He pointed.

Rhett kept Banjo walking while he studied the spot. "Speakin' of your pa, guess who rode into that wagon train camp the very next day?"

"Pa." Nate smiled, but his eyes searched the rim of the cliff.

"You guessed it." Rhett's expression didn't change. His lower jaw jutted out, eyes narrowed, as serious as that tall rock wall was sobering. "He rode up on that big bay of his, and the star pinned on his black vest shined. The men with him—US Marshal Joseph Huckabee, Deputy Tate Horn, Wild Bill Hickock, William Brooks, and Charlie Bassett—that was some posse. I didn't envy the men they were huntin'."

"What did Pa say? Was it those men you argued with that he was after?" Nate rattled off.

"Hold your horses." Rhett adjusted his hat, shading his eyes more. "Nothin' up there that I can see. But that don't mean we ain't bein' watched. We're well within rifle range."

They kept under the cover of the trees and turned direction. "Nolan questioned Kennedy. Three trunks of gold had been stolen from a British duke who'd come from overseas wanting to experience the American West."

"Man-o-day. All that gold." Nate thought of his wealthy aunt and uncle and the bounty they had stupidly put on his head. Some people should never leave their backyard.

"Right? It had me a'thinkin'. I looked over my shoulder toward the tree line where that wagon had been parked earlier. It was gone."

"No way." Nate gasped.

"I swear it." Rhett put a hand over his badge and heart. "I started over to tell your pa when Pernell, another of the hired men, caught me by the arm. Said that if I went over there, I'd only be ignitin' trouble."

"Pernell's a coward." Nate lipped off.

"Yup, spineless." Rhett agreed with a nod. "He told me that after my words with the fellas from that wagon, Kennedy was bad-mouthin' me to the hired men and some of the folks from the wagon train. He told 'em that there was an injured man in that wagon, and the reason they traveled behind was to make their hurt friend more comfortable. And with the youngsters of the wagon train doin' what kids do, the noise wouldn't allow for the victim to rest proper. It was nothin' personal that they weren't more social."

"Victim?" Nate raised a brow.

"You heard me right. Accordin' to Pernell, Kennedy was tellin' people that I shot the alleged man in the wagon back in Kiowa before we left. Kennedy assured the good folks that had he known I was so temperamental, he never would have hired me. And he feared I might shoot someone else if he tried to fire me."

"What a back-bitin' son of a bitch." Nate huffed.

"Watch your damn mouth. I already told ya once." Rhett frowned.

He shook his head while tugging the reins, leading Banjo into a gully at least ten feet deep, maybe four wide, with thick tree cover lining each side for a good half-mile ahead. If there was someone up on the cliff, it'd be near impossible to get a bead on them until they left the washout.

Rhett rubbed a hand down over his face. "Pernell was a friend. I trusted 'im 'til that day. Said he wouldn't back me up if I talked to the posse."

Nate understood trust issues all too well. There were very few men he put his faith into one hundred percent. Frankly, it was just Pa and Jesse, but Rhett was quickly becoming number three.

"Your pa and the others in the posse searched the wagons, talked mostly to the men, and come up empty-handed, as I knew they would. The wagon they were huntin' was hidin' somewhere. They sure as hell weren't gonna outrun a posse, but they could stay hidden 'til the posse passed by, then rejoin the wagon train and feel somewhat confident of a safe passage through that leg of their escape."

"Makes sense," Nate said.

"I was helpin' to fill a water barrel when your pa and the others came to talk to me. I had no idea what Kennedy had told them, and your pa's steely gray eyes are enough to shrink any man's confidence. He asked if I scouted for the train. I nodded. Had I seen anythin' unusual, spotted any strangers, or seen any wagons that didn't belong with the train?"

Nate held his breath.

"I looked at Kennedy, Pernell, and too many others scowlin' at me. Somehow, they blamed me for this inconvenience. As though I was the cause of all the trouble and not the men who stole the gold." Rhett stared off for a minute, probably picturing that day. "Your pa snapped his fingers in front of my face.

"Stop lookin' at them. If you know somethin', tell me.

"I shook my head, lyin' through my teeth. Said I hadn't seen nothin'.

"Yer a liar.

"Nolan said it right to my face. He might as well have punched me. Those words hurt 'cause I knew he was right, and that wasn't the kind of man I wanted to be, a chickenshit bucklin' under the pressure of men who didn't even like me. I glanced at Kennedy." Rhett swallowed hard. "Your pa grabbed me by the arm and spun me to face only him. He leaned in close.

"I will hang any man involved. There were some good men killed durin' the robbery. If you have somethin' to say, spit it out."

Nate got chills. He could almost hear his pa saying those words. He'd heard similar warnings come out of his father's mouth.

"It was that moment in time when I had to choose exactly who I wanted to be." Rhett tapped himself center chest, right where Nate imagined one's soul was housed. "I drew in a deep breath. I was afraid. I didn't know what I'd face from Kennedy or the others once that posse left. Your pa must have sensed my nerves. He put a hand on my shoulder.

"It ain't always easy to do what's right, but a man's gotta live with his choices. You ready for that?

"What he was really tellin' me was that if I didn't speak the truth, I'd be helpin' those criminals get away with their crimes."

Inwardly, Nate beamed. Always the teacher, Pa was.

"I let her fly. Told all of it from my first suspicion on. And pointed out where the wagon had been sittin' just hours ago. Kennedy's face turned ten shades of red, but he wasn't dumb enough to draw on me, not with the posse there. When they left, I followed. An hour later, I rode up on a wave of hills. There was a patch of cottonwoods. Underneath, the posse had the wagon. Two men lay dead on the ground. The other two who had stolen the gold were being tied at the wrists behind their backs. They were put on their horses and led under a branch."

Nate gulped.

"I didn't think anyone seen me 'til your pa gave a quick wave for me to join 'im.

"You come to watch 'em hang?

"Your pa stared me in the eyes. That wasn't why I was there. I looked right back at 'im and said I wanted to see justice served. Nolan grinned."

"That ain't the end, is it?" Nate wanted to hear more. "What about Kennedy? Surely, the posse went after him. Pa don't leave loose ends."

Rhett chuckled. "Yeah, the posse took Kennedy into custody, back to Kiowa. He hadn't been part of the killin's, nor had he been directly involved in the thievin'. He was the criminals' way out, for a price. One that led to prison."

They left the gully, keeping between the trees, weaving their own trail. Behind them now, the cliff appeared not so hateful, but shouldering that one, a small sister shelf of rock stood closer to them as Rhett turned Banjo again. If anyone was following, they had to be getting dizzy.

"Did you leave the wagon train and return with the posse?"

"Naw. Sheriff Brooks, one of the posse, asked me to. Said he was impressed with how I manned up, and your pa agreed. Brooks said there'd be a deputy's job waitin' for me. I was to drift his way."

"And you've been a deputy ever since," Nate added.

"Yup. I pinned on a badge, and life's been a whirlwind."

Nate slipped his arms farther around Rhett's middle, clasped his hands, and squeezed tight. "Thanks."

"I didn't do anythin'." Rhett's brow lifted.

That wasn't so. Rhett had given Nate something that not even Jesse could.

"The day I was adopted, I believed the rest of my life, every day, would be spent with Ma and Pa." Nate pressed his face into the back of Rhett's shirt. Leather and trail dust. It was the same fresh-air scent that Pa and Jesse wore. "Pa got shot because of me. If I hadn't tried to be a hero like him... Last I saw 'im"—Nate sniffled—"he had an infection, in bed, dyin'."

That wasn't how he should remember his father. Rhett's story reminded him of that. Nolan Crosson was a whole lot more than one bad memory.

"It's hard to get that picture of 'im lying there moanin' out of my head. Don't you ever wish you could somehow change that last memory of seein' your family die?"

Banjo blew as though expressing Rhett's feelings for him. "It ain't easy to switch that awful image." He nodded. "For some dumb reason, self-pity's easier to wallow in than the good times." Rhett lifted his hat off his head. "To buildin' new an' better memories. God willin'."

Blackhorse was out there somewhere. Nate hadn't forgotten, his gut twisting in a knot, recalling the cold, sharp edge of the bone needle against the skin on his neck.

"To what lies ahead," he whispered.

Simply surviving, food, shelter, those things wouldn't have worried him, but constant dogging from a hunter such as Blackhorse meant staying on his toes, always sharp and endlessly on the move.

CHAPTER 11

NATE SHIVERED ON THE BACK of Rhett's horse. Autumn had set in. Red and yellow leaves turned on the trees. Only a week ago, hints of weather change cooled the air, but the days were somewhat warm. Not today. It was downright cold.

Rhett looked over his shoulder. "Shit, boy, your lips are blue. If you shake any harder, you're gonna fall off Banjo."

"B-b-banjo." Nate's teeth chattered. It was an unusual name.

Rhett patted his horse's neck. "He's the only horse that can carry a tune that I know of. Watch this." He cleared his throat. "Oh my darlin', oh my darlin'…"

Banjo's head lifted, ears up, and the gelding neighed right along with Rhett's off-key tenor.

"He does that every time." Rhett chuckled. The horse threw his head, shaking his mane as though asking for more song.

"I think it's from standin' outside too many saloons and listenin' to bad music. He loves it. And who am I to deny 'im?"

Nate laughed. "Can I try?"

"Sure." Rhett sniggered. "But don't sing in key. Banjo might not recognize it."

"You ain't right in the head." Nate nudged the lawman.

"Don't tell anyone." Rhett winked. "I might lose my job."

As Nate opened his mouth with the words, "Oh my darlin'," belting out into the mountain air, a shot rang out. Lead zinged an inch over his head.

"Hold on." Rhett kicked Banjo's sides. The horse bolted in amid the trees.

On a rock ledge fifty yards above, the sun glinted off a rifle barrel. Nate squinted. Was he seeing things? Three figures, none of them with hair long enough to be Luther Blackhorse.

Rhett steered Banjo along the edge of a wide meadow, keeping close under the trees, which gave them some cover from above. On the other side of the field, Blackhorse appeared, his rifle raised. Rhett jerked on the reins. He grabbed for his Winchester as Luther's gun boomed. Lead shaved Banjo's rump, and the animal reared. Nate toppled over Banjo's tail and thudded the grass head first.

"Nathanial! Run!" Rhett charged across the field, working the trigger of his rifle.

Blackhorse yanked his reins, retreating into the tree line. Behind Nate, one, two, three shots rang out from overhead. Dirt kicked up around Banjo's feet. The horse kept a straight course. Then Rhett and Banjo disappeared into the trees where Blackhorse had gone a few seconds before.

Nate hightailed it in the direction of Green River, the opposite of the steep cliffside where the three gunmen had taken position. Not impassible but not easy ground to navigate a horse. That gave Nate needed time.

His heart pumped hard. Out of breath, he kept his legs running. He didn't know the area well enough to hide. Hoofing it farther away was his only chance. Distance was his weapon. What he wouldn't give for an army.

Out of the bushes leaped Montana, running alongside Nate. He wasn't alone now but still plenty scared, though not quite as much. By nightfall, the two of them had reached a bluff.

In the distance, lights, tiny specks, indicated a town. Green River? He was almost there … or somewhere.

Without thought, he patted Montana's head. The big wolf licked his hand. "I don't know what's down there waitin' for me, boy. S'pect I'll find out."

"Nathanial." Rhett's voice carried through the dark.

Nate crouched between a tall stand of weeds. Montana trotted off into the black.

"I know that was you I heard talkin'," Rhett said. "Let me help ya. Where ya at?"

There was a long silence between them. Nate curled up tighter, for the dark form of a man and horse appeared not five feet in front of him.

Rhett pulled up on the reins. Banjo's steamy breath blew the wisps of hair around Nate's face. Thank God there was no moon in the sky.

"Listen to me, Nathanial. Blackhorse slipped away again. I didn't even get a shot at those other three, but I did come across their tracks. They're followin' Luther. I'm bettin' they're countin' on 'im to lead 'em right to ya." Rhett turned his head toward the distant lights. "That's Green River. Please, git yourself there and stay put. I'm gonna try an' increase the odds in your favor." He tugged on the reins, turning Banjo. Then they halted. "Take care of yourself, boy."

And just like that, he was gone.

Nate fought his desire to have someone looking out for him, to have someone who cared close to him. As much as he wanted to call Rhett back, he just couldn't. Before pinning on a badge, a man had to swear to uphold the law, not just the ones he agreed with. They'd bonded over their losses and their shared praise for a certain man. As a deputy, it was impossible for Rhett to help Nate escape without risking his star. He would have no choice but to contact the Fletchers and turn Nate in, and he would never force Rhett into that choice.

When he no longer heard Banjo's steps, Nate slunk from his hiding spot slowly, for the ground was littered with sticks and stones common to any wooded area. He stepped with caution toward Green River, the specks of light in the distance that Rhett had pointed out.

Just before dawn, he stood at the edge of the dusty, weathered town. There were no lights on, nor did anyone stir out of doors. A snoring drunk lay in the middle of the street. Chickens clucked and pecked the ground around the water trough of the livery. A few horses stood lazily inside the fence, waiting for their breakfast. Nate's belly rumbled. He could use some grub himself.

A door opened. A woman wearing an apron tossed water out of a basin into the roadway. Then the door snapped shut. Above the porch, the sign read:

Boarding House

Meals Five Cents Extra

Nate pulled his deputy badge out of his pocket and stared at the star in his palm. It had to be worth at least five cents.

Down the alleyway, he kept out of sight behind the buildings. A cock crowed somewhere on the other side of town. Townsfolks would be coming awake soon. He knocked on the rear door.

It flew open. The woman he'd seen a few minutes ago stood there with her hands on her hips and stared at him. She was shorter than Ma, but the smear of flour on her cheek reminded him of his mother's early morning chores.

"Speak up, child. It's too chilly to stand here with the door hangin' open. I ain't heatin' the street."

A heartsickness pained him, but he lifted the badge flat on his palm. She leaned in, taking a good gander.

"Where'd ya get that?" She eyed him with her head cocked and brow raised.

"I didn't steal it." Nate felt the need to defend himself even though she hadn't exactly accused him of anything. "Is it worth a meal?"

The lines on her face softened, and she nodded as she stepped aside, giving way to him. Nate handed her his payment as he passed.

Heat from the cookstove warmed his goose-pimpled skin. He rubbed his hands together.

"You can wash up over there." She pointed to a pump.

When he was done, he took a seat at the table. A few minutes later, she placed a full plate of eggs, bacon, and a biscuit in front of him. And a tall glass of milk. Nate grabbed his fork, feeling her eyes on him.

She slid into the chair across the table. "My name is Sandra Bell. I'm a friend of Rhett's. He rode in here late last night." She broke the awkward silence between them.

Nate dropped his fork and jumped to his feet, nearly knocking the chair over backward.

"Sit down." Mrs. Bell's voice was stern. "There's no law here in town, and I ain't gonna hurt ya. What do I care if you don't wanna go back to your aunt and uncle?"

Nate didn't move. "They're offerin' ten thousand reasons for you to care."

"They upped it to fifteen." She unfolded a piece of paper from her apron pocket, then slid it across the table toward him.

Nate's jaw fell open. It was true. But whose picture was that under the headline of fifteen thousand dollars? The boy in the photograph carried strikingly similar features to those of Nate's: small frame, light hair, blue eyes. Even their faces were shaped the same. It was a close enough match that anyone could mistake him for the kid in the picture, but it was Nate's name in the caption. They'd referred to him as Nathanial Fletcher. This must've been Ashton Fletcher.

He crumpled the paper into a ball and threw it on the floor.

"What a bunch of bullshit." Nate smacked a fist on the table. The lady chuckled.

Nate had forgotten for a moment that he wasn't alone. "Sorry, ma'am."

"Understandable given the circumstances. Rhett explained everything to me." Mrs. Bell nodded toward Nate's food. "Eat."

He hesitantly sat. She hadn't made a move toward him, keeping a distance wider than arm's length. If she tried anything funny, he'd jump through a window if he had to. He picked up his fork.

"Rhett asked me to keep an eye out for ya. Said not to be too welcoming 'cause you wouldn't trust it and would run. That's why I kind of gave ya a hard time at the door. Sorry about that."

"Why ain't you interested in collectin' the money?" Nate took a bite. He didn't believe for a minute the reason had much to do with her friendship with Rhett. Fifteen thousand would make a person wealthy overnight.

"I don't agree with you being taken away. I can't put myself in your mother's shoes, but I can only imagine the heartache she feels. I lost both my husband and son in the war between the states. My life hasn't felt the same since. There's an emptiness, a void." She touched her heart. "Rhett and his youthfulness... When I look at him, I remember my son. He gives me joy that otherwise isn't there anymore. No amount of money can bring that back. I've learned to be happy with the day-to-day."

Nate crunched a piece of bacon. "You're a good cook." He didn't want to dwell on the sadness of her dead family, and he believed she was telling the truth about not caring about the cash.

"Thank you." Mrs. Bell grinned.

"Did Rhett ask ya to try and keep me here?" Nate picked up his milk glass. His plate was empty.

"No." She shook her head. "He said to feed ya and give ya a bed to rest in. He's hoping that you'll stay on your own accord. But if you leave, I'm not to try and stop ya." Mrs. Bell stood. "I do have something for you." She disappeared into the next room.

Nate had no idea what it could be. He swallowed the last of his milk.

She reappeared, holding a coat. "This was my son's. I don't know why I saved it. He outgrew it years before he died. He wasn't much older than you when he wore it. It might be a tad big, but it'll keep ya warm, better than just a shirt."

She held open the coat. Nate stood and slid his arms into the sleeves. The thing swallowed him, but she was right about one thing. It was wool-lined and warm.

"I don't have any boarders right now. Why don't you go upstairs, pick a room, and rest for an hour or two?"

That sounded good to Nate.

Bang, bang, bang. Someone rapped at the door.

"Who on earth?" Before Mrs. Bell took a step, the door was kicked in, smacking off the wall.

Mrs. Bell screamed. Nate froze. Luther Blackhorse, in his bloodstained shirt, stood in the entryway. Hot air snorted out of his flared nostrils.

"I will kill you." He took his thumb and made a slicing motion from one ear down across his throat and up around to the other ear.

"You get out of my place!" Mrs. Bell pushed Nate behind her.

"Stay out of the way, woman." Blackhorse shoved over a table, sending a lamp crashing to the floor. Glass fragments shattered everywhere.

Nate backed away. Blackhorse lunged, throwing a shoulder into Mrs. Bell. She twisted up onto her tiptoes. Her head smacked the wall, and she slumped to the floor, a red smear painting the wallpaper.

Nate bolted into the kitchen and grabbed a greasy frying pan. He spun, swinging with all his might, bacon fat splattering the cupboards, and he whacked Blackhorse on the knee. He yelped, grabbing that leg. Nate swung again. Blackhorse caught the iron skillet, ending Nate's assault. With a hard jerk, both Nate and the pan went sailing across the room. He hit a table, flipping it, and toppled over a chair. Luther stormed toward him, shoving a chair out of the way, knocking that one over too.

Nate leaped to his feet. Up the stairs, he ran by twos and threes. Behind him, Blackhorse's boots thundered on the steps. A shotgun boomed. Pieces of horsehair plaster fell from the ceiling where the buckshot had broken off chunks. Nate glanced over his shoulder. Mrs. Bell stood at the bottom of the steps, gun readied and shoved into her shoulder, finger on the trigger.

Luther twisted around, his pistol in hand.

"No!" Nate screamed. He spun and kicked the back of Blackhorse's knee, the one he'd hammered a solid shot with the frying pan. The bounty hunter's leg buckled. Headfirst, he tumbled down the stairs.

Mrs. Bell's rifle belched a great racket inside the small space. Half of Luther's face was torn off and splattered against the wall.

Nate slapped a hand over his mouth, vomit seeping through his fingers. Mrs. Bell dropped the rifle and crumpled onto the floor, sobbing into her hands.

Voices carried from outside. A rush of feet came through the door. From where Nate stood at the top of the stairs, he was hidden from the onlookers.

"Mrs. Bell, are you okay?"

Nate recognized the voice and ducked into a room.

"Sheriff Coleman." Mrs. Bell choked up.

Nate ran to the window. Mrs. Bell would have to tell the sheriff why Luther Blackhorse had busted up her place. Then the boarding house would be searched. Nate looked down into the alleyway. Loaded with a mound of hay, a wagon sat directly below. This was his lucky day. As quiet as he could, he lifted the window.

Nate crawled out of the hay, picking yellow strands off his clothing. A crowd had gathered around Mrs. Bell's front door. Everyone's back was turned. Nate slipped up to the hitchrail and pulled the knot on Luther's horse.

He walked the animal down the street and out of town so as not to draw attention. Nate buttoned his coat as he went. Thank God for the rare person, like Mrs. Bell, who'd been willing to help him, but it almost cost her life. That would've been worse than him getting killed.

He'd barely slipped away from Blackhorse. A much closer call than when he'd fled Grannie's place. Rhett had warned him that the three from the cliff were following Blackhorse. Where were they?

Nate hopped up onto a stump, then slid over into the saddle.

CHAPTER 12

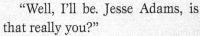

JESSE TILTED HIS HEAD BACK. The sun wasn't quite overhead. It'd be about noon when he reached Green River. Freckles was holding up fine, though the trail he'd taken had been much rougher than expected. The coach road would've been smoother, but it was the long way around the mountain. The other way, straight up and across the top, cut near a week off his travel time.

There was an excitement in him, wishful thinking that he might find his little partner on the first try. It was a long shot, but his fingers were crossed. Jesse pulled up his coat collar. Fall was settling in too soon.

Green River bustled with folks along each side of the boardwalk, not the lazy little town he had imagined it to be. He pulled up reins in front of the telegraph office, stepping down off his horse. A man strolled out, but Jesse didn't pay much attention.

"Well, I'll be. Jesse Adams, is that really you?"

Jesse looked up and grinned. "Rhett McCrea, good to see ya." They clapped one another's shoulder.

"I didn't know Green River hired itself a lawman." Jesse hadn't passed a jailhouse on his way in.

"They didn't." Rhett shook his head. "I followed Nathanial here."

Jesse grabbed Rhett by the arms just below his shoulders. "Partner's here?" His heart skipped a beat.

"Naw. He took off." Rhett jerked his head toward the far end of town.

"We gotta go after 'im." Jesse turned, yanking loose the slipknot that he had just tied on the rail.

Rhett caught him by the arm. "Don't be in such a hurry." He shifted his eyes toward the saloon. Three dusty, trail-ridden men, hard cases judging by the leathery faces and tied-down six-shooters, lounged on the porch.

"Who are they?" Jesse worked the fingers on his trigger hand.

"The one in the checked shirt is Smoky Joe Rawlins. His brother's the one with the cigarette pinched between his lips. They call him Slim. The fella behind them on the bench, their partner, that's Cord McNitt."

Jesse didn't have to ask why they were there. He recognized all the names. Bounty hunters. "Why they hangin' around if Nate's gone?"

"'Cause they don't know that. I started a rumor that we got Nate guarded at the boardin' house."

"Why?" Jesse wasn't seeing the point.

"To further discourage 'em and keep 'em off Nate's tail." Rhett pointed to the boarding house. "Early this mornin', Luther Blackhorse burst in there attemptin' to kill our little friend."

Jesse squeezed the reins in his head.

"Don't worry. Nate's fine. Scared, no doubt, but not hurt. He stole Luther's horse. But since the bounty hunter's dead, Sheriff Coleman has decided to call it borrowin' the horse."

"You sure partner's okay?"

"Yeah. Mrs. Bell said she didn't see a scratch on 'im, but if it makes ya feel better, you can ask her yourself." Rhett tilted his head toward the Rawlins brothers and their sidekick.

"Our friends over there"—he rolled his eyes—"rode into town shortly after I did. They got quite an eyeful. Sheriff Coleman and Deputy Long were draggin' Blackhorse's dead body up the street. Half his head was missin'. That ain't a sight ya forget." He paused, letting the details sink into Jesse's brain. "And Coleman ain't a fan of bounty hunters. Hates 'em worse than maybe horse thieves. He stopped dead center of those three hounds and told 'em to have a good long look."

"Too bad it didn't scare 'em off." Jesse tied his horse.

"It's got 'em stalled, and that's good for Nate. The longer they're here, the better for 'im."

Jesse nodded. "Any idea where he's headed?"

"Naw. But when ya leave to go after 'im, ya got yourself a partner." Rhett patted Jesse's shoulder.

"I won't say no to that." He grinned. "I need to wire Sheriff Crosson."

"I just did. Told 'im most of what I told you." Rhett smirked. "Minus the half a head thing."

"Then I'll just tell 'im I've arrived and that we're partnerin' up."

"Good, you do that." Rhett patted Freckles' nose. "I'll take your horse to the livery and see that Clayton gives 'im a good grainin'. When you're done here, meet me at the boardin' house. We might as well fill our stomachs before sneakin' out of town." He rubbed his midsection. "And there's somethin' ya gotta see. Nate left ya a surprise."

What in tarnation would the boy have left for him? Jesse turned and went inside. Nate had no way of knowing he was coming there.

The wire clerk handed him a message. "This just came across the wire."

Urgent from Sheriff Crosson.

Jesse read the slip of paper. "This has got to be a bad joke." He slammed his fist on the countertop. The clerk jumped.

Not only had the Fletchers upped the price on Nate's head, but they had extended their search beyond the neighboring territories and states. Every newspaper in the country was running the headline and would continue to do so once a week until Nathanial was found.

"I need paper," Jesse barked.

The clerk, his hands shaking, slid a pencil and a sheet of parchment across the counter. Jesse scribbled his message.

He marched down the boardwalk, then crossed the street toward the boarding house. He knocked once before entering. Rhett stood from where he was lounging. Sheriff Coleman and Deputy Long joined him. Ernie, Coleman's son-in-law who also wore a badge, sat at a long table, shoving pie into his jib.

"Hello, Jesse." Coleman shook his hand. "It's been a while."

"Yes, sir." Jesse nodded.

"How's Nolan?" Deputy Long handed Jesse a cup of coffee.

"Doin' better. Before I left, he was on his feet. At least he ain't bedridden."

"Glad to hear it," Coleman said. Deputy Long nodded in agreement.

Rhett squeezed Jesse's shoulder, a big grin on his face.

"What's so amusin'?" Jesse nudged Rhett

"You'll see." Rhett chuckled.

"Does this have anythin' to do with what Nathanial left for me?" Jesse looked from Rhett to the others.

All the lawmen smirked.

"Follow me upstairs." Rhett led him to a stairway.

A lady carrying a tray with empty plates glided down the steps.

"Mrs. Bell, this here's Deputy Jesse Adams." Rhett offered an introduction.

"It says sheriff on his badge." Mrs. Bell corrected.

Rhett stared at the star.

"I'll explain later," Jesse said.

"Either way, it's nice to meet you." Mrs. Bell stepped past, dishes clinking on the tray. "When you boys are finished talking to the children, there's fried potatoes and pot roast in the kitchen. Help yourselves."

"Children?" Jesse's eyes widened. What in the hell? Nate didn't have friends here. All the kids he knew were in Gray Rock. Jesse couldn't come up with any explanation.

Rhett opened the door. Jesse stepped inside first. Both children stood from the edge of the bed. The little girl squeezed tight to a doll. The boy stepped closer to her side.

"Leslie, Minnie, this's Deputy Adams. The one Nathanial told ya could help ya." Rhett pointed at the bed. "Take a seat."

Jesse looked over at Rhett. His mouth hung open, for he was experiencing an utter loss of words. Who were these kids, and what did they have to do with partner?

Rhett backhanded Jesse's shoulder, not hard, just enough to wake him from his bewilderment. "The Harrisons are orphans. They were on the same train as Nathanial."

"Why did Nate say I could help you two?" Jesse glanced between the kids. They were pale, a little thin, and dirty but looked to be in okay shape.

"He said you and his father, Sheriff Crosson, could solve any crime, that you never failed to catch the guilty party. Our brother was kidnapped after our parents died. But I think they were murdered."

"What makes ya say that?" Jesse pulled up a chair.

Rhett plopped down on the bed next to the kids.

"I remembered something. Something my brother told me a few days before our mother and father were killed." The kid wiped his eyes. "Patrick—that's our missing brother—he overheard Pa saying that he was going to sell some stock."

Jesse shrugged. "So what?"

"You don't understand." The boy twisted at his shirttail. "Our father, he put money into companies. Pat called it..." The boy bit at his lip. "Investigating."

Jesse raised a brow. "You mean investing."

"That's it." Leslie nodded. "The two that Pat talked about all the time were Goodwin and Myers, and Fletcher Enterprises. Said they were competing, whatever that means."

Jesse snapped to attention. "Lem Fletcher? The New York Tycoon?"

"The very one." The boy stiffly nodded.

"Pat said one of the two was in trouble. I can't recall which. And if our father pulled his stock, the company could be forced into bank…rup-see."

"Now that your parents are dead, the stocks can't be sold. Not until the will is read." Jesse was thinking out loud.

"Yeah." Rhett chimed in. "If the kids ain't there to accept the inheritance, what happens then?"

"Who else would stand to inherit?" Jesse eyed the kids.

The boy shrugged, and the little girl was braiding her dolly's hair.

"Patrick, is he close to eighteen? With his signature, your family's wealth could be turned over to someone else."

"No." Leslie shook his head. "Pat's only sixteen. But he knows all the inner workings of our father's business affairs. Father was mentoring him to take over someday. And he always explained stuff to me. Said it was never too early to learn. That I'd be his partner someday."

Jesse looked over at Rhett, who returned the troubled look. That didn't sound good for Patrick.

"The day Pat was kidnapped, I remember seeing something white on one of the man's shoes and on the shoulder of the other one. I was so worked up I didn't think much of it because, at the same time, Minnie and I were being dragged away and ended up on an orphan train." The kid grinned. "I know what that white stuff was, and there's only one place in San Francisco that you have to dodge the bird droppings so much that two different men could be marked with poop." He paused, licking his lips as though Jesse should be able to guess. When he didn't say anything, the kid went on. "The dock. At the harbor, the stockyards. Both Goodwin and Mayer and Fletcher Enterprises have cargo ships. Patrick might have been taken there."

That made perfect sense to Jesse. "Why haven't you mentioned this before, to Sheriff Coleman?"

"I didn't think it was important at first, but it kept popping into my mind."

Jesse nodded. "I'll wire Sheriff Crosson. He knows lawmen all over the country. He'll get to the bottom of this. I promise. And I'll help as soon as I can." Jesse stood.

"Wait." Leslie sprang off the bed. "Won't you be escorting us to Gray Rock on the stage tomorrow? Nate said you'd take us in. We don't have any place else to go, and he said we'd be safe there."

"I'll let the sheriff and Ma know you're comin'. You stay as long as you need. But I can't go with ya." Jesse hunkered in front of the kid. "Nate's out there somewhere all alone. I gotta find him before he gets hurt. There's too many people huntin' him."

"He ain't alone."

Jesse's brows shot up. "What do ya mean?" Nate had Luther Blackhorse's mount, but that was all, and that wasn't protection.

"No one was with 'im when he left town," Rhett said to the kid.

"I'm talking about that crazy wolf." The boy glanced between Jesse and Rhett. "The thing almost ripped apart an old lady who was about to whack Nate with a stick."

"I saw it too," the little girl said. "It growled at me." Tears filled her eyes, and she hugged her doll.

"This wolf," Rhett said, "is its name Montana?"

The boy nodded. Jesse and Rhett stared blankly at one another. Neither of them knew what to think.

A wolf! Jesse rubbed his temple. Wouldn't Ma and the sheriff just be thrilled to hear that tidbit of news? A wild animal. Unpredictable to say the least. Jesse decided right then that what Nate's folks didn't know wouldn't hurt them.

He and Rhett left the kids as Mrs. Bell entered with a slice of pie for each of them.

"I hope you saved a slice of that for me." Rhett tugged on her apron strings as he passed.

"There's plenty." She swatted at him.

Jesse thought of his family and how suppertime always brought them together no matter what any one of them had been into that day.

After the two of them ate enough to feed a small family, Jesse sent the telegraphs concerning the Harrisons. He sent one to Judge Prescott with the same details.

Clayton from the livery brought Jesse's and Rhett's horses around to the back of the boarding house. "I got some bad news, boys."

"Well, spit it out," Jesse snapped.

"The Rawlins brothers and that friend of theirs, they done got Virgil, the town drunk, all liquored up. He told 'em the kid they were lookin' for skipped town hours ago."

"When did they leave?" Jesse scowled.

Rhett jumped into the saddle.

"An hour maybe."

"Dammit," Jesse muttered under his breath.

Mrs. Bell came to the back door. "Jesse, wait." She held out her hand. "This belongs to Nathanial." She handed him Nate's deputy's badge.

Jesse stared at the star. The kid never took that off. "Thank you." He shoved the star into his shirt pocket.

Side by side, he and Rhett rode out of town. Jesse recalled his promise to Sheriff Crosson. He would bring Nate home—alive. He glanced at his Winchester. No one would stand in his way.

CHAPTER 13

FOR FOUR DAYS, Nate kept the stolen horse running as often as he could without killing the animal, resting only when necessary. He barely slept, nodding off in the saddle a few minutes each hour during the day. At night, he had to stay alert, keeping an eye open for anything on the ground that might trip his mount and for any bounty hunters trying to sneak up on him.

On a hillside, Nate pulled up on the reins. The black was snorting, and Nate was tired too. He glanced over his shoulder. Miles behind, over the treetops, dust swirled in the cold air. Whoever was trailing him was still there.

"Dammit," he cursed under his breath.

What both he and the black needed was a good night's sleep. With men hunting him no more than four, five hours behind, he had to be smarter, or he and the black might never get any rest, and he would likely be caught.

Nate slid out of the saddle. It only took a minute to find what he was looking for. He reached deep among the prickly pine branches and snapped off a small limb. With a swish motion, he swept away the horse prints made by the black. He'd tried this before and hadn't fooled the men behind him, but it couldn't hurt to try again.

He steered the black farther up the mountain. He zigzagged, led the men behind in a circle once or twice, and walked his horse in a creek for two miles, but those bloodhounds hadn't lost his scent.

Nate crested the summit. The black's hoofs clicked as she stepped on a flat slab of rock that jutted out from the anchor of a spruce standing taller than the others. "Whoa, girl."

Spread out before them, rich, earthy colors of sky and land appeared to never end. The wind whistled through the needles on the trees. An eagle circled overhead. If there was a top of the world, this quite possibly was it.

Nate's ears stung from the wind. He pulled Mrs. Bell's coat tighter around himself and hiked up the collar. "Time to go, Blackie." He nudged the horse's sides.

It was slow going down the other side of the mountain, for the ground was damp and slick in a few spots. This was a place he had not yet led his pursuers. Boulders lined the steep goat path he followed, and he gave the black her head to weave her way along the narrow trail. He was headed in the general direction of Missouri, so a minor sidestep wasn't a worry. But the men behind him were cause for concern. Hard telling what those others were capable of. Things just as bad as Blackhorse, if not worse, had tried.

Nate reached around and fished inside one of the saddle-bags. Luther's belongings included jerked beef, a half-full box of shells, a length of sinew, fifty-three dollars including some coinage, a collection of five or six hawk feathers, and a knife with a bone handle. Too bad there wasn't a pair of gloves in there. Nate's fingers were stiffening around the reins as sunlight dwindled, and at night, in an elevation greater than ten thousand feet, the air could be hellish frigid. Several peaks were snow-capped to the west of him.

Blackie jerked up her head, her front hooves dug in, and Nate whiplashed in the saddle.

"Blackie, what the hell's wrong with ya? 'Bout threw me on my head." Ten yards ahead of them, Montana stood in the center of the trail, a dead rabbit hanging limp in his jaws.

"Is that where you've been all day, huntin'?" Nate smiled. "Ya gonna share that supper with me. Rabbit sounds good after fillin' myself on jerky for the past however many days."

Montana dropped his kill on the ground. Nate leaned forward, patting Blackie's neck. "See, there's no reason to be scared of 'im. He's a big softy."

An hour later, he picketed the black behind a wall formed by a cutout in a stony bank, which gave the three of them needed relief from cold gusts blowing down off the peaks above. Nate rubbed his hands near the flames, then picked up the pieces of flint and shoved them back into his pocket. Without a frying pan, he made do with a flat rock. The cooking meat sizzled. Montana lay at Nate's side.

"I think we're safe for now. Those men behind us, if I have the timin' right, won't even reach the base of the mountain for another couple hours. Too dark to climb up and over without risking your horse goin' lame." He ran his fingers through Montana's thick scruff, rubbing the back of the animal's neck. "I figure they'll stay on the other side 'til mornin'."

Montana laid his head on his paws in the dirt.

"Exactly, my friend. After we eat, we can get some sleep." Nate stretched out next to his warm, furry companion and waited for supper to brown.

It wasn't long after gnawing every morsel of meat off the bunny bones that he curled up next to his fuzzy pal and closed his eyes. Not that he was expecting anyone, but if by chance anyone did come nosing around, Montana or Blackie would stir and wake him.

When Nate woke, it was with a chill. Montana was gone, and the groundsheet Luther had left fastened to his saddle wasn't thick enough to keep the cold, hard ground from seeping into his bones. He stretched out the stiffness.

Blackie pawed the ground as Nate crawled into the saddle. One good night's rest had done them all good.

A dark-gray overcast dulled the morning. Snow wasn't unlikely in October. Maybe God was going to skip fall and launch the world straight into winter. Maybe it was his way of slowing Nate down, giving him time to think about what he was about to do.

Missouri. That was a long trip to end up finding out the trouble-hunting Younger family had disowned him. After all, Jim Younger and his brothers had been caught that day in Northfield, and Nate's job during that robbery had been to spot a trap from his position inside the bank. The Youngers, Nate knew firsthand, weren't known for being forgiving.

The black made good time as if a born mountain horse, and Nate didn't know that she wasn't. In the valley below, he let Blackie stretch her legs, setting the pace. Rectangular in shape, the field was wide-open, full of dried grass. A herd of eight, nine elk grazed at the far end. Two or three lifted their heads and watched as he and Blackie passed at a distance.

Behind him, a smoke-colored cloud the size of Texas crowned the mountain he'd just come out of, and the peak was no longer visible. Up on top, it must have been snowing.

Nate rubbed Blackie's shoulder. "We got outta there just in time."

It'd be treacherous to try and cross that elevation now. If it was snowing up there, any amount would make the trail awful slick, too dangerous for a horse. Unless the men tailing him were plumb crazy, they'd have to wait out the nasty weather.

Nate would take any breathing room he could get. Could be he didn't have much at all. It was likely others were hunting him as well. Men on this side of the mountain, men who had seen the wanted picture of him but hadn't cut his trail yet. His enemies could be riding in around him from all directions.

CHAPTER 14

B Y WEEK'S END, Montana was eating out of Nate's hand, and Blackie rarely raised her head when the big wolf came around. Nate kicked dirt on the fire and glanced over his shoulder. A lifestyle he was once again getting accustomed to, only this time he wasn't running away from crimes with the Younger gang. But he might find himself doing just that if he returned to Missouri, to Jim Younger's family.

What was he thinking? He hated that man. Hated the life he'd had with that mean bastard. But what other choice did he have? New York definitely wasn't the answer. But neither was Missouri.

"It's just you and me now, Montana." They'd find someplace away from there where maybe no one would recognize him or until he came across another sweet lady like Mrs. Bell who would take them in, even if he had to be a farmhand like when he lived with the Harpers before he was adopted.

"Come on, boy." Nate whistled. Montana was trailing behind. "We'll be okay. I won't let anythin' happen to ya." Just because he couldn't see dust in the air behind him, due in part to the abrupt change in the weather, he wouldn't dare lie to himself. The men hunting him and the bounty on his head were back there somewhere.

He chewed on a piece of charcoaled backstrap from a deer that Montana had taken down earlier in the day, which Nate managed to badly overcook. The loins had curled tight in the flame, nothing like a fresh dish of Ma's eggs and bacon, crispy but never overdone. He glanced over at the deerskin lying in a fresh heap, then stared down at his boots. Why hadn't he thought of this before?

With the sharpened blade that had belonged to Luther Blackhorse, Nate sliced the furry pelt into four square sections of the same size. He rooted in the saddlebags. The honed piece of bone Blackhorse had tried to puncture him with was attached to a length of sinew. Perfect.

"Easy, girl." Nate patted Blackie's shoulder. "This won't hurt a bit. I promise." He squeezed Blackie's hock, and the horse lifted her leg. Nate wrapped one square of the deerskin around that foot. Then, with the needle and thread, he stitched the furry sock into place around Blackie's hoof. Twenty minutes later, he had all four of his horse's iron shoes covered.

Nate smirked. "Now let's see how well those arseholes behind us can pick up our trail."

Blackie swished her tail. It wouldn't be easy without horse prints, and the deerskin barrier should naturally do a fine job of wiping out the tracks.

Blackie pranced a bit as the feel of fur stitched around her ankles was unfamiliar.

"You're okay." Nate spoke softly for a few minutes before the animal settled. Buck, his horse back at home, trusted him one hundred percent. Theirs was a good bond. It would take time for him and Blackie to form that kind of relationship. Whether he decided to go on to Missouri or find his way through life, he needed a good horse. That damn bounty would keep him running for years. As dishonest as the Youngers were, they might even turn him in for the cash.

When they reached a fork in a road, a sign with a red arrow pointing east read:

Denver

One Hundred Miles

"Golly geez. A hundred miles. That'll take us a few days." He rubbed his sore behind, needing some time out of the saddle. Blackie's trot was like a mean spank.

Montana plunked his bottom down in the dirt, his tongue hanging out, panting.

"Been a long day, hasn't it, boy?" Nate turned Blackie into the tree line in the direction of Denver. "Let's find us a place to rest."

Montana trotted alongside.

A mile or so later, a crooked shack blackened by the pounding given by years of wind, snow, rain, and shine creaked against a gust. Vining weeds with leaves of three had climbed up the walls and across the roof. Many of the side planks had a gap of an inch or two between them, and all the glass had been broken out of the lone front window. The wind blew the door open and closed. Each pass produced a clap of wood on wood.

There was a ten-by-fifteen corral that would house two, three horses at most, but a majority of the railings had fallen at one time or another, and the posts were covered in tall-standing weeds. Yet it was a good place for the three of them to rest. Far enough off the coach road that anyone traveling by would not see them, and if anyone were to come across the wreck, unless desperate, who would bother with the place? It was about as unfriendly looking as a scrap pile found in the middle of nowhere could be. Welcome wasn't the vibe it was putting off.

Cobwebs, big ugly spiders, and snakes came to Nate's mind. But he was tired, and he wouldn't push the animals any harder. They'd covered a lot of miles today, and there was still light in the sky. After a hearty rest, they could go an hour or two more.

He slid out of the saddle. When he had the downed fencing propped in a cross-rail fashion so Blackie couldn't wander off but had room to roll if she had the urge, Nate pushed the cabin door wider, Montana at his side.

They peered inside the musty dark space. The wind whipped against Nate's cheeks. A limb, high up, scratched an uplifted board on the rooftop, and he damn near jumped out of his skin. Montana backed up a pace or two. His eyes narrowed on the tree line. His hackles stood on end, ears erect, and a deep, throaty growl rattled out between his long fanged teeth.

Seven riders bunched into the meadow, faces shaded by their hats, but their tied-down guns identified them as trouble. Nate's heart caught in his airway. Out front, a fella a few years older than Jesse pulled his pistol.

A bang rippled through the air. Dirt kicked up an inch away from Montana, who jumped and sprinted off around the opposite side of the cabin. Nate was in no mood. That was his best friend.

"You asshole! Let my dog alone!" He snatched up a rock and buzzed that fist-sized sucker in a beeline for the bridge of that jackass's nose.

The fella jerked in the saddle. "Ouch!" He dropped his pistol as he grabbed the bleeding cut between his eyes. A couple of the others with him snickered. One man had drawn his gun.

Nate dove through the doorway, then kicked shut the only thing between him and a bullet. The rusty hinges groaned. He scrambled across the floor toward a window at the rear of the shack. Like thunder, the door cracked open. Men stampeded in, bumping one another, searching about.

"That's the kid from the article," one of them shouted. All eyes fell on Nate.

He jumped to his feet, turned, and threw up the stiff, cranky window as fast as he could. As Nate tossed himself out the opening head first, they lunged, the whole group of them, arms outstretched. A rough hand latched onto his ankle, jerking him backward. He kicked and hit at the man hanging partway out the window with him.

Out of the brush, Montana sprang, his jaws wide. He bit down on the side of the man's face, savagely tearing flesh from the bone. Screams shook the air. The others pulled their friend inside. Nate dropped to the ground.

Montana took off, and Nate ran toward the corral. No time for saddling Blackie. Over the top rail, he leaped with one leg outstretched and landed on his horse's back. Blackie snorted, but she must have sensed the urgency and ran straight through the rotted timber fence.

Gunfire sounded behind them.

Nate didn't glance back. He hoped Montana was out of range. For being tired, Blackie thundered across the land, but a great rumbling drowned out the sound.

A rifle boomed. A few seconds later, a second shot fired. Blackie screeched. One of her back legs buckled, and she fell. Nate barely had time to jump and hit the ground the same time Blackie did. They both rolled.

Nate sat up, his head spinning. Blackie tried to stand. Her nostrils flared, and she was panting.

Nate scrambled toward her. "It'll be okay, girl." Tears rolled down his cheeks because he knew Blackie wouldn't recover.

A boom sent the horse to the ground again. This time, the bullet tore through her chest. Blackie didn't make another noise.

Nate rubbed the dead horse's nose. "I'm sorry, girl. This's all my fault."

Riders bunched in around Nate. They jerked on their reins, their mounts prancing around the smell of fresh blood on the ground in front of them.

"You bastards!" Nate eyeballed every one of the men. What did he have to lose? A few teeth that they could knock out of his head for being a smartass? They'd killed his horse. Montana had run off, and Nate couldn't go home where he wished to be in the worst kind of way.

"Shut up, kid." The one who had shot at Montana stepped down off his horse.

Nate had been right. Up close, this man was maybe a few years older than Jesse. Same coffee-colored hair. Only, this fella had a lean build to him and a mean glint in his eyes. His walk was more like a slink that made Nate think of a weasel. And any man who would condone the senseless slaughter of a perfectly good horse wasn't much in Nate's book.

"You didn't have to kill 'er." He threw a handful of dirt at the man's eyes.

The fella blocked the shot with his arm. "Kid, if you weren't worth fifteen thousand, I'd kill ya." He grabbed Nate by the hair, jerking his head in the direction of the man who'd been bitten by Montana.

Although his mouth was closed, his teeth were showing through the grotesque open wound on his cheek. After a few seconds, the man pressed the bloody rag against his face, covering the seeping hole.

"Maybe I should cut off a chunk of your face." He jerked Nate to his feet. In his other hand, he held a glistening blade. "Killin' that mutt of yours was purdy satisfyin'."

"You're full of shit! Ya did not!" Nate shook his head, hoping it wasn't true. He wouldn't believe it. They couldn't have killed Montana. He'd run, gotten away. He had to have. They'd shot and killed Blackie, not Montana too.

Nate jumped and kicked out like a mule. The heels of his boots smashed against the braggart's man parts. He dropped to the dirt and groaned.

"You little bastard!" He cursed a blue streak while holding his crotch and rolling on the ground as the others dove at Nate, swiping and missing as he dodged each grab.

Nate had just swung his leg over a saddle when an Indian fella clubbed him with his fist. Nate saw stars as he slid out of the saddle and thudded to the earth.

When he came to, the sky was black, other than a few stars. There was a fire flickering, but he wasn't close enough to feel the heat. He was tied to a tree, and he squirmed, wanting to rub his splitting headache, but his arms were drawn tight to his sides.

Six of the seven men he'd taken on earlier were around the flames. Two of them were holding down the fella Montana had attacked while a third man stitched his face. A fourth man poked a stick into the fire, and embers flew up into the night. Two others sat on their blankets, passing a bottle between them, maybe trying to drown out the moans of their injured friend. Where was the one who'd said Montana had been shot?

"You finally wake up?" Out of the dark came a voice, one Nate would rather forget. The fella he'd kicked stepped out of nowhere, rifle at his side, and he hunkered next to Nate.

"For a half-pint, you sure can put up a fight." He jerked Nate's head back by a fistful of hair, leaned in, and eyed the knot on his temple. "You're lucky Yooko didn't kill ya. He's Yaqui." The fella grinned. "His name means Tiger. Don't get any ideas 'bout runnin' off, or I'll set 'im free to hunt ya. And he's twice as mean as that wolf of yours."

"I doubt it." Nate put on a smirk. "I watched him rip a man's throat out." He glanced at the rifle in the fella's hands. "You better guard your men. Montana's out there somewhere, and he's watchin'. He'll creep in and kill when ya least expect it, kill anyone who lays a hand on me, so ya best sleep with one eye open," he said without fear and snapped his jaws, letting out a little of the wild inside of him toward his enemy. The fella jerked back, staring at him as though he were plumb loco.

Not that Nate wanted to witness another brutal attack, but if he could keep the seed of fear growing in these fellas, then he had an edge. Something to work with that might present an opportunity for escape. And unpredictability would do just that. He leaned heavily toward his capturer, the ropes around Nate's arms pulling tighter, and he growled.

The fella forced a scoff but swallowed hard at the same time. "I told ya that wolf's dead." He stood, sweat beads glistening on his forehead.

"Then what's got ya scared? Little ol' me?" Nate batted his baby blues. "'Cause ain't nobody else around." He sensed somehow that Montana was alive, and just as the wolf had once found companionship with Amos's partner, he'd taken a liking to Nate.

A fierce howl echoed through the trees. The fella standing next to Nate snapped up his head, gun raised in the ready position. The boys around the fire all stopped. The ones sitting jumped to their feet, pistols in hand.

"You best keep that fire bright," Nate said nonchalantly.

The fella marched toward the flames and his men.

CHAPTER 15

"**G**OOSE!" the fella marching away from Nate boomed.

A tall man stood from where he'd been squatted next to the man being held down, getting his cheek sewn back together. Not far away but outside the line of firelight, the horses snorted. Their hooves stomped the dirt as they pranced.

"Go check on the horses." He tossed a few sticks on the fire, and sparks flew up.

"Jasper, I ain't sure that's such a good idea." Goose didn't move away from the light, and Nate didn't blame him. No one in their right mind would willingly risk getting their face chewed off.

"Chickenshit," Jasper growled. "Why my brother ever let ya join with us…" He spit. "Don't know what he seen in ya. All I see is yella."

Goose's hands balled at his sides. "Believe me, I wish your brother was alive and callin' the shots. We always had money in our pockets when he was leadin' us." He pointed at the bleeding man who was passed out while the sewing continued. "Nothin' like that ever happened when Richard was in charge."

"Shut up!" Jasper snarled.

Nate cringed, but Goose straightened, standing taller than a few seconds ago. That man was anything but a coward.

"I'll do it." One of the two fellas who were passing the whiskey took a long swing, shoved the bottle at his friend, hitched up his belt, then shouldered past Goose. "Finch is right. You're spineless."

"I'd rather be that than ripped apart by a loco wolf. So you have at it, Anderson." Goose's hand rested on the butt of his holstered pistol.

"Anderson knows how to take orders. You could learn a thing or two from 'im." Jasper Finch pointedly glared at Goose. And as though Finch weren't holding a shotgun, Goose puckered his lips and made a smooching noise, basically telling his boss to kiss his ass.

Nate burst out laughing. Finch shot him a hard look. Nate bit his tongue, holding back his snickers.

A deep growl rattled through camp. They all twisted their heads. Panicked horses yanked on the ropes that held them tethered in a line. Montana leaped into the light and chomped down on Anderson's arm. Bone crunched. Nate's gut squeezed. Anderson's screams shook the trees. Montana savagely shook his head. Blood gushed out of the man's dangling arm. Human and beast rolled across the ground. Anderson clubbed at Nate's wolf with the butt of his pistol.

The men around the fire held their guns ready, but no one could dare shoot. Anderson and Montana were tightly wrapped together. Growls and shrieks echoed through the night.

Finch stormed toward Nate. "Call 'im off!" He shook Nate by his hair.

Son of a bitch, his teeth rattled. "Montana!" he managed to yell before getting his head bashed off the tree he was tied to. "No! Run!" Tears stung his eyes.

And just like that, Montana was gone. Finch shoved Nate's head, smacking it off the bark one more time.

The line holding the horses snapped, and the animals fled into the night. Finch hustled and dragged Anderson farther into the light, but not one of them ran into the dark after the horses.

"Shit!" Jasper yelled.

All his men were staring down at Anderson bleeding all over himself, his arm dangling by no more than a trace of skin connected to what had been muscle but was now shaped like a blob of mush.

"Damn, that arm's gonna have to come off," Goose said and leaned over into Anderson's face. "I surely do hate to rub it in, but I told ya so." His lips spread into a mean grin.

Finch shoved Goose out of the way. "Let me have a look."

Yooko stood next to Finch and watched Anderson reeling in the dirt. The Yaqui pulled a ten-inch blade out of the sheath strapped on his belt. The edge gleamed in the firelight. Nate swallowed hard.

Finch nodded, and Yooko dropped to his knees next to Anderson, who was white as a sheet and violently shaking his head. Anderson's drinking partner shoved a thick stick in his mouth, then pinned his shoulders down. Anderson's heavy breathing could be heard from where Nate was stuck ten feet away.

"Who's the pussy now?" Goose leaned back against a tree and lit a smoke.

Finch looked up from where he was on all fours, holding down Anderson's legs, and glared. His neck and face grew red. Yooko lifted the knife.

It was a safe bet that if Jasper wasn't caught in a life-and-death situation, he'd have punched Goose or maybe shot him.

Yooko sank the blade. Anderson screamed.

Nate wished he could shove a finger deep into each ear. Oh dear God, he burped out yellow juices from his stomach and down over the front of his coat.

Five minutes later, which felt like four seasons of the coldest, most brutal winter ever, Anderson's amputated limb was tossed into the fire. Skin sizzled. An instant stink filled the camp. Nate shivered, but it wasn't the cold wind that had him shaking. Anderson's eyes rolled in his head, out cold. His drinking partner cut up a spare shirt and wrapped the bandages around the bleeding stump. Yooko wiped the red off his blade in a tuft of withered grass. Goose, who didn't even glance at Anderson, flicked the butt of his smoke into the flames.

Finch, with a gun in his hand, walked toward Nate. He shrank back, but the tree was hard and unforgiving. Finch untied the ropes and managed to keep his pistol aimed at him. He jerked him to his feet. By the back of his coat, he was dragged toward the fire.

"Call in that wolf of yours." Jasper searched beyond the ring of light, his gun aimed into the dark. "Boys, get ready." The others all drew their guns, searching the same as Jasper.

"No, you'll kill 'im." Nate wouldn't do it. He yanked out of Jasper's grip, but before he could turn and run, the back of Finch's hand whacked him across the mouth, sending him flying. He hit the dirt on his back.

This time, Goose pulled Nate onto his feet, then shoved him behind. He stood between Nate and Finch. Both men held a weapon and hatefully eyeballed one another.

"Goose, you're askin' for a belly full of lead." Finch's tongue jetted out.

"Turnin' the kid over for money's one thang, but I ain't goin' along with beatin' 'im around." Goose took a step closer to Finch. "If this's how you prove yourself as a man, then reckon I was right. You ain't nothin' compared to Richard."

Finch spun his six-shooter and clubbed Goose on the cheekbone. He stumbled back, then regained his balance and lunged, buckling Jasper in two at the waist. They thudded the ground together and punched at one another.

"Git 'im, Goose," Nate cheered.

Anderson's drinking buddy, a stocky fella, shoved past Nate. He grabbed Finch, another fella getting a grip around Goose's arms, and they ripped the two apart, still swinging at one another.

"Hold on, you two," the stocky fella yelled. "We've got two injured, a wolf huntin' us, and a brat that's turned out to be more of a damn headache than any of us ever thought possible. We don't need any fightin' amongst us."

"Lutz is right," Goose said, looking at Finch. The fellas holding them let go. Goose snatched his pistol off the ground and jammed it into his holster.

"Someday." Jasper snarled when Goose had his back turned.

Nate hadn't relaxed yet, not that he ever would around these men, but the crazy look in Jasper's eyes kept him holding his breathing. He wasn't so sure Finch wouldn't snap and shoot Goose.

Goose turned, making direct eye contact with Finch. "The sun'll be up in two hours. A new day. Why not then?"

Lutz pushed Finch toward a corner of camp away from Goose. All the while, Finch glared. Nate was beginning to think Goose was better with a gun. Otherwise, why would Lutz have run interference?

Goose walked past Nate, not glancing at him, and stretched out on his blanket, his head pillowed on his saddle. Nate stood there baffled by the carnage. He scratched his head. At the moment, running away wasn't in his best interest. These men were stirred up worse than a hornet nest. Any one of them, other than Goose, might shoot him if he tried an escape now.

Nate sat down next to Goose.

The man slid his hat up over his face and onto his head. "What do ya want, kid?"

Nate hesitated, fiddling with a button on his coat. "May I sleep here next to you?"

"Let's get somethin' straight. I ain't yer friend. I ain't nobody's nothin'. You'd be wise to remember that." Goose placed his hat over his face.

Nate didn't care what Goose said. He didn't feel completely safe around the man, but at least if he stayed close, Finch might not hit him.

He laid his head to the ground. His lips were smarting from the backhanded slap, a good reminder of why he wasn't going to look for a home among the Youngers. He touched softly at the swollen skin.

Nate had been taught how to work people. This man would be a challenge, but Nate needed someone other than Montana on his side. "Thank you," he whispered.

Goose rolled onto his side, facing away from Nate, and ignored him.

* * *

Nate was still awake when a pink morning began to crawl over the mountaintop and stretch across the sky.

He glanced over his shoulder. Yooko lifted Anderson's shoulder with a boot toe, then let him flop. He shook his head at Finch. Jasper's face pinched tight, and he looked over at Nate and glared.

Nate scooted back, bumping into Goose who sat up with a start, and then his eyes fixed on Anderson's limp body.

"That ain't my fault." Nate pleaded. Without thought, he grabbed Goose's sleeve. Goose and Anderson had been at odds, but they'd also been riding companions. Nate didn't want to lose any ground, not even an inch, that he'd gained with this man.

"Settle." Goose peeled Nate's hands off him. "Anderson ain't worth the sweat it'll take to bury 'im." He stood and strode toward the fire. After pouring himself a cup of coffee, he joined Finch and the others all standing over the remains of their friend.

No one was watching Nate. He slowly stood and stepped backward into the tree line, holding his breath the whole time. A twig snapped under his boot, and Nate froze. Finch and his men all twisted around. They stared at him, and his eyes grew wide.

"Get 'im!" Finch bellowed.

Nate bolted deeper into the woods. He clambered over a mound of rocks. On the other side, he ducked a couple of low-hanging branches. Voices carried in the air, prickling his skin. They weren't far behind him. Where could he hide? He headed for the ridgetop. Climbing might slow those behind him, but he was used to running the hills around Gray Rock with his buddies.

Near the top, Montana appeared and charged down the hill straight at Nate. He glanced over his shoulder, hoping he didn't trip as he ran. Three feet behind him was Lutz, his hand reaching out until he focused on Montana. Lutz skinned his pistol. Nate scooped up a thick dead branch and swung with all his might. Wood collided with iron. A shot rang out just as Lutz's gun went sailing through the air. Lutz lunged for Nate, and Nate stepped wrong, catching his ankle between two rocks. Before he knew it, his hands and knees dug into the dirt.

Montana flew over Nate and, with one harsh slash of his teeth, tore out Lutz's windpipe.

"Over here!" Finch hollered.

A shot kicked up dirt between Montana's front feet. He turned and ran.

Nate jumped to his feet. "Ouch." He could hardly step, let alone run. But he wasn't about to give up and get caught.

Yooko and another fella came out from between the trees behind Finch. Where was Goose? Finch squeezed the trigger a second time. Lead bore into a tree a hair above Montana's ears.

Nate forced his paining foot to run. He cut straight up the ridge along the same path Montana used as he disappeared over the top. He let out a gust. At least Montana was safe.

Three-quarters of the way to the top, Goose jumped out from behind a spruce and grabbed him by the arm.

"Let me go!" Nate hollered, then sank his teeth into Goose's wrist.

Goose whipped him around and pressed him against a rock taller than him, holding him there. Nate heard the too-familiar sound of leather being pulled out of belt loops.

"Don't you ever do anythin' like that again." As Goose raised his arm, leather swooshed.

The first lick stood Nate on his toes. The second had him squinting his eyes tight shut. His behind pinched solid, stinging something fierce. The third and fourth, tears began to roll down his cheeks. The fifth, he was crying out loud.

Goose whirled him around so Nate was facing the man. He rubbed at his smarting backside.

"Quit your bawlin'. You asked for it." Goose shook the folded leather strap at Nate.

Finch stepped up next to them. "Now that's more like it." He clapped Goose on the shoulder.

Goose jerked his body away. "Swattin' his ass ain't the same as bustin' 'im in the teeth with yer knuckles. The boy needed taught a lesson. And he got one." He rubbed his hand where Nate had bitten him.

Jasper snatched the belt away from Goose. "Maybe he needs a few more lashes as a reminder." He looked hard at Nate. "That fifteen thousand will be ours. No one, not even you, will stand in the way of that." He drew back, holding the strap.

Goose caught him by the wrist. "Marv's face was bleedin' again when we left camp. I'm thinkin' we oughta check on 'im."

Goose and Finch pushed away from one another.

"Let's go." Finch grabbed Nate and shoved him in the direction of the camp.

Nate spun and clung to Goose's sleeve.

"I'm not goin' with you!" Nate wasn't a fool. He glared at Finch. The minute Goose wasn't around, Finch would likely pound his hide. Another of his men had been killed by Montana.

Finch eyed the two. "Goose, git 'im back to camp, and if he escapes on the way, I'll hold you responsible."

Nate could only imagine what that meant. Finch turned his back, as did the others, following a step behind their leader. They passed Lutz's carcass and stared at the bloody remains. Nate looked up at Goose, who was staring over his shoulder at the skyline. Montana stood watching down over everything from his rocky perch. The fur around his mouth was stained red. He snapped his powerful jaws several times. Goose's hand began to slide toward his revolver.

"No." Nate grabbed Goose's wrist before he could draw.

"Kid, I ain't about to let some wolf rip out my throat." He pulled at Nate's hands, but he held tight, yanking in the opposite direction.

"I'll promise I won't run away—from you."

They both stopped struggling for control of the gun. Goose lifted his chin toward Montana. "If he attacks, that promise don't mean a thang if I'm dead."

"I'll talk to 'im. He won't hurt ya." Nate raised his right hand.

Goose's brow arched. "Talk to a wolf? And he's gonna listen." The man chuckled.

"It ain't as strange as it might sound." Nate looked down the trail toward camp. The others had disappeared among the trees. "It ain't a trick. I swear."

Now that the others were gone, he could call Montana if he would come. Goose wasn't a friend, but the man had kept Finch from beating on him twice now. Nate owed him something.

"Let me have your bandana," Nate said.

"What for?" Goose eyed him.

"Just give it to me." Nate held out his hand. Goose untied his neck ribbon and handed it over, one eye on Montana the entire time.

Nate started up the hill.

"Where d'ya think you're goin'?" Goose's hand clamped down on Nate's shoulder.

Montana growled.

"Stand back," Nate said.

Goose needed to trust him, but he had no reason to. Two of the gang he rode with were dead and one badly injured because of Nate's wolf, and now the three of them were alone. He couldn't blame the man for sweating.

Slowly, Goose let go.

"Whatever ya do, don't pull that gun," Nate said, then walked toward Montana.

The big wolf trotted toward him, but his eyes were on Goose. Nate hunkered. Montana brushed up against him, licking his face. Nate hugged around the thick, fuzzy neck. Montana backed up, his nose lifted, sniffing at him. Nate was wearing Goose's bandana. A new and different scent that the wolf didn't recognize altogether as Nate's.

He patted between Montana's ears. "He can help us, Montana. You can't do it all. One of these times, they're gonna get lucky and put a bullet in ya. I don't wanna see that happen. I'd never forgive myself." He looked over his shoulder at Goose. Montana licked Nate's hair.

He looked back and smiled. "I'm glad to see you too, boy. But I gotta leave ya for a little while. I'm gonna go with 'im."

Montana pushed at Nate with his nose.

"I know ya don't want me to go. And I'd rather be with you. But they'll hunt us down and kill ya." He rubbed a hand the length of Montana's back. "You need to go. Stay away from 'em, away from me. As soon as I can, we'll be together again. I give ya my word." He stood.

Montana nosed his hand. He smoothed the hair over the top of the wolf's head.

"Don't make this harder than it has to be." Nate sniffled.

He walked toward Goose. Lately, it seemed that life had a way of tearing him away from everyone and everything he loved.

"I can't believe it." Goose stared past Nate.

He glanced over his shoulder. Montana had retaken his perch. He sat like a lord and watched Nate.

"Give me your hand." Nate wanted Montana to know that his human was safe.

"What?" Goose stared at the kid. Before he could question or protest, Nate slipped his fingers between Goose's. He turned his back on his beloved wolf and walked, holding to Goose, who was half a step behind and still watching the wolf over his shoulder.

Tears welled in Nate's eyes. What if he never saw Montana again? What if he returned to the wild? What if he was betting on this man to help him when he might truly be no better than Finch or the others?

Near the edge of camp, Nate let go of Goose and wiped a sleeve across his eyes.

"Took ya long enough," Finch barked.

"Saw that wolf. Thought I could get a shot at 'im, but the kid warned 'im off." Goose picked up his gear.

Only five men and Nate walked away from camp.

The wind picked up, pushing against them, slowing their efforts to find the horses. Marv, the man that had his face bitten, was shouldered by Goose on one side. A fella named Jackson carried Marv's rig plus his own. Finch was out front by a few paces, and it'd been that way for hours. Yooko brought up the rear, a step or two behind Nate, poking him in the back with his rifle every other step to move faster. Nate hadn't slept at all the night before, so his feet were dragging, and his belly growled.

"I'm hungry," he whined. And he was too blasted tired to care who it irritated.

Goose dropped his saddle off his shoulder. "Finch, the kid's right. You been pushin' all of us. Marv needs to rest, and it wouldn't hurt to get somethin' hot into our bellies." He eased Marv down against a tree where he leaned his head back, eyes closed, mouth open, breathing heavy. His tack was dumped in a lump at his feet. Blood trickled from his wound and down his chin.

Goose lifted his hat and mopped his hairline, though the air was cold.

"Marv either keeps up, or we leave 'im behind with a bullet in his head," Finch snapped. "Never cared much for 'im," he said as though the man weren't right there within earshot.

Neither Jackson nor Yooko lowered their rigs, but they stood, chests heaving, and caught some breath.

"Junior's place ain't far from here. Less than a day's walk. We could have Marv there by tomorrow." Goose pulled the makings of a cigarette out of his shirt pocket.

Finch's gaze roamed over what was left of his men.

"Could be the horses went there," Goose added.

"An hour, then we head to Junior's." Finch dropped his saddle.

Nate plopped on his butt right where he stood. God, he was beat. He stretched out and stared up through the treetops. A blackbird sat on a high-up branch. According to old man Pike, a blackbird was a sign of death among most Indian tribes. Nate hoped he wasn't the only one to see it.

Without warning, he was yanked off the ground. "Gather some wood but stay where I can see ya. If ya try an' run"—Finch glanced over at Goose—"I'll drill a bullet straight through his head."

Goose folded a piece of cloth for Marv, who pressed it against his leaky wound.

Nate picked up what sticks were close at hand. He straightened his achy back and glanced amid the trees for more wood. Montana lay in a ready position under a thicket of brush. His tail wagged.

Nate turned and dropped the armful of sticks next to Jackson. Bent over and blowing on a small flame, Jackson had his focus on his work. Yooko, on his knees, was filling the coffeepot at the creek. Goose rested near Marv, who was slumped on the ground. Finch had his beady eyes on Nate. From where he sat, he couldn't see Montana, for there were lots of branches between them.

Nate danced a little. "I gotta go." This time, he would run off Montana. He couldn't risk him crawling any closer and maybe getting shot.

"Well, go over there and take a piss." Finch waved toward a tree.

Nate shifted from one foot to the other, glancing every other second at his feet, wishing he could somehow produce a flush in his cheeks. Instead, he softened his voice. "I don't have to make water." He glanced around at the others, paying him no mind, then looked at Finch and whispered, "I gotta make stink."

"Goose!" Finch called. "The kid's gotta squat in the bushes. You take 'im. Don't let 'im out of your sight."

"Like hell," Goose said. "If you're that damn worried, you go sit beside 'im."

Nate pranced. "I'm gonna have an accident."

"All right. Git." Finch jerked his head. "You got exactly five minutes. If I have to come after ya, it won't be Goose who slaps leather to ya this time. And I'll whip ya raw. Ya won't sit for a month."

Nate nodded. He wasted no time running straight to Montana and leading the animal behind a hedge of brush. Montana pawed at him. "I can't follow ya, boy. It ain't safe for us. My ankle still hurts." He rubbed his leg. "Not bad, but I won't be runnin' anywhere soon."

"Who ya talkin' to?" Finch must not have trusted that Nate wouldn't run. It sounded as though he were near the edge of camp. It hadn't been five minutes. Three at most.

"Myself." Nate moaned. "My belly hurts." He pressed his lips against his arm and blew hard. Bubbles of air popped and burped against his skin. It sounded awful. Worse than when Jesse broke wind.

"Just stay there and finish your business."

Nate rolled his eyes. "I think what that idiot means is that I have more than five minutes," he whispered to Montana.

He untied the bandana Goose had given him. His sweat, his scent had soaked into the material.

"You have to go away this time." He slipped it around Montana's neck and fastened a loose knot. "If we don't find our way back together, maybe this'll keep someone from shootin' ya." He traced his fingers along the edge of the bandana. "They'll know that you were tamed—sort of." He grinned.

Montana rubbed against Nate. He pushed the wolf away. "No. Git," he said as loud as he could without being heard in camp.

He stood and, with an ache in his chest, he kicked at Montana. The wolf jumped back. Montana cocked his head and stared at Nate.

"I mean it, boy. Go." He shooed the animal away.

"You okay, kid?" It was Goose's voice, and footsteps were closing in on him.

He turned and, at a fast gimp, rounded the edge of the brush and smacked into Goose. Nate fell back on his bottom.

Goose eyed him. "You're pale."

"I don't feel good," he whimpered, and this time, he meant it. Nothing was physically wrong with him, but a case of homesickness swept over him worse than ever. Because of the Fletchers, the trial, and the stupid bounty, he'd lost another best friend. Montana wasn't safe as long as he stayed close to Nate.

He already had to leave Buck and his buddies from school. Not to mention his big partner, Jesse, Nate's best friend of all time. They'd probably all forgotten him by now.

Goose pulled him to his feet. "When's the last time you et anythin'?"

Nate shrugged. "Does it matter?"

"There's jerky in my saddlebags. Help yourself." Goose turned and headed farther in among the trees.

"Where ya goin'? Finch said an hour. It's gotta be close. He'll leave without ya." That was the last thing Nate wanted. To be honest, he just wanted to be left alone to sulk.

Goose looked over his shoulder. "Kid, you oughta know by now that I don't think much of anythin' Jasper says."

"Then why don't ya leave and take me with ya?" Nate threw the idea out there.

"I had every intention of leavin' the gang. Right after Jasper's brother died, had my saddlebags packed." Goose stared off as though recalling that day. "Then Jasper strolled into the hideout, waving a newspaper with your face on it."

"I'll help ya get the fifteen thousand—somehow." Nate promised. "But you have to swear you won't turn me over to the Fletchers."

"I don't want the money, kid." Goose passed his rifle to his other hand. "I know your father. Nolan and I grew up together on neighborin' ranches. Walked to school together, hunted together, and when we got older, we chased the same pretty girls." Goose grinned. "For a long time, we were the best of pals."

"I don't understand," Nate said. "Pa never mentioned ya."

Goose shrugged. "Why would he? He became a lawman, and I went the other direction. We ain't exactly on the same side anymore."

"But you said you weren't after the cash."

"That's true. The only reason I'm here is that I owe your pa, and I know what Jasper's like. He'd just as soon carry your dead carcass to the Fletchers. Said as much. I thought I had convinced 'im that, alive, ya might be worth more than fifteen grand. But I wouldn't bet on it." Goose walked off into the woods, leaving Nate with his mouth hanging open.

CHAPTER 16

NATE SHUFFLED INTO CAMP, ignoring the stares from Finch and the others sitting around the fire and sipping coffee. Colored leaves with curled edges blew across the ground. He wrapped up in Goose's groundsheet. Why did he owe Pa? And what exactly did that mean for Nate?

He pillowed his head on Goose's saddle, yawning. The sun was behind a cloud, which made the day darker than usual. It wasn't yet suppertime, but he wasn't hungry. Too many thoughts filled his mind. Questions only Goose could answer.

"Where's Goose?" Finch nudged Nate with his boot.

"I don't know. He just walked off." Nate closed his eyes.

When he woke, Goose was sitting with the others next to the flames, warming his hands while venison cooked.

Nate's eyes stuck fast on the bandana around Goose's neck. He dropped the blanket off his shoulders as he popped to his feet. "You backstabber! You killed 'im. How could you?"

Everyone turned and stared at Nate.

"What are ya talkin' about, kid?" Finch sipped his coffee.

"Not you—him." Nate pointed at Goose.

He nodded. "Yes, I shot the deer."

Jackson and Yooko snickered. Finch grinned. "Don't eat any if ya don't want to."

"I'm talkin' 'bout Montana." Nate charged Goose at a full run. Before the man could get to his feet, lifting from a squat, Nate threw himself and tackled Goose around the shoulders. They rolled over Jackson, who wasn't laughing anymore but groaned when Nate's knee caught him in the gut.

Goose peeled Nate off his back as he stood. He swung at any part of Goose he could. As the man jumped to miss his strikes, he also grabbed at Nate's arms. "Kid, I ain't sure what this is about, but ya need to calm down." He held up his hands while dodging a few kicks. "Let's talk."

Nate didn't want to talk. He drew back to throw another punch. Two big arms clamped around him, squeezing him tight. Nate wiggled. Finch threw him facedown against the ground and stomped a boot into his back, holding him pinned in one spot. Nate coughed on dust. Jasper's bootheel dug in, pinching the knobs of his spine.

"I wanna know what this is all about," Finch thundered.

"That." Nate couldn't move his body for Finch's weight, but he was able to lift a hand and point at Goose's neck.

Goose touched the bandana. "This?" he said. "Found it in the woods. Thought ya dropped it."

"What?" Nate said, blinking a few times and clearing the sleep out of his mind. "But I put that on..." He thought better of saying Montana. Finch would question when and where and know that Nate had slipped away, even if for only a few minutes, and that the wolf had once again been close enough to kill. What if these men decided to hunt Montana down instead of just keeping a watchful eye?

"I..." He looked about camp, then rubbed his lids. "Must've been dreamin'." Nate hoped his performance was believable. "Montana was right here. Just a minute ago." He stretched. "Could've sworn I put that on 'im. Then Goose took aim and pulled the trigger."

"A dream?" Finch smacked his hat on his leg. "You're a damn headache, kid. Just go back over there where ya were." He gave Nate a shove. "And do not say another word or move from that spot." Jasper mumbled curses under his breath, eyeing Nate as he hurried and retook his place on Goose's blanket.

It wasn't long before the meat was done. Goose joined Nate with a tin full of venison.

"We'll have to share. I only have one plate." Goose set the heaped tin between them on the blanket. Nate picked up a piece and juggled the hot meat between his fingers, blowing for a few seconds.

"It wasn't a dream, was it?" Goose stuck a small hunk of venison in his mouth.

Nate stiffly shook his head. He didn't want to discuss it. How could he one hundred percent trust Goose when he was part of this gang? But Nate did need help, and Goose had been good friends with Pa. That had to count for something.

"Tell me somethin' 'bout you and Pa."

Goose grinned. "I haven't thought that far back in a long time."

"Please," Nate begged. "I miss 'im…a lot." Anything to keep the people he loved alive in his mind. He didn't care if it was only memories Goose had to offer. His recollections were better than nothing, and Nate's mind was so clouded with the results of the trial and being torn away from his family that it was hard to focus on those good times they'd had.

Goose chewed a chunk of meat. "There was this one time when your pa and I were maybe twelve, thirteen at most. That year, the town had elected its first sheriff, a rancher, a good, honest man who was as stern and tough as they came. To celebrate, the council decided to hold a dance." The skin around Goose's eyes crinkled, and he stared at Nate.

"What?" Nate picked up a big hunk of meat.

"This story don't sound familiar?" Goose bit down and tore off a piece of venison.

"No." Nate's mouth was full, and bits of chewed meat sprayed out.

Goose wiped crumbs off the front of his shirt. "Everyone was excited, most of all your pa. And being his best buddy, I was just as thrilled. Figured on buyin' myself a store-bought shirt for the occasion, and I had my eye on a cute girl, Anna May."

"Wasn't your Sunday best good enough?" Nate was finding his appetite and chowing down, bite after bite.

"Not for that particular dance. It would mark a special night for a family well thought of in the community and for the town as a whole. There wasn't a single lawman in the territory at that time, and a finer man couldn't have been found for the job."

Nate giggled. "That's funny comin' from an outlaw." He didn't figure Goose would mind him saying so. It was the truth.

Goose grinned, then took a bite of meat. "Are ya sure ya ain't ever heard this story before?"

Nate shook his head while shoving venison into his mouth, filling his cheeks.

"Your grandmother planned on makin' your pa a new shirt and tie."

Nate coughed. He sat straight up and cleared his throat. "My grandmother."

He'd never thought about that before. He knew Ma's folks had died, but Pa never mentioned his parents. Nate assumed they were gone as well.

"What did she look like?" After being adopted, he hadn't thought to ask about grandparents. He had just been happy to have folks who loved him.

"Dark hair, and she had the same steely blue-gray eyes as your pa. Tall for a woman, but I remember that when she walked, she was graceful. A beautiful lady."

"What was her name? Was she nice?" Nate wanted to hear all about his father's mother.

"Ellen was her name." Goose smiled. "She liked to bake. Without fail, every day, she'd have cookies or a pie, warm out of the oven, waiting for when Nolan and me would show up after school. It was always our first stop. Until I took a job at the livery. Twenty-five cents a day, before and after school for a few hours. I'd earn more than enough money for the shirt I wanted. Had it picked out."

"What did Pa do while you were workin'?" At twelve or thirteen, Nate figured his pa had lots of chores on a cattle ranch.

"After he done his chores at home, he'd come help me at the livery."

Pa was loyal to his friends.

"Go on," Nate said, waiting to hear more.

"Well, the night of the dance came. Your pa waited at the door for me. Gave a wave. Before I got to him, Isaac Bowen and Billy Chambers, two boys from school, stopped me, said Jeffries, the man who owned the livery, wanted to see me. He was waiting at the stables. They walked along, talking about the decorations in the town hall."

Nate could picture the grand evening. Men dressed in suits. All the ladies decked out in frilly lace, maybe pearls. Ma wore pearls on special occasions. Black carriages and plain buckboards lining both sides of the street.

"When we got inside. Jefferies was nowhere to be seen. Isaac and Billy grabbed me. Turns out I wasn't the only one interested in havin' the first dance with Anna May Gibson." Goose pulled a paper and tobacco out of his shirt pocket. "Those two worked me over some." Goose struck a match on his bootheel. He cupped the flame between his hands, lighting the smoke dangling from the corner of his mouth. "They tossed me into the manure pile out back of the barn before they returned to the music."

"Let me guess." Nate smiled. "Pa came to your rescue."

Goose nodded. "When I didn't show up for the big announcement, though the whole town knew who had been appointed sheriff, Nolan came searching. Found me bent over the horse trough, trying to wash the bloodstains and the stink of horse shit off my new shirt."

"So you didn't get to go to the dance?" There was a pretty yellow-haired girl back in Gray Rock that Nate had a secret crush on. Abby was the first girl he'd ever danced with.

"I didn't want to, but your pa talked me into it. I remember what he said. *If I get ya a new shirt, will ya come?* He said it with such confidence that I said yes. More so because I was curious."

"But the store would've been closed. You said the dance was an induction for the newly appointed public official, so the whole town must've turned out for that." Nate was only guessing.

"Indeed." Goose nodded. "Nolan told me to stay there, and he headed toward the many people mingling there at the hall. Ten minutes later, he returned with not one but two shirts." Goose began to chuckle until he roared with laughter.

"What's so funny?" Nate licked the crumbs of meat off his fingers.

"Oh, I recognized the shirts. One belonged to Isaac Bowen, the other to Billy Chambers. I got my pick." Goose ruffled Nate's hair. "I wore Isaac's checked one and looked damn good."

Nate burst with laughter.

Goose drew in on his smoke, the end glowing red. "Isaac's folks, nor Billy's, said not a word. Likely 'cause I was sitting at the table with the guest of honor, William C. Crosson."

"My grandfather?" Nate nearly sprang to his feet.

"That's right." Goose flicked his smoke into the dirt. "I can't believe Nolan never told ya that his father was a sheriff. He was mighty proud."

Before Nate could ask even one of the dozen questions that rolled in his head, a shadow fell over the two of them.

"Havin' a good time?" Finch eyeballed both of them. Nate scooted out of kicking distance. The pointed toes of Finch's boots were decorated in silver, which would hurt. "If yer done amusin' yourselves, it's time to go." He wheeled and marched toward the fire.

"I don't believe I've ever met anyone so full of hate." Nate stood.

Goose took his time getting to his feet. "After his brother was killed, he snapped, turned rabid mean. Richard's death was Jasper's fault, and he damn well knows it."

"What happened?" Nate glanced up at Goose.

"Never you mind. Just remember this: Finch ain't my friend, never was, even when his brother was alive. Me being here doesn't make ya safe. Finch would rather see me dead and you too." Goose picked up his tack, looking over at Nate. "When I was huntin', shortly after I found my bandana and two of the horses, I come across three sets of tracks followin' us."

Nate twisted in the direction of their backtrail. He'd nearly forgotten the men who'd trailed him out of Green River on the far side of the mountain.

Goose turned Nate by the shoulders. "I know what they want, but who are they?"

"Goose! Help Jackson get Marv on a horse." Jasper was readying the other with his own saddle.

Marv's face was gray and swollen, his one eye all puffed out and crusted shut. At least his wound wasn't bleeding, but he was swatting to keep the flies away.

"In a minute," Goose hollered back. He stared down at Nate. "I'm waitin'," he said.

"I don't know. Honest." Nate raised his right hand. "They've been after me since before Luther Blackhorse was killed."

"You killed Blackhorse, a dog soldier?" Goose straightened, his saddle over his shoulder and a Sharps rifle in hand.

Nate shook his head. "But I am the reason he's dead."

"Good job, kid." Goose patted Nate's shoulder. "No one'll miss that cold-blooded killer." He left Nate standing and, with Jackson, shoved Marv onto a brown horse.

Jasper was on his mount, holding the reins of Marv's transportation. Yooko slid the blade side of a hatchet across a razor stone.

"For yer wolf friend." Yooko zipped the sharpened edge along the stone another time.

Nate wouldn't let that happen. "If I were you, I'd be more worried about the armed men trailin' us. They want the bounty on my head just as much as you." Nate pointed to a branch high up in a tree. Yooko looked up. The blackbird screeched.

Yooko's eyes narrowed. "I am not afraid."

"You should be," Nate said.

In a twenty-four-hour period, Montana had killed two members of this gang and badly injured a third. Jackson paused as he and Goose adjusted Marv, sitting hunched far forward in the saddle.

Jasper jerked on his horse. "How d'ya know there're men followin' us?" He stared over Nate's head toward the tree line.

"They followed me over the mountain." That much was true.

Nate wouldn't tell on Goose. There must have been a reason he hadn't told Jasper. It was important information that a leader should know and a bit of a shock because he was in charge, not Goose, and Goose wouldn't want to die in an ambush any more than the rest of them.

"I saw their tracks that day I tried to run away." Nate would use whatever means available to give himself an edge, keep himself safe, including a blatant lie. And he didn't want Finch to fly off the handle and shoot Goose for not informing him.

There was already enough tension between the two to light a powder keg.

"Is that true?" Finch barked, eyeing Goose. "You were with the kid that day. Did you see any tracks?"

"Not that day, I didn't." Goose standing on the far side of Marv's horse would not be an easy target to plug. Finch, though, atop his horse in the open, might as well have been wearing a red bull's-eye on his shirt.

Nate held his breath. Goose's hands could not be seen, but Nate would bet his right gripped his pistol. Jasper pushed his coattail behind his holster. Jackson backed up a few paces, his gaze flicking between the two. Nate didn't blame him for getting out of the line of fire.

"I saw some tracks earlier when I found the horses," Goose said too casually, as though Finch wasn't steaming at the ears.

"But you failed to mention it. Why?" Finch's face contorted into something so ugly that Nate was sure he was staring at Satan himself. Jasper's nostrils flared. A big blue vein near his temple throbbed.

Goose stepped around the rear of Marv's horse. Within his field, all three of the others stood. Goose's hand rested on the butt of his revolver. He could fire upon all three without turning. That advantage might have kept Finch's hands on his reins. Nate didn't dare blink. He wished he hadn't mentioned the tracks.

"I just hadn't gotten around to it. But now you know. So what's the problem?" Goose was no fool.

Finch was ten feet in front of him. Yooko's loyalty belonged to Finch. That was evident in the way the man took orders. Jackson, Nate believed, could be swayed to either side of the fight. He had stood by when Lutz had talked sense into the two and split up what could have ended in far worse than a word battle. At the moment, it was two against one. Jackson's hands were nowhere near his gun belt, but he might choose to back up his boss.

"Yer my problem." Japer's hand swept down.

"No!" Nate screamed.

Two guns boomed within a second of one another. Goose twisted at the shoulder and rolled on his feet behind Marv's prancing horse. Finch held to his side. Blood leaked between his fingers.

"Kill 'im!" Finch ordered.

CHAPTER 17

NATE RAN TOWARD Marv's panicked horse. Yooko raised his gun as Goose's pistol cracked. Sparks flew the instant his bullet hit iron, and the Yaqui's weapon fell to the ground.

"Grab the kid!" Finch was off his horse and still holding his bleeding ribcage.

Jackson lunged, his arm outstretched. Nate jumped to the side, missing the swipe but not by much. A blast from a rifle kicked up dirt at Jackson's feet, stopping him in his tracks. Gunfire lit up everywhere. Smoke clouded the air.

Nate picked up the reins of Marv's horse.

"Give me the reins, kid." Marv was leaned forward on his horse's shoulder, but he had his six-shooter pointed at Nate.

"Go to hell!" Nate grabbed with both hands and yanked with all his weight, tearing Marv out of the saddle. When he hit the ground, his gun boomed. Nate screamed as he clutched his hip. A red stain formed near the loops on his pants.

"Git outta here!" Goose yelled from behind a tree inside the forest.

This was no time to cry. Nate blinked back his tears.

Marv swung at Nate's leg. He kicked at the man's hand. Jasper and Jackson pumped lead from their rifles toward Goose.

Where was the Indian?

Nate turned, heaved himself up into the saddle, and walloped the sides of that horse the best he could despite the pain stabbing through his hip. The animal sprang forward, knocking Jasper and Marv, who was half on his feet, out of the way. A flash of buckskin and fringe caught Nate's eye. The Yaqui!

"Goose! Over there!" Nate pointed as his horse weaved at a run through the trees. Behind him, shots fired. He didn't glance back. This was his chance. He had to run for it. Goose had told him to.

Nate didn't feel good about leaving him behind, but other than this horse to help Goose escape the battle, what could Nate do but get in the way? Finch wouldn't stop fighting if Nate were with Goose, but he might leave that fight to come after Nate. After all, he was the grand prize. Hanging around to maybe catch lead from one of Goose's shots wouldn't make Jasper any richer, but it could kill him.

When the gunfire faded out behind him, Nate slowed the mare's pace. She was breathing heavily. Nate pulled up on the reins and glanced behind him. "Goose," he said into the open space. "I hope they didn't kill ya."

Again, he wondered what Goose had meant when he'd said he owed Pa. The price of a new shirt wasn't worth a man's life. Besides that, they'd been kids when that happened. And Goose had risked his life to save Nate. He could have just sprinted off into the woods, defended himself against Finch and the others. But he had covered Nate during his escape. He didn't have to do that. What had Pa done for Goose that he was willing to lay down his own life to repay him?

The thigh of Nate's pant leg was covered with dried blood. Every little move caused him pain, but he had to keep going forward. To stop would give them behind him time to catch up, and he didn't know the area around him well enough to find a good hiding spot.

Nate walked his horse through the night. Finch and his three men had one mount between them. Goose was on foot—if he was still alive.

Whoever those other three horsemen were that were following him since Green River likely would take this opportunity to catch Nate. If they'd been following Finch, as Nate suspected, and were waiting for a chance at him, then they'd know by now that he had gotten away from that bunch, so this was their ideal chance.

Come morning, Nate yawned. He could barely keep his droopy lids open. For all he knew, he was riding away from Denver. But he no longer had the money left in the saddlebags that once belonged to Luther Blackhorse. He couldn't buy supplies without cash. And he needed bandages. His hip had stopped bleeding but thumped something awful.

Ahead of him, the sound of an ax cutting wood echoed across the hilltops. He nudged his horse. What he expected was trouble. It seemed everyone knew his face and the price he was worth. Instinct was telling him to ride wide around the fella throwing that ax, but the men behind him were searching for a brown horse and by now knew the tracks of the animal he was riding. There were too many hunting for him not to use every trick he knew.

Nate pulled up reins twenty feet away. A white dog barked. The man lowered his ax. His eyes widened at the boy's sudden appearance. Nate was filthy, and blood stained his clothes. It was doubtful the fella came across too many people way out there. Especially a banged-up kid. But Nate had thought that about Amos. News traveled fast when the prize was fifteen thousand.

"Hello," the man said. The sun was barely in the sky, and this fella mopped his head with a handkerchief. The dog stayed at the man's side. With a snap of his fingers, his dog stopped barking.

"Hi." Nate glanced around.

No one else was there. That didn't mean this fella was without a partner, maybe at a nearby cabin. Cutting timbers was no small chore. The gate of the wagon bed was down, and the jagged teeth of a duel saw pointed toward him, along with other logging implements, shiny new ones.

"You hurt?" The man eyed Nate's leg. "You must be lost." He glanced at Nate's lathered horse.

"I was on my way to Denver when I got sidetracked. Can you point me in the right direction?" Nate leaned back without taking his eyes off the man and fished in Marv's saddlebags. The first thing he brought to the surface was a pair of stinky, balled-up socks. A Bible, the black cover worn thin and a few pages loose. Three dollars, which Nate shoved in his pocket. And a ten-inch hogleg and a full box of shells. "I'd like to do some tradin'."

"You in trouble, kid?" The man took a step toward him.

Nate's hand, of its own will, spun the weapon, aiming at that lumberjack. "Trouble's my name, mister. Now don't come any closer." His heart pounded, the gun in his hand. The movement had been so fast, instinctual.

The fella slowly reached down and patted his dog's head. "When I ride out and scout an area for certain wood, I never keep my spare loaded. Could go off."

He was right, and Nate knew it. Pa never kept his spare loaded, nor Jesse. But they always kept shells close at hand, same as Marv had the box stored with the hogleg.

"I can thumb bullets quicker than you can blink." Nate was honest.

"I don't doubt that." The fella scratched his thick beard. "You're awfully young to be mixed up in the shootin' kind of trouble. I'd bet you ain't ten yet."

"Nine," Nate said, lowering the gun.

The fella rubbed his thumbs along the inside of his leather suspenders, stretching them out from his barreled chest. His eyes were gray, the same color as Pa's.

"I got a son your age." The fella sat on a stump and rubbed behind the dog's ears. "I'm gonna give this dog to 'im. It belonged to one of my workers. A young fella. The top of a tree split and fell, crushed him. I had the awful job of writing his folks and didn't have the heart to send his remains."

Nate was sorry to hear that. What an awful thing to happen. But what did any of that have to do with bartering for a little food and a bandage? Nate needed a fast horse too.

"In that valley below"—the fella pointed—"I have a crew of forty men. There's a camp there, a well-armed camp. You and your horse can rest there if you'd like."

Nate didn't want to say too much, but he needed this man to understand the seriousness of doing more than trading a few supplies with him, then sending him on his way. Even that much could cost this fella. But Finch and his crew and the other three horsemen would think twice about starting any trouble with an army of brawny lumberjacks.

"All I need is a fresh horse. I'll give ya everything in these saddlebags and this horse. After she rests, she'll be good as new. I just don't have the time to wait."

"Who ya runnin' from?" The fella spit.

"Nobody ya wanna tangle with. They ain't afraid to kill." Nate stared at the hand holding the pistol, remembering the speed with which he'd handled the weapon.

His hands began to shake. The hogleg dropped to the ground. His eyes were stuck fast to the iron. In his veins flowed the blood of a bad man, a killer. Was that nature born in him? He'd told himself over and over that it wasn't true. He wouldn't grow up to be like Jim Younger. He was the son of Nolan Crosson, a lawman.

Maybe everything he'd told himself was a lie. Maybe the choice of what he'd become was made the day he was born, and there was no stopping it.

The lumberjack picked up the gun and shoved it in his belt. "I'll keep that. I wouldn't want ya to accidentally hurt yourself or someone else." He patted the neck of Nate's horse.

Nate snapped to attention. He hadn't realized the man had walked right up to him until he had spoken.

"Son, I'm not gonna hurt ya. But you're bleedin', or were, and from what little you've told me, it sounds like the men followin' have evil intentions. Let me help."

There was something Nate needed to know. "How often does any news reach your camp? Is there a town nearby? Any frequent visitors?"

The fella's brow arched. "Denver's a day's ride. That way." He pointed. "My foreman and a few others are there now, gone with a couple wagons for supplies. They should be back the day after next. When they can, they'll pick up a newspaper. The one or two we have in camp must be at least a month old, maybe older. And we occasionally see a trapper, but they tend to keep to themselves."

"Good." Not so much news. Nate grinned. He could use some sleep, but he didn't want this man or his companions getting hurt on his account. "I should warn ya. Helpin' me is the same as askin' for trouble."

"Kid, your cheeks are sunken. Ya look starved. And I ain't ever seen such deep, dark circles around a child's eyes. Sleep-deprived, I'm guessin'." He shook his head. "I can provide ya with food and a place to rest. I'm not worried about whoever's followin' ya."

"Japer Finch and his gang are not just followin'. They're huntin' me. Besides them, there's another bunch, three men. Don't know their names. But I'm sure they're just a mean as Finch and his lot." Nate paused.

At the mention of Finch's name, the lumberjack picked up his ax.

"If you've changed your mind, I wouldn't blame ya none. If I was you, I'd think twice about helpin' me." Nate nudged his horse. He'd make it easy on the man. Who wanted to look a kid in the eyes and tell him to leave, knowing he might get killed by outlaws?

"Wait!" The lumberjack crawled up onto the wagon seat. As he did, the white dog jumped into the bed. "You don't have to tell me why those men are after ya. I can't get past the fact that they'd be huntin' a kid. I'll post guards and send another of my men to town, though I'm not sure there's a lawman in Denver."

Nate wasn't going to argue over involving the law. He could sleep, eat, then be gone before anyone reached Denver to report his whereabouts and that of Finch and his gang. But he still needed to switch horses.

The fella slapped leather to his team. Nate trotted his horse behind the wagon. When they reached the edge of the ridgetop, the camp below appeared. Rows of white canvas indicated the living area. There were men and teams of horses everywhere. Trees were being pulled toward the river. Crews of men stood on the logs, heaving axes, chopping off branches. Voices shouted back and forth.

As they neared the camp, a line of partners pulled their double saws back and forth, singing the same tune as they worked. A few men nodded at their boss passing by in the creaky wagon.

He pulled up next to one of the tents. "You can rest here. This is my home away from home."

Nate slid out of the saddle and tied his horse to the back of the wagon.

"I'll be back with food." The lumberjack clucked at his team, and the wagon jerked forward.

Nate stood there a minute. Finch would have to be plumb crazy to come after him here in the heart of this encampment. But he was unpredictable. He'd shot at Goose, one of his own men. However, Marv was injured, and there'd been mention of taking him to a place owned by someone named Junior, whoever and wherever that was.

The other gang of men, Nate knew nothing about, so it was hard telling what they would do. Maybe try to sneak in and kidnap him.

Nate flipped open the canvas flap. It wasn't the cot that held his attention. A desk sat in one corner. An oil lamp hung over the desk on a hook, and sheets of paper and a pencil waited for use. Nate plopped down in the chair. Writing home was a bad idea. Staying hidden, that was his goal. Not leaving a trail to follow. And a postage stamp would do just that. He twiddled the pencil between his fingers.

CHAPTER 18

NOLAN LEANED AGAINST a porch post in front of the ticket office while waiting for the stage to arrive. The short wagon ride into Gray Rock had tired him out. This was his first outing off the ranch, and Kate had insisted on keeping an eye on him.

He scratched his side where the stitches itched under his shirt. The town looked different. Busier than he remembered. Folks in and out of shops, carrying their goods, congregating on the boardwalks and talking to one another. Buckboards rattled in the street as they passed by. Horses dotted the length of the hitch from one end of town to the other. Everyone who saw him stopped, said it was good to see him, asked how he was doing and when did he think he'd return to his duties.

To the last question, he had no answer. On the outside, he didn't allow his bitterness to show. Inwardly, he was an angry man. He believed in the law, always had. For years, he worked to establish order in an untamed land, upheld the oath to serve, and for what? For the law that he enforced to bite him in the ass. His little boy had been ripped away. Nolan wasn't sure he could pin on a badge and support a system that had worked against him and his family.

He had his own ways of dealing with problems, and as soon as Jesse found Nathanial and, God willing, both boys made it home safe, the Fletchers would find out just how hard Nolan, when not flat on his back and ill, would fight for Nathanial.

Nolan looked at his pocket watch. A quarter past ten. The stagecoach was late, as always. Couldn't Dutch tell time? How hard was it to get from point A to B in a timely manner? He sat down on a bench near the door.

Kate walked out of the Henderson's store with Elizabeth toddling beside her, holding her hand, coming toward him. A swinging basket of goods was hooked on Kate's elbow. The stage rattled across the wooden planks of the bridge at the end of town and into the street at a hell-and-gone pace. Dust rolled off the wheels, forming a cloud. Dutch must've been trying to make up time. He yanked on the reins, and the team of four brown horses skidded to a halt.

Nolan stood.

Jesse's telegram about the Harrison children was a shock, but it wasn't surprising that Nathanial had given his word that Nolan and Jesse would help the kids arriving on the stage. His son was a good little deputy.

Kate stood beside Nolan as he reached to open the coach door.

"Sheriff, wait." Dutch jumped down from the driver's seat and grabbed Nolan's shoulder. The stage door swung open. "There's somethin' I need to tell ya," Dutch blurted, but it was too late.

Lem Fletcher was the first person to step out of the coach, followed closely by his wife. Nolan's jaw tightened. He grabbed Fletcher by the shoulders and slammed him against the side of the stage, not once but twice.

"What in the hell are you doin' here?" Nolan growled. His teeth gnashed together, his nose all but touching Lem Fletcher's.

"Release my husband at once," Deloris Fletcher screeched. "Driver, do something. Don't just stand there."

Dutch chuckled. "Lady, if you wanna try to take the bull by the horns, be my guest. This ain't my fight."

Deloris huffed. Lem Fletcher's eyes were wide, and he stood stiff as a board.

"Nolan, the children." Kate touched his arm.

He looked over at a boy and girl fitting the description Jesse had given. Their eyes were as wide as Fletcher's, but tears glistened in the little girl's and she squeezed her doll tight in her arms.

Kate bent in front of them and smiled. "Hello, I'm Mrs. Crosson, Nathanial's mother." She looked down at Elizabeth. "This is—"

"Elizabeth," the boy said in a soft voice. "Nate told me all about his sister, about all of you."

Nolan hadn't let go of Fletcher. "Kate, take the kids to the wagon. I'll be there shortly."

According to Jesse's telegram, Minnie was the little girl's name. She was on her knees next to Elizabeth, playing with the rag doll his daughter loved so much. How many times had Nathanial taken Ticklebug, that chewed-on dolly, and tormented his sister until she would squeal like a piglet?

"You're not taking Leslie and Minerva anywhere." Deloris grabbed Minnie by the arm, pulling the child to her feet. Tears sprang out of the little girl's eyes.

"Let go of my sister!" The boy pushed Deloris Fletcher's hand off his sibling. "Why do you think we'd want to go with you? Because we talked to you a little bit on the stage ride? Because you were friends with our mother and father? They're dead, and Patrick's missing." Leslie's hands balled at his sides. Wetness magnified his pale eyes. "I think you had something to do with it. I don't want to be anywhere near you."

With a turn and a quick step, Kate had all three children herded behind her. She and Mrs. Fletcher were face to face and glared at one another.

Nolan spun Lem and shoved him stumbling headfirst into the stagecoach, and he slammed the door shut. In one step, he planted himself between his wife and that mouthy woman. What was her damn problem? The Harrison children were none of her concern. This had little to do with Nathanial's disappearance, if that was the reason the Fletchers were interfering with this matter. Or did it have something to do with him investigating Patrick Harrison's kidnapping and the suspicious death of the Harrison kids' mother and father?

Nolan leaned down into Deloris's face.

Mrs. Fletcher looked around, her husband picking himself up off the floor of the coach. She backed up. Nolan marched forward until she couldn't retreat any farther, her back flat against the side of the stage.

Nolan's narrowed eyes bored into her, and he yanked open the door.

"Git the hell out of my sight." And he for damn sure meant it. He'd shove her ass right into that coach the same way he'd done her husband.

"Deputy!" Deloris waved her beaded handbag at Big John walking down the boardwalk toward them. "Please help us. This..." She eyed Nolan from head to toe. "Brute has threatened me and has forced my husband back onto the stagecoach." Her breathing came in short, rapid spurts.

"Nolan." Big John tipped his hat. "Are these folks botherin' you and Kate?"

Mrs. Fletcher's mouth fell open. She'd expected help.

"Nothin' I can't handle," Nolan said.

John nodded, ignoring Fletcher, who now stood next to his persnickety wife and brushed the dirt off his trousers and sleeves, grumbling under his breath.

After the trial, John and his wife, Cora, close friends of the Crossons, were as stunned and angry about the verdict as the Crosson family. The Fletchers wouldn't find too many friendly faces in Gray Rock willing to give sympathy or lend a hand to the couple in any way. Nathanial was one of the community and a child, Nolan's little shadow, a constant presence. His being taken away had been a blow to the entire town.

"You're no longer the sheriff of this town or even a lawman." Fletcher had found his backbone. "You have no authority over us or anyone. You can't make us leave." He straightened his suit coat. The little wifey, wearing a smirk, slipped an arm around her man's.

"Nolan, we're ready," Kate called from the wagon seat. The two girls were sitting in the bed, playing with their dolls. Leslie stood behind the seat. His eyes were still wide, taking in all the commotion.

Nolan turned. Fletcher caught him by the arm. Nolan had his fill of Mr. and Mrs. Lem Fletcher. He jabbed with his right, popping Lem square in the nose. The man yelled. His hands flew up, covering his face.

Mrs. Fletcher gasped.

John turned and walked in the other direction.

"I just want to talk," Fletcher said while holding his bleeding nose, staining his silk neckerchief.

"I ain't in the mood." Nolan fought down his urge to punch Fletcher a second time. Because of this man and woman, his little boy's life was in danger. Both of his sons were out there somewhere, and God only knew what dangers they'd come face to face with. Greedy people could be ruthless.

Around them, the other passengers quickly exited the stage. Dutch and Harv were unloading trunks from up top. Dutch dropped a number of them near the Fletchers.

"Yes, we're staying until Nathanial is found," Deloris snipped at Nolan, staring at the stack of bags around her feet on the boardwalk.

"Don't bother." Leslie appeared next to Nolan. "Nathanial would rather die than go to New York with the two of you."

"He said that?" Nolan felt a pang in his chest.

The Fletchers huddled closer to the boy.

"Not those words exactly." Leslie shook his head. "I don't know how to explain it, but he jumped off a moving train, fought a wolf and somehow sort of tamed it, then escaped an old lady who wanted to kill him, and Luther Blackhorse got his face half shot off."

"Luther Blackhorse!" Nolan lifted his hat and ran a hand through his thick hair. "My God."

"Who's that?" Fletcher gawked at Nolan.

"A killer. He makes his livin' by bounty huntin', and none of the people he brings in is ever alive." Nolan was about two seconds from jumping on a horse and running after Nate. He knew such men might go after his son, but hearing Blackhorse's name caused a painful tightness throughout his entire body.

Both Mr. and Mrs. Fletcher gulped. The missus fanned herself with her dainty clutch. "Lem, what do we do?"

"Should we call off the search?" Fletcher looked at Nolan for the answer. "I mean, should we cancel the reward?"

Nolan grabbed him by the collar. "If you do that, then Nathanial's lost his value. Now that you put a price on 'im, you can't take it away. You'll get 'im killed for sure."

"Please." Lem peeled Nolan's hand away. "Believe it or not, we are on the same side."

Kate stood next to Nolan and slipped her hand into his, giving him a squeeze. He looked over his shoulder. The girls were crawling around the wagon bed, giggling. Leslie was close at Nolan's side. Fletcher was right. These kids and Nathanial, they were what was important. Not Nolan's or Fletcher's personal feelings toward one another.

Nolan extended a hand. "I apologize."

Both Fletchers smiled. "Thank you," Lem said.

"Nate kept Minnie and me alive." Leslie spoke up. "We wouldn't have survived without him. He dodged a posse, twice, before we left Green River. He's not going anywhere he doesn't want to. I'm certain after all I've seen—and believe me, I wish I hadn't seen any of it—that Nate will die trying to get to Missouri."

"Missouri!" The voices of all four adults boomed as one.

Nolan squatted in front of Leslie. "Are you sure that's where Nate is headed?"

"Yes, sir." The boy nodded. "I overheard him one night. He was talking in his sleep. Seemed like he was scared. He was fussing like maybe he shouldn't go."

Kate clutched her chest. Her eyes welled up. "Nolan." She sniffled. "He's going back to where his life started, back to those roots that nearly killed him."

Nolan stood. "Leslie, stay with the girls. Kate, follow me." He headed toward the jailhouse.

When he opened the door, Big John stood from behind the desk. "Somethin' wrong?" He watched the line file in, including the uninvited Fletchers.

Nolan went straight to the large map that hung on the wall behind his desk. He tapped a finger on a spot, indicating Green River. "Nate left here on horseback about a week ago." He rubbed his chin. "If he's headed to Missouri, then likely, he would take this route." He traced his finger along the mark representing the mountain ranges. "Tougher travel but off the beaten path. And if he's already had a couple run-ins with people wantin' to catch 'im, he'll stay off the well-traveled roadways." He was thinking aloud.

"How do you know that for sure?" Lem Fletcher wasn't being smart.

"I know my son," Nolan stated as a matter of fact.

"Do you think Jesse caught up to him?" Kate wrung her hands.

"Hard to say. Depends on if Jesse and Rhett or Nate ran into any other trouble." Nolan didn't want to scare the ladies any more than they were. Both quivered where they stood.

Deloris dabbed at her eyes. "You mean other bounty hunters like that Blackhorse fellow?"

"Yes." Nolan wouldn't lie.

"Oh, Lem." Deloris threw herself into her husband's arms. Tears rolled down her cheeks.

Lem peeled her back, gripping her shoulders. "I tried to tell you nothing good would come from taking Nathanial from his home, from his mother and father. But you wouldn't listen." He rubbed his head. "Selfish as always."

"Are you blaming this entire mess on me?" She took a step back, breaking his hold.

"No." He dropped into a chair. "I blame myself. I know very well that when you look at Nathanial, you see Ashton. That first day in Birch Creek, I saw the resemblance too, but for me, it stopped the moment that boy barged through the doors of the Songbird Saloon and knocked us spinning." His face reddened. "Do you recall the ruckus he started in that restaurant in Fort Sherman? It was basically a bar fight, leaving us dealing with a mob of angry people while he slipped out the door and hopped a train." Lem took a deep breath, then blew out.

"To get away from us," he said slowly, giving the missus time for those words to sink in. Fletcher stood and spread his arms as though displaying the inside of the jailhouse and beyond. "Given the circumstances, I would definitely say we are not what is best for him."

"He belongs to us. You heard the judge. Nathanial is ours," Deloris snipped, keeping her eyes on her husband, but she had to be feeling the mean stares from Nolan and Kate and even John because Deloris shifted back and forth from one leg to the other.

Nolan had to bite his tongue. This was a squabbling couple, not the time for him to interfere.

"For God's sake, Deloris. The boy fights Indians. He tamed a wolf. Were you not hearing Leslie? Nathanial knows how to trick a posse. He is *not* Ashton. Our son could barely tie his own shoes."

Nolan opened the bottom drawer of his desk and pulled out a bottle of whiskey and a shot glass. He slid them across the top toward Fletcher.

"Thank you." Fletcher greedily accepted. He tossed his first one back and poured another.

Mrs. Fletcher twisted her satin and lace handkerchief. "I know," she said in a hushed tone. "But he is a small piece of my sister, and I miss Lucinda. We didn't always get along, but that doesn't mean I didn't love her." She dabbed at her eyes.

Fletcher pulled his wife into his arms. She buried her face in his chest, and sobs rose up. Nolan glanced at Kate, then picked up the drink Fletcher had poured and pressed the glass to his lips, swallowing it down. He'd thought this day would be as simple as picking up two kids from the stagecoach.

Fletcher led his wife to a chair and eased her down. "Since the trial ended, Nathanial's behavior has become reckless. He's taking risks that most boys wouldn't. My fear is that the path he is on can only lead to him getting hurt or killed." He looked over at Nolan. "Correct me if I'm wrong."

"I'm readin' it the same way." Nolan then glanced at Kate, who was pale.

Big John smacked his forefinger against the map. "Sheriff, if what you've said about Nate's course is accurate, Denver would be the next town. He might stop there."

Nolan patted John's shoulder. "That's exactly what I was thinkin'."

Fletcher stared at the vastness of the land map, the space between Gray Rock and where they believed Nathanial was headed. "We should notify the marshal there."

Nolan lifted a hip and sat on the corner of his desk. "Two months ago, the marshal there was killed. Shot by Richard Finch, an outlaw guilty of mostly small-time robberies. He was killed too." He recalled reading about the shootout in the newspaper. The marshal hadn't shot Finch. He'd been shot by one of his own men, or so a witness had claimed.

"Y-y-you mean there's no law there? Who will help our nephew?" Deloris glanced away from Nolan to her husband.

Kate squeezed her eyes tight shut, then opened them. "Dear God, keep him safe." She supported herself, leaning on the desk. Her round middle seemed more pronounced.

Nolan hurried around the desk and took her by the arm. "I should git ya home. All this stress ain't good for you or the baby."

The others in the room stayed quiet, watching the two of them.

"How can I rest? Our little boy is being hunted by God knows who." Her teary gaze met his. "I know that glint in your eyes, Nolan Crosson." She shook her head. "As much as I want our boys at home, you can't go after Nate. You've only been out of bed a few days. Your strength isn't what it should be." Her tears teetered on the rims. "What if you get yourself killed? You can't help anyone then." She blew her nose. "I need you here." She rubbed her belly. "This baby, Elizabeth, and the boys, they need a father."

"Kate, we'll discuss this at home." He couldn't be upset with her, but this was not the time. The Fletchers' curious stares were fixed on them. Since before the custody trial, under their roof, everyone's emotions had been raw. Being in a delicate condition, Kate's were a mite worse. Perhaps a bit irrational, but he'd never say that to her.

"Yes, husband." She headed for the door. "I'll be waitin' in the wagon. Please don't be long."

He nodded.

"Sheriff." Big John pulled a sheet of paper and a pencil out of the top drawer. "I'll make a list of those towns between Denver and Missouri that we know have a lawman. I'll have Ned send wires. Nathanial has to show up somewhere."

"Much appreciated." Nolan headed after Kate.

"Wait," Fletcher called after him. "What can we do?"

"Stay out of the way." He eyed the polished couple. "And don't run any more foolish newspaper articles."

Fletcher straightened, his face reddening. "I would like your word that you will inform us upon hearing any news concerning Nathanial."

Nolan stood in the doorway, his broad shoulders filling the space. He was a tall man, and nothing about him was scrawny, not even after being ill for a few weeks. He pointed a straight finger at the couple. "Get this straight. Nathanial is my son— *my* son." He tapped his chest. "When he's brought home, he will remain with me, with his family."

Nolan had no reason to doubt what Leslie had said. In Nate's eyes, he'd lost everything. Otherwise, he wouldn't have jumped a train to escape. He'd be on his way to New York right this minute.

"But the judge said—" Deloris Fletcher's nostrils flared as her man grabbed her.

"Quiet, darling." Fletcher kept her held at his side.

"I've filed an appeal." Nolan knew that his son's behavior would only get more daring. The boy had to be thinking that he had nothing else to lose. "We'll be goin' back to court." He wasn't about to let any form of harm come to his son. "Some colleagues of mine in San Francisco are investigating the suspicious deaths of Mr. and Mrs. Harrison and the sudden disappearance of their son Patrick."

Nolan tugged at his collar. He hadn't planned on telling the Fletchers anything about the inquiries and what he'd found out, but he'd always been able to easily read people by their reactions.

"Interesting fact. Your friend, Judge Parker, happened to visit the Harrisons the very day they went missing." Nolan smirked. "I'm sure you're aware that he owns stock in your company. Something that wasn't brought up at the trial but should've been."

Fletcher cleared his throat. "I don't know every stockholder. After I found out, I had one of my people in the New York office look into it. Parker owned a few hundred shares."

"But you hid the fact. Your lawyer never mentioned the connection to my attorneys. I reckon because you knew we'd have asked for another judge. That would have delayed the trial you were so confident about because of Mrs. Gill's testimony, and people would've thought you and Parker were scratching each other's backs." Nolan waited for a rebuttal.

Fletcher stiffly nodded. "I swear, though. We knew nothing about Mary Ann's and Frederick's deaths or that Parker was even acquainted with the Harrisons. When Leslie became angry and blurted it out, that was the first we heard. I didn't want to ask questions then and further upset the child." He ran a hand through his well-manicured hair. "It was hard to hide my shock."

Mrs. Fletcher dabbed at her eyes, a genuine emotion after the loss of a friend. Mr. Fletcher spoke with confidence. Not one syllable had wavered off-key.

"I believe you," Nolan said.

The Fletchers glanced at one another, then stared at Nolan.

He leaned out the door and held up one finger. Kate gave a nod.

Nolan turned back to the Fletchers. "What you might not know is that Parker is largely invested in your prime competitor, Goodwin and Myers. My sources have reported that Parker was at the Harrison home that day, trying to get the inside scoop. Harrison planned on pulling his funds out of either your enterprise or Goodwin and Myers. I'm going to guess it would have been the other company since you had a friendly relationship with Harrison. Either way, Parker would take a financial hit." Nolan straightened his hat. "Harrison had enough stock in Goodwin and Myers that if he backed out on them, that company would sink, and Parker would lose his shirt. But if he knew which company Harrison had decided to support, Parker could roll over his entire initial investment into shares in that particular company and stand to make a mint."

"What does any of that have to do with Nathanial?" Deloris's brow shot up.

"Not a damn thing." Nolan smirked.

Deloris looked at her husband for perhaps more of an answer. Lem's head hung low. "Lem, what's wrong? I don't understand."

"If Parker is convicted of inside trading, or even suspected, any rulings he's made within that time period in question might be thrown out, at least investigated. And if anyone finds out that he owns stock in Fletcher Enterprises, of which Frederick Harrison owned thousands of shares, our custody case will more than likely be overturned. It would appear to be a case of co-conspiracy. Parker becomes wealthy overnight, and we secure Nathanial."

Mrs. Fletcher snorted. "That's not true!"

Nolan tipped his hat. "You folks have a good day." He slammed the door behind him.

CHAPTER 19

WHEN NOLAN STEPPED UP into the wagon, Kate was grimacing and holding her abdomen.

"You okay?" He sat next to her.

"I'm not feeling too good." Beads of sweat glistened on her forehead.

"I better fetch Doc." He turned to jump off the wagon, but Kate caught him by the arm.

"Haven't we seen enough of that man? I'm thankful I had his help while tending to your wounds, but after all those weeks, we finally have our spare room back. I just wanna go home." Kate took a couple deep breaths. "I'm sure I'll feel better after I lie down for a while."

He nodded. She was too sensible. Had she truly thought anything was wrong concerning the baby, she would have gone straight to Doc Martin herself.

Nolan flicked the reins. The buckboard rolled forward. Before they reached the edge of town, Ned from the telegraph office ran toward them with a slip of paper in his hand.

"Sheriff! Sheriff Crosson!" Ned called.

Nolan pulled up on the reins. Now what? He just wanted to get Kate home and these kids settled in. But the message could be

important information concerning Nathanial or the Harrison case.

Ned handed him the wire. "Thought you'd wanna see this right away." He glanced briefly at the children who had arrived not long ago on the stage.

Kate leaned over, pressing against Nolan's side, and silently read the short sentences. A bloodstained shirt and cap had been found during a search of one of the two ships that Leslie had told Jesse about, but no Patrick. "That doesn't sound good," she whispered.

Nolan cursed under his breath. It was looking less likely that these kids' brother would be found alive.

"Will you tell them?" Kate looked over her shoulder, and Nolan's gaze followed.

Leslie's arms hugged tight around his knees, and he rocked himself while staring out over the lip of the wagon bed at nothing in particular. Minnie held Elizabeth on her lap, braiding the younger girl's hair, but her eyes were red. The Harrison kids had been through a lot. Could they handle more bad news?

"I don't know. That shirt could belong to someone other than Patrick. Hard to tell who or how many people are involved." Nolan had some questions. He needed more facts and didn't want to upset these two for no reason.

Other than the creaky wheels of the buckboard, the ride home was quiet. Nolan couldn't fathom receiving a similar message, applying what he had possibly learned about Patrick Harrison to Nathanial's situation. Nolan wasn't typically a worrier, but he also wasn't usually stuck at home while a member of his family, one of his kids, was in trouble. His colleague in San Francisco stated that he wasn't hopeful of finding Patrick Harrison. He didn't have to be told that a body dumped in the harbor might never be recovered. However, the search continued.

His mind repeatedly landed on one conclusion concerning Nate. He looked over at Kate.

"I've seen that spark in your eyes too many times to misinterpret it." She slipped an arm around his. "I was wrong before. I want you to go after Nathanial. Elizabeth and I and the baby will be just fine." She paused for a moment. "I'm sorry. I let the Fletchers' unexpected arrival, what Mrs. Fletcher was saying about *her nephew*…" Kate drew out the last two words. "Like Nathanial, our *son*, means nothing to us. And just everything that was going on at that moment at the jailhouse got to me."

Nolan leaned and kissed her face. "I know none of this is easy on ya." She was a strong woman, though. It was one of the reasons he'd fallen in love with her. "I do believe—goin' after Nate—we're making the right decision."

She gave his arm a squeeze. "You find our boys, and all of you come home safe."

Nolan halted the team in front of the house. Kate ushered the kids inside while he unhitched the horses, then stored the harness.

After supper, Kate retired early. When he checked on her, Minnie and Elizabeth were curled up and fast asleep, one on each side of his loving wife. A book lay open across her round middle. She must have fallen asleep before finishing *Goldilocks and The Three Little Bears*. He set aside the book and eased the blanket up over the sleeping trio.

On his way downstairs, he looked into Nathanial's room where Leslie would stay while with them. The boy was sitting at the window overlooking the pasture of dry, withered grass and, beyond that, the mountain range. Many colorful leaves had fallen, leaving the limbs barren, gray, and cold-looking. A bleak picture of the season they were enduring. Wind rattled the glass panes.

"You okay?" Nolan sat on the edge of the bed.

Minnie had taken to Elizabeth right away and had settled in wonderfully, as though nothing in her life were amiss. Kids had their own way of dealing with hardships. The little girl was clingy with Kate earlier that evening. The boy was older even than Nathanial. Harder maybe for a kid his age to feel at home with strangers, and that was exactly what Nolan and Kate were.

"I can't stop thinking about Patrick." He turned his watery eyes on Nolan. "At home, I liked to sleep with my window open. I can hear the waves splashing up against the rocks along the shore followed by the sprinkling of foam. Puts me right to sleep usually." He grinned. "The night before my parents were killed, I was restless. I heard voices below my window. But it was late. Too dark to see faces. Though, I recognized one man's voice as my father. The other man, I think, was short, but I was staring down from above, so maybe it was just the odd angle. There were so many stars in the sky that night." The boy brushed strands of hair away from his eyes. "It must have been after midnight. I remember thinking it was strange that someone would show up at the house at that hour. And of all things, they were arguing about work."

Nolan straightened. "Do you recall anything that was said? Think hard."

The boy shook his head. "The next day, the same man came to the house again. I recognized his voice. He talked to Father and Patrick. In Father's office."

"Did ya get a look at him—see his face?" Nolan licked his lips. A possible murder suspect or at least a new avenue to travel for clues toward finding Patrick.

"I'd know him if I saw him again." The boy's voice held strong and clear. "Minnie and I were playing hide-and-seek. I'd been hiding behind a chair next to our grandfather clock in the entryway. He placed his coat on the headrest of the very chair I was crouched behind."

"Follow me." Nolan hurried down the stairs. Leslie was on his heels.

Nolan pulled open a drawer on his desk. Three different newspapers had covered Nathanial's custody trial. One of the papers had printed a picture of the presiding judge. A short man. And Nolan's informant in San Francisco had an eyewitness, the butler who had answered the door the day Mr. and Mrs. Harrison had been killed, which coincided with the meeting Leslie had just told Nolan about.

Nolan unfolded the picture. "Is this the man you saw?" He tapped the photograph of Judge Bartholomew J. Parker.

"That's him!" The boy's eyes stretched wide. "Do you think he killed my mother and father? But he wasn't one of the men who took Patrick or Minnie and me." Leslie shook his head. He appeared to be arguing with himself. "The kidnappers, those men were much bigger, taller. They had masks on, so I didn't see their faces."

Men that worked for Parker, no doubt.

Nolan returned the paper inside the drawer. "I do believe Parker's the mastermind behind the crime, but I doubt he was the one who committed the assault that caused your parents' deaths. It's been my experience that men like Parker hire others to do the dirty work while he makes sure he has plenty of witnesses around that can give 'im an alibi."

Leslie's shoulders sank.

Nolan winked at the kid. "Don't let that worry ya. We'll catch 'im. I've called in favors. There are a lot of good lawmen on this case. Parker'll be behind bars before ya know it."

Leslie beamed a big, wide smile. "Nathanial was right. You are the best sheriff."

Nolan chuckled. "I don't know about that. Nathanial's opinion might be a little biased. After all, I am his father."

"I'm sorry." The boy stared at his feet.

"About what?" Nolan didn't have a clue as to what the kid was referring to.

"I feel bad because … I'm glad the Fletchers took Nathanial," Leslie blurted.

Nolan sat down at his desk. "Would you care to explain that to me?" He pointed to a chair.

The boy plopped down, biting at his lip.

"Son, look at me." Nolan's voice was firm.

The boy slowly raised his head. "Minnie and I would still be wandering around in the woods or have starved or gotten ourselves killed had it not been for Nathanial. He told us to come here. That you would help, that Jesse, your deputy, would help us. Everything he's said has been true. If it weren't for him, I wouldn't be any closer to finding out who murdered Mother and Father or locating Patrick. I might have stayed on that orphan train. I was scared. Nate wasn't. Because of him, me and Minnie were able to make it this far, closer to home." The boy wiped a sleeve across his eyes.

Nolan could understand the boy's perspective. He didn't agree with it, but he was a man and a father, not a ten-year-old kid who had suffered many losses in a short period of time.

"Will you still help us?" Leslie's eyes were full of tears. "Are you going to kick us out?"

Nolan rubbed a hand over his face. "No one is gonna throw ya out. And believe me, I wanna see Parker jailed just as bad as you."

Murder wasn't the only reason he wanted Parker locked in prison. He was counting on Parker's crooked dealings to lead to disbarment. He'd been an attorney first, then a judge. His career would be ruined and, with any luck, Nathanial's ruling overturned.

"Can I say one more thing?" the boy said in a soft voice.

"Why not?" Nolan shrugged. He was growing a headache. What a day. He reached for the whiskey bottle in the cupboard behind him.

"If Jesse and Rhett find Nathanial, then I hope the Fletchers change their minds and let Nate stay here with you and Mrs. Crosson."

Nolan poured himself a shot. "I'll drink to that." He raised his glass.

The boy's simple way of thinking, his solution, would certainly make things easier. But Nolan wouldn't bet a wooden nickel on that happening. The Fletchers had fought them every step of the way right up to the custody trial, and they were still a thorn in his side. He expected more of the same. Though, this time was different. The Fletchers weren't holding all the cards. He would expose their crooked judge.

Nolan wasn't a sheriff anymore. The gunshot wound he'd sustained weeks ago, days before the trial for Nate's custody, had kept him in bed until recently, but he still felt that sense of duty. He never did tolerate those who manipulated their position of authority for personal gain. Just as a sheriff was an elected official, so was a judge. Put in that territorial seat by citizens to be in service, not to serve oneself. Even if Nathanial were not involved, Nolan would do what he believed was right.

He leaned back in his chair and stared out the window. The evening shadows stretched across the ground as the moon rose higher in the sky. He hoped the boys were both safe.

"Good night, sir."

"Good night," Nolan said over his shoulder.

Leslie's feet patted on the stairs.

Nolan corked the whiskey bottle. The long day had caught up to him. He stood and yawned.

Nolan woke to the invigorating smell of Kate's good coffee wafting up the stairs. When he walked into the dining room, the kids were chowing down, and Kate poured him some fresh brew. He'd no sooner sat than she placed an overflowing plate of eggs and bacon in front of him.

"I must look hungry this mornin'." He smiled at her.

"It might be a while before you get another woman-cooked meal." She returned to the kitchen and a second later reappeared, carrying a sack and a supply of coffee, salt pork, and beans. "I thought you'd want to get an early start." She set what would fit in his saddlebags on the table, then placed each item inside the canvas tote.

"Where are you going?" Leslie stopped chewing.

Nolan picked up his fork and took a bite. "I'm going to track down Nathanial."

Leslie jumped out of his seat. "What about Patrick? He doesn't know how to survive like Nathanial. And with that wolf around, I don't think anyone could get near Nate."

Minnie looked up from her plate. "It's mean. It sticks its fangs out like this." The little girl bared her teeth, which made Elizabeth squeal.

"Sit down." Nolan nodded toward the boy's chair. Leslie flopped on his seat. Nolan wouldn't say it, but his gut was telling him that Patrick Harrison was dead, and his hunches were right more often than not.

"Son, there's only so much I can do from here. I've already told ya. I have trusted men on the case there in San Francisco. Not only are they in correspondence with me, but they also answer to Judge Prescott. He can handle things while I'm gone. If the judge or anyone else"—he looked over at Kate—"should need me for any reason, I plan on leaving a list of towns where I can be reached along my tentative travel route." What Nolan was saying was that the investigation was well under control. He hoped Leslie understood that.

The boy nodded.

"I don't hear ya," Nolan stated.

Leslie stared at him. "Yes, sir. I understand."

Kate sat next to Nolan with a plate of food in her hands. His gaze was on the boy.

"While I'm gone, you will help Mrs. Crosson with any chores around the house and with the girls. You're plenty old enough to take on some responsibility." He lifted his coffee cup. "A friend of mine, John Filson, and his son Johnny will come by each evening to care for the stock." Big John and his family were lending a hand since Jesse left and Nolan wasn't yet at full strength. "You're to help Mr. Filson too and do anything else that's asked of ya."

"I will." Leslie picked up his fork.

Nolan nodded. It wasn't good for a body to wallow in pity or spend every minute worrying. Nolan knew that firsthand.

"Mr. Crosson, sir." Leslie set down his glass of milk. "I know you don't like the Fletchers, but they're not all bad. Father and Mother would take us to their estate. It was as big as a hotel. We would picnic in the gardens, play croquet. Their son and I went to school together before we moved to San Francisco." The boy glanced at Kate. Then his gaze fixed once again on Nolan. "Mr. Fletcher is well-known in the business world. My father had great respect for him. He knows lots of people. I wouldn't mind talking to him now that I've identified Parker. I honestly don't believe Mr. Fletcher would get involved with a man like that, not on purpose anyway. I was just scared before. I didn't know what to believe, what to think. I mean, look at what they did. According to Nate, they stole him away. After talking to you, I'm thinking clearer. With Mr. Fletcher's resources, I know he would do everything he could to help find Patrick."

Nolan swished the coffee in his mouth. Leslie had a good point. There was no reason to refuse help, and it sounded as though the Fletchers would be more than willing given the close relationship of the two families. Nolan would not allow his personal feelings toward the couple to interfere with an investigation, especially when a child's life was at stake.

"I'll allow it." He put up his hands. "But only if Mrs. Crosson agrees to oversee the visits. If she's not feeling up to it, then the answer is no, and you are not to argue with her." Nolan had faith in his men looking into the murder and kidnapping, but extra eyes and ears couldn't hurt. "And you will not speak of Nathanial with the Fletchers." Nolan wagged a finger. "If you disobey me, there will be consequences when I return."

He didn't entirely trust the Fletchers. They, or at least Mrs. Fletcher, wanted Nathanial as much as Nolan and Kate wished to keep him, their son, under their roof. Lem Fletcher had admitted the boy belonged here.

"What does that mean exactly?" The kid shifted in his chair.

The boy must have been weighing the risk of doing what he thought was best to help himself. Nolan would open Leslie's ears. "What I mean is that I will wail the tar out of you on the spot. Am I makin' myself clear?"

"Yes, sir." The boy adamantly nodded.

An hour later, Nolan had everything he needed in his saddlebags, and his horse stood ready. "I'll stop in town and let Big John know I'm leavin'." He didn't want Kate worrying about barn chores or doing too much. Having three kids underfoot would be enough for a pregnant woman, but they'd better get used to it. Soon, they would have a third of their own. Four if they counted Jesse.

Kate and Elizabeth hugged and kissed him three, four times before he could peel himself away. The Harrison children waited on the porch and watched.

Nolan stepped up onto the bay. "As soon as I can, I'll bring 'im home."

Water glistened in Kate's eyes. "You take care." She touched his leg. "We'll be here waiting." She stepped back, holding their daughter on her hip.

Nolan touched spurs to the bay.

When he trotted his horse over the bridge at the edge of town, Nolan wasn't feeling tired. He was ready to be on his way. At that hour, the street was alive with folks. Mr. Henderson pushed a broom across the boardwalk in front of his store. Cooper, the smithy, was banging away with a mallet, shaping a glowing hot horseshoe pressed on an anvil. One of the horses at the livery whinnied. Old man Pike tossed hay over the top rail. At the granary, several men loaded a wagon with full sacks.

Nolan pulled up reins in front of the jailhouse, his second home, though he wasn't even wearing a badge. He touched his vest where the star had been pinned for the past couple of years.

Mr. Fletcher walked out from inside. They stared at one another.

"What are you doin' here?" Nolan didn't want to be tied up in some ridiculous argument about custody or anything else. He planned on sparing only a few minutes to explain to John. That was it.

"I asked your deputy if he would ride out to your ranch with me. I want to talk." Fletcher straightened his bowtie.

Nolan stepped down. "Not now. I'm busy." He stepped past Lem Fletcher.

"Where are you going?"

Nolan turned and faced Fletcher. The man was eyeing the blanket roll and sack of supplies tied to the back of Nolan's saddle.

"That ain't none of your damn business." Nolan stopped at the door. He looked over his shoulder. "Do not bother my wife while I'm gone. You and the missus aren't welcome on our ranch. If either of ya so much as cause Kate a headache, God help ya when I get my hands on ya." He walked inside and slammed the door shut behind him.

He glanced out the window. Fletcher was hurrying in the direction of the hotel.

It took all of five minutes to fill John in on Nolan's plan, including a list of non-negotiable rules he rattled off about Leslie possibly meeting with the Fletchers and why.

"Keep a close eye on that couple. I don't want 'em causing Kate any more stress than she already has." Nolan picked up a box of shells out of the gun cabinet.

"Don't worry." John patted his shoulder. "I'll watch those two like a hawk. Most importantly, I'll keep tabs on Kate and all the kids. I'm sure Doc will check in at the ranch too."

Nolan opened the door. He stopped midstep. Big John bumped into his back, pushing him stumbling out the door. He straightened himself but still stared at Fletcher sitting atop a horse. The man wore a warm coat and a fur hat that resembled a derby style. No rifle, but somehow, he managed in a short period of time to load his horse with a rather large bag of goods.

"No!" Nolan thundered. "You are not goin' with me!" He pointed a straight finger. "Absolutely not! You'll just slow me down." He slipped the reins of the bay off the hitch rail, cursing under his breath.

"Deloris and I want to find Nathanial as badly as you and Mrs. Crosson. It makes sense for us to work together." Fletcher's saddle creaked as he shifted his weight.

"Like hell it does! As far as I'm concerned, you're the enemy." Nolan stowed the extra box of bullets. "If Nathanial gets one glimpse of you, he'll run faster and farther. And he's already proved himself hard to catch." He threw a leg over his saddle. "I go alone."

"You can't stop me from following." Fletcher straightened. "I believe I can help, or I wouldn't insist on going."

Nolan burst out laughing. "You, Mr. City Slicker, track me?" He grinned. "I'm positive hell would freeze over first. I'd bet I could lose you on a short one-way street."

Fletcher scowled. "Here." He thrust a folded piece of paper at Nolan.

"What's that?" Nolan didn't move to accept.

"Please read it when you have a chance. It's a thought I had. I couldn't sleep last night, and while I was thinking, I drew up this agreement. Nathanial can benefit from both of our worlds. He doesn't have to choose between the two."

"Wake the hell up. Nathanial has made his choice. And it ain't either one of us." Nolan rubbed a hand over his mouth. "I doubt you'd know this, but Nate hates the Youngers. He doesn't like to tell people he's adopted. I've heard him straight up lie that he's come from my flesh. I never corrected him 'cause, as far as I'm concerned, he is my blood." Nolan swallowed. "There are mean scars all over that boy's body where he was beaten by his so-called father, and those aren't the only reflections of pain he carries. The others you just can't see 'til his insecurities flare up or he acts out because of some awful memory. So think about this: He'd rather return to Missouri to a life of God knows what—if any of the Youngers will even accept him now that he's a Crosson—instead of livin' with you in New York."

Nolan took a breath. "You wanna help Nathanial? Leave, go back to the city. I have an eyewitness that places Judge Parker at the Harrison home the night before and two witnesses that can identify him as being there the day of the murders. He won't be a judge much longer, and I will make sure Nathanial's custody case is first on the docket to be thrown out, seeing how the deaths of Mary Ann and Fredrick Harrison have everything to do with stocks involving your company. I don't need your agreement." He turned his horse, trotting away from town. He would take the trail past Blue Sky Lake. It was the most direct route to Denver.

CHAPTER 20

"I DON'T UNDERSTAND why we're still here. It's been a goshdamn week, and still no sign of partner. I doubt the boy would stop at this pisshole. More than likely, he skirted around it," Jesse grumbled more to himself than Rhett.

Rhett stepped down, tossing his reins over the hitchrail. "The kid's gotta eat, and Denver's a big town. Lots of places to hide."

"Yeah, and I'm sick of seein' it." Jesse tied a slipknot in his reins next to Rhett's horse.

Three whores prowled past in nothing more than garter belts and pantaloons. One wore a shawl off her shoulders. However, her titties were half hanging out, the same as the other two. The skinny one with the black eye smiled, her front tooth missing.

Rhett nudged Jesse's arm while eyeing the petite one with long dark hair and a spattering of freckles on her cheeks. "It 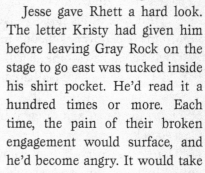 ain't all bad, is it?" He grinned.

Jesse gave Rhett a hard look. The letter Kristy had given him before leaving Gray Rock on the stage to go east was tucked inside his shirt pocket. He'd read it a hundred times or more. Each time, the pain of their broken engagement would surface, and he'd become angry. It would take

time for him to get over such an unexpected split. He needed to forget Kristy and focus.

The whores rolled over a drunk lying in the middle of the street. His pants pockets were already turned inside out, as were his vest pockets, but they patted him down anyway. Jesse wasn't sure if the odor making his eyes water was coming from the man who had saturated himself in rotgut and the large puddle of piss and vomit he was sprawled in or the three dirty-faced women.

Rhett kicked the crud off his boots against one of the hitch posts. "Nathanial might gamble on bein' able to slip in and out without notice. We've been askin' around, questionin' different people every day, and only a handful of folks has so much as glanced at our badges. And most of those were the business owners."

"Excuse me, Deputy Adams." A man wearing garters on his sleeves handed Jesse a message.

"What's it say?" Rhett leaned over Jesse's shoulder.

"Give me a damn minute." He turned.

It was from Big John. Nathanial was believed to be headed toward Missouri. Sheriff Crosson had left Gray Rock five days ago. He would catch up to them somewhere along the trail. John apologized for the lateness of the telegram. There had been a situation involving the Fletchers and Mrs. Crosson.

Jesse cursed under his breath. The Fletchers were in Gray Rock. Heat rose in his neck. What had they done to Ma? He flipped the paper over as though the answer would be there.

"That's good news—the sheriff comin'." Rhett adjusted his hat. "Bet he can pick up Nathanial's trail where we lost it."

Jesse's jaw tightened. "If the Fletchers hurt Ma..." He crumpled the paper and threw it in the dirt. "I'm gonna need me a good lawyer."

"Don't you worry. I'll bail ya out even if I have to bust ya out." Rhett clapped Jesse's shoulder.

"Let's get somethin' to eat." Jesse needed coffee.

A few minutes later, they walked into one of the restaurants at that end of town. Jack Murphy sat at a table just inside the door. Near him, Hansen Snyder and Roy Billings ate their supper. All were known bounty hunters. Jesse and Rhett sat where they could see the door and had a view of the street from the windows. Jesse looked at every kid that went by.

"Do ya see who's sittin' over there in the corner?" Rhett kicked Jesse's shin under the table.

Smoky Joe Rawlins and his brother Slim ate steak and potatoes ten feet from the two lawmen.

"Where's the other fella, the one we seen with them in Green River?" Jesse looked around the room. There were a lot of men wearing guns, maybe lesser-known bounty hunters.

"Cord McNitt," Rhett said. "Cord's a tracker. I'm only guessin', but I'd say they're here for the same reason we are."

Jesse was suddenly thankful that Nathanial could cover his trail so well. But if Cord wasn't in town, such as Rhett was hinting, that meant he was scouring someplace for the boy's tracks. Maybe closer to finding Nathanial than Jesse and Rhett.

Jesse stood, shoving back his chair. He marched toward Rawlins and his brother. They looked up as he flipped over the table holding their meals. Dishes crashed to the floor. Jesse grabbed Joe by the collar and slammed him against the wall. "Where's McNitt?"

Slim's hand jerked toward his holstered pistol.

"I wouldn't do that." Rhett's voice thundered behind Jesse. The room had fallen silent. The click of the hammer on Rhett's Colt was magnified inside the space.

Slim put his hands up.

"Couldn't tell ya," Joe said in a too-smooth tone.

"Can't or won't?" Jesse slammed him a second time against the wall. "My patience is thin today. You best start talkin'."

"Go to hell," Joe spat.

With the butt of his pistol, Jesse whacked that cocky bastard upside the head.

"You son of a bitch!" Blood tricked along Joe's hairline.

"Where?" Jesse drew back the handle of his gun.

"I'm not sure." Joe put up his hands. "We lost the boy's trail."

Jesse dragged Joe outside before he said more. He didn't want a roomful of money-hungry bounty hunters overhearing the information. Rhett was beside Jesse, still holding his gun on Slim.

"Now tell me. Where's McNitt searchin'?"

Smoky Joe glanced at his brother. Slim shrugged. Jesse gave Joe a hard shake.

"Okay," Joe said breathlessly. "We ain't sure, but we found a lumberin' camp after we lost the kid's trail. We didn't actually see 'im there, but where else could he be hidin'? We've hunted everywhere. No tracks. He's gotta be somewheres close."

Jesse let go of Joe. Depending on how big the camp was—and it must have been rather large if the Rawlins brothers didn't just ride in—Nate might lie low there. And it would explain why Jesse and Rhett hadn't found any tracks. Over the past days, they had searched five miles in every direction surrounding Denver. No sign of partner had been found.

Joe and Slim went back inside. Jesse and Rhett stood on the boardwalk. They stared toward the golden palette of the sunset.

"I saw a couple of wagons the other day. Docherty Lumber was painted on the side. They picked up supplies." Rhett shoved his gun into his holster.

"You see which way they went?" Jesse had lost his temper in there, and Sheriff Crosson had taught him to be smarter than that. Though, the sheriff wasn't always level-headed either.

"Sure did." Rhett grinned. "And wagons as heavy as those were loaded won't be hard to follow."

"Let's get the horses." Jesse took a step, but Rhett grabbed his arm

"We should take a few minutes and buy some supplies." Rhett jerked his head toward the restaurant. "All those bloodhounds'll be watchin' us. Let's not look as if we're in a big hurry."

"I'm sure most of 'em will follow us anyway," Jesse said in a flat tone. They'd have to watch their backs every minute.

"That's why we're gonna leave town in a different direction." Rhett stepped off the boardwalk toward the general store.

Jesse was glad Rhett was with him. Too often, he was ready to react without much thought. He just wanted, more than anything, to secure his little partner. His cute face was all Jesse could focus on at times, not meaning to put on a blinder to the other stuff like heeling bounty hunters. And the thought of anyone hurting Nate, well, Rhett did a fairly good job of keeping Jesse reined in. They were a good balance of headstrong, strength, and savvy.

Jesse fell into pace next to Rhett as they crossed the street. "Thanks for coverin' my back."

"You would've done the same for me. That's what partners do." Rhett chuckled. "But I would've bashed that bastard upside his head a second time. Just for the hell of it."

Jesse laughed. Rhett opened the door. Jesse stepped inside first, but his mind wasn't on supplies. Many an evening around the hearth in the Crosson home, Sheriff Crosson imparted tales for Jesse and Nate from when he rode posse with Marshal Huckabee. The two were not only best friends but worked in sync, complimenting each other's strengths and weaknesses and somehow always at the right time. Jesse couldn't help but think that he and Rhett were much the same, only in the early stages. Unless there was a side of Rhett that Jesse hadn't seen yet.

Rhett plunked a few cans of peaches on the counter, a slab of bacon, beans, coffee, a plug of tobacco, and Jesse had a handful of gumdrops.

"Didn't know ya had a sweet tooth." Rhett added two apples to the order.

"I don't. They're Nathanial's favorite." Jesse put the small brown bag of candy inside his coat pocket.

Rhett crunched one of the apples. "Don't get your hopes up. Rawlins wasn't sure the kid was at the lumber mill. And that little stinker's too damn smart."

"Just in case we're lucky," Jesse said.

Rhett patted his shoulder. "I hope we are, but McNitt's already watchin' that camp. And there could be others we don't know about." He dropped some bills on the counter.

CHAPTER 21

NATE ROLLED AROUND the floor inside the tent with Montana and the female white dog. The canvas flapped opened. In stepped Mr. Docherty with a small kettle of food and a couple of plates. Montana stood, bared his teeth, and growled.

Nate patted the wolf's head. "Stop it, Montana. Mr. Docherty's a nice man. He patched up my leg, and he's been feedin' us for how many days? You should say thank you." He pushed Montana's butt down until he sat.

Mr. Docherty slipped into the chair at his desk. "One of my men spotted a fella circling camp. It's one of those three that came in huntin' ya shortly after you arrived." He dished stew onto the plates, then set one on the floor for the two animals.

Nate plopped down on the bed. Where were the other two? "Well, I can't hide here forever. But I'm glad you talked me into stayin' a few days." He was feeling much better after consecutive nights of wholesome sleep and regular meals.

Nate took the plate he was handed. "I can't say I'll miss your cook's rock-hard biscuits." For the third day in a row, he couldn't bite through. He hoped he didn't crack a tooth. "Tell 'im to stick to bakin' bread. Least it's eatable."

Docherty chuckled. "He's heard it all before." The man poured himself a whiskey. "In the mornin', I'm gonna take ya into Denver. My foreman saw two deputies in town."

"Ya know I can't go." Nate took a bite of stew. Montana lay at his feet. "You read the *Denver Press* that your men brought after gettin' supplies. The list of bounty hunters there alone who are huntin' me is a mile long. Two lawmen aren't gonna stop all of 'em."

Docherty nodded. "I remember readin' about your custody battle." He waved a hand as if that had been years ago. "And I don't agree with the verdict, but those deputies are the best way of keepin' you safe. I can't let ya leave alone. Your mother and father must be out of their minds with worry. I'd never forgive myself if I just let ya go and then something happened to ya. You're not old enough to be on your own."

Mr. Docherty sounded too much like Pa. There was no sense in arguing. The man had made up his mind. Nate finished his stew, then curled up on the cot. That first night, Docherty had a second one brought in for him.

"I have to check on one of my crew. A saw busted, and he was hurt. I might be a while." Docherty collected the dishes. "Let's go, girl." The white dog that Nate had named Timber followed Docherty out. The canvas cover fell shut.

Nate reached down over the edge of the cot and rubbed behind Montana's ears. It was likely Rhett was one of the deputies because Pa had called him relentless once he was on someone's trail. Nate didn't want to see him get hurt against an army of bounty hunters. He'd gotten shot fighting a single old lady but a darn mean one. Who was the other deputy? One of Sheriff Coleman's other men?

Nate didn't wait long after Docherty left. He slipped on his boots and coat. The man didn't fully understand the risk he'd be taking in trying to get Nate to Denver. The man Docherty had mentioned, the one watching the camp, he was a bounty hunter. Those types of men killed for what they wanted. Docherty had a family, a wife and son. Nate needed to leave before he returned.

He pulled back the canvas just an inch and peeked out. A short distance away, men stood around a fire jawing with one another. Laughter carried on the wind. Behind them was the corral. Nate's was the only saddle horse. The other animals were all draft horses. He owed Docherty something for the food and doctoring. He'd leave the horse. Besides, that animal was known to the men following him.

Nate ducked around the side of the tent. Montana was at his side. They made their way quietly along the darkened row of canvas dwellings. The moon overhead lit the ground between the black spaces. He kept to the shadows until he reached the edge of camp, then darted into the tree line. It was black among the trees, so he paused a moment to let his eyes adjust.

Montana led the way, and Nate stopped running only when he had to suck wind. By morning, he was pushing himself to walk. Most of his steps were stumbling. When the sun was directly overhead, his legs quivered so badly he couldn't force another foot to lift. He crawled between a cropping of stone slabs and closed his eyes. Just a few minutes, that's all he needed. He yawned.

Nate woke to Montana tugging at his pant leg. The sun was far to the west. Shit! How long had he slept? Clothing snagged on brush, and a leaf crunched underfoot not far outside the rocks he'd found shelter behind. Montana's ears pinned back, and he growled.

"Quiet, boy," Nate whispered.

Another dried leaf crunched, and this time, whoever was out there drew closer. Too many leaves on the ground not to make some noise. Nate didn't dare move. Montana wiggled out from behind the rocks and took off running. A shot rang out.

"Dammit!" a man cursed. "I thought it was the kid."

"How do ya mistake a wolf for a kid?" said a deeper voice than the first one. "And we don't want 'im dead … unless he's too much trouble."

"Shut up, you two. Slim's right. The boy's tracks come this far," a third man said.

"Well, he ain't here now. That wolf might've scared 'im into hidin' somewhere." It was the voice of the first man.

"Spread out. Holler if ya see 'im," the deep voice ordered.

Nate peeked out.

Three men, two sitting atop their horses, and a single horse in tow. The third man, wearing a checkered shirt, stood with a rifle in his hands. One of the others tossed the reins of the riderless horse, and the man on foot caught the leather straps in the hand not holding his gun. He stepped into the saddle. These were the same men who had trailed him to the lumber camp from Green River.

Nate waited until they were out of sight. Then he slipped out from between the rocks. The bounty hunters had split in separate directions. Nate chose the way none of them had gone. That didn't mean he couldn't run into one of them. They were on horses and could cover a lot more ground. At the moment, he didn't care that he was running in the wrong direction to get to Missouri. He should have been headed southeast. Instead, he was hightailing it west.

On the ridge behind him, a shot rang out. Nate skidded to a halt. Montana hadn't caught up to him, but he'd been leading those men away from Nate. Two more shots echoed through the trees. Birds flew up out of the branches into the sky maybe seventy-five yards away.

Nate bit his tongue. He wanted to scream for his wolf, but he couldn't give away his position. Another shot fired. Then a volley of rifle blasts shook the mountain. Someone was shooting at someone else. Had to be. Sounded like a damn battlefield.

Nate knew a chance when one presented itself. He just hoped Montana was safe. He took off running. The bounty hunters were stalled, caught up in a different fight. That was precious time since he was on foot.

He scurried down a rocky bank. At the bottom, he followed a dry creek bed for about half a mile, but the rush of a current nearby drowned out the sound of the leaves crunching under his feet as he ran. What it didn't kill was the rumbling of the gun battle drawing closer to Nate rather than farther away.

Ahead, the brush opened up, exposing a cliff. Water gushing over the falls produced a great mist in the air.

"Nathanial!"

Nate twisted around, stopped dead in his tracks. He recognized that voice. But it couldn't be.

Jesse charged out of the tree line on Freckles.

Nate's heart leaped. "Jesse!"

A rifle boomed, and Jesse jerked in the saddle. Blood stained his coat sleeve. He grabbed his shoulder as he wheeled his horse. One of the bounty hunters raced toward him, gun raised and aimed at Jesse. Jesse squeezed the trigger of his Winchester. The man called Slim flipped backward over the rump of his horse and smacked the dirt.

On the hill behind Jesse, among the aspen, Rhett and the man in the checkered shirt popped off shots at each other.

"Gotcha!"

A rough hand grabbed Nate, yanking him in front to serve as a barrier between the third bounty hunter as Jesse swung his Winchester and took aim.

"Let the kid go, McNitt." Jesse's jaw tightened.

McNitt spit. "Can't do that. He's worth too much. Dead or alive." McNitt backed toward his horse and closer to the edge of the cliff, keeping Nate flat against him facing Jesse.

The gunfire on the ridge died. Someone had lost.

"Take the shot!" Rhett yelled from somewhere on the hill.

Nate stared straight down the barrel of the Winchester. Jesse's eyes squinted in line with the rifle's sight. There wasn't a better rifleman. Jesse was dead-on accurate, but if the fella pinching Nate tight moved even a tenth of an inch, he might end up the target. He swallowed hard, his heart thudding against his chest wall.

"You don't have to die, McNitt." Jesse's aim held steady as he walked cautiously forward.

McNitt grabbed his saddle horn, one foot in the stirrup, hauling Nate up with him.

"Kill 'im!" Rhett raced his horse out into the open to the left of Nate, not fifteen feet away.

McNitt turned that direction, his eyes on Rhett. Jesse pulled the trigger. A great boom echoed. McNitt jerked backward with a hole in his forehead. As he timbered, Nate dropped away from the dead man. Rhett's horse skidded on its haunches, slammed the side of McNitt's sorrel, and Nate went flying, screaming his head off. He hit the ground and rolled four, five times until he stopped, his head spinning circles.

No more than a foot away, the rocks dropped away, thirty feet at least to the bottom of the river basin. Water gushed over the falls. The roar was deafening. Below, the churning white filled the entire alley between the two stone walls.

"Partner! Git away from there!" Jesse hustled toward Nate.

Rhett was picking himself up off the ground.

Nate pushed up, facing Jesse, and he backed up half a step without thinking. His instinct to flee anyone who would return him to the Fletchers came second nature. Pebbles skidded under his boots, tumbling off the edge.

"Don't come any closer, Jesse." Nate shrank back an inch, his one heel hanging off the drop. He teetered on the rim.

Jesse skidded to a halt. "Partner, what are ya doin'?" He dropped his rifle and reached out. "Give me your hands!"

Knees bent and his arms pulled back, ready to spring, Rhett posed next to Jesse whose eyes were wide. Stones under Nate's feet trickled off the cliff. The wind pushed with a mighty gust. Leaves swirled through the cold air. Nate's and Jesse's eyes held.

"Your pa filed an appeal. He's gonna try to overturn the verdict." Jesse's chest pumped up and down.

"Pa's alive!" Nate smiled from ear to ear.

His foot slipped. Arms flailing, he began to timber backward over the edge.

"No!" Jesse screamed as Nate plummeted.

Nate smacked atop the water with a mean slap against his spine, then sank as quick as a stone. Air blew out of his lungs, filling in an instant with cold liquid before he could catch a single breath. The force of the fall drove him toward the bottom of the river.

Nate kicked and grabbed against the current, which pulled him downward. His head broke the surface. High above, two silhouettes stood where he had fallen off the cliff.

"Nathanial!" Jesse's voice echoed down through the canyon.

Nate opened his lips. "J—" A splash poured into his mouth. A second later, he was swept around a bend where the water quickly calmed. He grabbed hold of a floating log. His clothing was soaked and heavy, making it hard to move, and his muscles were stiffening in the cold river. He bobbed with the wet timber for half a mile or more until the wood drifted close to the shoreline and he had caught his breath.

On the sandy bank, dripping wet, Nate's arms and legs buckled as he crawled away from the current. He lay facedown in the dirt. His chest hurt. He coughed out water, then rolled over onto his back. The sky had turned crimson.

"Ain't it just my lucky day?" A shadow fell over him.

Nate jolted into a sitting position. "Who are you?" Though, he knew the answer. Another damn bounty hunter.

"Jack Murphy." The man squatted in front of Nate while holding the reins of his horse. "Let's get you dry." Murphy pulled up his coat collar against the stinging air.

"Sounds g-g-good." Nate's teeth chattered. Still, he knew better than to trust this well-armed fella. Two .45s, one on each hip, and a rifle on his horse. But freezing half to death wouldn't be any good either. Nate just had to be smart. He could use this sharp-eyed fella to get warm, maybe fed, then escape. Somehow.

Murphy pulled Nate to his feet. "You don't give me any trouble, and I won't tie ya up. Any problems and I have a couple lengths of rawhide in my saddlebags."

Nate nodded.

"All I want is the money, kid. I don't wanna hurt ya." Murphy threw a leg over his saddle, then extended a hand.

Shortly after nightfall, riding away from the river, Murphy pulled on the reins. Nate didn't recognize where they were in relationship to Denver, a town he now had to steer clear of. Too many men there hunting him.

"Where ya takin' me?" Nate believed he had a right to know, yet Murphy might not think so. Nate slid out of the saddle.

"Denver." Murphy picketed his horse. "Rumor has it your father's ridin' this way. I figure those two deputies in town can keep ya under lock and key until he comes to fetch ya."

"Pa's comin' here?" Nate said more to himself. This was bad news. As excited, tingling all over, as he'd been to see Jesse, he would feel twice that for Pa. Nate couldn't go through being torn away a second time if he didn't win the appeal Jesse had mentioned.

Murphy fed sticks to a small flame. "Overheard one of those deputies talkin'."

Nate warmed his hands. How long would an appeal process take? Not knowing and hanging on for an outcome was awful hard on a body. And there was no guarantee he would get to stay with his folks while the court fight ensued. What if the Fletchers had another witness from his past such as Mrs. Gill tucked in their deep billfold?

Nate pulled off his wet boots and soaked coat, placing the wet garments near the fire. He couldn't again go through all that court stuff and what his family endured that first time. Nate laid his head to the cold, hard ground and stared into the starry sky. His arms wrapped tight around his chest, for he shivered badly.

Nate's lids sprang open to an earth-shaking boom. Murphy, who stood next to the fire with his cup raised to his lips, jerked. Coffee spilled down his front as the tin cup dropped out of his hand onto the ground at Nate's feet. Blood poured out of Murphy's stomach. One knee buckled, and he hit the dirt on his side. A second blast tore through his chest, which flopped the bounty hunter over face up, flat on his back.

Nate screamed as he jumped to his feet.

Finch walked his horse out of the tree line. Smoke rolled off the end of his pistol. "I told ya, kid. No one'll stand in my way of that fifteen thousand."

Behind Jasper by a horse length, Jackson, Yooko, and two others that Nate didn't recognize bunched, two on either side of Finch. Marv wasn't with them. Either dead or he'd stayed behind. Nate recalled the gang discussing taking him to a place owned by a man named Junior. Must've been where Finch had picked up the two new recruits.

Nate's eyes shifted. Could he make the distance into the tree line before one of them scooped him up? Maybe he should try for the river, but the current was at least a mile away and not very swift.

Finch began to chuckle. "I know what you're thinkin'." He opened the cylinder, feeding two bullets into the empty chambers. "You try an' run, I'll shoot ya in the leg." Jasper's face was stone sober.

It didn't matter that Nate was a kid. All Finch saw were dollar signs.

"Then again," Finch said, "your aunt and uncle might pay more for their poor little nephew in desperate need of medical attention." He sneered.

Two of the men with him grinned. Jackson snickered. Yooko stared at Nate with hate-filled eyes.

Nate stood there in stocking feet and damp clothing. His cheeks were chapped from the biting wind. Not that he had a death wish, but he was right miserable, and what else did he have to lose or even live for? If Jasper had wanted him dead, he could have shot Nate when he killed Murphy. And there were just times when he couldn't control his fiery tongue.

"Has anyone ever told ya what an asshole ya are?" Nate snatched up a stick. One end had been hanging out of the smoldering fire, but the other end of the wood glowed red. He whipped the hunk of branch whizzing through the air straight at Finch.

Jasper's horse jumped sideways, bumping into Yooko's gelding, which reared. A shot fired from behind them. Red blew out from Jackson's chest. Face first, he fell out of the saddle, dead before he thudded the ground. A second boom put a bullet into the shoulder of one of the new recruits. Before he could yank his carbine out of its boot on his saddle, he ate lead right through the neck.

Finch and his men pulled their guns, returning fire. It had to be Jesse and Rhett. McNitt and those other two were dead. That left only the deputies, or so Nate hoped. Maybe it was more bounty hunters. Nate grabbed the reins of one of the riderless horses, jumped into the saddle as quick as could be, and madly walloped the sides of the animal with his stocking feet. No time to grab his things.

Nate lit out at a thunderous pace. The roan had legs that stretched longer than any horse he'd ever ridden. Boy, could that horse run. Nate's hair blew. The gunfire behind him faded as he kept the mare racing. He'd recently had too many close calls with death. Maybe he should find Pa, give himself up, and hope for the best as far as the appeal.

Nate recalled the picture of Ashton Fletcher in the newspaper that Mrs. Bell had shown him. That was no way to live, as a replacement child. It wasn't love. Whatever Mrs. Fletcher thought she felt for him wasn't real. At the trial, according to Mrs. Gill, Deloris Fletcher had said no to taking him in when his mother had asked before she took sick and died. Mrs. Fletcher was seeing her dead son. That was all. Nate didn't want that kind of life. A life of pretending or, rather, being expected to be a person he wasn't. No doubt he and Ashton Fletcher were opposites. How could they not be? Ashton would have been raised with the best of everything at his disposal. Nate barely had a roof over his head until he'd been adopted by the Crossons, and before that, he rode with a gang that robbed banks.

He kicked the mare's sides. No, he couldn't turn back, couldn't seek Pa. He needed to get away from there, away from Finch and his gang, away from Jesse and Rhett, away from the bounty hunters in Denver, and away from Pa who might have no choice but to turn Nate over to the Fletchers.

For a few miles, he ran the mare off and on, giving her a little breather but keeping them moving forward. The morning brought with it a mite of fog in the bottomland. Rising off the ground, the mist gave his skin a clammy feel. Dark-gray clouds hung in the sky.

Nate pulled up reins inside the tree line skirting a long stretch of flat meadow. To the east of him, a half-mile away, two riders, one mounted on a gray and the other on a dun, crossed the far end of the field, keeping under the trees. They studied the ground as they trotted their horses in the direction of Denver. Could be they were hunters tracking their kill, but no gunshots had come from that standpoint. More likely, they were searching for him.

They were covering ground at a steady pace. Thankfully, they weren't headed in his direction. Nate turned his horse west. The farther he got from Denver, hopefully, the better off he would be.

Nate let the mare walk and patted her neck. She was breathing hard. There was an ache in him to see Montana, to know if he was alive. What if he was hurt, lying back there somewhere in pain and Nate too busy running? Maybe he should go back. He slowed the mare's pace. Montana might need help. But if he ran into Finch, there would be no helping anyone, including himself. Jasper likely would just put a bullet in him.

He wiped a sleeve across his eyes. As much as he wanted to, he couldn't go searching for Montana. The big wolf did make Nate feel safer. At least when he was around, Nate could close his lids at night and sleep without keeping one eye open for trouble. Montana never failed to alert him to danger.

Nate turned his horse into a shallow gully, following that for a mile or two. What brown leaves that still clung to the branches gave him some cover, and the animal he was riding matched the earthy hue. He skirted the hills and stayed away from the open fields he passed, all the while keeping his eyes open for any sign of Montana. It was noon or better before his shoulders were warmed by the sun.

In the dirt at the mare's feet, the track of a buckboard grooved the sod. It had passed by three, four hours ago. No wolf tracks. He sighed.

The wagon couldn't have been one owned by Docherty Lumber. The hoofprints weren't large enough to belong to one of the Percherons that pulled the logs. The work was too heavy for a standardbred horse, even a good solid one. This was a single carriage animal, not a team of horses, and the stride was short, not a long-legged pony.

Bounty hunters didn't drive wagons, but families did. Nate had dragged a branch behind him here and there to wipe out his trail, and he'd kept the mare on hard ground when possible. Tricks that men accustomed to living on the trail would be familiar with. What Nate needed was a new scheme that would completely throw anyone following off his scent. Too many men were chasing him, and it wasn't unlikely that rumors or even a news clipping had reached a family way out there. What kind of fella wouldn't want to improve his family situation? And fifteen thousand dollars would certainly do that. With Nate's sweet smile and soft blue eyes, anyone could mistake him for an easy catch. But there was a chance he wouldn't be recognized.

He had time before catching up with the wagon to come up with a good story about how he got lost. Sad eyes, thrust out a quivering lip, all that crap. But how he was going to steal a weapon, he didn't have the faintest idea.

CHAPTER 22

NIGH TO DARK, Nate pulled up reins alongside a fenced meadow that blocked his path. At the end of the fence rails, the pale glow of a lantern warmed the appearance of a bland, weather-weary board-and-batten cabin. A green-painted wagon sat near the barn. Inside a round pen, a black horse munched hay. Short legs, fourteen hands high at the withers at most.

Something was strange about the place. Nate studied as Pa had taught him. Tall weeds stood everywhere in the yard as though it had been abandoned. It shouldn't have been that way if indeed a family lived there. There would have been lots of foot traffic in and out of the house and barn. Paths in the yard. Where were the stock animals? Not even a manure pile. This was just a stop for whoever was inside. That might be better yet for Nate. Perhaps he could somehow hide in the bed of the wagon.

Finch, his gang, Jesse, and Rhett were all following the tracks of a lone horse. An animal Nate could set free. No one would expect that. Plus, he wasn't heavy enough that the mare's hoofprints set any deeper when he sat in the saddle or led the animal on foot. No difference at all between the two sets of tracks he made. Inside a wagon, he couldn't make tracks.

Nate crept into the yard, his eyes on the cabin. A fair-haired woman walked past the window. Surely, a woman hadn't come way out there alone. He gripped the sill and peeked over the lip. It was one large room. A table and chairs sat near the fireplace. The woman's back was to him, and she was bent over someone lying on the bed in the corner. A bowl of water and bandages sat on a table next to them. Who had been hurt? She stepped aside as the man sat up on the edge of the mattress, his left arm cradled in a sling.

Nate's eyes bugged.

"Goose!" he said without thought of hiding himself.

Both Goose and the woman twisted around, facing him. Goose's pistol was in his hand.

"Nathanial!" Goose jumped up.

The door flew open. Goose grabbed him by the arm and shoved him inside. Nate stumbled.

Goose was alive. Bleeding but breathing.

"Why did ya follow us?" Goose pushed Nate into a chair.

"I didn't know it was you. I just saw wagon tracks." He was honest.

The woman plunked a plate of stew in front of Nate. "Goose told me about you." She shook her head. "They'll find us for sure now."

Nate understood the woman was talking about whoever was following him, that his presence there put the two of them in greater danger. If Jasper were to cross paths with Goose, that would lead to another shootout. This woman could get killed for helping either of them. One man against a gang of cutthroats.

"I'll leave." Nate pushed aside his plate and stood. He owed Goose one. That hurt arm was because the man had aided him in an escape.

"Sit down," Goose said. He pulled out a chair and sat. "I'm glad you're okay, kid."

Nate grinned. "That day." He gave a low whistle. "I was hopin' Finch hadn't killed ya."

"He almost did." Goose rubbed the arm in the sling. "One of the horses spooked at all the gunfire and bumped Jasper. Otherwise, his bullet would've plugged my heart instead of my arm."

The woman slapped a hand on the table. "He'll kill us all if he finds us."

Goose lifted his chin. "Nathanial, this is June."

June lifted the hem of her tight-fitting baby-blue dress before sitting. Her face was painted, and her bodice dipped low. Ma would never wear such a getup. June's shawl slipped down, exposing a bare shoulder.

When Nate had ridden with the Younger gang, he'd been in a number of saloons scattered throughout the West and knew a working girl when he saw one. Besides, his mother had been a whore, one of the reasons he was in this feud with the Fletchers.

"We can't stay here," June said. "Bowman knows I come out this way sometimes. He doesn't know about this place, but it wouldn't be hard to find. It isn't too far off the road. A few miles."

Nate didn't recognize that name. Another bounty hunter maybe. He glanced between June and Goose.

"Bowman is the man who owns the saloon, and he's a good friend of Jasper's." Tears glistened in her eyes as she looked away and stared at Goose. "What if he saw us leave town together?" She drummed her painted nails on the tabletop. "If he were to mention that to Finch…" She shook her head. "He might come anyway. Hunt down the kid and finish the job of killin' you."

"June, ya worry too much." Goose spun the chamber of his pistol, checking his load. "You're gonna cause wrinkles on that pretty face if ya don't ease up."

"How can you joke about this? Jasper Finch's a killer." She huffed.

Nate stood, scooting back his chair. "I got an idea."

There was a place he recalled hearing about, a safe haven tucked somewhere near the Denver mountains. Jim Younger and his brothers and the gang Nate used to ride with, all those men had talked of a hideout, more of a gathering place for anyone dodging the law. A canyon that, once inside its walls, turned into a maze of twists and turns. Alone, neither Nate nor June would be welcome there—if they could find the place—but Goose, he was a wanted man, a known hunted man. Surely, he knew the whereabouts.

"Death Canyon." Nate stared at Goose.

Lawmen didn't tread there. The few who had were never seen again. This was their chance. They could hide inside one of the canyon's corridors. Maybe they wouldn't even be noticed by any other outlaws. But if Goose knew the place, how to find it, then it was a safe bet that Jasper Finch did too.

Goose shook his head. "It's too dangerous. We don't know who we could run into in there. I'd rather take my chances on the outside against Finch and whoever else is huntin' ya."

"Pa's on his way." Nate sat down with a plop. "You know as well as I do that my father has the nose of a bloodhound. But even he doesn't know where the entrance to the outlaw canyon is. He would have told me somethin' like that."

It was almost the perfect place for him to hide. The law, which meant the Fletchers, would never find him. But there was a risk. Finch likely would follow them inside, and there was the danger of other criminals.

Nate chewed on his lip.

Goose pushed back his hat. "Well, I'll be. I haven't seen Nolan in years." He stared off.

"Goose." Nate shook the man's uninjured arm. "I'll go alone if you don't help me." His gut knotted at the thought of going all by himself. He crossed his fingers. Without Goose, he had no chance. He'd gotten lucky too many times over the past couple weeks since jumping off that train.

Goose was quiet for a long minute. The skin at the corners of his eyes crinkled. His gaze never wavered off Nate, and slowly, he nodded.

"Are you two crazy? Death Canyon!" June threw up her hands. "I don't want to die." She dabbed at the glistening sweat beads on her top lip with a frilly handkerchief. "Guaranteed, we'll all be killed. Including you." She pointed at Nate. "Don't you think those criminals hiding out in there will know about the bounty on your head? I swear the whole country is talkin' about it. We're askin' for trouble if we go in there."

Goose shoved his pistol into its holster. "That's why it's the best place to hide. No one would think to hunt for us there."

"That's because it's a ridiculous idea." June flicked away a stray strand of hair that had fallen out of the bun atop her head.

"Have you been inside the trail, the canyon?" Nate pictured the many hideouts he'd stayed in years ago. God, he hated that life. And here he was again.

"A few times," Goose said. "We won't go to the main encampment. There are a lot of dead ends that shoot off the main trail. We'll slip into one of those, brush out our tracks, and lay low for a week or two."

"That's plenty of time for your arm to heal. And we have enough supplies for four or five days," June added, but her lips pressed into a thin line.

"We'll need more supplies. I won't be able to hunt once we're inside the canyon. Any gunfire and those hard cases in the area'll come snoopin'." Goose pulled a roll of bills out of his pocket. "June, you'll have to buy what we need. Neither of us"—he nodded his head toward Nate—"can risk bein' seen in town."

"What about Bowman? He's gonna be expectin' me to return to work. And if I show up in town with a wad of cash, buying supplies, what do you think he's going to do? He don't let any of his girls just go. Unless they're carried out in a coffin." June was breathing heavy.

Goose shoved the bills back into his pocket. "I'll go." He stood. "You stay here with the boy for now."

"What do you mean?" June grabbed Goose's hands. "I'm just scared." She went on before he could say a word. "You're right. It isn't safe for either of you to go." She reached into Goose's pocket, retrieving the bills. "Bowman's never liked you. And if Jasper's in town, now that the two of you have split…" She was quiet for a minute, fiddling with the money. "It's hard to tell what either of them might do if they were to see ya." She wiped at her eyes. "I'm a fool for you, Jim."

June headed for the door. Goose's mouth opened, but he didn't say a word. Why was it hard for a grown man to tell how he felt? Pa wasn't so good with mushy words either, but he had picked Ma flowers a time or two.

Nate stomped on Goose's foot. "Say somethin', dummy," he whispered.

Goose gave him a hard look. Maybe it wasn't any of his business, but Nate knew time was precious, especially those minutes with people who mutually cared for one another. Goose had to feel something for this woman or he wouldn't have sought her help in digging the bullet out of him.

"Wait," Nate called June back. He handed her a letter, the one he had written days ago at the lumber camp.

She looked at the address.

"You sure about this?" She waited.

"Yes, ma'am."

Earlier that day, Nate had briefly thought about turning himself in. Jesse never lied to him, not once, ever. So if he said Pa was going to fight the Fletchers in court, then that was exactly what would happen.

He glanced up at Goose. "How hard is it to get a judgment overturned?" His adoption had basically been thrown out. Why not Judge Parker's ruling that gave Nate to the Fletchers?

"I don't know." Goose scratched his head. "Why?"

"Pa's gonna take the Fletchers back to court." Nate was more than tired, and he had blisters on his heels. He couldn't keep running day and night at this pace. Someone would eventually catch him. And there were worse men out there than Jasper Finch. Nate had been born to one such man. His blood was tarnished, so deep down, he was just as bad as Finch.

June tucked his letter under her arm. "How do you know that?"

"Jesse, my pa's deputy, I talked to 'im the other day." Then Nate had slipped off a cliff and later convinced himself that it was better to be on the run than right back where he started when he had first bolted after the Fletchers had gained the legal right to take him away. But one of these times, he wasn't going to slip through the hands of his captors as he had today when Jesse and Rhett shot at Finch. Nate's luck was sure to run out.

Goose's eyes brightened. "You sure about that?"

Nate nodded. Goose patted him on the shoulder. What did he know that Nate didn't? Something about the legal process, or was it something else entirely? He had certainly caused this man a few headaches.

"S'pose you'll be happy to be rid of me." Hence, the smile.

"You have been a pain in the ass, but no." Goose rested his hand on Nate's head for a few seconds. "One thing I've always admired about your father. When he fights for somethin' or someone, he don't ever give up." He flicked Nate's nose.

Nate smiled. Goose was right. He had confidence in Pa, but not so much in the law, not anymore. Judge Parker had him torn away from a happy home and placed with strangers. Kin or not, that didn't matter to Nate. Blood didn't make them family.

June tightened her shawl around her shoulders. "I need to get back to town." Her hand was on the knob. "I'll bring the supplies as soon as I can. You can hide here as long as it takes for the kid's pa to show up."

"Whose place is this?" Nate glanced around. Things were neat. Not fancy, but there wasn't any dust on the furniture or that musty odor that comes with sitting empty. Someone at least took care of the inside.

June smiled, but tears welled in her eyes. "My husband and I bought this place shortly after we married." She twisted the gold ring on her finger.

Nate didn't have to ask where her husband was. June was a painted dove. That was a profession chosen in desperation. Her husband had either run out on her or was dead. Nate would bet that somewhere outside, he'd find a grave.

June was willing to help him, a stranger. Yes, he was a child and she was in love with Goose, but mean-hearted people didn't risk their lives for others. And she would be doing just that. She could run into Finch or any number of other criminals hunting him while trying to get them supplies. Plus, she handled the letter addressed to his ma and pa with gentle hands. She was a sweet person under all that makeup.

With the door half-open, June looked over her shoulder. "That deputy of your pa's, if I see him, should I fetch him here?"

Before Nate opened his mouth, Goose stepped in front of him.

"No. I'll only turn the boy over to his father. Remember, June, I'm a wanted man. The law ain't just gonna forgive my past crimes because I helped the kid."

Nate didn't know Rhett as well as he knew Jesse, but Jesse and Pa were firm believers that if a man was guilty, he shouldn't go unpunished. Why wasn't Goose hesitant to face Pa? Because they were old friends? Did this have something to do with repaying the debt Goose had told Nate about when they'd first met? Maybe he wanted to pay off that favor face to face.

Nate was okay staying with Goose. The idea of turning himself over to go through another court battle was still settling into his head. And as excited as he'd be to see Jesse, Nate couldn't forget the awful proceedings he'd already been through, recalling Jesse had lost his temper and almost punched the Fletchers' attorney in the face had it not been for Marshal Huckabee.

Goose pulled June close. They kissed, then kissed again. Nate thought of Ma and Pa.

"You be careful, June." Goose closed the door behind them as he likely went to hitch up the little black horse to the wagon.

A few minutes later, Goose stepped inside to the rattle of the carriage departing the yard behind him. "We're leavin'. Let's go."

"What about June? She'll be back. Shouldn't we wait for her?"

This wasn't the plan they had discussed five minutes ago. They would need supplies. The three of them were to travel into the outlaw trail together. She was helping them, going into town, taking a big risk. Someone bad might find out. That put her in danger. Surely, Goose wasn't turning his back on her. He had just kissed her.

"I don't want June gettin' hurt. And I told her that just a minute ago before she left," Goose said. "Keepin' ya away from the wrong people until Nolan arrives will be tough enough."

"Ya gonna marry her?" Nate understood that instinct to protect a loved one. Just yesterday on the ridge side with

Rhett, Jesse had squeezed the trigger and killed to keep Nate from harm. If anything were to happen to his big partner, he would want to shrivel up and die.

"Thought about it." Goose poured the remnants of the coffeepot on the fire. Steam hissed.

"Where we goin'?" Nate grabbed a couple biscuits off a plate on the table, filling his pockets. Since Goose had changed his mind about June going with them, he might have decided on another place to hide.

"Death Canyon." Goose donned his bloodstained coat. His face was pale, his wounded arm moving with stiffness. Thank God it wasn't his pistol hand.

"You sure this's a smart idea?" Nate tugged lightly on the sleeve of Goose's injured arm. He hadn't thought about the injury when he first suggested riding into the outlaw trail. "And how will Pa find me?"

The windows rattled against the wind. Nate wrapped a blanket around his shoulders.

"Because Nolan's been on the inside. We hid out there once." Goose was at the door, his rifle in one hand and a sack with the coffeepot and a few food items in the other.

Nate's eyes widened. "Pa broke the law?" Was Goose pulling his leg? "I don't believe it."

Goose grinned, and with the supply sack slung over his shoulder, he stepped out the door.

Nate hustled out on the man's heels toward the corral.

CHAPTER 23

NATE PRANCED AS GOOSE saddled the horse that Nate had taken while escaping Finch and his gang, but not because he worried about the two of them getting caught. "Are ya gonna tell me or make me beg? I wanna know what Pa did."

Goose swung a leg over the mare. "It ain't what you're thinkin'." He pulled Nate up into the saddle behind him. "I'm positive your pa ain't proud of what he did. That's likely the reason he never mentioned it." He nudged the horse.

They started east, following the moonlit ridgeline. Overhead, stars twinkled. The night was clear, the air crisp. Nate drew the blanket around him tighter, glad for the warmth.

"Your pa…" Goose broke the still silence. "He'd been ridin' with a posse, trackin' men who robbed a stage carryin' a mining payroll."

Nate, waiting for more, squeezed Goose's waist.

"As I recall"—Goose adjusted his hat—"the shotgun rider was killed. And a couple undercover lawmen." His voice softened. He shook his head, and if Nate could have looked into the man's eyes, he'd bet on the shine of regret being there.

"That sounds awful," Nate said. He'd seen too much killing

lately, enough that one more bloody body and he would crack. It was one of the reasons he was willing to give the appeal process Pa had facilitated a try.

Goose nodded. "The posse caught up. Lead flew from every direction. Three of our boys were cut down. That's when the gang broke. We scattered."

Nate couldn't imagine having to arrest a best friend.

Goose turned the mare. "There's a rocky gorge six, seven miles thataway." He pointed into the black. "That day, I raced my horse right for it."

"Why chance your horse going lame with a posse on your tail?"

Goose steered the mare, crossing a pale moon-bathed stretch of grass. "Beyond the gorge is the mouth of Death Canyon, better known as the outlaw trail. It's a narrow, rough path for better than a mile, lined with boulders that offer plenty of concealed spots for an ambush. I figured no lawman would follow me inside."

"But Pa did." Nate took a guess.

Goose chuckled. "He tackled me right out of the saddle. We hit the dirt and rolled."

Nate grinned, picturing it happening.

"We got to our feet. Had it been anyone but Nolan, I would've been swingin' or grabbed for my iron. Instead, we just stood there starin' at one another. I'm not sure either of us was even breathin'."

"But you're here now, so you must've outsmarted Pa some-how." Nate's father wasn't easily fooled. He hadn't gained a famed reputation because he was dumb. He was the best at tracking down criminals. Never lost a man that Nate knew of.

"It's been too long, my friend." Goose cleared his throat. "That's what I said to 'im. Then I extended a hand. Your pa grinned, grabbed me, pulled me close, and clapped my shoulder."

"So he didn't arrest you?" Nate tucked his hands inside the blanket, away from the biting wind. That didn't sound like Pa. He wasn't typically a rule-bender.

Goose pulled up reins at the edge of the steep, rocky gorge. Moonlight shone on the many stones. Barely visible was a single rabbit path that weaved down into the black bottom of what appeared to be a pit about a mile wide and even longer. Nate quivered, clinging to the back of Goose's coat. It was strange to think that Pa had ridden in this exact place at one time.

"I wasn't sure what your father's intention was, and I didn't care. It was just damn good to see 'im." Goose paused, looking up into the starry sky as if to say that had been a lifetime ago. "We spent the next three days talkin' about where the years had taken us. Nolan bragged 'bout bein' a father. Matthew was four or five at the time. I didn't even know he had a boy. When I heard about Mary and their son bein' killed, I wrote Nolan and conveyed my deepest condolences." Goose nudged the mare.

They started the descent into the outlaw trail. The air grew colder. Nate wrapped his arms around himself. Clouds now hung over the moon, blackening the path before them. Every step the mare took was a risk. If she fell, it'd be a hell of a tumble for all of them. He had to stop looking down.

"After the three days, what happened then?" Nate needed to focus on something other than his pounding heart.

"We rode out together." Goose jerked a thumb over his shoulder. "Right there where we were just stopped, Nolan and I shook hands. I went my way. He went his."

"That's it?" Nate slumped. He thought for sure Goose would tell him something way more exciting than that.

"Before we parted, your pa did give me a fair warnin'. At our next meetin', should there be one, he'd have no choice. He would hang me."

Nate gulped a mouthful of cold air. "Then why are ya helpin' me? You know he's comin'."

"I have my reasons."

Not one shaky syllable, not a hint of worry in Goose's voice. Was he nuts?

Nate pinched Goose's arm. The man looked over his shoulder and frowned. Now he had his full attention. "I get it. He saved you. You save me. But why risk swingin' by the neck on a rope?" He drew out the last few words.

Goose's gaze was on the path in front of them. "Nolan let me live when, by all rights, I should've hanged. I hadn't killed any of those men on the stage, but I'd been part of the robbery. He had caught me. And with the list of crimes behind my name by that time, I would've been strung up had he turned me over to the posse. But that ain't why I'm helpin' ya."

"Then why?" What other reason could there be? A life for a life. That's how Nate figured it. More importantly, he never knew Pa to have a blind eye. "Maybe he'll let ya go this time too. Since you're helpin' me."

They struck the bottom of the gorge where the ground leveled off. It was still rocky, but the mare was surefooted and walked at a slow but steady pace. Nate released his grip on Goose.

"I wouldn't bet on that, kid. Your pa's a man of his word." Goose pulled up his coat collar, then blew into his hands, still holding the reins.

"Ain't you afraid?" Nate didn't want to see Goose dance at the end of a rope. Maybe he could stop his father, but how?

"It ain't the thought of dyin' that troubles me. I failed Nolan. I haven't been able to forgive myself since." Goose pulled up on the reins. The mare was breathing heavy.

The moon peeked out from behind the clouds, and before them, tall stone walls formed the jaws of a deep canyon. Jagged rocks sticking up out of the ground reminded Nate of a mouthful of fanged teeth, which made him momentarily think of Montana.

"What did ya do?" Nate wasn't sure if he'd get an answer. Goose must've let Pa down in a big way for him to take a bullet in the arm, risking his life while helping Nate escape.

Goose remained quiet. His breath misted white, the same as the mare's. "I'd gone to visit my brother. I wasn't known as an outlaw in that area, so it was safe. We were headin' down the boardwalk when the stagecoach rattled past. I couldn't believe my eyes. It was Mary. As I recall, she had the most beautiful black hair." Goose stared off into the darkness ahead as though that moment were replaying right before his eyes. "I hadn't seen her in quite a few years, not since she and Nolan had married. Matthew was with her, but I didn't see Nolan. I had never met their son but hoped to right then and there, and I started to turn to follow. I couldn't wait to talk to Mary, to both of them."

Goose touched spurs to the mare. "My brother caught me by the arm. He wanted me to look over a horse at the livery that he was thinkin' 'bout buyin'. It would only take a few minutes. He promised me." He drew in a deep breath. "I should've followed my gut instinct and run after Mary and Matthew. If I had, they might still be alive."

Nate stiffened. "Where was this?" He didn't have to ask. He knew the answer. The memory sent a shiver of cold through his spine. Would there ever be a time in his life when his awful past didn't overshadow him?

"Northfield," Goose said and blew out a long exhale. "I left the stable and hurried along the boardwalk toward the stage office. I was at the coach door when the first shots rang out. They weren't on the platform outside the office. I never figured they were still inside the stage. It looked empty. I didn't know they had ducked onto the floor." Goose cursed under his breath. "I was right there, dammit. I hunkered next to the wheel and fired at the gang involved, knowing Mary and Matthew were somewhere. All I could think about was protecting them. I should've searched inside, made sure the coach was empty. I could've got them out of there, got them to safety, protected them better. It was my fault they died."

Nate wiped at his eyes. Goose wasn't to blame for the deaths of Mary and Matthew Crosson. He needed to fess up. He still carried some blame. "Jim Younger, my old pa, he's the one, not you." He grew from bad seed, one of the reasons he needed to throw out the idea of going home, of going back to being a Crosson. He wasn't a good enough person.

"I know you were there." Goose glanced over his shoulder. "I rode to Nolan's ranch after the murder of his family. Planned on beggin' his forgiveness. But when I got there, he had sold the place. The new owner couldn't even point me in the direction Nolan had taken off. I heard later he was scoutin' for the army. I wrote him. He sent a letter to my brother's place, knowing I visit there when I can. He told me 'bout marryin' a woman named Kate James and all 'bout you." Goose grinned. "He's a proud father."

"Did Pa forgive ya?" Nate figured that's why Goose had written Pa, though he wasn't guilty and doubted Pa would think otherwise.

"Said the apology was unnecessary. He called me a brother." The saddle creaked as Goose shifted his weight. "I won't fail 'im this time."

Nate hated to disappoint Goose. He wasn't going to hang around and force Pa's hand. When Pa said he was going to do somethin', you could bet your life he would, and that included hanging Goose. Before morning, Nate would slip away. If he could find his way out. It was awful dark, and they'd turned at least ten times. What if he went the wrong direction and ran smack-dab into more outlaws? And there was a chance of that happening even if he did find his way out.

He had no choice, though, and hopefully, Goose wouldn't come after him.

CHAPTER 24

JESSE STEERED FRECKLES into Denver's main street. Lanterns had been lit along each side. For as late as it was, there were a number of men milling about. More voices carried out from the saloon. Town had become too crowded with prize hunters. Jesse cursed under his breath. Horses—fifteen or twenty, maybe more—stood lazily along the hitchrail in one long line. One rider per animal—that was a lot of opposition. And he and Rhett had lost partner's trail.

Jesse shifted his eyes, glaring at Rhett. "You had no call to shoot Finch's man, Jackson. We're lawmen, for God's sake. You know better than to shoot a man in the back."

Rhett's jaw tightened. "I'm tired of yer bitchin'! Finch threatened to shoot Nathanial. You heard 'im! I did what I had to. I got their attention off the boy before he got hurt."

"You killed a man without warnin'. And in case you haven't noticed, partner got away thanks to you startin' a damn shoo-tin' battle." Jesse stepped down in front of the hotel.

Rhett jumped off his gelding and leaned into Jesse's face, chin to chin. "Finch wasn't gonna just put up his hands and turn the boy over. And Jackson was a no-account." Rhett straightened. "So was the one you killed."

Jesse slapped his reins around the hitchrail. "I ain't sayin' guns wouldn't have been necessary, but Nathanial's nine, Rhett. A little kid. And behind 'im so far, there's a string of dead. How many people does he have to see die? Maybe we could've spared 'im one." Jesse was quiet for a long minute. "I don't know." He rubbed his hand over his face. "I just can't help but think that havin' so many men huntin' 'im and seein' all those bastards cut down has to be takin' a toll on the boy." Jesse patted Freckles' soft nose. "I'm just worried."

"We'll find 'im." Rhett rested a hand on Jesse's shoulder. "I hadn't thought 'bout Nate that way. He's such a tough little bugger. I reckon I didn't think 'bout 'im gettin' scared."

Jesse nudged Rhett.

"What is it?" Rhett turned in the direction Jesse was staring.

Jasper Finch, the Yaqui, and the one other man who hadn't been killed during their gun battle pulled up reins in front of the saloon.

"I could use a drink." Rhett backhanded Jesse on the arm. "How 'bout you?"

Jesse nodded. "Yeah, I'm awful dry." He stepped off the boardwalk, heading across the street.

Before they pushed through the swinging doors, two men came running out, tossing a third fella, head first, into the dirt. He rolled five, six times over the rutted lane.

"And stay out!" one of the two hollered. The other one snickered as he brushed his hands of the matter.

Jesse couldn't help but picture the scene in Gray Rock a few weeks ago when he'd been drunk as a skunk and tossed out of Pete's saloon. He'd been an idiot. Alcohol wasn't the answer to any problem but thirst.

Jesse, with Rhett a step behind, shouldered past and into the packed house. A thick cloud of smoke hung low over the many gambling tables, card games in full swing. Men lined the bar three deep. All the voices nearly covered the twang of a mouth harp. On the balcony above, men stood along the rail. Some of them had drinks in hand. Doors up there opened and closed. The working girls were busy tonight.

"Over there." Jesse lifted his chin toward a table near a far window. Finch picked up the five cards in front of him, shuffling them front to back. Leaned against the wall with a beer in his hand was one of the two he showed up with.

"Where's the damn Yaqui?" Rhett said, scanning the room.

"Maybe upstairs." Jesse pushed through the crowd toward the bar where they shouldered in and picked up two drinks. Fact was that if Finch and his men were here, they had lost Nathanial's trail too. But they weren't the only ones hunting the kid.

"I don't like it," Rhett said. "That Injun should be here. There ain't too many whores who'll lay with a red man." He pressed his glass to his lips, then swallowed. "S'pose he slipped out the back."

"I don't think they seen us." Jesse waved at the barkeep for another beer. "From what I've heard, he sticks pretty close to Finch. Ya don't see one without the other. I'd bet he's here somewhere."

Rhett set down his empty glass on the bar top. "Yer probably right. And there's a couple girls here that only charge a nickel a ride. Doubt they're all that particular, not like the two-, three-dollar girls."

Jesse raised a brow, a smirk on his face.

"Well, I don't spend every minute of the day with ya." Rhett grinned.

Jesse chuckled.

"My oh my, what do we have here?" A blond harlot pressed herself against Jesse. "A sheriff." She traced a painted nail along the stubble on his jawline. "You want to go upstairs, handsome?" She smooched his cheek, but her eyes shifted toward Finch.

He might have shrugged that off since the room was filled with men, but Finch stood, heading toward the bar. The whore turned Jesse, keeping him directly between the two. His back was now facing Finch. Rhett stood behind him, so Jesse wasn't worried. Tears glistened in the woman's eyes. Fear. She was shaking, and her grip had tightened.

Perhaps Finch thought of this whore as his woman when in town, and she wasn't receptive. Jesse had learned during other investigations that outlaws who traveled within a particular area tended to have a favorite girl or two. But Finch hadn't glanced at her once. Jesse had enough trouble with that man. He didn't need any more. Women were a headache sometimes. Kristy had just up and left him. Her ring was at home in his top dresser drawer, under his socks.

"I ain't interested." He peeled her off.

Rhett tinged the star on his chest. "Don't let the word deputy fool ya, darlin'. I'm just as powerful." He smiled, showing all those straight white teeth.

She grinned, then slipped her arms around Jesse's neck. "Sorry, but I got my eyes on Sheriff Crosson."

Jesse and Rhett threw each other a sideways glance. That information, that the sheriff was expected, wasn't public as far as Jesse knew.

"What makes ya think he's Sheriff Crosson?" Rhett's firm tone was a big change from just a second ago.

Her arms loosened, and she slid off Jesse. She glanced about. Again, her shining gaze fixed on Finch, who had returned to his seat and tossed a couple bucks into the pot. There was something between those two. Although, he was talking and drinking, not bothered at all on the outside, not by her at least. Inwardly, he might have been stewing about Nate's disappearance. His so-called jackpot had gotten away. It all left Jesse unsettled.

"I-I-I do hear things," she stuttered as she backed up a few steps, bumping into customers at the bar. A few men glanced, then turned their attention back to their drinks and conversations.

Jesse caught her by the wrist, jerking her forward. Why so curious that she would seek him out in a barroom full of men with money? She was a looker too. High cheekbones, full lips, and a shapely posterior. She no doubt could have her pick. He was dusty, and anytime he raised either arm, the odor nearly turned his stomach. Too many weeks on the trail. Had this whore not believed him to be Sheriff Crosson, she wouldn't have gotten in his face.

"I don't know what you're up to, whore, but you best start talkin'." Jesse kept a grip on her arm.

"Jesse." Rhett bumped him.

The Yaqui walked in the rear door, not far away, eyeing the three of them, but his gaze lingered on the woman. He shouldered past Rhett.

"Stop starin', Injun. I'm already workin'." She cupped Jesse's face and planted a smooth one right on his lips. Her face caressed along his cheek as she kept kissing until her mouth touched his ear. "In my room," she barely whispered.

Heat rose in Jesse's face. Damn. She had him half turned on, though he knew this had nothing to do with her usual business. And for whatever reason, she didn't want Finch or his men to know she was about to talk. About what exactly, Jesse wasn't sure. He would, however, oblige her and maybe more. He swung her up into his arms and carried her toward the stairs. She let out a loud hoot. This time, he kissed her. But he wasn't forgetting the reason he and the numerous dangerous men downstairs were all there.

"Don't worry about me," Rhett called after them. "I'll just have another beer."

On the landing at the top of the staircase, she said, "Room three."

At the door, he put her down and glanced over the balcony. Rhett pressed a glass to his lips. Finch was laughing, arms wide, gathering the large pot he'd just won. The Yaqui and the other in the gang huddled along the wall near their leader, passing a bottle. Everyone was engaged in their own doings. No one appeared to be hunting trouble.

A hinge creaked behind him, and he turned. The whore led him by the hands into her room. With a short kick like a mule, he shut the door with a bang. To his surprise, the space was well-kept and clean. The bed was made, the floor swept, and other than a tall dresser holding a pitcher and washbasin, there was a small table with a lace runner, a chair near the window, and a fancy, intricately carved beside table wearing the same dark stain as the other two pieces and the poster bed. It looked like a hotel room, not a whore's sin palace.

"The badge fooled me." She glanced at the sheriff's star. "I'm assuming you're Sheriff Crosson's deputy."

"That's right." Jesse pulled her close and kissed her neck. His hands lingered on her hips.

"We need to talk." She pulled away.

"I'm listenin'." He scooped her up and tossed her playfully onto the bed. The springs squeaked. He jumped, landing on the quilt beside her, and rolled over on top of her. His lips pressed against hers.

She turned her head. "I know where Nathanial is."

Jesse jolted, sitting upright. He just stared.

She pushed up next to him. "Here." She handed him a letter off her night table. "I told him I would send this."

Jesse unfolded the piece of paper. It was partner's handwriting all right. He rubbed a finger over the words. "Is he okay?" He looked deep into her eyes.

She smiled. "Yes, he is."

"Where's he at?" Jesse stood and adjusted his gun belt.

Her eyes turned down. "I can't tell ya."

Jesse grabbed her by the shoulders. "Do you understand that over three-quarters, if not all, of those men downstairs are huntin' that little boy?" He shook her. "Tell me!"

"Stop it!" She jerked free and slapped his face. "He's safe. He's with a friend." She sat back down on the bed.

"Who?" Jesse wouldn't leave without an answer. He rubbed his stinging cheek.

"His name is Jim Reed. He's a friend of Sheriff Crosson's." She patted the bed next to her. Jesse sat, holding the letter in his hands. "I can only tell ya where they were. I'll take ya there if ya want."

"He's runnin' again." Jesse cursed under his breath, talking to himself.

"No." She touched his arm. "He and Jim went to hide until the boy's father shows up. Then the kid will give himself up."

Jesse looked down at the letter. Maybe it contained a clue as to where they would hide.

> Dear Ma and Pa,
> I ain't sure what to say. A lot has happened since I had
> to leave home.

Jesse touched a discolored splotch or two on the paper and figured they were teardrops that had dried. His chest ached.

> I figured something out about myself. Something that
> frightens me. Pa once told me that I was born to be a
> Crosson. That I was his blood, but that was nothing
> but a lie. As much as I love you all. I don't believe that
> anymore. Truth is in my veins runs the blood of a killer.
> I'm just not sure that I should belong with anyone. It's
> hard to explain, but I felt it. The pistol was in my hand,
> aimed in a blink. My finger was on the trigger, but I

didn't want to squeeze that shot. But the natural ability to do so was there. It was a mistake for me to think I should return to Missouri where my newfound skill will be put to full use in a bad way. I thought I could start life over again and be happy. I was wrong.

Jesse didn't know what the kid was talking about, but it seemed he had pulled a gun on someone. Nate was too young for all this trouble. He had lots of scars to begin with, mental ones too. God knew this wouldn't help any of that and might mess with his head more. For as tough as he was, he was a very insecure child.

P.S. I got myself a dog. Actually, he's a wolf.
Nathanial

Jesse folded the paper and slipped it into his vest pocket. "Take me to 'im. Please. I'm beggin' ya."

"I'm June, by the way." She wiped at her eyes. She had read the letter over Jesse's shoulder. "Promise me one thing." She rested a hand on his arm. "Jim, the man Nathanial is with. He's wanted by the law. I'll take ya to the boy, but Goose goes free."

Jesse hadn't recognized the name Jim Reed, but Goose he knew from a wanted poster. Sheriff Crosson had balled the picture and tossed it into the potbelly stove, cursing under his breath the entire time. He'd nearly kicked a leg off the stove. Otherwise, Jesse might not have recalled the name. He didn't know what crimes the man had committed, and at the moment, he didn't care.

"Deal." Jesse extended a hand.

June kissed his face instead.

"I'll get my shawl." She stood. "But we can't let Finch see us leaving. He wants Goose and the boy dead."

Jesse headed for the door. An almighty crash shook the walls outside the room. He threw open the door. Down below, a pistol blasted. Chips of plaster above showered onto his hat and shoulders as he ducked. "Stay in there!" he hollered at June. The door slammed shut.

From above, Jesse couldn't tell who was fighting who or why? It was one big boxing ring. Everywhere he looked, men were throwing punches. Tables were flipped, chairs thrown across the room. One man got hit and went sailing through a window. Glass shattered everywhere. Another fella was bashed over the head with a beer mug and dropped to the floor. Someone went cartwheeling over the bar. Across the room, someone else was tossed rolling over a table. In the middle of the madness, Finch landed a solid right hook to Rhett's chin, turning him on his toes and stumbling backward into a table. Rhett pushed off and dove, buckling Finch at the waist. The Yaqui appeared out of the crowd behind Rhett, holding a knife.

Jesse hustled down, taking the steps by threes, knife in hand. He lunged at the Indian before Finch's buddy had reached Rhett. Jesse swiped at him but missed. Unfortunately, the Yaqui hit his target. His blade slashed Jesse's coat along his side but only scratched his skin.

They circled one another, which wasn't easy with all the bumps from the men fighting around them. A spittoon flew over their heads. Whiskey bottles rattled, a few smashing to the floor. They jabbed at each other. Groans and grunts rose from every corner of the room.

Without warning, a rifle bellowed. The large antler chandler fell from the ceiling, smashing the table directly under. Everyone stopped mid-strike and turned toward the door.

"Sheriff Crosson!" Jesse blurted.

The man stood just inside the batwings, all six feet four inches of him, Winchester in hand. His jaw clenched, eyes narrowed. No one would guess by the firm stance that he'd been flat on his back for weeks. He certainly wasn't displaying weakness of any kind.

"Git out! All of ya!" He jerked his head toward the door.

And as though he had an army behind him—more than just his reputation for being a hard man and fast with a gun—men scrambled. They grabbed up their hats off the floor and filed past him at a rushed pace into the night. One fella jumped out a broken window. Others retreated out the rear. The pack of gunslicks was too liquored up for any one of them to chance their luck against a stone-sober lawman, especially one of Sheriff Crosson's caliber. He wasn't the average tin star. In no time flat, the place was empty, except for the barkeep who cursed a streak as he picked up broken glass.

"Just what in the hell have you two knuckleheads been up to? You're supposed to be lookin' for Nathanial. Is this how ya do that?" Sheriff Crosson shoved Jesse into a chair.

"No, sir," Jesse said.

Rhett picked up a chair and sat. He rubbed at the bruise on his cheek.

Sheriff Crosson eyeballed the two of them.

"I oughta strip ya of your badges." He pulled up a chair.

"We didn't start it." Rhett piped up, and Jesse cringed.

Anytime Jesse's behavior was unbefitting that of a lawman, or at least in Sheriff Crosson's eyes, Jesse got his ass royally chewed out. He knew when to shut up. Rhett would learn.

Sheriff Crosson reached across the table and tore Rhett's star off his shirt, throwing it down on the table. "You swore an oath to keep the peace. Sometimes that means using your fists or guns, but you should always use your words first. This town is a tough one, but remember, it is your job to keep people safe, even the bad ones. This brawl should've never happened."

How could the sheriff say that? Jesse didn't even know what started the fight, and he'd been there.

Rhett shifted in his seat. "How do ya know we weren't tryin' to break it up?" His voice lacked confidence, and Jesse knew Rhett was lying.

Sheriff Crosson grabbed Rhett by the hair, knocking his hat off, and smacked his face into the table. "Don't you ever lie to me, boy."

"Aw, my nose." Rhett grabbed his face.

"You might not care if you have my respect, but once a man has lost it, there's no gainin' it back." Sheriff Crosson whistled at the barkeep. "Bring the boys a beer, and I'll take a whiskey." He looked over at Rhett. "I've always liked ya, Rhett, so I'm gonna give ya some sound advice. If you wanna work for me, I do not tolerate dishonesty—especially when the liar has influence over my son." The sheriff glanced at Jesse. "Who should know better."

Jesse winced.

Rhett nodded.

"I can't hear you!" Crosson thundered.

Jesse sat stiffly.

Rhett wasn't being fired, which was good.

"Yes, sir, I understand." Rhett held eye contact with the sheriff.

But Jesse was still left wondering. Rhett was Sheriff Coleman's deputy. Yes, he was helping Sheriff Crosson, but Crosson hadn't said working *with* him. He'd said working *for* him. Jesse must have misunderstood. Surely, the sheriff wasn't thinking of hiring himself a second full-time deputy.

The barkeep set their drinks in front of them.

"I was standin' outside the door when you and Finch were arguin'. I wanted to see how ya handled yourself. And I agreed with everythin' you said to 'im ... right up to the point where he started to turn away and you sucker-punched 'im." Sheriff Crosson took a drink.

Rhett fiddled with his beer mug.

Jesse grabbed Rhett's arm. "Is that true?" He didn't want to believe it. They were a good team, or so Jesse had thought. They'd had that one misunderstanding about shooting Jackson in the back, but Rhett had done a fine job of explaining himself, and Jesse had been willing to forget the matter. Until now.

"Yeah, I lost my temper and hit 'im first." Rhett didn't sound pleased with himself.

Jesse was disappointed too.

The sheriff smacked down his whiskey glass. "And low and behold, who should come chargin' down from upstairs but my idiot son, jumpin' headfirst into a knife fight?" He gave Jesse a hard look. "Now don't get me wrong. I'm glad you kept Rhett from gettin' stabbed, but did either of you think for one second that with all the bodies in the room, two lawmen might become the prime targets? Kill the two of you and there's no one within a hundred miles to keep those lowlifes from the prize they're all huntin'."

Jesse and Rhett glanced at each other. It was clear that neither had looked at the situation that way.

Sheriff Crosson poured himself a second drink. "Rhett, I'm willin' to forgive your misdemeanor—this time. I am aware of how Sheriff Brooks, the man who took ya underwing all those years ago, operates. He likely encouraged this kind of behavior or at least never corrected it. And Coleman is cut from the same cloth." The sheriff picked up Rhett's badge. He spit on it, then rubbed it on his coat sleeve. "I could use a second deputy. And I still think you'd be a good fit. But you will listen and do things my way, or you can get on your horse and leave now." He handed Rhett the star.

Jesse knocked over his beer. Liquid poured off the table onto his lap. He jumped up, knocking his chair backward. It smacked the floor. "Sheriff Crosson, sir, can we talk about this?" Jesse didn't need help. He could handle things around Gray Rock. It was mostly a peaceful town. But it had been without law since before Nate's trial when the sheriff had gotten shot. Then Jesse had taken to drinking. Was the sheriff still mad about that?

Rhett reached across the table. "I accept." He shook the sheriff's hand.

"Good. Now that that's settled, let's have another round, and you boys can fill me in on your investigation." Sheriff Crosson looked over at Jesse. "Why don't you go dry your pants by the stove. Ya look like ya pissed yourself. Rhett can catch me up on things."

Already, Jesse was being pushed aside. He suddenly understood Nathanial's jealously. "I know where he's at."

Sheriff Crosson and Rhett both sprang out of their chairs. The sheriff grabbed Jesse by the shoulders, squeezing him. "Then what're we waitin' for? Let's go."

"June, the whore I was talkin' to upstairs, she wouldn't tell me partner's location but said she'd take me there."

The sheriff's eyes narrowed. "How do you know it wasn't a trap?"

Jesse pulled the letter Nathanial had written out of his pocket and handed it to the sheriff.

"What's that?" Rhett watched as the sheriff scanned down the lines. When he finished reading, he thrust the paper toward Rhett.

"Where's she now?" The sheriff's eyes were on the balcony.

"June!" Jesse hollered. He hustled toward the stairs, calling her name several more times. At her door, he knocked.

Rhett turned the knob, shoving it open. The sheriff patted his shoulder.

Jesse grumbled under his breath, catching a harsh look from Sheriff Crosson. Jesse needed to focus on finding Nate.

The three of them stepped into the empty room. The place was a mess. It looked like downstairs. Her table and small nightstand were knocked over. The water pitcher lay in pieces on the floor, same as the lamp broken into shards.

"This is all wrong. It didn't look like this a few minutes ago. Everything was in order, nice and neat." Jesse's heart was racing. June had said Finch wanted the boy dead.

"Look." Rhett picked up a shawl off the floor. Blood drips stained one corner. "Finch must've took her."

Sheriff Crosson nodded. Jesse agreed.

"Rhett, when you and Finch were arguin', a man was standin' next to 'im. Finch called him Bowman. Do ya know 'im?"

"I know who he is." Rhett shrugged. "He owns the bar."

Sheriff Crosson ran for the stairs. Jesse and Rhett were on his heels. The bartender looked up from sweeping the floor as they marched toward him, their boots pounding the floor, echoing inside the room. He dropped his broom and put his hands up.

"Where's Bowman?" Sheriff Crosson snarled.

The barkeep's hand shook as he pointed to a door at the rear of the building.

Sheriff Crosson didn't bother knocking. He kicked down the door. Bowman, or who Jesse believed was the bar owner, popped out of his chair, dropping the glass of whiskey in his hand, and ran for the back entrance, throwing that door open. The sheriff grabbed him by the collar, smacked his back flat against the wall, and held him there.

"I wanna know why you said June knows where my son is," he said through gritted teeth.

There wasn't enough space between them and where the door swung as cold air spilled in. Rhett moved over, nudging in between Jesse and the sheriff. Jesse gave him a hard shove. Rhett fell into Sheriff Crosson, who then pressed into Bowman, and all three of them toppled through the moonlit doorway.

"What the hell?" Rhett cursed at Jesse.

Bowman scrambled to his feet.

Oh shit! Jesse cursed himself.

The sheriff picked himself up off the ground. Jesse took off running after Bowman. Rhett, a few strides ahead, dove at the bar owner. The two hit the ground and tussled a minute before

Rhett slugged him once. Bowman stopped fighting, gasping for air.

"The sheriff asked you a question. Now answer 'im!" Rhett held him pinned to the ground.

The sheriff walked over, giving Jesse a mean scowl. He withered under the hard glare. Good thing there was urgent business at hand. His tongue-lashing would come later, though hopefully not in front of Rhett.

"I seen June earlier." Bowman was breathing heavy. "She was with Goose. He used to ride with Finch. The two of 'em rode out in her buckboard. He was injured. I didn't think much of it. She's always had a sweet spot for 'im."

"Let 'im up," the sheriff said. "You sure it was Jim Reed you saw?"

Rhett hauled Bowman to his feet.

"I don't know 'im by that name." The man brushed the dirt off the knees of his pants. "But then Finch showed up, said he shot Goose for helpin' the kid escape." He straightened. "I thought about followin' June's wagon tracks, but then she showed up, no Goose, no kid. But I know her. She loves children, helps at the school sometimes. Even has a special plain dress she wears and wipes off all her makeup so the kids' folks won't complain. She looks all motherly." Bowmen frowned. "I figured she returned for supplies or somethin', and I'd wait and follow. But then Finch got into that damn argument with you." He pointed at Rhett. "And I opened my big mouth. I hadn't planned on tellin' 'im. I wanted that money for myself."

Sheriff Crosson turned, marching through the black alleyway toward the front of the building. He swung into the saddle.

"Where we headed?" Jesse grabbed the bridle of the bay. His and Rhett's horses were across the street.

"I know where Jim took Nathanial. They're waitin' for me. You two can't go." He jerked the reins, but Jesse held tight, not letting the bay turn.

"What about the woman?" Jesse understood that the sheriff's focus was on his little boy. "We don't know if she'll lead Finch elsewhere or straight to Nathanial." He feared she would give in to save herself if Finch got mean. Jesse couldn't forget that Finch had threatened to shoot a child. Why not a woman?

"Finch has two men with 'im. Could be others," Rhett added, standing next to Jesse.

Not that either of them believed the sheriff to be afraid of the odds, but he should be informed.

The sheriff nodded. "Get the woman. Then get your asses back to town. I'll meet ya here."

"Why can't we go with ya? We're your deputies." Rhett scratched his beard.

"Where I'm goin', I need to know the two of you are out of the way. I don't wanna shoot at the wrong man."

Rhett nodded. Jesse let go of the bay. Rhett hurried toward their horses. It would be dawn in two hours, but the moon was bright. Fresh tracks wouldn't be that hard to see if June guided Finch along the road. And a bright girl like June would realize that.

"Wait," Jesse called to the sheriff. He halted the bay. Jesse hustled. He unpinned the sheriff's badge. "This is yours." He wanted to tell him to be careful, that he had almost lost him once. Jesse blinked back the wetness in his eyes at the thought of going through that hell again.

Sheriff Crosson pinned the star on his coat, then spurred the bay. Jesse couldn't take his eyes off him as he headed out of town. He had promised to bring Nate home. Did the sheriff not trust him to make good on that promise? Was that one of the reasons he was there and that he'd hired Rhett? Had the sheriff lost faith in him? But he'd sent him searching. Why do that if he didn't believe Jesse could handle the job? Then again, the sheriff had still been mostly bedridden at the time he'd given this assignment to Jesse.

"Wake up!" Rhett snapped his fingers. He tossed Jesse's reins at him.

As Jesse swung into the saddle, he glared at Rhett.

CHAPTER 25

"IS THIS THE SPOT?" Nate yawned and slid off the horse.

Goose stepped down. "Yup, this is it." He rubbed at his eyes.

A rock overhang formed a natural dugout. On one end stood a hedge of brush taller than Goose. At the other end, the wind had blown dirt over the remains of a fallen tree. Over the course of years, nature had produced a barrier. They were sheltered somewhat on three sides and deep inside one of the canyon's corridors. It was a good hideout. Nate could picture Pa there. But Nate and Goose had turned so many times while riding in that he wasn't sure how to get out. Still, he had to try. It was his turn to help Goose.

Goose pulled the saddle off the mare, dropped the tack under the roof of rock, then picketed the animal behind the hedge out of sight of the main path they had ridden in on. Nate gathered sticks. After they had a small fire jumping, he waited 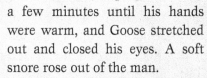 a few minutes until his hands were warm, and Goose stretched out and closed his eyes. A soft snore rose out of the man.

Nate slipped out of camp. He had no more than an hour before the sun would be up. Though, as tired as Goose was, and he was injured, he might sleep half the day. Nate would need every second in case he took a wrong turn. Being on foot wouldn't gain him any ground either. The poor mare was so exhausted that she didn't even eat what tufts of grass stood at her feet.

Nate tiptoed in his stocking feet until the dugout was no longer in sight. Then he ran. He was huffing and puffing long before the sun crested the mountaintop. The farther he could get from Goose, the likeliness of Pa hanging him lessened.

By midmorning, Nate stumbled into the rocky gorge. It'd taken him longer than he thought to get this far. He had taken a couple wrong turns, hit dead ends, then backtracked. His chest heaved to suck in air. Could his legs hold up, let alone his lungs?

A shadow fell over him. Nate's head snapped up. Montana stood above him on a slab of stone that was perched on an angle over a round boulder. He wagged his tail.

"Montana!" Nate scrambled over the mounds of rocks. Montana dashed between pillars of stone. They tackled into one another and rolled on the ground. Nate threw his arms around the animal's neck. "I've missed you, boy." Lots of licks wet his face and hair. "I'm glad you're okay." He believed if Montana could talk, he would've said the exact same thing.

Montana suddenly lifted his head, his ears standing tall. He pressed a big paw on Nate's chest, and somehow, he knew the wolf wanted him to stay down. That suspicion was confirmed a few seconds later when the hoofbeats of a single horse carried on the wind into Nate's ears. Montana eased down, covering him with his body but not crushing Nate with his full weight. The wolf turned his head, his sharp eyes on the rider until the hoof claps faded.

Montana stood.

Nate crawled out from underneath him and patted the wolf's head. "Let's get outta here," he whispered.

When they left the gorge, it wasn't by the main route. Nate followed Montana up over the rocks. He couldn't be tracked that way, not on horseback anyway. And after that close call, he suddenly had more energy.

They stopped and drank at the first water they came to. Nate dropped on all fours, lapping the coolness up next to his wolf. He was sweating from being on the move, but the wind was hellish chilly. He had left the blanket he'd taken from June's house rolled up back at camp, so if Goose woke and gave him a glance, he might be fooled into thinking Nate was there wrapped in the quilt. He shivered. It hadn't taken his body long to cool off.

Montana crossed the creek. He halted on the other side and looked back at Nate. No stepping stones were sticking up, and the water from bank to bank was too wide for him to jump.

Twice since leaving the gorge, riders had passed them. Montana had warned Nate in time that they were hidden before the hunters came into sight. So far, he'd let Montana lead, finding their path through the woods. Without a destination, their direction didn't matter. All Nate knew was that they were headed away from Denver and all the danger back there and deeper into the mountains. Yet Jesse was there somewhere, and he would be worried. And Pa was on his way there too … to find him, to protect him. Nate patted his chest. Nathanial Crosson. A son, a brother, part of a family, a family that was always there for one another no matter what, including his past.

But how could he find those two without getting caught? He couldn't just wander around the countryside on foot in the cold when there was an army of bounty hunters after him and expect to get lucky. Killed was what he'd get.

Nate didn't like the thought of going on without them. There were too many hunting him, but he now had a plan. If it went well, he would eventually be reunited with them. At the moment, he also hated the thought of getting his feet wet. He might never get warm. But Montana had steered him clear of harm that Nate might have otherwise walked right into. Plus, he hadn't slept in twenty-four hours.

He splashed through the current. "I hope I don't catch the sniffles. We have a long walk ahead of us."

At least they were headed in the right direction.

CHAPTER 26

NOLAN SLOWED THE BAY as he turned his horse into the corridor he and Jim had hidden in years ago. He hadn't gotten all the answers during those three days eons ago, and he wasn't there to start any arguments. Out ahead, a rider approached. Even from that distance, he recognized the slouched way Jim Reed sat in the saddle. Nathanial must have been behind him. Nolan touched spurs to the bay.

On the ground were kid-size toeprints, had to belong to his son, but why wasn't he wearing boots? His chest lifted. He hadn't smiled this wide in a long time. Though, the tracks were facing the direction Nolan had just ridden in from. Strange, but Jim, who had Nathanial underwing, was right there not ten yards away.

When they were close enough to shake hands, they each pulled up the reins. "Hello, Jim."

"Ain't you a sight?" Jim shook Nolan's hand.

Nolan leaned forward, looking behind his friend. He had expected Nate to pop out. "Where's Nathanial?"

"You ain't gonna believe this, but he slipped away from me. I'm sorry. I told 'im how we hid out here once, and I think I might've scared 'im off."

"Did you tell 'im that cockamamie story about me threatenin' to hang you the next time we met?" Nolan scowled.

Jim nodded. "I wasn't gonna, but he looked disappointed when he found out we parted on good terms."

"Dammit, Jim. Stop tellin' people I said that. I never did. You made that shit up. Now my little boy believes I'm gonna kill ya." Nolan shook his head. "Geez, you can be a real ass sometimes."

Jim grinned. "I only lie so you can save face. You're a lawman. A well-known one at that. It wouldn't do to have anyone know we're friends. But I swear." Jim put up a hand. "I'd have confessed everythin' had I thought for a minute Nathanial would run off."

Nolan wheeled the bay. "Well, you can help me find 'im."

"Planned on it." Jim's horse fell into pace.

They weaved through a maze of crossroads inside the canyon walls for fifty, sixty yards, following Nate's occasion footprint, then made a sharp right into a dry basin where the path widened. At the far end, they pulled up reins at a seep and let the horses drink.

Nolan looked over at Jim

"What?" Jim said. "If you're worried, don't be. We'll find 'im. He couldn't have gotten that far on foot."

"It's not that." Nolan shrugged. Nate's prints were less than an hour old. He'd have his son in his arms soon. "I don't know." He shook his head. "It's just that I always imagined our kids growin' up playin' together."

Jim chuckled. "You mean when we were twenty, you didn't picture this?" He waved a hand at their cold, hard surroundings. The wind howled. His face sobered. "This ain't my dream either. And I don't want ya thinkin' it ever was. I shouldn't have run away." Jim was quiet for a minute. "I was scared. I didn't wanna die."

They turned their horses.

Nolan touched spurs to the bay. Who wouldn't be afraid of a noose? But there were witnesses.

"I saw the whole thing." Nolan thumped his chest. This was an unsettled rift. "And my father loved you like a son." He pointed a straight finger. "He would have done everythin' in his power as sheriff to make sure ya didn't swing."

"I know that. It wasn't the trial I was afraid of," Jim snapped. "Believe me, I wish I would've stayed and faced all those big ranchers and their money and had my name cleared. But there's more to it. And I don't wanna rehash the past."

They steered their horses into an adjoining stone alleyway. No horse tracks. No one else had ridden through. Nolan didn't see Nathanial's prints either. His gut tightened. He turned in the saddle, staring down another long path. Every stone wall looked too similar.

Jim searched the dirt ahead of them. "What if the boy took a wrong turn?"

"Nathanial has a good sense of direction." Nolan wasn't forgetting the facts, but as a father, he was worried. "I also taught him to map using the stars. There was a full moon last night. Plenty of light." His son also knew how to use land-marks to backtrack.

"I do envy you that boy." Jim pulled the makings of a smoke out of his coat pocket. "At the mention of your name, his eyes light up." He licked the paper before rolling the tobacco inside the parchment.

"It ain't too late." Nolan clapped his friend's shoulder. "You can still have a family."

One corner of Jim's mouth lifted. "You're still dreamin', ain't ya?" He shook his head. "Are ya forgettin' I'm a wanted man? Besides that, do ya have any idea how long it's been since I lived with a roof over my head? And I don't know if I could get used to a woman constantly squawkin' at me." He puffed on his cigarette.

"Marriage ain't like that." Nolan frowned. "Kate and I are a complement to one another. We both know when to give and take. I ain't sayin' we don't bicker, because we do." He looked down at the gold band on his finger. "But every time I walk in the door and set eyes on that woman and the kids…" he smiled. "Other than this damn mess with the Fletchers, I am a happy man."

They pulled up reins at the bottom of the gorge, letting the horses catch their wind before the climb.

"That all sounds great." His friend sighed. "But be realistic. Say I get married. Then what? We have to hide out the rest of our days so some bounty hunter don't shoot me down? I don't wanna leave behind a widow and kids." He flicked the butt of his smoke into the dirt.

Nolan wouldn't give up. He'd always hoped his friend would amend his ways and go straight. "You can change your name. Others have done it. I'm sure you can find honest work. I'd vouch for ya."

He meant every word. Though they'd taken different paths in life, they still had each other's back. Jim was a criminal and Nolan a lawman, but he trusted that man with his life.

Jim stepped down off his horse and tossed the reins to Nolan. "I can't ask ya to do that." He picked up one of his horse's front legs, pulled his knife, and scooped a stone out of her hoof. "I won't let ya jeopardize your career. It might sound silly, but I'm proud of ya."

Nolan's saddle creaked as he shifted. "I appreciate that. But some things are more important than a job." he handed over the reins. "It hurt when you just disappeared without even sayin' good-bye. You could've said somethin'. I thought our friendship meant more to ya than that."

"I've apologized for that—a couple times. Let's not dig it up again." Jim began to swing a leg over, then stopped. "What do ya make of this?" He pointed near the remnant of his cig.

A child-size footprint stopped at the face of a wide boulder. Nolan searched the mound of rocks that formed this side of the gorge. Then he scanned the path they would use with the horses. No footprints.

"Nathanial climbed up over the rocks." Nolan stepped down. "Here." He handed his reins to Jim.

Nolan climbed up through the stony gorge. He stopped where there was a circle of dirt between two large slabs. He cocked his head. Scuff marks, lots of them. He picked up several short strands of gray fur. Then he pressed a finger into what he was certain was Nate's heelprint. The sign he was reading didn't make sense.

"What'd ya find?" Jim hollered from below.

"Wolf tracks." Nolan shook his head. "The smudges in the dirt, it almost looks like Nate was rollin' around with the thing, but no blood." Thank God. His heart was pumping hard.

"That would be Montana, Nate's pet," Jim called, hands cupped around his mouth.

"What?" Nolan's brow arched. He stared down over the rocks at him.

"Ya heard me right." Jim lifted his hat, pushing back his hair. "And that damn beast is a man-killer. Seen it myself two, three times. But for whatever reason, the animal has taken to protectin' Nathanial as though he was its pup."

Nolan didn't like the sounds of that. Not one damn bit.

At the top of the gorge, Nolan picked up Nathanial's trail or, rather, a large wolf print. An hour later, they let the horses drink at a creek where Nate had stopped before them, as evidenced by the partial imprint in the dirt of a small foot. The ground around the print was still wet where the boy must have splashed water.

"Nathanial ain't that far ahead of us. Half an hour at most." This was going to be a good day. Nolan's arms ached to scoop up his little boy.

"If ya don't mind, I could use some coffee." Jim flipped open his saddlebags. "I know we're close, but I only got a few hours' sleep. If I don't do somethin' to wake up, I'm gonna fall right outta the saddle."

Nolan yawned. Judging by the boy's stride, he wasn't in a hurry as though he were being chased, and they hadn't come across any bounty hunters or others hunting the child. There didn't seem to be any immediate danger. "I could use some myself. Make it strong."

He picketed the horses on some tall blades of brown grass along the creek. "I rode into Denver last night, thinkin' I'd get a hotel room," he said over his shoulder as Jim gathered wood. "Instead, I find one of my deputies startin' a bar fight and the other runnin' to the rescue."

Jim set the pot on the flames. "Sounds like us at that age."

Nolan squatted next to the flames, warming his hands. "Don't repeat that to them. I'll never hear the end of it."

His friend laughed.

Nolan pulled up his coat collar. "I just want 'em to take the job serious. To do their very best to bring justice to the wronged. And they do, but they're young and—" Nolan was quiet for a minute. There was a reason he never quit when in pursuit of a criminal. He was known to always catch his man. His friend had everything to do with that. "Do you know why I'm such a hard ass when it comes to stoppin' crime?"

The coffeepot hissed. "Well, it can't be the company because everyone I know on this side of the law is an asshole." Jim poured them each a cup.

Nolan smirked. "I would agree. Present company excluded." He took a drink.

"Don't count me out." Jim grinned. "I have my days." He raised his cup.

Nolan did likewise. "Don't we all?"

They drank their coffee, and Jim chewed a piece of jerked beef as a few quiet minutes passed. Nolan cleared his throat. Jim looked up.

"I never forgave my father." Nolan dumped the remains of his coffee. "The look on your face when he told you that he didn't have enough evidence to press charges against that rich cattleman, Doolittle, for the murder of your folks. It still haunts me."

Jim froze. Nolan wasn't sure his friend was breathing.

"We argued. I told 'im he should press the smaller ranchers to testify against Doolittle. To have 'em band together. The fact that Doolittle had his men gun down your ma and pa—he would do it again. It was just a matter of time. He was pushin' all the smaller ranchers one by one off their grass, grabbing land. But even the ones he burned out wouldn't speak up." Nolan rubbed a hand over his face. "Maybe my father was afraid of 'im too. I went as far as to call 'im a coward."

"Is that why you and Mary packed up and left town? Your letter said only that you had a fallin'-out with your pa."

Nolan nodded. "Before that, before you shot Doolittle, I told my father I was going after the cattleman. Everyone in that valley knew he was guilty of murder. I aimed to prove it and bring 'im in."

"Why didn't ya tell me?" Deep wrinkles set across Jim's forehead.

"I didn't want justice twisted into revenge. But before I took a step out the door that day, my father stripped my badge."

Jim cursed under this breath. "Ya should've told me."

"I planned on it. Came to tell ya right away, but when I found ya on the street, Doolittle and his men were there tauntin' ya. He was askin' for a fight. And when his hand swept down, I thought he was drawin' a gun the same as you and everyone else." Nolan took a deep breath.

"But you didn't squeeze the trigger. I did," Jim said.

"No one realized it was just a flask in his right hand 'til we rolled 'im over." Nolan stirred the fire with a long stick. "Had ya stayed, I think it would've been ruled an accidental shootin'. Ya acted in self-defense."

"True. But a lot of people heard me threaten Doolittle before that day, includin' his son." Jim poured what was left in the pot over the fire, which produced a steam cloud.

"Yeah, but I never pegged ya for bein' a coward." Nolan stood, kicking dirt over the embers. "Ya just up and ran." He threw up his hands.

"Careful, my friend. That sounds a lot like an insult." Jim picked up his saddlebags.

"Wasn't meant to be a compliment," Nolan said in a dry tone. They eyeballed one another from across the outed fire. "Mary." He poked Jim's chest with a straight finger. "A new bride, my wife. And you stood as my best man. She could hardly console poor Amy, her dearest friend. You remember her." Nolan leaned in nose to nose. "The woman you were engaged to."

"Drop it, will ya? We've been through this before." Jim turned toward the horses, his saddlebags slung over his shoulder.

Nolan grabbed his arm, spinning him. "This time, I want all the answers." His jaw tightened. "Amy was with child. You left when she needed you most." He squeezed Jim's arm. "I hated you for a long time."

Jim jerked free. "I swear I didn't know 'bout any baby. I've told ya this before. And I did think 'bout comin' back, lots. How many times do I have to say it? Hours a day for months on end, I was tortured by thoughts of all of it. I hated myself. Is that what ya wanna hear?"

"Then why didn't ya come back?" Nolan stared straight into his friend's eyes, expecting to see anger because of the prodding to understand the truth. Instead, wetness magnified Jim's green irises.

He turned and picked up his reins.

"I couldn't face Amy. Not after what I'd done. I was afraid she'd have nothin' to do with me." Jim swung into the saddle and touched spurs to his horse.

Nolan stepped up onto the bay. "She was there. She knew that shootin' wasn't your fault." Water splashed his boots as his horse trotted through the creek behind Jim's.

Their mounts scrambled the rocky bank on the opposite side. Jim pushed a branch out of the way. He led as the path before them narrowed, forced into single file.

"It wasn't the killin'. I signed over the ranch to Doolittle," Jim blurted. "Everything Pa and I ever worked for. Amy's and my entire future." He was quiet for a long minute. His horse stepped over the trunk of a downed tree.

"Why'd ya do it?" This was the first Nolan had heard it direct from the source. "You ain't a man that buckles easy." He searched the ground for sign of his son. A snapped twig and a patch of parted grass caught his eyes.

Jim rubbed his temple. "Doolittle hired a man to kill me. This fella knocked on my door one night, shoved an iron in my gut." He turned his animal and stared at Nolan.

"Bold move." Nolan knew his friend wouldn't just bend for the average man. "Ya know a name?"

Jim stiffly shook his head, but his eyes shifted. Nolan didn't believe him. Why would his friend lie? There had to be a good reason.

The trail widened, and they started their horses forward side by side.

"The fella worked me over quite a bit before I agreed." Jim's hands balled, squeezing the reins. "When it came down to it, I couldn't sign. The fella who'd come to do Doolittle's dirty work hit me a few more times. I was nearly unconscious when he forced my signature, his hand atop mine." He blew out. "Our future home, the cattle, everythin' my folks left behind, it was all gone. How was I supposed to explain that?"

Nolan pulled up reins. He stared at the ground. Not that what his friend was saying wasn't important, but the length of Nathanial's stride had changed drastically. He circled his horse and found a hint of a footprint.

Jim halted his mount. "What is it?"

"Nathanial's picked up his pace." Nolan didn't see any other tracks besides the wolf prints.

Jim twisted in the saddle. "Do ya think it's Finch?"

Nolan shook his head. No hoofprints. "No one's chasin' 'im."

"Second wind, then." Jim turned forward, staring along the route he predicted Nate had taken. Straight ahead, flat ground, and easy, not thick with brush or too rocky.

"He went that way." Nolan pointed toward the white mountain peak.

He didn't have to see another track to know. The kid wasn't runnin' scared. And the speed with which he was now traveling suggested a purpose. His son had a vision, an endpoint in his mind. He knew where he was going. He had also completely changed direction from his previous days of running. He was now headed north. And from the peak, he could set a course. From up there, Nathanial might be able to see into Wyoming.

Nolan smiled.

"What in the hell are ya grinnin' 'bout?" Jim cocked his head. "That climb to the top could kill the horses."

"My little boy's headed home." Nolan nudged the gelding. But they weren't going to trail him up near the snow line and risk their animals. "It's the only reason I can think for Nathanial to turn around and go north."

"Maybe he's just tryin' to throw off anyone followin' 'im. Ya know, leadin' 'em in a circle." Jim fell into pace next to the bay.

Nolan couldn't explain his gut feeling. He knew without a doubt that his son was on his way to Gray Rock. "We'll skirt the ridgeline. Try to get ahead of 'im." He pointed where the mountain dipped into a valley." Hopefully, we can catch 'im there."

"If you say so." Jim agreed.

An hour later, they left the horses nibbling grass behind a cluster of evergreens and crept up through the rocks until they found a spot that not only hid them but gave them a clear view of the pass between the hills. They were maybe thirty yards off the trail at most.

They waited, hunkered between a cluster of tall boulders. Nolan chewed on his lip.

"Stop it. You're makin' me nervous," Jim whispered. Then he grabbed Nolan's shoulder. "Look." He nodded down the slope.

A wolf, a large male, biggest Nolan had ever seen, stood in the middle of the trail. The animal's nose was up, sniffing. If that was Montana, then where was Nathanial? Nolan began to ease his rifle up.

Jim caught his arm. "Don't." He kept his voice low. "That boy of yours'll never forgive ya." He lifted his gun, but the wolf had disappeared.

"Dammit." Nolan stood.

Jim straightened, his gun down at his side. "Nathanial can't be far away."

Behind them, a deep growl chilled the air. They both turned slowly toward the mean sound. On a rock that put the wolf a head higher than where the two of them stood, the wolf curled his lips back, baring his pointed fangs. He snapped his jaws and jerked his head.

"Montana!"

Nolan's heart started again. That was Nathanial's voice. He glanced toward the trail. The boy wasn't there, maybe back among the trees.

"Where are ya, boy?" Nate called a second time.

Wetness filled Nolan's eyes. His son was there somewhere within reach after all this time. He looked about, expecting to see him each time he turned. Where was he? Nolan opened his mouth. Before he could call his son, Jim slapped a hand over Nolan's face.

"Don't say a word and stop movin'," Jim hissed. "The only thing that's gonna keep us alive is Nate callin' that beast away."

The wolf lowered its head. The blacks of its eyes narrowed.

"Montana! Come!" Nate sounded close.

Nolan's heart ached worse each time Nathanial called the wolf's name.

With the thrust of its head, the wolf bit at them, then leaped over their heads. Nolan spun one way. Jim stumbled the other. When they picked themselves up off the ground, the wolf was gone, and Nathanial was silent.

Jim rested a hand on Nolan's shoulder. "Let's get the horses. We can still find Nathanial."

"We're gonna have to kill that wolf," Nolan said more to himself than to Jim. His friend was right. Nate would never forgive him.

"It'll be my pleasure." Jim ran toward the horses.

Nolan halted behind the evergreens. Jim stared at the empty patch of grass. They both looked around.

Nolan squatted and touched a wolf track. "Dammit!"

It could take them hours, if not days or longer, to track down the horses. A wolf as big as that one would have scared them for sure.

Nolan's chest was still pounding, and a heavy ache set in around his heart. He'd missed his chance.

CHAPTER 27

JESSE GLANCED AWAY from the little cabin, smoke puffing up out of the chimney. "How long we gonna wait?" He stretched his legs where he lay on the ground with his rifle held ready. The cold was seeping up through him. His damn clothes were drawing damp.

June had led Finch around in a circle through the hills until the sun was overhead, and nowhere along the way had a chance showed itself that they could safely take her away from the men holding her captive. Jesse didn't want her getting hurt. Rhett had agreed. So they had followed at a distance, waiting for the right time.

Rhett shrugged. "You'd think someone would have to take a piss by now. They've been in there for a few hours." He worked his fingers. "There ain't a back door. They gotta come out the front."

All Jesse could figure was that June had led Finch there in hopes of keeping the gang stalled and away from Jim Reed and Nathanial. This was likely the spot where she had left the two. How else would she have known about the place? It wasn't likely that they'd stumbled across it. It also wouldn't be hard to believe that a man would return for her. She was a little on the short side, but the curve of her hips and the way she kissed made up for that.

"If we're gettin' tired of waitin', Finch probably is too," Rhett said.

Not that they believed Jim Reed and Nathanial were returning, but Jesse would bet June had told Finch something along those lines, and that's why Finch was waiting at the cabin. And with three men and one woman, the place would be crowded. Too tight to stir comfortably. With June in there, they couldn't just announce themselves as lawmen and risk a gunfight. She might get shot. And Finch wasn't the type to surrender.

The door creaked.

Jesse's eyes narrowed on the cabin once again. Finch shoved June outside. Her ankle twisted as she stumbled off the porch and fell, hands and knees in the dirt. One corner of her mouth dripped blood, and a dark bruise marred her eye. Finch or someone had obviously smacked her around, but she hadn't made a noise or Jesse would've burst in. That poor woman had been through enough.

Jesse stood and walked out of the tree line across from the front of the house. "You're under arrest, Finch." Kidnapping. Murder. Jesse would hang him.

Finch ripped June up off the ground, holding her between them. "Take another step and she's dead." He retreated toward the corral and horses, the Yaqui and the other fella a step off his pace, both holding guns.

Rhett stepped out from inside the open barn door. "Drop those guns."

The Yaqui swung his rifle. Rhett's gun boomed. June screamed.

Rhett ducked as the boards above his head splintered with buckshot. Finch threw June against the ground and ran for the horses. The other fella fired at Jesse. He dove behind a water trough. They exchanged shots. Finch jumped his horse over the fence and into the tree line. Dammit. He was getting away. Before the one firing at Jesse reached his horse, Rhett turned his aim in that direction and pulled the trigger. The fella timbered forward with a hole through his chest.

June jumped up, breaking for the house. The Yaqui pitched his hatchet, spinning it through the air.

"June!" Jesse hollered.

She screeched the second the blade sank between her shoulder blades. She dropped to the ground, flat on her stomach, blood staining the back of her dress, and she groaned.

Jesse ran toward her. A bullet kicked up dirt at his feet. Then Rhett's rifle exploded. The Yaqui, bleeding from his gut, turned on his toes, lifting his pistol. Rhett squeezed the trigger a second time, saving Jesse's life. The bullet nailed the Yaqui near the heart, and he fell over, face in the dirt.

When Jesse reached June, blood had begun to pool around her body. He gently turned her, holding her in his arms. She choked up red. But her tear-filled eyes were focused on him.

"I don't wanna die." She clung to him and gasped for breath.

"June, I—" He didn't know what to say. There was nothing he could do. She was bleeding out right before his eyes.

"Get her inside. Make her comfortable." Rhett touched Jesse's shoulder. "I'm goin' after Finch." He hustled in the direction of their horses.

Jesse lifted June off the ground and carried her into the cabin. Once he pulled that hatchet out, blood would gush. It wouldn't take long, seconds maybe, for her to bleed to death. But if he left the blade in her, she'd suffer just the same.

"Help me," she pleaded in a weak voice. Her eyes rolled, and her grip on his shirt slipped off.

He touched the soft side of her wrist, finding her weak heartbeat. He wiped his forehead. She'd just passed out. He laid her carefully on her stomach. What he was about to do might not work, but it was better than just watching her die.

He pulled shells from his gun belt and used his knife to pop the caps off the tops. After tearing away the back of her blouse, he dumped the black powder along each side of the hatchet. Once he pulled that thing, he might have to cauterize her a second time if the bleeding didn't stop.

"One, two, three." Jesse struck match to powder.

A flame sizzled, and June screamed. He yanked out the blade. She was still bleeding, not much, but she'd already lost a lot of blood, enough that she couldn't afford to lose any more. He repeated the steps as quick as he could. Flame sparked along the line of skin, then expired once the powder burned off.

June didn't move.

He shook her a little. "June?"

A hoarse moan rose out of her, but her eyes remained shut.

Jesse flopped into a chair. He ran both hands through his hair, knocking his hat off and onto the floor.

What was he supposed to do now? Rhett was gone, or one of them could have ridden into town and fetched the doctor—if there was one. The sheriff was on his way to wherever to fetch Nathanial, and Jesse had no choice but to wait it out there until June was able to travel—if she didn't die. He rubbed his temples. Perhaps Rhett would get Finch, then come back when Jesse didn't catch up. When he left, it hadn't looked good for June.

Jesse stood and walked outside the cabin. He'd best gather some firewood and bring in his horse. He filled the empty chambers of his gun. Finch wasn't the only one in the area hunting the kid, and if word had spread that June knew where the boy was, others might come hunting her.

Nigh to dark, Jesse put more wood on the fire. Then he went outside and took a turn about the place. All was quiet. No one had come around or even passed by.

He went back inside. The hours ticked away as Jesse sponged now and then at June's head. She woke for a few minutes, drank, then fell back to sleep. He stood, stretched, and kept the coffee hot. It was hard not to worry about everything else going on.

———

Jesse leaned against the window frame. Four days had drifted by with no sign of Rhett or the sheriff. A deep shade of winter blue lit the morning, though it wasn't that time of year yet. Flurries twirled in the air. The loft door on the barn banged open and closed. Tumbleweeds collected overnight between the horse trough and the fence rail.

A horse and rider appeared in the not-too-far distance. Jesse hustled to the door with his Winchester.

Rhett pulled up reins near the barn. He held two horses in tow. The big bay, Jesse recognized.

Rhett put up his hands. "Don't ask 'cause I don't know. I found 'em both wanderin'."

Jesse patted the bay's nose. "Wish ya could talk."

"Finch got away," Rhett said. "I stopped trailin' 'im when I found these horses."

"You think he did this?" Jesse couldn't imagine that Finch had outgunned Sheriff Crosson. But Finch might have shot him and the man with Nathanial in the back, then took the kid. There were two horses. So the sheriff must've been with Jim Reed and Nate.

Rhett shrugged. "I searched. Didn't find any blood or even boot prints." He stepped down off his horse.

A bad situation had just turned worse. Sheriff Crosson was either injured, dead, or on foot out in the mountains. God only knew where Nathanial was or who had him.

"You stay with June. I'll ride to town and fetch help." He nodded toward the house. "Then we can go after the sheriff."

Rhett's eyes widened. "You mean to tell me that whore's still alive?"

"Barely," Jesse said. He'd done for her what he knew how. She needed someone with more knowledge of wound care.

"I'm sorry for her, but we need to search for the sheriff. Finch could have the boy for all we know." Rhett led his horse into the corral where he stripped off the saddle. "I just want coffee. Then I'll be ready to ride. If ya wanna fetch a doc, you go on, but I ain't waitin' around."

"You're a prick." Jesse grabbed the reins of the sheriff's bay. "She's a person like any other." Not that Jesse was dismissing the danger concerning Nathanial, but this was a result of that, and it just wouldn't be right to leave her there alone, unable to fend for herself. She would die. Maybe he should check on her before he left. Would Rhett even give her a glance?

"You're just mad 'cause the sheriff hired me." Rhett walked toward the house. "You practically fell out of your chair."

That was true, but—

"I like workin' with ya, Rhett. I just don't always understand your attitude." He left the bay standing in front of the cabin.

Rhett stepped inside, and Jesse followed.

They both halted.

June's arm hung limply over the edge of the bed. She stared blankly at the ceiling, her eyes waxen.

"Huh." Rhett patted Jesse's shoulder. "That settles that, don't it?"

Jesse scowled.

Rhett picked up the coffeepot and a cup. "It ain't like she was someone's wife." There was something bitter in his eyes.

In two huffing strides, Jesse jabbed Rhett in the mouth, knocking him backward into the cookstove, spilling his coffee. "Get a shovel."

"The hell I will." Rhett tossed what remained in his cup in Jesse's face. "There's only one kind of sweatin' I do over a whore."

Coffee dripped off Jesse's chin. He lunged, buckling Rhett in two at the waist. They hit the wall. A shelf holding tins fell and clanked on the floor. Rhett drilled an elbow into Jesse's ribs two, three times. God, he could hardly breathe. He thrust an uppercut into the underside of Rhett's chin.

"Aw! I bit my tongue!" Rhett cried, then walloped Jesse upside the head with the first thing within reach, a wooden batter bowl.

Stars burst inside Jesse's head, and he dropped to his knees.

"What in the hell is wrong with ya?" Rhett shoved him.

Jesse fell onto his back and held his thumping skull, not moving to get up off the floor.

"Are you really that upset over a prostitute?" Rhett slumped into a chair. He held a rag against his bleeding tongue.

Jesse pointed to a picture on the wall. Rhett stood. After a long minute of staring, he turned toward Jesse, and what he saw was deep hurt. Rhett's eyes glistened.

Jesse pushed up. "I found her husband's grave out behind the house. And that of a child, a daughter, Anna."

"I'll get a shovel." Rhett headed out the door.

Jesse wrapped June in a quilt, and they laid her to rest with her family.

"I'm sorry," Rhett said as they packed the dirt mounding her grave. "Sometimes I don't think straight. I haven't stopped worryin' since findin' those horses." He rested against the spade in his hands. "I shouldn't have assumed there wasn't any more to June than bein' a saloon girl."

Jesse nodded. He had jumped to the wrong conclusion more than once in his life. He believed Rhett's apology was sincere. Otherwise, he wouldn't have helped dig June's grave.

Twenty minutes later, they were riding toward the mountains. The heavy breathing of their mounts and the hiss of the wind between branches were the only sounds. What would they find? The bay wasn't a spooky horse, and the sheriff was a better-than-average rider, excellent in fact. He'd never gotten thrown that Jesse had seen. But it wasn't just the sheriff's horse that had turned up. And horses didn't run off for no reason. Jesse hated to think the worst. And where did that leave Nathanial?

They'd ridden about five miles when they crossed a flat meadow. On the other side of a grove of trees at the far end, the earth opened into a steep, rocky gorge. The mountains were on their right.

"Jesse!"

Jesse twisted in the saddle.

Sheriff Crosson walked out of the tree line, and there was a man with him. Jesse could only guess that was Jim Reed, the outlaw June had made him give his word not to arrest.

He pulled up reins in front of the sheriff. "Good to see ya, sir."

Sheriff Crosson smiled. "I can't tell ya how good it is to see those damn horses. I'm sick of chasin' 'em. My feet hurt."

Jesse handed over the reins of the bay. Rhett tossed the lead of the other horse to Jim.

"Jim." The sheriff swung into the saddle. "This's Jesse Adams. Jesse, this is a good friend of mine, Jim Reed."

"I've heard a lot 'bout you, son. It's nice to meet ya." Jim offered a hand.

Jesse accepted and shook. He trusted Sheriff Crosson. If he wasn't concerned about having a wanted man tied up, then Jesse wasn't going to sweat it. The sheriff was too smart to be double-crossed. And Jesse wasn't forgetting that Jim had helped Nathanial.

Jesse looked around. "Where's partner?"

Sheriff Crosson lifted his chin toward the mountains. "He was gone when I found Jim."

"Maybe that bastard"—Rhett pointed at Jim—"handed the boy over to one of his partners and is leadin' you around, keepin' ya off their trail." Rhett spit. "I've seen you before. I know you ride with Finch."

Sheriff Crosson jerked his reins, butting the bay right alongside Rhett's horse.

Before he could say anything, Jim spoke up.

"Nolan, let it drop. He's right." Jim looked around at each of them. "I told ya no one would accept a friendship between an outlaw an' a lawman."

Jesse had to admit he was a bit bothered by the fact, but not enough to be rude.

Rhett glared at Jim. If he was trying to impress the sheriff by showing his toughness, this wasn't the right way. The sheriff's jaw set in a clench. How would he handle this? Rhett had the look of wanting to string up that other fella, and Jim was way too calm, slouched in the saddle, for Jesse not to feel uneasy. But Jim's hand rested on his pistol.

"We're wastin' time," Sheriff Crosson snapped. "Our objective is to find Nathanial. That means workin' together." He gave Rhett a hard look. "Jim's no sidewinder. If I didn't trust 'im, he wouldn't be here." The sheriff grabbed Rhett by the front of his coat and jerked him forward. "My patience only runs so thick. I do not tolerate my judgment bein' questioned—Deputy."

Jesse waited for Rhett to be fired. Inwardly, he grinned. Gray Rock wasn't big enough for two deputies. One of them would end up being more of a note runner, and Jesse would be damned if he'd become the jailhouse filing clerk, demoted to a paper pusher. Not that he didn't do some of that in the day-to-day, but this was different.

"Sheriff Coleman and your old job are that way." Sheriff Crosson pointed. "I don't need a man who's so quick to start fights without good cause."

Jesse never figured that the sheriff was kidding about his one-time allowance. He had already forgiven Rhett for instigating the barroom brawl.

The sheriff shoved Rhett away. "I can understand your mistrust of Jim. You don't know 'im the way I do. All you're aware of is his criminal record. But then you should have said somethin' to me, either out in the open or pulled me aside. I would've answered any questions you had."

Rhett looked around at the ground as if the right thing to say was waiting there behind a rock or tree. Leather creaked as he shifted.

Jesse adjusted himself in the saddle too. He felt kind of bad for Rhett. It was a privilege to work each day with Sheriff Crosson, a lawman of such high standing. Not many men received the opportunity. It was an honor. Rhett had to be realizing his loss.

"Sheriff Crosson, sir." Jesse's mind was on his little partner, and Rhett was another pair of eyes and ears to search for the boy. Jesse might regret opening his mouth. They didn't know who might have Nathanial, so as far as he could figure, they weren't in any position to turn away help. Rhett wasn't as accurate with a gun as Jesse, but he for damn sure wasn't afraid of a fight.

"What?" Sheriff Crosson turned and stared at Jesse.

"Finch got away." Jesse straightened in the saddle. "The four of us combin' the woods for Nathanial would be better than only three."

"He's right," Jim said.

Sheriff Crosson looked over at Rhett.

Rhett's Adam's apple bobbed as he swallowed hard. "If you'd allow me, I would like to ride with ya 'til we find Nathanial." There was a humbleness to his tone.

Crosson nodded. "All right. But if I see your hand anywhere near your gun and Jim's back is turned, I'll make you eat that iron."

"Yes, sir." Rhett backed his gelding off a step or two.

They turned their horses. Rhett stayed a length behind and didn't engage in any talk. Jesse, on the other hand, was learning all kinds of things. He grinned as Jim went on.

"Nolan and I couldn't have been more than ten." Jim snickered. "We snuck into the local cathouse for a peek of what we weren't exactly sure of at the time."

"Did ya get caught?" Jesse leaned forward on the horn.

The sheriff laughed. "The madam chased us right out the front door into the street."

Jim nudged Jesse. "And you'll never guess who was standin' there."

Jesse scratched his chin. "Who?"

Jim jerked a thumb toward the sheriff. "His pa, the sheriff."

Jesse burst out laughing. "I bet ya got a heck of an ear-chewin'."

"Shit. We got more than that." Jim smirked. "We were marched into the alleyway, thrown up against a wall, and got our asses smacked with his belt."

"I couldn't sit for a couple hours." The sheriff chuckled. "Then I caught the devil from Ma all night."

Jim patted Jesse's shoulder. "It was worth seein' all them titties."

They all chuckled.

"It's hard to believe Pa ever pinned badges on the two of us." The sheriff shook his head.

"You were a lawman?" Rhett said from behind them. Everyone turned. He stared at Jim.

"I was a deputy for a time." Jim reined in enough to allow Rhett to fall into pace. "Nolan and I worked for his father."

"What made you turn against the law?" Rhett might have been being nosey, but Jesse was curious too. He liked Jim a lot.

"My father had just bought some land that adjoined his property. I always wanted to be a rancher like my pa." Jim smiled. "The land was to be a weddin' gift for me and my soon-to-be wife. The two parcels together amounted to a little over three hundred and forty acres. Plenty for us to raise cattle. And both places had good water. Amy and I even had a spot picked out to build a house."

Sheriff Crosson pulled up reins. They had reached a dip between the mountains. Jesse and the other two halted, bunched in around the sheriff. On the ground, there were wolf tracks, days old.

"This's where our horses got spooked and ran off." The sheriff's eyes glistened.

Jesse didn't know what to make of the emotion other than Sheriff Crosson was seeing his little boy being taken farther away. Jesse had imagined it himself more than once.

"There's a footprint." Jim lifted his chin. "Looks like Nathanial went that way." He nudged his gelding.

"Wait." Rhett caught him by the arm. "Finish what you were sayin' 'bout the land. What happened that you would leave what sounds like a great life, good friends, family, and turn criminal?"

Jim took a breath. "Okay, but let's keep searchin'."

They started along a trail wide enough for two horses. Jim and the sheriff led off. Jesse and Rhett, side by side, bunched in behind.

"A cattleman with a much bigger spread aimed to have our land. His men gunned down my folks. A week later, I shot 'im. It was an accident, but I kilt 'im." Jim glanced at the sheriff. "The rancher's son then hired Salazar Null to kill me."

"The assassin?" Rhett's face wrinkled up.

Jesse didn't know the name. He looked over at the sheriff who was leaned in listening and stiffened.

"He strung me up. But it was dark, and he couldn't see that the branch was rotted. When I dropped, there was a crack. He must have thought it was my neck. The branch gave way, and I fell and hit the dirt. I lost consciousness. So he had to've believed I was dead. When I came to, Salazar was gone."

They veered around a cluster of boulders. On the far side, as a tight group, they turned where the sheriff pointed at a dislodged pebble, a scuff mark from five little toes dragging in the dirt.

"Why didn't ya go to the town sheriff?" Jesse would have.

"I thought 'bout it." Jim rested a hand on Sheriff Crosson's shoulder, their horses moving in rhythm side by side. "Your father was no match for Salazar Null. The only reason he hung me instead of shootin' me was that Doolittle's son demanded it." Jim took a breath. "I know my best friend too well. You would've ridden after Salazar and gotten yerself killed."

"Why didn't ya go after 'im together?" Rhett picked up his canteen.

"He never told me. This is the first I'm hearin' it," Sheriff Crosson grumbled. "Instead, he skipped town."

Jim nodded. "I did. I knew that if Salazar ever found out I was alive, he'd come back and finish the job." He faced the sheriff. "I knew you wouldn't stay out of the middle of it. And I didn't believe Amy would want a coward for a husband. I told ya how Salazar forced me to sign over the ranch."

"Fearin' a man like Salazar Null isn't bein' a coward. You should've come to me. And you should've let Amy decide," the sheriff boomed.

The horses all pranced.

"Even if she had agreed to still marry me, what kind of life would that have been? Lookin' over our shoulders every day, her worryin' herself to death. And we would've had to start over from scratch!" Jim's voice rose above the sheriff's boom.

"Women worry. That's what they do!" Crosson snapped.

Jesse and Rhett glanced at one another. Both remained quiet while tugging on the reins of their horses.

"To answer your question, son." Jim looked over at Rhett. "I hid out in the hills for 'bout six months. I didn't know if word had reached Salazar that I was alive. I couldn't sleep. I practiced my draw all the time. I was goin' mad in the solitude of my own misery. Then one day, I find this fella lying in the woods, bleedin'."

"Richard Finch." Sheriff Crosson spit out the name through gritted teeth.

"Dammit, Nolan! How many times do I have to apologize? God! You weren't the only one that was hurtin'!" Jim wheeled his horse and smacked into the bay.

"You should've let 'im die. He ruined your life." Sheriff Crosson tackled Jim out of the saddle. They hit the ground with a thud. "He wasn't your friend." The sheriff gripped Jim by the shoulders, shaking the shit out of him. "How could you even compare 'im to me?"

Jesse and Rhett grabbed the reins of the horses. Jim smacked the sheriff in the nose. Sheriff Crosson slugged Jim in the mouth. They both sat on the ground, holding their bleeding faces.

"Coffee anyone?" Rhett said. They all looked in his direction. He shrugged.

"I'll get some wood." Jesse stepped down off Freckles.

"Hold up, boys. I want ya to hear this." Jim looked at the two of them. Then he stood and gave the sheriff a hand-up. "It was never my intention to replace ya." He stared at the sheriff. "But I was alone, scared, and he was the first human interaction I'd had in a long time. All he did was fill a void." He wiped at his eyes. "Richard didn't force me to follow 'im. I chose to do that. I didn't have to, but I did. I was livin' like a criminal anyway. I didn't know if I was bein' hunted for killin' that cattleman."

Sheriff Crosson kicked the dirt. "I blame myself for not goin' after ya. I was just so pissed off that you deserted everyone and figured you'd come back of your own accord. But then weeks passed, months went by, and you didn't. I wasn't the tracker I am now, or I would've hunted ya down even after all that time."

Jim brushed some dirt off his shoulder. "Believe me, I wish I would have made better decisions. I wish things could be different."

"Me too," the sheriff said and walked away.

It was quiet around the fire as they each drank their coffee. It was close to suppertime, and Jesse chewed on a piece of jerky.

"Mount up, boys." Sheriff Crosson stood, holding his empty cup. "Keep an eye out for that wolf. Only shoot if necessary."

Nathanial believed that thing to be a pet. Jesse would hate to have to kill Montana in front of the boy.

"Does that go for Finch too?" Rhett chuckled.

Jesse gave him a sideways glance. He just never knew what was going to fly out of his mouth.

The sheriff grinned and shook his head.

"You'll have to get in line behind me," Jim said.

CHAPTER 28

NATE PEELED OFF what was left of his holy socks. They'd been covering lots of rough miles over the past week, but every step was one closer to home. He rubbed his raw heels. At least his socks were a thin covering against the wind. The temperature dropped more each day. It was freezing by day or night. Flurries whipped in the air.

Montana sank down next to him. The fire and the wolf's fur felt good against Nate's bare skin. If it got any colder, they might have to hole up for the season on this side of the mountain. There had to be a thick layer of ice on the peak. It was pure white up there.

Nate turned the turkey Montana had taken down. He sliced off a hunk of semi-cooked meat and fed it to the wolf, then patted his pet's head. "I hope Ma and Pa let me keep ya. If not, I'll hide ya out in the barn."

The appeal hadn't been won yet, but Nate was counting on things going his way this time. He'd been through too much for it not to work out.

"Isn't that sweet?" Downwind from camp, Japer Finch stepped out from behind a tree.

Montana leaped to his feet, his teeth bared, and he snarled. Spit flew. Jasper pulled the trigger as Montana lunged. The wolf's back end whipped around, one of his hind legs buckled, and he fell hard against the ground.

"Yip, yip, yip." Montana tried to stand, but his ass end wouldn't hold up.

Tears sprang to Nate's eyes. He dove in front of his wolf before Jasper fired a second shot. He hugged around Montana's neck. "Please don't kill 'im," he begged. "I'll go with ya. I swear."

Montana stood on three legs. He growled at Finch while holding his injured leg up under himself. Nate snatched up a thick stick. Jasper would have to kill him too.

Finch pulled the trigger, shooting Nate's club in two. Then a third time, he fired and broke the branch off right above his hands, stinging his skin. Tears rolled down his cheeks. He and Montana were about to die.

"Up there on the ridge!" a familiar voice hollered.

Nate froze. Was that Goose? Had he followed him?

Finch twisted toward the sound of running horses. Goose wasn't alone. Who was with him? He'd be dead if Pa had found him. Finch glared. Down below, maybe fifty yards, four men charged up the hillside. Nate's eyes fixed on the big bay and its rider.

"Pa!" he cheered.

Montana circled Nate's legs, pushing him toward the space between two rocks that they'd slept in last night.

Finch ran toward Nate. "I'll kill ya both!"

Nate pushed Montana. "Git outta here!"

Montana turned and, on one hind leg, he pillared off the ground. His massive paws hit on each of Finch's shoulders, and the two fell backward and rolled in a tangle of screams and fur across the rocky dirt toward the slope.

Goose charged onto the rim first, followed close by Pa, Jesse, and Rhett. They all held guns. Their horses nearly trampled over Finch and Montana tearing at each other on the ground.

"Don't shoot!" Nate dove for his wolf.

Teeth sliced his arm, and Nate let out a scream. He rolled, and Montana came with him. The mighty jaws clamped down on the back of Nate's shirt, and Montana began dragging him away into the brush.

Finch rolled up, his gun aimed at the two of them. Gunfire blasted. Finch jerked one way then the other as bullets drilled him. He spun as he managed to get to his feet and fired three times at the four horsemen. Goose toppled off his gelding.

"No!" Nate couldn't take seeing anyone else die.

Pa hadn't hanged him, so maybe he had planned on letting Goose live. Now this.

Pa's Colt barked in his hand.

Finch grabbed above his belt and wobbled backward. He tripped over a rock and landed flat on his back within arm's reach of Nate. His arm thrust out, gun in hand, aimed right between Nate's eyes. His breath caught. His eyes widened. Finch pulled the trigger. The chamber clicked empty.

Nate swung his leg around and hoofed the iron out of Jasper's hand. It spun through the air, then stopped when it clanged against a boulder and dropped into the dirt.

"You bastard!" Nate unleashed the beast inside. His fingers curled, and with a wild furiousness, he clawed and kicked at Finch, who struck back. Nate howled, his muscles burning under each hit. Montana growled louder. A hard punch sent Nate flat on his back, gasping for air.

Montana plowed over Nate. Piss warmed the crotch of his pants, and he shook violently. He couldn't breathe. Montana rammed Finch, knocking him head over heels. He pounced on top of the man's chest and clamped down on Jasper's throat until he stopped kicking.

"Partner!" Jesse scooped Nate up off the ground. "You're bleedin'."

Nate didn't care about his cut. He threw his arms around Jesse and squeezed. Had that chamber not been empty... Nate burst out crying. He had almost lost everything. His part of the fight had been over in all of a few seconds, but within that time, he realized he'd chosen to fight for the right reason. He hadn't just snapped. He wasn't coldblooded like the Youngers.

Montana lifted his head and snarled. Jesse backed up a step.

"No, Montana. Jesse won't hurt ya or me." Nate sniffled. "And that's my pa over there. They're here to help us."

"I got 'im in my sights, sheriff," Rhett called. "At your so-say."

Nate wiggled, but Jesse wouldn't put him down. "Please, Pa. Don't." Tears gushed out of his eyes. "He's my best friend."

Pa glanced at Goose who held to this bleeding shoulder.

"Put down the gun, Rhett." Pa walked cautiously toward Montana. The wolf's head swung between growling at Jesse and snarling at Pa.

Nate sobbed and held tight to Jesse. "Don't hurt 'im." He wasn't sure if he meant Pa or Montana. Each was fierce in his own world. And a hurt animal, especially one that felt cornered, could be twice as mean.

Montana snapped up at Pa's face. Pa grabbed with one hand around the wolf's muzzle, the other hand latched onto the scruff of his neck, and he slammed Montana down on his back. He dropped a knee like an anvil into Montana's chest, then bent forward and sank his teeth in over the top of his nose. The wolf whimpered and kicked, but Pa held him pinned down, not letting any pressure off his bite.

Blood began to stain around Pa's lips.

"Stop it! You're hurtin' 'im." Nate cried harder. He twisted and pulled away, but Jesse was stronger and kept Nate confined to him.

Montana suddenly lay very still. His chest was rising and falling, so he wasn't dead. Pa stood and let go of Nate's wolf. Montana stayed crouched belly side up.

Nate held out his arms toward Pa. "What did you do to 'im? Is he okay?"

Jesse passed Nate to his father. He hugged Pa around the neck, and Pa kissed his forehead.

"Montana's fine. Female wolves will correct their young by bitin' 'em over the muzzle. So will the pack leader in order to maintain dominance over the lower-rankin' wolves. I just established that I am the alpha male." Pa spit fur out of his mouth.

"Can I try it?" Nate wiped a sleeve across his cheeks.

Pa laughed. "Only if ya wanna get bit. Wolves can see size. Montana knows I'm bigger than him, and now he understands I'm stronger too. You're just a pup. I don't think he'd tolerate such an act of control from you."

Nate grinned. It had been so long since he'd heard his father's voice. Pa could have told him the sky was purple, and it would make no difference. Nate had missed those moments of teaching. He hadn't realized just how much until now.

"I love you." He rested his head on Pa's shoulder. There was no safer place.

"Let's get you home." Pa walked toward his horse. "But first, we need to bandage that arm."

"What about Goose?" Nate looked over at the man.

Jesse was fingering around Goose's bleeding wound while Rhett had his nose in there close and was checking the bullet hole over good. It was Goose's neck, not his injury, that had Nate squirming.

"The name's Jim, Jim Reed, not Goose." Jim grinned at Pa, who smiled. "I'm good." He lifted his shoulder. "It's just a mean scratch. Nothin' a few stitches won't fix."

"But..." Nate glanced between Pa and Jim. He didn't want to bring up the fact that one was an outlaw, the other a lawman who had sworn to hang his best friend the next time they met.

"I'm not gonna turn Jim over to the law or hang 'im." Pa lifted Nate onto the bay. "I'm hopin' he'll come to Gray Rock with us." He glanced at Jim. Then he untied his bandana and wrapped Nate's arm.

Nate smiled. "You would like Gray Rock. Everyone's real nice. And you can meet Buck, my mustang."

Jim chuckled. "First, I'd like to talk to June. There's an important question I'd like to ask her. But I don't see any reason why we couldn't settle near Gray Rock."

Pa stepped into the saddle behind Nate. He rested back against Pa and caught all the sideways glances thrown between Jesse and Rhett. Both deputies sat oddly quiet on their horses as Jim swung a leg over his saddle.

"I'm happy you've finally come to your senses. I've been waitin' for this day." Pa shook Jim's hand.

Both men chuckled.

Nate couldn't wait to hear more stories about the two friends growing up together. But Jesse's and Rhett's long faces had him wondering what bad news was about to pass over their lips.

"Mr. Reed," Jesse said in a sad tone.

Rhett tucked his chin and stared straight down at his saddle horn.

Nate's gut tightened. What had happened to June?

"That's awful formal, son," Jim said while rubbing at his injured shoulder.

Pa turned his horse. All eyes, except Rhett's, were on Jesse.

Jesse removed his hat. "I'm sorry to say June was killed by one of Finch's men."

Jim's face drained of color, and his eyes shined. Pa stiffened, which made Nate sit up straight.

Rhett looked up from where he'd been focused on nothing. "Jesse did his best to save her. And he made sure she was buried proper."

Why did death seem to follow Nate everywhere? He wiped his eyes. Poor June.

Jim nodded. "Thank you, boys" He was quiet for a minute, taking a few deep inhales. "Did ya kill the bastard who done it?"

Rhett grinned. "Damn right, I did. That Yaqui was 'bout to cut down Jesse too."

Pa leaned, and the saddle under them creaked. He patted Rhett's shoulder. Jesse's face turned bright red. Nate wasn't sure what to think about that. He must have been embarrassed for some reason.

Jim wheeled his horse in the direction the others were facing. "I'll buy the first round when we get to Gray Rock."

"We can't leave Montana." Nate had been distracted while reuniting with part of his family and with the worry of Jim possibly being hanged by Pa right before his eyes. He hadn't forgotten Montana, but the wolf wasn't his only focus.

The four men turned their heads in unison. Montana lay curled up not far from the spot where Pa had set him straight on who the boss was, and he licked at the cut on his hip.

"A wolf isn't a pet," Pa said in a firm voice.

"But he's hurt," Nate whined. "He was protectin' me." He needed backup, so he batted his teary blue eyes at his big partner.

"S'pose I could fashion a sling sack like a gurney. We could use branches to hold the groundsheet." Jesse didn't move to untie his blanket roll. He stared at Pa for the go-ahead.

"Don't you start too." Pa wagged a finger at Jesse. "You boys know better. Wild animals can turn on ya, and I won't have that wolf around your ma or Elizabeth or the baby."

"Yes, sir." Jesse then shrugged at Nate as though he were saying sorry. He had tried.

The throatless remains of Jasper Finch lay not six feet from the group, a bloody reminder of what Montana was capable of, but Nate wasn't afraid and didn't believe Montana would attack anyone who wasn't asking for it.

"He'll die without help." Tears streamed down Nate's cheeks. He shook his head. "I won't go. Not without Montana." He was sure that Montana would in time become familiar with the others. He was a good wolf.

"Look," Jim said.

Montana was gone. He had disappeared into the forest while everyone was focused on Nate.

Pa gave Nate a squeeze. "Montana can take care of himself. All animals have instincts." He nudged the bay.

Nate twisted in the saddle. Montana wasn't anywhere. He wanted to call out but knew that Pa would get mad, and he didn't want to upset his father. He had just explained why Nate couldn't keep Montana. Nate understood but didn't agree. He had to give it one more try.

He wiped his nose across his sleeve, then the tears on his face. "Montana would never hurt Ma or Elizabeth."

"This subject is closed. Now that is enough. Not another word." Pa frowned.

Nate held his tongue, but he glanced at their backtrail. Montana had followed him before. This time, he was hurt. Could he trail Nate the whole way to Gray Rock?

"I think Rhett and I should track Montana." Jim broke the silence.

Nate's head whipped around. "No! Let 'im alone!" It was a fact that Jim knew exactly what Nate did. Montana would likely follow. The pit of his stomach churned.

Jim ignored him. Instead, he was looking over at Pa. "Montana trailed Nathanial and killed some of Finch's men in the process."

Pa rubbed the stubble on his chin.

"Don't let 'em go after Montana, Pa," Nate begged. Wetness filled his eyes once again.

"I'm sorry, son, but that wolf's a man-killer." Pa nodded at Jim. Though, he eyed Jim and Rhett.

Nate didn't understand the strange look, and he didn't care. All he wished was for Montana to be okay.

"Are ya sure ya wouldn't rather have Jesse with ya?" Pa rested a hand on his Colt.

Jim shook his head. "You just enjoy this time now that ya have both your boys together." He spurred his horse. "We'll catch up as soon as we can."

Rhett followed, and the two trotted their horses away.

Nate was torn between obeying what he knew Pa expected—for him not to have a fit—and Nate's love for his wolf. "Will they shoot Montana or just run 'im off?" His voice shook. As much as he didn't want to know, he needed an answer.

"Jim will do whatever he thinks is necessary," Pa said.

Jesse's horse fell into pace next to Pa's. "Sorry, kid."

Nate sobbed.

CHAPTER 29

FIVE DAYS LATER, the weary trio lumbered into the ranch yard on skinny horses, all of them, including the animals, beaten down by the harsh weather and the hard travel over the ice-topped mountain. Nate had strips of the spare shirt Pa had cut up wrapped around his feet so they wouldn't freeze. He couldn't stop worrying about Montana, and there were tears in his eyes every other minute. They hadn't seen a hair of Jim or Rhett. They were cold and tired and dirty from sleeping on the ground.

Smoke floated up out of the chimney. The house hadn't changed a bit. Nate couldn't wait to get warm and eat some of Ma's good cooking. Parked outside the picket fence at the hitchrail was a fancy black carriage. Nate didn't recognize it at first, but then Pa jerked up on the reins and stiffened in the saddle. He cursed under his breath.

"What in the hell are the Fletchers doin' here?" Jesse fumed.

"Pa, don't let 'em take me." Nate pressed back into the front of his father.

Pa slipped an arm around him as the front door opened.

"Don't worry. They won't be here for long," Pa growled between gritted teeth.

Ma ran out across the porch. Well, she wobbled at a brisk pace.

Her belly was huge. Elizabeth barely fit on her hip. A wide smile lit up Ma's face, and tears shined on her cheeks. She hustled down the front steps toward them. Elizabeth squealed the entire time, kicking her legs and reaching for Nate.

"Mama!" Nate hollered and slid off Pa's horse. He ran with arms stretched wide. They threw themselves together, all three of them landing on the ground in a tangle of hugs and kisses.

"Oh, sweetheart." Ma couldn't have squeezed him any tighter.

"I can't breathe." He wiggled, peeling himself away.

Ma chuckled. Elizabeth clung to the front of his shirt with both chubby little hands.

Pa stepped down off the bay, tossed his reins to Jesse, then gave Ma a hand-up. Nate's folks were both smiling. This was a day to celebrate. For a while, he never thought he'd see home again. Ma smelled just the same, like fresh bread. Elizabeth's yellow curls bounced as she giggled. Not much could have ruined this moment for him or any of them. That was until Mr. and Mrs. Fletcher showed their faces outside the house.

Pa suddenly straightened. Jesse was now at his side, holding the reins of the two horses. The faces of both men were stern, their eyes narrow.

Leslie pushed between the couple and appeared at the top of the porch steps. No coat. Just a shirt, suspenders, and a bowtie to keep the nasty wind from scratching at his skin. He ran toward Nate. The air in front of the other boy puffed white with each hurried breath. Minnie, decked out in a fur-trimmed stole that matched Mrs. Fletcher's in color and style, wasn't far behind her brother. Her dainty shoes clicked across the hard ground. Nate couldn't help but smile.

Pa took a step forward. The Fletchers were closing in quick. Ma caught Pa's arm.

"It's over, Nolan." She squeezed his forearm. Her lips curled, widening her smile. "Parker was arrested two days after you left here. Judge Prescott has already had Nathanial's case reviewed."

Leslie skidded to a halt, plowing Nate over. They hit the ground laughing.

"The case was thrown out," Ma announced.

Pa swept her up and planted a big one on her.

"Woo-hoo!" Jesse grabbed Nate out of the dirt and tossed him in the air. Nate let out a gay holler. Jesse caught him and spun them a few times. Giddy voices filled the air.

When Jesse planted Nate's feet on the ground, even the Fletchers were smiling. Mr. Fletcher extended a hand toward Pa. Pa raised a brow, and Nate could almost read his mind.

"What are ya still doin' here?" Nate blurted. It was what Pa was thinking too.

"Nathanial." Ma tapped him on top of the head.

Leslie chuckled. Minnie slipped her hand into Mrs. Fletcher's, and the faces of both adults sobered. Lem Fletcher withdrew his hand.

Ma wagged a finger. "Don't be rude. Your aunt and uncle would still like the opportunity to get to know you." She then pointedly looked at Pa, silently scolding him with that sharp look in her eyes. "Judge Prescott is in town. With him present, I have already heard the Fletchers out." Ma smoothed Nate's hair with both hands. "I have to say I am in agreement, as is Judge Prescott." She looked up at Pa. "I know the decision is yours, husband. I just ask that you please listen to what they have to say. They're not the people we thought they were." Ma squeezed Leslie around the shoulders, and they both grinned.

Nate wasn't so sure. Deloris Fletcher's face pinched as she eyed his torn and bloodstained clothing from his head to his wrapped feet. Pa's big coat hung off Nate's shoulders and draped over him, but it was warm.

Pa nodded. He extended a hand and shook with Mr. Fletcher.

Nate pressed against Pa's side. The fight for his custody was over. He was no longer afraid that the Fletchers would whisk him across the country. Nate liked the way things were before the Fletchers had ever interfered with his family. But like it or not, Lem and Deloris Fletcher were part of his life now, and life didn't move in a backward motion. He couldn't erase them out of his memory. They could only go forward from there.

Trust wasn't easy for Nate to give. He quivered, and Pa rested a hand on his shoulder. He would, however, try if his folks thought it best for him because he did trust them. One hundred percent. No one loved him more.

"Where's that crazy wolf?" Leslie looked around.

Nate's gaze fell toward the ground. He couldn't even say if Montana was still alive.

"Here he is!" Jim called from the end of the lane.

Nate's head snapped around. Leslie twisted in the same direction.

"Well, I'll be," Jesse said and ruffled Nate's hair.

Nate's folks, his aunt and uncle, and Minnie all had turned too. Behind Rhett's horse on a makeshift litter lay Nate's wolf. He lifted his head, ears perked.

"Montana!" Nate sprinted.

Montana slapped his bushy tail against the sling. Nate dropped next to his wolf. He began to lick Nate's face. He ran his fingers through the fur, ruffling the gray around his wolf's thick neck.

Rhett pulled up reins not far from the group of awestruck adults. Mr. and Mrs. Fletcher took a step back. Minnie was clinging to Deloris. Jim stepped down off his horse next to Pa, who scowled.

"I'm sorry, Nolan. I just couldn't do it." He nodded toward Nate patting his furry playmate's head. "For a first in a long time, I thought about bein' the hero."

Nate couldn't stop smiling. Leslie slowly stuck out his hand. Montana sniffed, then licked him, and he grinned.

"Be careful," Mr. Fletcher said. Neither he nor the missus came any closer.

Minnie hid in the folds of Mrs. Fletcher's skirt. Ma allowed Elizabeth to crawl onto the sheet with Nate, though she remained close. Montana nosed Elizabeth's belly, and she giggled.

"Just great." Pa shook his head. "Now I'm stuck with a damn wolf."

"He'll be a good watchdog," Jesse offered.

Pa raised a brow.

Jim rested a hand on Pa's shoulder. "He didn't let me stitch that cut on his hip, but Rhett and I got him onto the litter without too much trouble."

"Please, Pa, can we keep 'im?" Nate thrust out his lip.

Jesse stroked Montana's head, and Ma was grinning at Elizabeth who had her head laid against Montana's middle like a fluffy pillow.

"What a picture." Pa chuckled. "How can I say no to that?"

"Come on, boys." Jesse hauled Nate and Leslie up off the litter. "Let's go make a place in the barn for Montana." He looked over at Rhett. "Ya wanna help us?"

"Sure." Rhett grinned, then sobered and glanced at Pa. Tension filled the air.

Nate didn't know what was going on between the two, but something wasn't right.

Jim stepped between Pa and Rhett. "We all got a past. That young man's no different. He has a strong temper and has made some bad decisions. Underneath that, he's a good kid. Guidance is what he needs." He lowered his voice. "I wish I would've had some at his age. Then things would have turned out different, and I wouldn't be startin' over after all these years."

Ma slipped an arm around Pa's before he had a chance to say anything. "You men must be hungry for a good hearty meal. Give me a few minutes." She gently snatched Elizabeth off of Montana and headed toward the house.

"Excuse us," Mr. Fletcher said, his missus and Minnie at his side. "We would like to stay if we're not intruding. Nathanial's home now, but we are curious to know what all happened out there."

"I don't know that my son'll feel up to talkin' about it, but you're welcome to stay," Pa said in a tolerant tone. "Besides, I have some questions for ya."

Mr. Fletcher nodded. Deloris and Minnie turned, then headed for the house with chins tucked and shoulders into the wind.

Lem pulled open the barn door. "Are we going to fix a spot or what?" He clapped his hands together.

The rest of them were just standing there being bitten by the cold air.

Nate smiled. "Yes, sir." He hesitated. "Uncle … Lem." The expression came out awkward, but Nate had forced it anyway. He had a gut feeling he'd best get used to the words.

Lem Fletcher smiled.

Rhett steered his horse with the litter carrying Montana into the barn where Jesse, Nate, and Leslie waited. Pa, Jim, and Mr. Fletcher filed in behind.

"Leslie, git up there and throw some hay down from the loft." Jesse gave orders.

Nate and Leslie did most of the work with some help from both Jesse and Rhett who held the planks together as Leslie hammered in nails. Nate waited for his turn and patted Buck's soft nose. It was good to see his horse again.

So far, their open-box idea looked more like a big, flat, square chicken roost. Nate glanced over at Pa. He was leaned against the workbench, talking to Jim and Fletcher. Nate overheard enough to know that Patrick Harrison was mur-dered. Pa agreed. As sheriff, he would tell the Harrison kids about their brother with the Fletchers present, since they'd known the family. Lem and Deloris would be taking Leslie and Minnie back to San Francisco to an aunt they had met twice and didn't like. The Harrison kids had begged to live with the Fletchers. At that, Pa smirked.

"You should let them stay." Nate walked over and leaned against Pa, but his gaze was on his uncle. "They know you and feel comfortable with you. They've lost a lot of important people. It ain't right to give 'em to a stranger." Nate wasn't thinking of replacement children for the one the Fletchers had lost. He only wanted what was best for his friends.

Lem brushed hay off one of his sleeves. "Deloris and I are discussing the matter. It's hard not to consider after what we put you through."

"It's done," Jesse boasted loudly.

Everyone turned and eyed the lopsided box. Montana sniffed it. Two seconds later, he hopped on three legs toward the door.

Nate looked up at Pa. "I think Montana should just sleep with me."

Everyone chuckled.

"No." Pa swung Nate up over his shoulder and gave him a playful swat. "Let's go eat."

Pa helped turn Nate so he hung piggyback on him, arms around his neck and legs twisted around his middle. One by one, they all filed out as Pa held the door open, and jokes about the ugly dog box were being made, followed by snickers. When Rhett stepped past, Pa slipped a hand around the scruff of his neck and gave him a shake.

"You have Jim to thank for me givin' ya another chance." Pa tapped the star on Rhett's chest. "Don't let that piece of tin go to your head again, or I'll bust ya down to size."

For whatever reason, it made Nate think about the day he'd drawn the pistol on the lumberjack. He thought briefly of telling Pa. His hand had moved with a speed far beyond his years. His stomach tightened just thinking about it. He needed to forget it. With any luck, his letter explaining the discovery of such a skill hadn't arrived and never would.

Nate leaned down. His mouth touched Pa's ear. "It's good to be home," he whispered.

"That it is." Pa patted Nate's threaded fingers holding the base of his neck.

Montana followed them right onto the porch and curled up next to the door.

"You'll always have a home with me," Nate mouthed.

ABOUT THE AUTHOR

J.B. Richard, author of the Western Promises and Gold Country series, resides in the Seven Mountain region of Central Pennsylvania with her two sons.

When she's not writing, she can be found hiking in the mountains, horseback riding, or sketching. She is an enthusiast of the "Old West" and loves a good-fitting pair of cowboy boots.

Visit J.B. at:
JBRichard.com
FB: juliebethrichard
Instagram: j.b._richard
Twitter: JBRichardwriter

CPSIA information can be obtained
at www.ICGtesting.com
Printed in the USA
LVHW040056170621
690399LV00005B/134